A Blue Moon
in Poorwater

Books by Cathryn Hankla

Phenomena / poetry

Learning the Mother Tongue / short stories

A Blue Moon in Poorwater / novel

Cathryn Hankla

A Blue Moon in Poorwater

Ticknor & Fields

New York

_1988_

For information about permission to reproduce selections
from this book, write to Permissions, Ticknor & Fields,
52 Vanderbilt Avenue, New York, New York 10017.

Library of Congress Cataloging-in-Publication Data

Hankla, Cathryn, date.
  A blue moon in Poorwater / Cathryn Hankla.
    p. cm.
  ISBN 0–89919–534–2
  I. Title.
PS3558.A4689B5   1988   87–33561
813′.54 — dc19   CIP

Printed in the United States of America

S 10 9 8 7 6 5 4 3 2 1

The author is grateful for permission to quote from the
following songs by A. P. Carter: "Keep on the Sunny
Side," copyright 1928 by Peer International Corporation,
copyright renewed, and "Gospel Ship," copyright 1935
by Southern Music Publishing Co., Inc., copyright renewed
assigned to Peer International Corporation. International
copyright secured. All rights reserved. Used by permission.
She is also grateful to the Reverend Howard Finster for
permission to quote from his artwork number 4427.

The blear-eyed escapeth a pit into which
  the clear-sighted falleth;
And the ignorant, an expression by which
  the shrewd sage is ruined.
The believer can scarce earn his food,
  while the impious infidel is favoured.
What art or act can a man devise? It is
  what the Almighty appointeth!

— the story told by the Christian Broker in
The Arabian Nights' Entertainment

Acknowledgments

I would like to thank the friends and family who encouraged me throughout the writing of this book; especially Donald Fairey, for offering valuable information about unions; Michael Verdon, for reading and commenting free of charge; George Garrett, for practical counsel; the Snack Bar Poets; and Richard Dillard. I would also like to thank Hollins College for a Faculty Research grant and for allowing me a leave.

Several books I found most useful were *We Be Here When the Morning Comes*, text by Bryan Woolley, photographs by Ford Reid; *Snake Handlers: God-Fearers? or Fanatics?* by Robert W. Pelton and Karen W. Carden; *Appalachia in the Sixties: Decade of Reawakening*, edited by David S. Walls and John B. Stephenson; and *Some Old-Fashioned Mountain Recipes and Some Folk Remedies*, edited by Hubert J. Davis.

Contents

Chronicles a pivotal year in the life
of an 11-year-old girl who lives in
the Appalachian town of Poorwater,
Tennessee.

The Christmas Train, 1942

I saw an article in the newspaper last December about something called the Christmas Train that's been going through mining country for over forty years, delivering gifts to folks who don't have much at Christmas, or at any other time for that matter. It made me remember a story my daddy told me about his childhood back up in the hills. I kept after him to tell it again but he never felt like it, so I've had to fill in the details here for myself. If he ever reads it he'd probably say, "That's not exactly how it was, but it'll do for a story."

It is snowing fast and furious but the walk is easy, even into the teeth of a wind that pushes back his ears and whips his pants legs back and forth, brushing the tops of his feet with a gathering crust of ice. He has no shoes but barely feels the cold earth, frozen husks of scrub grass, the falling snow; his tracks fill in behind him as he goes. Last night he saw the ring around the moon, the circle of light that predicts bad weather. It did not matter in the least; his plan was set. Before dawn he would rise and begin hiking through the mountains, along the paths and dirt roads, finally into the meadow where the train tracks darted like twin deer trails, dark and constant across the sudden opening of land. So now he walks there, like a ram or a bull, head forward, chin down, instinct and purpose guiding him where nothing but a scattering of animals has passed. In minutes the sun will rise, but it will take another hour for light to penetrate the blowing snow, into the nooks of life below the mountaintops. He knows where he is going and why he must go.

At the general store, a mile from the holler where he lives, he has heard the old men tell about a new scheme the merchants down in Tennessee have hatched. He has heard how a train full of toys will wind up from the south, leaving all kinds of presents in its path. It sounds too good to be true, but he is the oldest boy, with two sisters longing for dolls. He cannot go to war — he is too young — but he can walk through the mountains to the tracks and see if it is true. As he walks, he thinks again that maybe the story is just that, a story, and he will come here and the train will not even pass by, or if it passes it will not stop for him, will not drop anything to fill his paper sack. Faith pulls him forward, though the snow is thick: if this does not work he will just have to think of something else, another way. There are things he could do — he could sweep out a store. Boys younger than he had worked in the mines, but his daddy had said no, told him, "Son, you got to tend to your mind first. Get all the schoolin' you can. Then we'll look for you a job."

It is not money he wants; no, not that simple. It is not what money can buy either, not exactly. He does not mind that his feet are bare; last year he had shoes and would have some now if he had not outgrown them. He'll probably get a new pair for Christmas; there is money enough for shoes or material for dresses, but it is dolls his sisters want, more than anything, and that is what he wants for them. He cannot think of anything he wants more for himself than to be the one who gets them their dolls. When he was younger he had worn himself out wishing for things he knew he could not have. It started with a dump truck, then an air rifle, then a bike. Could not ride a bike up a holler anyway, his daddy had said. Now he is thirteen, and past wanting things; he has given up wishing. But from the minute he understood that a train might come, that old feeling, old longing, had risen up in his heart; the old quiet hope for better things. At first he had beaten it down, like butter in a churn, beaten it down into his chest the way his mother beat biscuits, but the hope stayed there, a lump too large to swallow; it stayed there and pushed back against his heart each time it beat. He knows he can stand it, though, if the train does not come; this was the only way he would allow himself the journey. Until he knew that he could walk home alone, swinging an empty paper sack at his side, he had not finally decided to meet the train.

In another mile, which twists like the path, he will be within sight of the meadow. The snow has let up, but the wind blows stronger. The boy cuts a silhouette against the landscape, bends down and rubs each foot between his hands for a minute before going on. It surprises him, but he does not seem that cold. His face radiates color, warm as a baked apple to the touch. Only his fingertips and lips hold a slight purple cast, and he tries not to lick his lips so that the wind will not chap them so badly. It is hard to think of anything except the effort of putting one step in front of the other — the closer he gets to the meadow, the heavier his steps bear down into the snow. An old song runs through his mind until he begins to hum the tune while the words turn over and over, out of sequence. "She'll be comin' round the mountain when she comes . . . she'll be drivin' six white horses when she comes . . . she'll be comin' round the mountain . . . she'll be drivin' six white horses . . . she'll be comin' round the mountain . . . we'll all go out to meet her when she comes . . . when she comes." He can hear his grandma's voice in his head; his humming is her accompaniment.

His grandpa plays the fiddle, not as good as some, but passable. He often plays a song he got from a real good fiddler, who got it from someone else, called "High Dad in the Morning." That and "Laughing Boy" he can play as good as anyone else, and slide out of one song right into the other, just like they belong together. As the boy picks up his pace, he slaps his knees in time. And the words to the song keep running through his mind, drowning out the chugging of wheels, climbing the steep grade, so distant still that anyone would have to believe with all his strength that a train was coming, to be able to hear its engine's music in spite of the beating of his heart.

1

The Black Ball

I used to think that the past was like an irreproducible inkblot. It was an unanswerable question, like the inkblot, open to free association and a lot of interpretation. A question with a million different answers, and none of them right. Lately, the past grows closer and closer to the idea of a black hole, when I point my telescoping memory into the space where it lingers, revealing its presence only by the behavior of the matter around it. That matter might be my life and how I'm going to live it in the future, for all I know. The size of black holes can vary from the point of a pin to the ellipse of Jupiter's orbit. But even one of them could easily consume a life as short as mine if it felt like it. A black hole spends its existence trying to disappear, trying to achieve infinite density, zero radius; that's its nature, but it leaves a trail of gravity behind it whipping like a rattler's tail.

I keep playing with the idea of that impossible zero, a radius without a number, but it doesn't seem to lead anywhere but into memory. If I take a memory and shape it into a ball, pack it tighter and tighter between my hands, adding some gravel to the snow so that it will carry straight and sting when it gets there; if I begin a memory and stop to begin a memory and stop to begin a memory and so on, ad infinitum, et cetera, world without end, and so forth, packing layer over layer, how many times can I interrupt my own story before it falls into itself, like the light circling a black hole, hooked into its own impossible exit?

I don't know the answer, or even if the question makes any sense in the long run, but what I remember is how one thing led to another even though it didn't seem to be heading anyplace in particular at the time. Everything started going to hell on a stick the summer of 1968, when I was ten and reading a condensed version of *The Arabian Nights*. I guess it had really been on its way for a long time before I had sense enough to notice what was happening. By the time I looked up, things were rolling downhill faster than the Gingerbread Boy, and I felt more mixed up than Dorothy ever felt when she visited the Emerald City, just thinking the whole time that she'd rather be at home if only she could find the Wizard. I was at home, one way or another, and that was part of the problem. There's no place to return to when your own home town turns inside out and you feel like that yourself too. Part of my story is dead and buried, but part of it goes on. That's the part of me that started changing that summer and hasn't finished yet. Parts of the story I still don't know completely and probably never will, but those are the parts it seems I need most to tell. So I'm going to try to tell it all, or as close as I can come, like Shahrazad, and if it kills me, well, at least I had the nerve to try to get what's inside on the outside, where it belongs, before I disappear.

My best friend, Betty Grayson, skipped out of the screen door of her red brick house, dangling her Chatty Cathy by one arm. I hadn't seen that doll since we'd pulled its string one time too many and it stopped talking. The next thing I knew Betty would drag out Thumbelina and make me stare at its head while it rocked back and forth.

I raised my hand to wave hello and called into the trailer, "Mom, you got any Kool-Aid made? Betty's on her way over." Betty tried to wave back but all she could do was shake her fist; she had something in her hand.

"No," Momma answered. "If y'all get thirsty, Miss Priss can just take you to her house, where everything's hunky-dory."

I wished Momma wouldn't say things like that; Betty was practically in the square of dirt we called our front yard. But I don't think she heard. She zinged her fist to the ground, letting go of a ball like she was trying to find China and it bounced right over the trailer. Thank God it didn't hit the top. It would have made a dent the size of a moon crater. Betty eyed me and asked, "Well, aren't you going to get it?"

"You bounced it, you get it," I said.

"But I'm your guest."

Betty had a way of saying *guest* that I could never explain or duplicate in a million years, so I got off the concrete stoop and scrambled around behind the trailer until I found the black ball, like a lump of coal on the edge of the alley. It had a little scratch from nudging a clinker, and as I was bringing it to her I rubbed it up good, hoping the hard rubber would meld back and the shine would take like it did with apples. Sure enough she noticed the flaw right away.

"What did you do to my new Superball?" She held it to one eye.

"It was like that when I picked it up."

"It wasn't like that a minute ago."

Betty cradled Chatty Cathy, smothering it up against the smocking of her white dress while she studied the scratched Superball, lengthening her arm as she placed the black ball between her eye and the sun like a newly discovered moon. I thought she'd never say another word, but she wasn't about to go home. Finally she slipped the ball into her dress pocket. She knew I wanted to bounce that ball and see how high it could go.

"My mommy says your mommy feeds you too much sugar and that's why you're so mean all the time," Betty said at last, in her Sunday School recital voice. Just the week before she had stood at the altar to say her verse: "I applied mine heart to know, and to search, and to seek out wisdom, and the reason of things." Betty always selected the hardest verses she could find just to show everyone up, and I knew she was trying to start something now, but I couldn't stop myself.

"Your momma's mean as a snake and ugly as Michael Dale," I said. Sure enough, Betty took the bait.

"I was going to let you bounce my ball but now I'm not."

She snuggled up to Chatty Cathy and stared a hole through me, her nose scrunched up like a prune.

I wanted to ask her why she was dragging that old doll around, but I was afraid she'd accuse me of having broken it. "I've got a ball of my own," I said.

"Not like this one." Betty spoke the truth.

"I don't care."

"My mommy says your mommy ought to wash your clothes more often."

I hoped Momma hadn't heard that one. "At least I don't have to wear dresses in the summer like you do." I was aware that the word *dresses* sounded enough like a cuss word.

"I don't have to do anything I don't want to." Betty set her jaw. Her momma just then started calling her to lunch.

"You want to come eat?" asked Betty.

I was so surprised that I yelled to Momma that I was going up the hill to Betty's. The argument seemed to be at a standstill; I watched the bulge in Betty's pocket all the way to her house. Once, when Betty tripped on a rock, I thought the ball had to fall out, but that pocket seemed designed for that ball — just the right size with no room left over except for Betty's hand to dip it out if she ever decided to.

Mrs. Grayson met us at the door and gave Betty her "guess who's coming to lunch without my permission" look. But she was too polite to say anything out loud.

"Hello, Dorie. Are your hands clean?"

"No, ma'am," I said. Mrs. Grayson looked in the direction of my beat-up Red Ball Jets; their red dots were almost completely rubbed off.

"Betty, show Dorie to the bathroom." Mrs. Grayson said this like Betty's hands had never been dirty and I was the only person she'd heard of to admit that they had dirty hands before lunch.

I didn't mind too much, because I liked their bathroom. It smelled like sandalwood soap and had the biggest basin I'd seen. Betty said she'd seen bigger, and she was probably telling the truth. The floor was covered with little squares of black and white ceramic tile. Ours had cracked linoleum rumpled at the seam where the glue was coming unglued. Betty didn't go in ours; she always went home and came back without explaining.

The Graysons' house looked like a Monopoly hotel to me; I'd never been on the inside of anything but a motel, and that wasn't to sleep but to eat in the restaurant once in a blue moon. It was the only motel in the county. "The meeting place of big fish and small," Daddy would say when we jumped down from the truck. "And you know which kind you are," Momma would shoot back. The Graysons' house rose two stories high, with the bedrooms on the second floor and a big staircase right in front of the foyer. At the top of the stairs (Betty's mother was refinishing the banister for "the natural look," so you couldn't touch it most of the time) was a bigger bathroom than the one I went to downstairs. You could pace back and forth in there and actually get tired after a few turns. Little white squares covered the floor, and bigger squares, black and white, inched halfway up the walls and all over the walls and ceiling in the tub corner. The towels hung around neat enough to be decorations, all baby blue, all cotton, with matching bath mat, sink mat, toilet mat and cover. I was sure I'd track mud on something if I ever went all the way in there. Betty's room was painted pink, and she kept a turtle in a bowl until he got out and "expired" (Mrs. Grayson's word) behind the bookcase, leaving nothing but his shell. Betty called him her "specimen" after that. I thought it was grisly, because I could remember the way Tom Turtle had felt crawling over my palm, leaving a trail of brown water like a snail.

You couldn't go in Betty's sister's room, and nobody really wanted to except Betty, who would sit on her bed wrinkling the spread, trying to think up ways, or excuses, to get in there. Barbara's room let off turpentine fumes because Barbara was going to be a famous artist someday. I saw some of her paintings. A seascape was hanging in the dining room downstairs, of the ocean where Betty and Barbara and Dr. and Mrs. Grayson vacationed every summer for two weeks and came back practically black. It didn't look so hot to me, but then I'd never seen the ocean or a painting before. I preferred Betty's Instamatic snapshots, where everything was clear. Mrs. Grayson smiled at Barbara's painting a lot, almost like she'd done it herself, or maybe she was waiting for somebody to notice it so she could brag on Barbara. Barbara did everything right except get a suntan. When they'd come home from the beach Mrs. Grayson would look strange, but Barbara looked about the same because she stayed on the screened-in porch reading or painting the whole time, except at night, when she'd beg to go out to the amusement park and ride the Rock-'n'-Roll cages and the Wild Mouse. Last year when Mrs. Grayson went Piggly Wiggling the day after they got back, the mouths of the check-out ladies shot open like they were little robins waiting for thrown-up worms. Ed refused to tote her bags out to the station wagon until he realized who it was. Then butter wouldn't melt; for all the world they treated her like she was Elizabeth Taylor and they would be pleased to have her autograph. My momma was there, so she told me the whole story. She thought it was pretty funny that "Mrs. Grayson got mistaken for a nigger."

I held my wet hands over the sink and shook them because all the towels were cross-stitched with golf tees and clubs. Betty saw me hesitate and said, "Don't use those. I'll get you a paper towel."

When we came back into the kitchen, Mrs. Grayson was trimming the crusts off the bread for our sandwiches. I liked the crust.

"Do you want mayonnaise on yours, Dorie?" she asked.

"Yes, ma'am, lots," I answered, just to watch Betty's face screw up. She couldn't stand mayonnaise unless it was mixed in.

We had pimiento cheese sandwiches on Roman Meal, Fritos, and iced tea. If we'd been at my house it would have been baloney with mustard on "grab a tiger by the tail" bread with the crusts, potato chips, and soft drinks. Mrs. Grayson wouldn't have bought any of those things, especially not the Coke or Crush, because they were full of sugar. Betty had never had a cavity in her head in her life. But she admired mine. One time she asked me if she could get rich on my fillings after I died. I told her that if anybody could it'd be her. They weren't even gold.

In between bites of Frito and sandwich and gulps of bland tea, Betty tapped her foot and touched her bulging pocket under the table.

"Stop that tapping, Betty Gray," Mrs. Grayson called from the dining room, where she sat reading the rest of the paper. She could've heard Betty tapping her foot a mile away.

"It's Dorie," Betty said.

Mrs. Grayson caught my eye through the archway, and I looked blank. She couldn't see Betty and wasn't about to get up.

"You'll tell the truth this instant or face the corner for an hour after lunch," she said, still bowed over the news.

"Okay," Betty said, in the same tone that *uncle* usually is spoken. "But I don't see how you can tell who it is when you can't even see me."

Mrs. Grayson laughed and tried to stifle it. "I have x-ray vision like Superman."

I thought a truer sentence had never been spoken. After a few moments of silence, Mrs. Grayson folded the paper and picked up the mystery she was halfway through and headed into the living room, far out of range.

"Is she gone?" whispered Betty. If she hadn't been she would have heard for sure, because Betty wasn't good at whispering. I nodded affirmative.

The last inch of tea and the last Frito disappeared from the table before Betty suggested we see who could hold their breath the longest. I knew she'd been practicing up at the country club, doing underwater laps faster than Tarzan's 'gator, but I was a fool for a contest and Betty knew it. I had to either beg Daddy to drive me to the Wileys' pond on Sundays or pay fifty cents to swim at the public pool, and by mid-July you needed a steak knife to slice through the slime, so I hadn't been much lately. You couldn't swim there to save your life, it was so crowded.

I could tread water and dog-paddle like Lassie but my head stayed out on both counts. I didn't know if I could hold my breath or not, so I said, "I'll bet you a million dollars you'll turn blue first."

"You're on," Betty said.

She wasn't the least bit afraid, and that should have clued me in.

Betty decided we would start at the count of three. We turned our chairs to face the second hand of the wall clock; we counted together, "One, two . . ." Our chests pumped forward as we sucked in air, and the race began. The second hand swept each little space between the black lines. I'd never looked into seconds before, and it was odd. Maybe the gravity that held things together, like the moon in its orbit around us, had spaces in it, like these free spaces between the black second lines of the clock, where things could fall apart. I felt like my watching could just about slow time down to a stop, but not quite. It would keep going whether I watched or not. Funny, I hadn't noticed the design on their clock face before now: two wings on a stick with two snakes crawling up. Each time the inner end of the second hand moved it cut a piece of a snake in two. Ten seconds went by like ten minutes, but I felt fine. I didn't look over at Betty even though I wanted to ask her about the snakes; I was afraid I'd get tickled and lose. Our cheeks must have looked awfully funny, puffed out with our mouths puckered like grouper. Twenty seconds felt the same as ten, except that my throat tightened up and some air escaped from my nose and my stomach muscles were beginning to hurt like they had after too many sit-ups in the President's Physical Fitness Test. I was thinking about that time I'd spotted a dime on the bottom of the shallow end. My hand sped toward the shiny money, and before I knew it my face slapped the water, my eyes were stinging, and I was about half choked to death. The lifeguard plucked me out and held me while I sputtered for air.

Then something happened, but I kept holding my breath. I looked at the clock but couldn't remember where it had started exactly. Those twined snakes started wriggling. Black balls of light encircled my head, bounced toward my eyes like planets trying to find an orbit around a star. I didn't let go. The circles looked dark and light, dark and light. And the snakes' tails thrashed the wings.

The next thing I remember was waking up on the cold kitchen floor. Mrs. Grayson stared down at me as she held the phone to her ear.

"Charles, I'm sorry to bother you — I thought you'd never come to the phone — Dorie's over here and she's passed out on the floor for some reason. What do you think I should do? . . . Yes, her eyes are open now . . . Pink . . ." Mrs. Grayson cupped a hand over the mouthpiece and directed Betty to get me a glass of ice water. While Betty filled a glass, I sat up and started to cry. I tried to hold it in, but I couldn't.

"She's crying, Charles . . . Oh, okay," Mrs. Grayson said and hung up. She bent down and helped me back into the chair. Betty's hand shook when she brought me the water; she was white as a sheep, probably wondering if I'd tell on her. I sipped and sipped.

"How do you feel now?" Mrs. Grayson asked.

"Never felt better," I said. The crying had embarrassed me, I guess. This time, Mrs. Grayson didn't say anything about what she'd more than once labeled my "sarcasm."

"I think I'll go home," I said. Momma would be watching her program, *Edge of Night,* by now.

"Only if you're sure you're all right," Mrs. Grayson said. "I never know what's going to happen next around this house; excitement every second." She looked at Betty. Betty looked at her hands.

"I'll walk you home," Betty muttered.

"That's a good idea," Mrs. Grayson chirped.

"Thanks for lunch," I said.

"You're welcome," Mrs. Grayson said. "Any time."

We walked out the front door and up the steps to the sidewalk and down the sidewalk and down the steps to the court without talking. For some reason, I kept seeing Barbara's painting of the waves and wondering if her colors were true to life. If they were, there was a lot more to the ocean than just blue.

"Bye," I said.

Betty squeezed the bottom of her pocket until the black ball erupted. She caught it before it fell, and smoothed down her dress. "Close your eyes and open your hand," she said.

I opened my eyes a few seconds later and watched Betty skip back up the sidewalk before I looked hard at the palm of my hand. With the scratched ball caged in my fingers, I felt strange, excluded from something, when I should have felt good. After all, it was nice of Betty to give me her ball. Maybe it was because I knew she could tell her daddy she'd lost it and get a new one. Maybe he'd buy her a prettier one, see-through with glitter stars trapped inside.

2

Strange Feelings

"Stand still, Daddy. I haven't even gotten to your shoulders yet." I was hosing the coal dust off his back. The six o'clock train had just whistled past. Daddy was real late that day because he'd missed his car pool and walked part of the way home before he thumbed a ride into Poorwater. At times like this I wished we'd never moved from Raven. It was closer to the mines, and Momma didn't have to worry so much all the time, wondering if anything was going wrong. But Daddy thought the Poorwater school system was better, so we moved into town when I started first grade. He'd been to college for a year, but nobody would have believed it if he'd told them, which might have been the reason he never told anybody and forbade me to mention it. Momma had told me, to encourage me to go to school one day when I was bellyaching. Daddy didn't speak for a long time after I asked him if it was true he'd been to college.

"Are you about finished? Your momma's gonna have our hides if her supper gets cold." I guess he was tired of bending over to keep the spray off his pants.

"If you don't want me to do this, get Momma to," I said.

"Hold on, hold on. You're doing a fine job." He bent farther down, picked up a big bar of Lava, and squeezed it between his gritty palms and over each hand.

I could hear Betty practicing piano in her den. The windows must have been open. Betty could look out one of those windows and see the turquoise roof of our trailer, but I don't think she could see me and Daddy, because we were behind the trailer next to the alley on a little square of concrete we never could figure out what was for. Maybe the last people had faced their front door to the alley. The slab served our purpose. I must have heard Betty play that same piece a thousand times. It was the same one she'd played in her last recital in the high school auditorium. Practically the whole town went; there wasn't much chance to hear classical music in Poorwater. Daddy took me. I could play "Heart and Soul" with Betty and some old hymns by ear, but just about the time I had something almost down, Betty got bored and told me it was her piano and I better not break it or her mommy would kill me. I don't really think you can break a piano by playing it, but if it happened I'd be sorry even if Mrs. Grayson didn't kill me with her meat tenderizer.

The dust swirled into strange, dark, muddy silt that pooled around Daddy's shoes until it streamed off the concrete block and into the alley over clinkers and gravel until it hit the gutter, rushed down the gutter until it disappeared through the grate at the lowest part of our U-shaped street. We didn't know what street we lived on, but the U street was where we parked the truck. Our mail came to a box tacked to the trailer or that might have solved the mystery. Our address didn't specify anything beyond Hareem's Trailer Court, Poorwater. Everyone in town knew where it was because they'd tried three times to turn it into a public park, with swing sets and basketball courts. Only two families lived in the rectangle of land about the size of a tenth of a Poorwater block. Daddy liked it. It was the most land we'd had to ourselves. And you didn't have to listen to anyone's fights but your own. Daddy constantly seeded and strawed the square of dirt right in front of the trailer, but somehow it wouldn't take. Over to the side, a sunny strip of grass where Momma took sunbaths and I pulled up dandelions sloped to the truck. In the shade outside the front door I had an eighteen-wheeler tire filled with good dirt where I grew pansies. Daddy wanted me to go back to growing tomatoes like I had the first summer, but I loved the pansies. They were the prettiest flowers on earth. I called them my little faces. Some, usually the purple ones, looked sad; the mixed yellow and purple looked the cheerfulest to me. I tried to cheer up the dark velvety ones by giving them the most to drink. That summer I named the biggest purple one Sam. When Sam looked up at me I felt miserable through and through.

After I finished with Daddy I kept the hose running and walked it to the tire garden. I stuck my thumb against the end of the water to make a spout arch up and land in the circle. I just about had the physics down when I heard Momma's voice.

"Dorie Ann, it's high time and then some. If you want any supper—"

"Coming," I said, to cut her off. She sounded sort of halfhearted, so there wasn't any sense in letting her get worked up. I turned off the spigot and wound the hose into its cobra pose beneath the trailer.

Sometimes our kitchen seemed so crowded I wanted to scream. I don't know why. It was worse in the summer because of the heat. Most of the time it cooled off after sundown because of the mountains, but we ate early. I thought if we had cooling potato salad once more that week I'd probably die of potato salad poisoning, if that was possible. It was hard to imagine there being too few of something like potatoes, but I'd learned about the potato famine in school. We ate slabs of fried Spam with our potato salad and drank lemonade Momma had made fresh. Daddy liked it more than I did. The biscuits melted in your mouth; we'd have the leftovers for breakfast. Even so, sweat stuck my shirt to my back and I was dying to leave the table.

"Momma, why don't we ever eat outside in the summer?"

"You don't want the whole neighborhood watching you eat, do you?"

"Dogs come and beg," Daddy added.

"The Graysons eat out in their back yard every night practically," I said.

"We ain't the Graysons, if you ain't noticed," snapped Momma.

"I just meant that they're not worried about folks staring, or dogs." I looked at Daddy. He kept up his rhythm, slicing his Spam while he chewed.

"Nobody can see into their back yard, if you ain't noticed the forest for the trees," Momma said.

She had me there. I could smell their steaks, though, so I knew they were cooking out tonight, like every weekend in the summer when Dr. Grayson wasn't on call.

"Dr. Grayson would make us move if he could, you know," Momma said.

"Now, Mary," Daddy said. "These biscuits are about the best *I've* ever had." He looked over at me for support.

"Sure as shit are," I said, immediately eating my words.

Momma pushed her chair back from the built-in, Formica-topped table and reached across to slap my face. I deserved it. Sometimes I didn't know what got into me.

"I'm sorry," I said. "It must be the heat. I feel funny."

My face stung, but I didn't hold it or anything. I just sat there wishing she'd sit back down and that I had some vanishing cream so I could disappear. She scraped off the fine line of congealed fat into the trash; she was watching her weight. All the time she looked in Daddy's direction like it was all his fault.

"I'm really sorry," I repeated.

"Well," Momma said, "you ought to be ashamed." Now it was coming. "David, did you hear what came out of your daughter's mouth?"

Daddy stayed quiet.

"She's barely ten years old, and did you hear that?"

Daddy spoke. "Dorie, go to your room."

"It's awful hot in there," I said. Momma burned me with her look.

"Then go out in the yard, but don't go out of it," Daddy said, like he was worn out.

"She ought to get a paddling," Momma said. "You've got her spoiled rotten. You'll live to rue the day, mark my words."

Momma was on her high horse now, with "rue the day" and "mark my words." I closed the screen as carefully as I dared. It hardly made a sound when it clicked to. It was their fight now.

I rubbed my cheek for a second, trying not to listen to them. They didn't used to fight; it was all my fault, I guess, for being such a smart ass. Daddy's arms could break somebody's neck off, but he and Momma would never hit at each other during an argument. They hardly touched, period; I couldn't remember having seen them kiss. It was like they were caught in a game of freeze tag. Or maybe they'd touched once, a long time ago, and gotten frozen instead of warm. All the things Daddy never said made a knot in my stomach. I could scream and kick, I guess, but he'd probably just look at me like I was crazy and shake his head. And maybe I would be then. Something hit the floor with a smash, so I walked around back and up the alley past the back of the Graysons' house. Betty saw me going by and came running to the gate.

"Where're you going?"

"I don't know," I said.

"What's wrong with your face?"

"I've got poison ivy, I think," I said, scratching at it for effect.

"Pop's got some sample ointment for it. You want me to get it?"

"No. I'm not sure what I've got yet."

"You know" — Betty was looking down — "if you go barefoot, you'll get worms."

I gave her my look.

"One time Barbara rubbed her legs with poison ivy and she couldn't do anything but lie in a tub of soda for a solid week. Are you sure you don't need that medicine?"

"No," I said firmly, "but thanks."

I thought whoever was stupid enough to rub poison ivy on their legs deserved whatever they got.

"You want to swing, then?" Betty opened the gate.

I stepped into her back yard and selected the swing lowest to the ground. My knees almost touched my chest, and it was hard to get started without breaking an ankle. I was taller than Betty. I looked across the yard to the picnic table where they ate. Under the umbrella Dr. and Mrs. Grayson sipped after-dinner drinks and shared a cigarette.

"You get a new umbrella?" I looked at the yellow floral pattern, the sickly green fringe.

"Yeah. Mommy didn't like the candy stripes on the other one, so she took it back. They didn't want to take it back but they gave her that one. I'd picked out the other one."

"I liked the other one."

"Pop said he liked it too, but it's Mommy's picnic set. You want to marsh some marshmallows?" Betty asked, like she'd just invented the idea.

Before I could say sure, Betty had run halfway across the yard to get the bag of marshmallows and the skewers. We toasted marshmallows for her pop and mom and some for each of us, and plucked them off the ends of the skewers with sticky fingers. I burned my mouth good, but I didn't care. Betty was an expert "marsher," browning each side perfectly medium golden before she'd touch the masterpiece to her lips.

I felt myself about to do something Mrs. Grayson would take as further evidence that I was a menace to society in general. My last marshmallow was nearly burned to a crisp just the way I liked them; in a second or two it was going to drip off the skewer into the coals, and all I wanted to do was see it stuck in Betty's dark pixie hair. If you told Betty her hair was black, she'd cry every time. I wanted to mash the marshmallow on the side of her head like a wad of old Dubble Bubble that would never come out. It wasn't that mean, because I knew it would rinse out when Betty washed her hair, which she'd have to do tomorrow night anyway because the day after that was Sunday. I was less than an inch from grabbing the crusty marshmallow off the end of the skewer and stuffing it close to Betty's ear instead of into my own mouth when she asked me a question.

"Will you feed Tiger while we're at the beach?"

"Huh?" I balanced the husk on the skewer, keeping it from falling into the coals.

"Tiger. You said you'd feed him, remember?"

I liked Tiger. I wasn't allowed to keep pets at the court. Once in a while ole Tiger would wake me up with his cry, and when I stepped outside to meet him, still in my pajamas, he'd rub my legs and purr up a storm. Most of the time he didn't pay much attention to anyone, Betty included. Whenever I fed Tiger he was real friendly, though. I could scratch his stomach a little without getting clawed. Tiger looked nothing like one; I don't know why he was called that. Probably one of Barbara's weird ideas. Tiger looked more like a polar bear, about that size, and as solid white as fancy tuna, with yellow eyes, really more orange. For a whole summer orange was my favorite color; that must have been when I decided the color of Tiger's eyes and that I liked him pretty much, and that was when Betty started asking me to be his official caretaker when they were gone. I had this thing about circuses, especially the tiger and lion tamers. I imagined myself taking one of our metal kitchenette chairs and a long whiplike switch and taming my Tiger, conning him to learn tricks while the Graysons were away. I thought maybe I'd try it again. Last time Tiger hadn't learned anything. I even gave him treats. I borrowed Tina's — she lives in the court — Hula Hoop and set up two stacks of cinder blocks as high as my waist. Tiger was supposed to jump through the hoop from one stack to the other. I held the Hula Hoop with one hand and tapped Tiger on the behind with the switch with the other. He raised up on his hind legs and swatted at the switch, opened his mouth, and nipped the end of it before I could raise it out of his reach. That was when he most resembled a real tiger.

I was saying, "Jump, Tiger! Jump! Come on, Tiger, you can do it — jump through the hoop and I'll give you some tuna salad!" Well, Tiger jumped all right. He sprang onto the front of my tanktop and sank eight of his claws into my shoulders and neck. I was too shocked for a second even to drop the hoop and switch. There I was, both arms outstretched with Tiger dug into my flesh worse than the leeches at the Wileys' pond. I screamed bloody murder, and Tiger let go. All but one claw, that Momma had to pry loose. I don't know why I still liked him after that. Ole Tiger didn't really give a shit about anybody.

I saw myself smash the marshmallow on top of Betty's head like I was doing the imaginary egg trick.

"Mommy! Mommy, help me!" Betty stumbled toward the umbrella with one hand over the mess on the top of her head. "Dorie's trying to *kill* me!" Dr. and Mrs. Grayson had slipped into the house, so Betty had to race through the basement door and all the way upstairs to get their attention. I picked up a piece of smoldering charcoal and threw it after her. I ran for the gate, shaking my hand, and bruised my feet bounding down the alley back to the court.

It was almost dark and Daddy sat in a lawn chair, smoking a cigarette, staring over the roof of the truck and up into the sky to the rim of the mountains. I hobbled into the yard, sucking my burned fingers.

"Didn't I tell you not to leave the yard?" he asked, without looking from the sky.

I watched Daddy stub out his half-smoked cigarette; he was trying to quit as an economy measure. He bought the cheapest cigarettes, made of the swept-up tobacco. I couldn't pronounce their name. I looked at Daddy and started to cry.

"Come here," he said. "What'd you do to your hand?"

I crawled silently into his lap, not worrying whether or not the old lawn chair would break. I was way too big to sit with Daddy, but I managed to wrap my arms around his very clean neck. His hard chest barely moved when he breathed. I sniffled into his collar before I blurted out a complete sentence between tears.

"Sometimes I feel like killing somebody."

"That's a terrible thing to say," Daddy said, so gently that I thought maybe he knew how I felt and wasn't going to hold it against me.

3

The Homecoming

About two weeks after Betty had to wash her hair a day early, the Graysons had already been on their vacation for a week, and I got a postcard with the same ocean picture as last year.

Dear Dorie,

I went on a vacation to Myrtle Beach, but you already know that. How's Tiger? Is he sleeping "you know where"? Is there enough cat chow left? Barbara's met somebody, as usual. He's too old for her though. See you next Saturday.

Your Friend,
Betty

Tiger was doing just fine, but he wasn't sleeping on the back porch like we'd planned. Right before they left, when the car was loaded and all anyone had to do was hop in, Betty made like she had to pee and went back into the house alone. She slipped out the back door onto the porch and unlocked the screen to the outside so Tiger could get up there to sleep. After locking the back door she ran to the front door, where her pop was waiting to pull that door to. She did it perfectly except she forgot to really go to the bathroom and Dr. Grayson had to stop the station wagon about half an hour down the road at an overlook so Betty could use the woods. She said he was really mad. I found the screen door unlocked like we'd planned, found an old towel and folded it into a cardboard box, and scooted the box into the corner for Tiger's naps.

Every morning I went up the alley and through the gate, across their back yard to the steps leading up to the back porch to whistle for Tiger. Usually I didn't have to whistle, because he just appeared, circled my legs, and brushed his tail up as high as my knees in his greeting ritual while I spooned out some smelly meat to top up his dry food and ran the hose to fill his water bowl in the shade beneath the porch. Betty's theory ran that if Tiger's food was left on the steps leading to the porch, no other cat or dog would have the nerve to touch it so close to the house. Tiger gobbled it down so fast I don't see how anything else could have ever gotten to it in time. I don't know where Tiger was hanging out, but it was probably underneath one of the hedges that fenced their back yard on either side. I checked on the box every other afternoon, but there was never any hair on the towel. The box stayed pressed exactly into the corner exactly as I had left it on the first day. Tiger was up to no good, though, you can rest assured. His ears looked intact, so whatever he was messing with, it was an undercover operation.

Momma stood beating up an orange box cake with a spoon when I got home from feeding and hanging out with Tiger. The fudge icing that always went with that cake didn't come out of a box, and boy was it good. I thought I'd stick around until it was bowl-licking time.

Momma saw me eyeing the batter. "Willie's coming home tomorrow. I got a letter last week."

"Oh," I said, cool as a cucumber. "Where's he coming in from?"

"He didn't say."

"What's the postmark?"

"It's in there." She motioned to her and Daddy's bedroom and added, "If you're bent on becoming a spy."

"How long's he staying?" I called over my shoulder.

"It ain't polite to ask." Momma sampled a finger lick of batter.

I picked up the letter; postmark read Knoxville.

"We're his momma and daddy, too, if you ain't noticed."

"He sure doesn't act like it. He might as well be anybody's brother but mine."

Momma didn't even answer that. When Willie was coming home you couldn't make her mad.

"Does Daddy know he's coming?"

"Course he knows! It ain't no secret. Here, hold the bowl."
No secret from anyone but me, I thought. Momma ran the
spatula around and around and across the bottom of the bowl
until hardly any batter was left to lick. Willie had dropped out
of Tornado High when I was in first grade. Daddy tried to
keep it from me, afraid that I'd figure it was the thing to do.
Some kid in my class told me about Willie. "Your brother's on
drugs," said Barry, the kid who traded everything on his plate,
including the hamburger, for extra onions. "He's a dropout too,"
Barry said when I wouldn't give up my onions for his sweet
pickle chips.

When the two round pans were in the oven Momma started
melting the squares of Baker's chocolate you couldn't eat for
candy, they were so bitter. The icing took about two sticks of
butter and a box of powdered sugar. Luckily there was always
way too much of it to go on the cake, so I'd have one bowl to
lick anyway.

About noon the next day Willie loped into the grassy part of
the yard, wearing a knapsack and looking sunburned around
the edges of his once-upon-a-time-white T-shirt.

"Hey, Dorie," he called, "it's your brother, Will. You look
like you've seen a ghost!"

"I remember you," I said. I stuck out my hand to shake, but
Willie bent down and kissed my cheek. I don't know why he
did that. We didn't kiss much in our family, especially not Momma
and Daddy. But when Momma heard Willie she rattled out of
the trailer into the yard for the first time in about two days.
Willie reached around and grabbed the dusty green pack off
his back, dropped it to the ground, and you've never seen such
carrying-on.

"Oh, Willie! Ain't you a sight! Oh, Willie, we've all missed
you to death." She threw her arms around his neck.

"I've missed you too, Momma." He hugged her some more.
"Don't you look fit to kill! You lost weight, ain't you?"

Willie always homed in on the right thing to say to Momma.

Almost like he had ESP. I thought I was going to throw up, but I just picked up the pack and carried it inside. I stuck my head back out the door and asked, "Where's Willie sleeping?"

"He's in your room," Momma said.

Before I could spit, Willie said, "I don't want to put nobody out."

"Daddy can string up the hammock," I said.

"That sounds just fine," Willie said. "I can look up through the trees to the stars. It suits me just fine," he insisted.

Momma said, "Dorie don't mind, do you, honey?"

"I left your stuff on the kitchen floor," I said. "What you got in there anyway? It's heavy as a dead horse."

Willie just laughed. I knew he wouldn't tell me. But I wanted Momma to know he was up to something. Which, count on it, he was. He and ole Tiger were just about alike in that department.

"Sit out here in the shade," Momma said. "I'll bring you some lemonade fresh made."

"Thank you. We'll just sit here and get reacquainted." Willie motioned me to the chair facing his.

After a pause I asked, "How'd you get here?"

"Oh, this way and that," he hedged, then added, in a strangely soft voice, "The Lord provides a way for His own."

"But how'd you get here from Knoxville?" I wanted him to know I wasn't taken in.

"I took the Greyhound," he whispered, like it was a golden chariot.

Momma delivered one glass of lemonade full up with clinking ice cubes and one giant slab of cake on our best plates, not the dishwasher-safe plastic. "Even your momma can't break these." Daddy had gotten a kick out of his own joke.

"Momma, you shouldn't have," Willie said, his mouth watering at the sight of that cake. It looked like something straight out of *Better Homes*. Every year Mrs. Grayson tried a new project from their Christmas Ideas issue. For some reason, she wanted Betty to learn to sew.

"Can I have some, too?" I stared at Willie's plate.

"It's on the counter. But you'll spoil your supper." When I got up she plopped into my chair to watch Willie eat his cake.

I came back out with my piece and sat on the stoop.

"Don't lean back, you'll bust the screen," Momma said.

Willie was scraping the icing off his plate, lapping it from the fork. He took his finger and wiped off every little smudge of chocolate before he handed Momma the empty plate and leaned back in the chair, crossing one big foot over the other. Striped cuffs encircled his ankles above each shoe but there wasn't a sign of a sock to be seen through the hole in his sole.

"What size shoe do you wear?" I asked.

"Dorie, that's not nice," Momma said.

Willie chuckled. "I reckon the last pair I bought they had to tan two whole cows to make them."

Momma laughed too long. "That's a good one," she snorted, after about five solid minutes of hee-hawing.

"That's the best cake I ever ate," Willie said, eyeing his empty plate in Momma's lap. He raised the water-beaded glass and slurped out some ice to crack between his molars. Momma got up and he handed her the glass.

"I'll get you another helping. Dorie, let me by."

"I think I'll have some more," I said.

"You've already spoiled your supper."

"Willie's having two."

"Willie's a grown man," Momma said, like that was the best thing on earth.

I didn't feel that hungry anymore, so I just took my plate inside and came back out and sat down in the chair. Willie had his eyes closed. If he hadn't been who he was he might have been fairly nice-looking, with a high forehead like Daddy and light brown curly hair like Momma. His nose looked as straight as Granddaddy's in the picture, and his greenish-blue eyes were like mine. The jeans he wore were so filthy they had trouble bending at the knees. Willie now had his feet stretched straight out in front of him. I was counting the freckles on his sparsely haired arms when Momma came back and he opened his eyes and sat up to accept the refilled glass and plate. His belt looked like a smear of grease around his middle.

"You got any clothes need washing?" Momma looked at his pants.

"I'll take them down to McClure's later on." Willie stuffed cake into his mouth.

"I never heard of such a thing. Dorie, where'd you put his bag?"

Willie bolted up so fast I thought he must have choked on his last bite of cake. "I'll get them for you, Momma." Willie put down the plate and hopped into the trailer. In about half a minute he emerged, carrying two handfuls of wrinkled-up under-wear and shirts.

"You can wear your daddy's spare while I wash those. Take them off." She gestured toward his jeans.

"I can't wear Daddy's pants."

"Why not? I bet you're about the same size. They're hanging on the nail behind the bedroom door."

In a few minutes Willie came back outside and handed Momma his stinking jeans. He kept on his filthy T-shirt. And Momma didn't insist. Daddy's pants fit him better than his own.

"Let's walk down to the Wye," Willie said.

I wouldn't have gone with him but without Betty there was nobody to do anything with except Tina next door; her daddy was a miner too, and she was only seven and wanted to play school all the time. More than an hour of that was more than enough. The summer was nearly over as it was.

The Wye River ran along the edge of town, with the railroad tracks beside it most of the way. It was only the length of a football field or so from Hareem's, straight downhill all the way after we'd climbed our U street and crossed the Graysons' street. We passed the crumbling wall of slate, where I picked out little chips good for drawing hopscotch boards on the sidewalk above the steps down to the court. I always drew Heaven in a half moon at the top of the board and Hell in a half moon slanting downhill toward the court. Willie wedged out a flat piece of rock and tossed it up and down. Whenever it slapped his palm it made me edgy. Then he'd flip it up like a coin and watch it tumble end over end over end, going up and coming down, before he'd catch it again. We stopped at the bottom of the hill at the light; no traffic, but the light was red, so we waited and Willie kept flipping and catching that rock. It was driving me crazy. We crossed the street and headed down the worn dirt path to the riverbank. Down a ways was an old man fishing with a homemade pole.

"How's the fishing?" Willie called.

"It ain't — so far," the man hollered.

Willie closed his eyes a long second, opened them, pulled back his arm like a slingshot, and sent the rock skipping straight across the Wye. I counted six hops. I bent down to find me a good rock. Willie sat and pulled off his shoes and scrappy socks. He rolled up Daddy's pants and stuck his feet into the green water.

"Gosh" — he caught his breath and jerked back his feet — "that's cold as a witch's —" He stopped himself and tried the water again; this time he got his feet in up to the ankles. "It feels so good," he said.

I stood and sidearmed the rock I'd picked out. It hopped once and sank.

"Pretty good," Willie said. "But you got to *see* it skip before it'll really skip. You got to see it in your mind before you let it go."

"That doesn't make any sense."

"Sure it does. Now try another one, but watch it skip a dozen times before you throw it in."

I couldn't help but squat and search for another flat rock. I might as well try it.

"Now wait," Willie said when I'd stood up with my rock in hand, poised to throw. "Close your eyes and see that rock hopping like a frog right out over the water."

I closed and opened my eyes.

"You didn't do it long enough. Close your eyes tight."

"Okay."

I closed them and sent the rock skipping and hopping across water as smooth as cream. I opened my eyes, drew back my arm, and released the rock. It looked like a Mexican jumping bean skimming the rippling water. I slurped in a breath of air, my eyes bugging.

"Try it again!" Willie said.

"It might not work," I said and sat down beside him on the bank. "Where'd you learn that trick anyway?"

"Oh, it's hard to say, but it ain't a trick."

I wished I hadn't asked. The old man let out a shout and we looked his way.

"He's finally got something," I said.

We hurried down the bank. He was winding the string around the end of the pole. The string pulled taut; the tip of the pole pointed toward the water.

"Need a hand?" Willie asked.

"I reckon not," the man said. His gray-streaked whiskers quivered and his breath stank. He clenched his jaw, pressing his tongue against the dark stubs of his eyeteeth. His fleshy tongue showed through the spaces left in front.

After the man had wound some more string, Willie reached into the river and pulled up the catch. A catfish about ten inches long dangled below a batch of little sinkers and hooks.

"Hot dog in the morning!" Willie said. "You'll have you a good supper tonight."

The old man bent down and lifted up his bucket to take the fish as Willie removed the hook. All the time the fish sounded like a crying baby or like air squeaking from a pinched balloon. I stepped back and focused across the Wye to a couple of kids walking along the opposite bank. I heard the catfish plop into the bucket and its crying stop.

"You want to try and catch something?" the man asked, setting down his bucket, picking up his pole.

"I might, but I don't have a pole," Willie said.

"Here, this here's a lucky one." The man thrust the stick, wound round the end with what looked like kite string, into Willie's hands by way of thanks. "Just leave it under that bush yonder when you're done. I'll fetch it tomorrow."

"Why thanks," Willie said, taking the pole.

"I got to get this critter home." The old man grabbed the bucket and started up the bank toward the path.

The rest of the afternoon Willie and I sat beside the Wye getting sunburned and waiting for a bite. I pushed my skin with one finger and drew it back to watch the white oval fill in with red. I had pretty hairy arms for a girl. Last fall in the lunch line I had put my arms up against the best-looking boy's in the class and nearly won. And I think he was the only boy who even had any hair on his arms, but he had a lot. After that he was my boyfriend until he and his mother had to move to Philadelphia right after Christmas. I missed him for a while. Nobody took his place, but I got used to being by myself again at the lunch table. Betty was a good friend in the summer but she wasn't much at school. She had a lot of other friends — the lunch box set. I had a ticket to get punched for dime lunches at school. The plate lunch kids and the lunch box kids didn't really mix, and most of the other plate lunch kids lived in the hollers. It seemed like I was the only in-between kid in the school. There were two blacks, though, a brother and sister, and I guess they felt worse. We ate all right at home, especially when Willie was with us. Daddy's sister, my aunt Sarah, farmed in Rural Retreat, and we'd ride up there to get stuff — two hams a year and lots of home-canned vegetables every fall.

Willie jumped up. "Whoo now! I think we've got something."

The line sprang taut, jerked back and forth, some inches of slack quickly settling back into a tight line again.

"It must be a big one," I said.

"I think you better get your hands tight on the bottom of the pole. I'll try to wind in some line when it swims this way."

I gripped the pole, the end punching into my stomach while Willie managed to keep one hand on the tip of it and the other on the line so he could feel the slack when it came. In a second Willie found some and wound the loose inches around a stick he'd clawed up from the ground. Whatever was on the hook didn't want to be there. Even as Willie gradually looped more and more string around the stick, I felt myself inching closer and closer to the river.

"Back up if you can," Willie said. "Here, let me."

He traded me the stick for the pole. Winding string was even worse, so we switched back after Willie had backed up the bank a few feet. As usual when hard times come or something special happens, nobody else was around to see it. We fought that weight into shore, winding until the catch was in view.

"What in hell!" Willie exclaimed, trying to get a look at it.

Instead of the thousand-pound catfish I had stored up in my mind, what was this muddy-looking monster? With a mouth the size of a baseball, and a set of sharp teeth to rival a bear trap. The ugliest thing about it was its disposition.

"It's a damn dogfish," Willie said.

"What's that?" I watched as scales like armor rippled the surface each time the dogfish bucked.

"Dogfish is the meanest fish God made outside of piranha. Got teeth like a shark and angry as a rabid coon. Dogfish'll eat anything, including each other. Regular cannibals."

"Yuck," I said, wondering what a piranha could be. "You gonna pull him on in?"

"He'll just start breathing and grow legs and follow us home if I do."

"That's impossible. I don't care what kind of fish it is."

Just then the line snapped with the quickness of a twig and the zing of an arrow letting fly. The dogfish squirmed off with our hook in his belly to make him that much meaner in the long run.

"Good riddance." Willie wiped his brow.

"I didn't even get a good look at him."

"You didn't miss much — that fella's worse-looking than Jo-Jo the Dog-faced Boy."

"Who's that?"

"A famous freak. He naturally looks like a werewolf."

"And horses can fly too," I said.

"What about that dogfish? You ever hear tell of anything like it?"

"No, but I've seen everything now."

"You've just got started on it — on seeing what there is to see in this wide world." Willie's eyes seemed far away. "Let's go home." He balanced the pole over his shoulder.

"You're supposed to leave it there." I pointed to the bush.

"I've got to fix the line, put on new sinkers and hooks too. That dogfish took it all. Daddy's likely to have some tackle."

"He doesn't fish," I said.

"Well, he used to, a while back," Willie said.

Daddy probably took Willie fishing, but if he did I suddenly didn't want to hear about it. As we climbed the hill home I remembered the face of the dogfish and thought it looked sort of like a bat. Daddy had to kill a bat with a broom one summer when it wriggled through an eye-size hole in the screen door. Momma nearly had a heart attack. Daddy dropped it in a paper bag and into the silver garbage can. Momma told me not to go near that trash until the men came to pick it up, but I opened the lid, unrolled the top of the paper bag, and let the dead bat fall out. I squatted next to the bat, took a stick, and flipped him over on his back. At first his two long, pointy teeth scared me, but after a while he started looking like a field mouse with triangle ears and phony plastic wings wrinkled up like the faces of dried apple dolls. Bats have tails, too. The dark brown fur didn't even smell bad yet. I stared into the bat's dull squinty eyes, then at what looked like thumbs at the top of his wings where shoulders might have been. I counted his ten taloned toes and thought about keeping him in my room. Before I realized I shouldn't have done it, I picked up the poor bat with my bare hands and slipped him back inside the bag. His drawn-up wings stayed stiff and still. I crimped the bag shut.

It was strange to think that dogfish came out of the same

water where, a quarter mile north, around the bend, the foot-washing Baptists dunked each other on Sunday afternoons. Then I got to figuring that maybe it was all that sin they left in the river that was responsible for making the dogfish so pugnacious.

Daddy was waiting for us when we got home from fishing. That night Momma cooked a meal to beat the feast for the Prodigal Son. We were all so stuffed up with biscuits and real country ham, snap beans, slaw, and more of that cake that we turned in earlier than usual, at the same time as Daddy. Willie put on his span-clean pants — I don't see how Momma got them washed — and looped his crummy belt around them. Just before he situated himself in the hammock he pulled his dirty T-shirt over his head in exchange for a freshly Cloroxed one; I saw him tuck a delicate gold cross inside the neck band before he tucked the shirt inside his pants and I said good night. As the lights turned off inside the trailer I could hear him whistling my favorite Carter Family song, "Keep on the Sunny Side."

I lay awake, remembering the end of a verse — "And when the ship comes in, I'll leave this world of sin, and go sailing through the air." I thought maybe it wasn't so bad having Willie home after all and wondered if he'd stay any longer than the three days he'd promised Momma. I still wanted to see what he had in his bag.

4

Holy Rollers

The next night, Thursday, I woke up about ten-thirty because Tiger was pitching a fit underneath my window. My copy of *The Arabian Nights* plopped onto the floor when I sat up. That afternoon I'd tried to return it to the library; it was due, but the librarian asked me if I'd read it all, and when I told her I hadn't finished she stamped it and gave it back to me. I thanked her, but I was disappointed; I thought I'd try another book. Maybe there's a rule that says you can't start a new book until you read all of the last one. *The Arabian Nights* was beginning to grow on me, but it seemed like I could never get through one story without another one starting. It was like a great big box with smaller and smaller boxes inside, but you couldn't ever tell where the treasure would be, if there was one. Whenever I thought something exciting was going to happen, it turned out to be the beginning of another story instead. People in Arabia like to tell stories instead of doing things, that's clear. It wasn't so bad, though. I'd read a few pages every night before going to sleep. All the same, my dreams had been pretty strange lately.

I tried to slide back the screen to stick my head out, but it jammed, and Tiger kept mouthing off like a maniac. I could sleep through the train whistle but not through that high-pitched *meow*. I tiptoed to the door and outside, hoping I wouldn't wake anybody; if they could sleep through Tiger, they'd earned their rest. I sat down on the stoop, and Tiger was right there, rubbing my legs and stretching up his head to have his ears scratched. On full moon nights, like that one, light filtered in through the trees like the moon was caught behind them. I rubbed Tiger's head and looked at the patches of moonlight, pale blue, scattered over the ground. It took me a minute to remember Willie in the hammock, but when I looked I could see it clear as day. And Willie was gone!

I raced back to my room as quietly as I could to put on my clothes and shoes. I thought I could find Willie before anybody knew he was missing. Tiger skittered beneath the trailer and I ran to the end of our street, toward town. Between the moonlight and the occasional streetlight, it seemed a lot earlier. Then I guess I hadn't gotten more than a quarter mile from home when I spotted Willie crossing the street down from the Sally Thomas Hospital. Just then the moon must have hitched on a mountain, because the light went dim all of a sudden, exactly like the end of a movie scene. I hurried toward the place I'd seen Willie, not knowing whether or not I wanted him to know I was there. I didn't call out to him. The next time I spotted him he walked under a streetlight in front of the Rexall Drug. He stopped at the corner, threw down a cigarette, its red flame falling like a shooting star, a quick flash to the street. One foot twisted it out and he walked rapidly on. I wasn't sure whether to follow or shout or go home. I kept following, like there was a magnet in my head. We crossed the railroad tracks and passed the junior high. Just before reaching the armory Willie took a sharp left into a field full of parked cars. As I got closer I could hear what sounded like a hymn but I couldn't make out the words. There in the middle of the field was a big tent meeting. Why on earth Willie was going there, God only could tell. I should have gone back home the second I saw where we were headed, but just as I recognized the tent for what it was, a burst of applause swept out of it and Willie vanished inside. The triangles of light formed by the canvas doors held his silhouette for a moment. Briefly, he looked like a backlit mountain just before the sun overshadows it and rises high enough to spotlight trees. Willie was in there, and there I was trapped on the outside with the riffraff, the drinkers and adulterators in their parked cars.

I made my way through the maze of cars, most of them with

the windows rolled down and country music wafting out. A few couples argued with the windows rolled most of the way up but not far enough. A man carrying a bottle in a paper bag reeled into my arm when I passed. If I could just get Willie and go home. The open doors of the tent nearly blinded me as I got closer and closer to the light. The singing had stopped by the time I slipped into the back row. From front to back I scanned row after row without turning up Willie. I knew he was in there, but where?

"Now, ladies and gentlemen," a familiar voice crooned, "will you kindly direct your attention and open your hearts for Brother Saul Blevins of the Holiness Church of God in Jesus' Name, of Chattanooga, Tennessee."

For some reason I was hardly surprised at Willie's oration. He sat down in the front row and Brother Saul appeared from behind the curtain at the right-hand side of the stage, wearing a checked suit and a string tie ornamented with a miniature of the praying hands.

"Y'all sang the words of the hymn just now," Brother Saul began. " 'Some folk don't walk with God, some folk do,' " he recited. " 'But only God knows who's who.' " A few amens fluttered through the crowd. Brother Saul hummed the chorus once while some of the flock furnished the lyrics. "Who's who, who's who. Only He knows who's who." Brother Saul made his way back to the podium, picked up his Bible like it was no more important than a wad of dirty diapers, and looked out into the faces of the crowd. A spotlight flooded onto his face while the houselights faded a bit.

All I could see of Willie was the back of his head, and now, with the fat head in front of me bobbing, even that was getting harder to keep an eye on.

"Jesus said," Brother Saul almost whispered. "JE-sus said," Brother Saul repeated in a lilting, much louder voice, " 'If you suffer with Me, you shall also reign with Me.' "

A few hushed amens from the crowd.

"Now listen very carefully." Brother Saul enunciated each syllable like he was mouthing to deaf mutes. "JE-sus said, 'If you
suffer with Me, you shall also REIGN with Me.' He didn't say
you was going to reign with Him first, now did He? Suffering
comes first for a reason, folks. Without suffering there can be
no blessing. Without you suffering first, there is no reward. There
is no reward, there is no KING-dom, unless you sweat a little for
it."

I heard low chuckles all around when he hit the sweat line.

"We're made perfect through suffering, and there's no other
way. If there was another way, don't you think God Himself
would have known about it? Praise Jesus on the cross — if there
was another way, don't you think He would have found it out?
And if there was another way, I'd surely tell you about it!"

Whenever Brother Saul weaved near the edge of the stage,
the spotlight followed, illuminating Willie's head like he was
wearing a halo. I got more and more wrapped up in Brother
Saul's words and less and less interested in what Willie's part
in things was. Brother Saul recapped Jesus' life and spent special
attention on His suffering on the cross. Even Jesus had to die
like a thief before inheriting the Kingdom, was Brother Saul's
main point. He spent a long time describing Jesus' wounds, in
His hands and feet especially, before moving on.

"Take a second and imagine a nail through your hand, just
one of them. Take a second and imagine a nail through one of
your feet."

I could feel the nails, the way I had seen the rock skip before
it skipped. I rubbed my thumbs into my palms, one then the
other.

"Suffering of the flesh might be torment, but it's nothing com-
pared with the eternal torment of a soul in Hell. Flesh can be
burned, flesh can be stoned, flesh can be ripped off like the
cloth of the Soul it is, but the Soul, the everlasting Soul, lives
on, either in Heaven or in Hell. And you've got a choice. Yes,
praise Jesus, brothers and sisters, there's a choice to be made.
It's up to you where your Soul spends eternity. You think it's

torture to burn a finger on an iron, ladies, consider having your Soul burned. If you think it's torture, more than you can stand, to have a tooth pulled, gentlemen, consider what torments the depths of Hell hold next time you're in that dentist's chair! I've never personally been to Heaven or Hell, you're thinking, so what do I know about it? What do I know about it? What the Bible says, ladies and gentlemen. And what the Bible says is that each sinner has a choice, and can't nobody else make that decision. And I've seen the faces of the saved just after the breath of life left them, may they rest in peace, and they died with a sweet Jesus smile across their lips. I hate to tell you, but I've also seen, been a witness to, what happens to the faces of sinners, unrepentant sinners, when they pass away. Folks, it's a terrible sight; it's the worst feeling on earth to know a soul is already halfway to Hell the instant death grabs it."

Brother Saul ambled back to the podium.

"I'd like to read to you now from the Word of God. In Second Peter it says, chapter one, verses three and four, read along if you will: 'According as his divine power hath given unto us all things that pertain unto life and godliness, through the knowledge of him that hath called us to glory and virtue: Whereby are given unto us exceeding great and precious promises: that by these ye might be partakers of the divine nature, having escaped the corruption that is in the world through lust.' That's a whopping big promise now, isn't it? Praise Jesus, He has promised us a part in God's very nature if we abandon our lust of the world.

"Let's think for a few minutes just what it means to be partakers of the divine nature. It means nothing less than being assured you're going to Heaven! Are you sure? Are you sure?" Brother Saul pointed at members of the audience, who obediently shook their heads no.

"It means assurance, blessed assurance, of a place in God's Kingdom, in Heaven and on Earth. When you get up in the morning, your back aches, you'd rather go back to sleep, am I

right? Praise Jesus, when you get up in God's image your back
might ache but your spirit's excited, hungry, not for scrambled
eggs and brains, but for doing the will of God all day long.
Every day is exciting when you're part of God's nature, when
you're part of God's holy plan. It's a plan for your life and it's
a plan for the whole world. Amen."

"Amen" came the crowd's response, right on cue.

"You see these mountains all around us? Well, you can move
them if you have faith no bigger than a mustard seed. If you
don't believe it, you're going against God's Word. If you don't
believe God can move a mountain, you're just not saved. 'He
that believeth not shall be damned.' Those aren't my words,
they're God's Words."

Brother Saul picked up his Bible again. "Now turn with me
to Mark, chapter sixteen, verses sixteen to eighteen. These are
the very Words of Jesus. Read verse sixteen silently to yourself.
It's black and white, ladies and gentlemen, black and white!
'He that believeth and is baptized shall be saved; but he that
believeth not shall be damned.' Does it say you have to dishonor
your parents to be damned? No! Does it say you have to lust
after your neighbor's wife to be damned? No!"

Several members of the audience shouted "No!" along with
Brother Saul.

"And does it say" — he raised his voice into a shout — "THAT
YOU HAVE TO RAPE AND MURDER TO BE DAMNED?"

"NO!!" The whole audience shook.

"Praise Jesus," Brother Saul said very quietly. "Praise His
name," he said again while the whole place chorused, "Praise
Him, sweet Jesus. Praise God."

"You must believe, that's all. You must believe Jesus is the
Son of Almighty God. That's all. You must believe that Jesus,
the Son of God, died on the cross and was buried and in three
days rose from the dead. And how can you tell who believes
and who don't? Read on, read on aloud with me, we're still in
Mark. 'And these signs shall follow them that believe; In my

name shall they cast out devils; they shall speak with new tongues; they shall take up serpents; and if they drink any deadly thing, it shall not hurt them; they shall lay hands on the sick, and they shall recover.' "

Scattered voices kept reading on but stopped cold when they realized they were alone. Brother Saul took off his coat and rolled his shirt sleeves.

"You might think it's easy to move a little ole mountain after you try wrestling the devil out of somebody! You might think it's easy to heal the sick with a touch of your hands after you try it the devil's way a while! Try Jesus! God doesn't lie!"

Near the front of the tent a man got up to his feet and turned toward the crowd, speaking with a strange voice, some kind of foreign language. More people rose to their feet — a fat woman, a man with a mustache, a farmer in overalls — moving their lips and raising their hands over their heads. Brother Saul started whispering "Praise Him, praise Him" into the microphone. More and more people stood and raised up their hands. A few fell to the floor and rolled while others stood over them shouting in that language I'd never heard before. Then Brother Saul closed his eyes and stretched out his hands. Willie sprang to his feet and retrieved a cage from behind the podium. He set it on a little table and unlocked the padlock with a key he produced from a pocket. Brother Saul looked like he might not be able to see, with his eyes rolled back in his head, but he dipped his hands into the cage and raised a snake. Brother Saul shook a little, like he was freezing from head to foot. His hands looked as stiff as a corpse. I'd never seen anything but a copperhead before. This snake was green and long as a picnic table. Brother Saul wrapped it around and around his waist. The snake hissed and slithered along one of Brother Saul's shirt sleeves, then along his bare arm to the wrist. Into the palm of his hand came the head of the snake; it shot around his hand, looping several times before stretching its head straight out from his hand. The hairs on my arms stood up.

Brother Saul opened his eyes and hurried to the cage. He flipped both his hands and unwound the snake. Willie snapped the lid closed.

"Does anyone among us feel the anointment?" Brother Saul asked. "I can feel the Spirit's power running through this tent tonight, right now. Praise Jesus, someone's got the Spirit! Do you feel the power of the Lord commanding you to prove God's word is true?" He looked toward the snake cage.

Nobody was rushing to the stage. Most everyone had returned to their seats, even those who had been writhing on the floor, when Brother Saul had first taken up the snake.

"That cobra's mean as a snake!" shouted Brother Saul. "But he can be overcome by the power of God. Think what He can do for you. God don't make promises He can't keep! If you hear the voice of Jesus whispering in your heart, I'll be waiting here during the hymn."

The audience, suddenly aware of what had taken place, rose to their feet and began shouting, "Praise God! Praise God!" Willie got up with the rest and began working his way among the rows, carrying a basket. Dollars and pennies and quarters flooded into the basket as it was whisked along each row.

Brother Saul started up "Amazing Grace" and set himself at the podium to receive the saved. By the end of the song a long line was gathered, and I slipped out the door into the night, hoping Willie hadn't seen me. I knew Brother Saul had more work to do. About midnight he'd have to lead the newly saved down to the Wye and dunk each one if he wanted to keep up with the Primitive Baptists.

I ran most of the way back home, afraid all the time that someone was following me or that Momma would be waiting at the door, holding a frying pan in one hand and a rolling pin in the other.

I don't know why but it was quiet as the world just after a thunderstorm when I slipped into the yard from the alley. I felt like I could hear my own heartbeat, my panting, especially my steps. I found Tiger curled up beneath the trailer sound asleep, and I tiptoed into my room, with my chest heaving up and down and my breathing so loud I was sure that would give me away. After five minutes I was able to hear Daddy's snoring from behind the wall. I felt safe, pulled off my clothes, and climbed under the sheet to sleep until morning, pretty sure that I'd seen the last of Willie for a while.

5

The Snake

As soon as I woke up I headed out to see if Willie had come home. The night before felt like a dream, hazier than a memory. Momma was beating eggs and smiling about something. Willie must be around.

"You want scrambled eggs this morning, Dorie?" Momma asked.

"Nope. Just toast and milk."

"Willie likes scrambled eggs, always has."

Bully for him, I thought and opened the screen door. There he sat, pinching little weights onto new line for the old man's pole. I could have dreamed the whole thing — the tent, Brother Saul, the snake. Part of me hoped it had been a dream, but the other part sensed the truth.

"Morning, Dorie," Willie said, like nothing was different.

"I thought you took that back yesterday." I decided to play along.

"Better a day late and good as new than on time and broke, don't you think?"

"He'll probably think we stole it. Where'd you get the sinkers?"

"Daddy's old tackle box. He said it was all right."

Momma called, "Eggs up in a flash. You want them out there?"

"If you don't mind. It's such a pretty morning," Willie said.

"Is my toast ready?"

"Just how many hands do you suppose I have?"

I went inside and put the bread in the toaster and poured a glass of milk. Momma scraped the eggs onto a good plate and poured Willie a mug of coffee to wash them down with. While I waited for the toast I was trying to figure out a way to find out more about Willie without letting on I knew anything. I probably should have told Momma what I'd seen and taken the consequences of having run around like I had. But I knew Willie would just take off like always and leave me in the doghouse. Then I spotted that knapsack of his, wadded into the corner behind the kitchen table.

"Since this is my last day at home," I heard Willie say, "I thought maybe we could all do something together."

I wondered what he'd done all day yesterday before the tent meeting when he could have been at home visiting, but I kept quiet and reached for his bag. I was going to blow the whistle on him just as soon as I had some hard evidence.

"We could take the truck and go for a picnic on Bald Mountain," Momma suggested.

"That's a great idea!" Willie said.

He'd had his eye on Daddy's truck the whole time he'd been home. I loosened the strap and lifted the flap.

"That okay with you, Dorie?" Willie called, like I could change their plans if I wanted to.

I had my arm down in the bag. Momma was going to march inside any second. "It's fine by me," I shouted and lifted the bag out of the corner. I could tell before I shoved my face in that I wasn't going to find anything; the bag was light as a feather. Nothing inside but clean clothes, a ratty Blue Horse notebook, and a raggedy old Bible.

Every place I looked for answers I found some more mystery. Willie should have had a question mark for his name, as far as I was concerned, the way he came and left without ever explaining himself. Each time he visited, Momma acted like Christmas had come, and each time he left she went back to getting through things the best way she could, watching her program and saying goodbye to Daddy in the mornings and hello at night, and yelling at me in between. There were so many things I didn't understand that to start asking questions seemed like another dead end. I didn't even know what questions to ask. And I used to have a notebook entirely devoted to hard questions. For starters I could've tried "Where're you going?" and "Where've you been?" But I knew I wouldn't get anywhere with those. There was something I wanted to ask Momma, too; I wanted to ask her why she couldn't love me the way she loved Willie. I wanted to ask her why I couldn't do anything right when I was trying so hard. I wanted to know why we'd ever moved to Poorwater if we couldn't ever really fit in. Most of all I wanted to know how you could be born into a family and not feel like you belonged there — how you could be blood-related to people you didn't know the first thing about.

In a couple of hours Momma had fried chicken, made sandwiches, cookies, lemonade, and the ever present potato salad, and filled our picnic basket to the hilt.

"I guess I'd better go get us gassed up," Willie said.

"We could get gas on the way," Momma said but handed him the keys. She was long accustomed to the enigmatic ways of men with their vehicles. "You think three dollars'll do?" She reached into her snap purse.

Willie took the bills and stuffed them into his jeans. "I'll be back quicker than you can shake a stick!" He looked at me like I was tapping my foot, raring to go. On my way up to the Graysons' to take care of Tiger I could hear the engine revving away.

About half an hour later I'd been back fifteen minutes. Momma looked at her watch. "I wonder what's keeping him?"

"Probably saw one of his old friends," I said.

Momma latched onto the idea. "Of course, ain't you smart? He ran into one of those Breedlove boys. Don't they work some at the Gulf?"

"I think so," I said.

They were the last thing Willie had run into — he didn't have any friends to speak of. But Momma thought he did. For some reason she'd decided the Breedlove boys were Willie's best friends in the world. Every time we saw one of them she'd tell him anything she could about Willie. They hadn't asked about him once that I knew of. But they'd smile when she gave news of

Willie. I think one of them was retarded or something. He smiled all the time. The other one hardly said a word except "That's nice" and "Y'all come back."

When an hour and a half had come and gone I heard the truck pull up. Momma had gone back into the bedroom to lie down.

"It's Willie," I called.

He met me at the door and by that time Momma was up and moving. "What took you so darn long?" I asked.

"Now, Dorie," Momma said.

"I'm sorry as I can be." Willie looked straight at Momma. "But I ran into some friends I hadn't seen for a while and had a cola with them."

"That's just what I thought." Momma looked over at me like I ought to be ashamed. "Get the basket off the countertop."

"I'll take that," Willie said, grabbing the food out of my hands.

We all three sat in the cab, Momma in the middle. Willie wedged the basket in the back between two big rocks for the twenty-minute ride to Bald Mountain. As we rounded the curve out of town I looked back and read the shrubbery sign on the hillside. POORWATER it spelled out backward in the mirror, just like it was saying HOLLYWOOD. Our town council had some strange ideas about making Poorwater a tourist center of the Appalachians. Another Gatlinburg.

Willie switched on the radio, tuned to the usual station. A Flatt and Scruggs number was just winding down. The disc jockey came on: "This is WMTN — where 'hillbilly' is a compliment and mountain music is tops!"

"Willie, I thought we could talk," Momma said.

"Sure thing. I don't much care for that station anyway." He clicked it off.

"What do you mean? If I was going to listen to music I'd take WMTN over that drug noise any day of the week."

"I like the Beatles," I piped up. "They're not on drugs."

"You ought to listen to their songs, Momma," Willie said. "They've sure got some good songs."

"I like Paul the best," I said, amazed that Willie and I had something in common.

"Well, I wouldn't know about that." Willie laughed.

"Well I never," Momma started. "With the most famous musicians in the world coming from right down the road, too."

"They haven't recorded anything new in twenty-five years!" Willie said.

"I reckon that's because they haven't needed to," Momma said.

"I like the Carter Family," I said.

"So does Willie," Momma said. "He's just getting above his raising with all this talk."

Outside the truck window the mountains flicked by, some so close I couldn't trace across the tops. My hand would go up, up, up, then down, down, down, skiing the slope of a mountain, turning a sudden V, and sailing up the next one. Sometimes I'd let my hand rocket off into the sky and pick up with a down slope when I could. The road twisted through solid rock walls, walls that had been blasted out with dynamite for there to be a road at all. I could trace telephone lines and hop the top of each pole as we passed. I never bothered hopping cracks in the sidewalk — there weren't too many sidewalks in Poorwater; maybe that's the reason — but I always felt kind of doomed if I let my hand pass through a pole instead of jumping it. Blip! Quick hop over a pole. Blip! Then a long, straight stretch of wire with voices all along it. Blip! Skip over the glass knobs where all the conversations got crossed before going on past each other in the proper directions. I took my eye and hand along the stretching voices, counting the poles to a mile, trying to imagine how many poles it took to get to Liverpool, where Paul was from. He wasn't married, but he probably had a girlfriend. It seemed like Willie was driving too fast and I couldn't figure why Momma didn't tell him to slow down like she did Daddy. Maybe she was making up for what she'd said about the Beatles. But I wished she'd tell him to take it easy. I wasn't going to be able to eat that chicken if he kept it up. The telephone poles whipped by in a blur; whenever we'd hit a curve either I or Willie would be squashed flat against our door of the truck. I reached back and locked my door.

"Where's the fire?" I asked.

"You could ease up some. We're not that hungry." Momma gave a nervous little laugh.

"I'm sorry, Momma." Willie let up on the gas. "I guess I haven't driven in so long I just got carried away."

"Watch the road!" I said. The truck was headed smack for a bend. Beyond it was a sheet of rock. Willie jerked back the wheel.

"You seem awfully skittish," Momma said. She settled back against the seat and pressed her feet to the floor.

Willie apologized and I held on tight to the door, one arm out the window, wondering if I could jump in time if anything happened. Only the man from U.N.C.L.E. could survive the jump. The road steepened past the turn-off to Bald Mountain, and Willie automatically slowed. You couldn't go but so fast, climbing that gravel road. He shifted down to first, made second, and stayed there to the top. Bald Mountain got its name from the big open field where its top should have been. From the air it must have looked like a big bull's eye. In spring it would have been covered in wildflowers. A few black-eyed Susans and some chicory still bloomed around the edges of the clearing.

We parked the truck under a big pine and started unpacking the basket onto a towel. Except for some red ants where I was sitting, it was a pretty nice spread. When we'd finished eating and lain around a while chewing grass, Willie and I played a game of catch. "Burn 'er in here!" Willie would shout as I wound up for my pitch. "Whew, Momma," he'd say and blow on his glove after making the catch. "This girl's got herself a pair of major league hands!"

Willie loped out of the yard around five-thirty, right after supper; he had hugged Momma practically to death while Daddy and

I looked on awkwardly, and shaken Daddy's hand three times. He just looked me in the eye and said, "Goodbye, be seeing you." Daddy's "Good luck" followed him nearly to the curb. Willie looked back then and waved one giant palm, flat as a placard, into the air. That's that, I thought. I didn't know where he was going, but I was sure nobody else knew either. If he was bent on living his gypsy life like everything was a big mysterious secret all the time that was worth someone's while to figure out, then so be it, but I wasn't going to waste any more of my time. He probably didn't know beans about himself — that was his great big secret.

Late that night I lay in bed hot as blazes, kicking off the sheet and wishing the walls of the trailer would blow apart and an arctic breeze would sweep over me like a million tiny ice cubes on the loose. Living in an igloo would be the answer to a prayer. Crickets chirped so loud it was like a universe of fingernails raking across a universe of chalkboards. It reminded me most of the squawker in the Tornado High band, the clarinetist who couldn't manage to make it through a parade without honking on the reed, letting out a sound resembling a goose, or a peacock defending his turf. Whoever it was, they couldn't even get through the school fight song without making one of those amazing squeaks. I lay there trying against my will to forget about Willie and to "think cool thoughts," like Momma always ordered me to do when it was stuffy. Most nights it would cool way down, even in the hottest part of the summer, but that night after Willie left the humidity was two hundred percent and the temperature at the boiling point. The same kind of night must have prompted Thomas Jefferson down in Charlottesville to invent his air conditioning. If I'd known where to get a big hunk of ice, I'd have tried it. It might have worked better to climb into bed, curl up with the ice, and hope you'd just float away.

I couldn't stand it — I got up, into my clothes, and out the door without making a sound. I walked straight across town, that magnet in my head pulling me again, the way the moon pulls your bloodstream along with the tides. Some strong gravity was working on me from the inside.

The only living things I saw along the way were a couple of stray dogs lumbering through the grocery store parking lot, rummaging for scraps. I rounded the Rexall corner and practically ran the half mile to the field where the tent meeting had been. There again was the sea of cars, parked bumper to bumper. I'd hurried there, halfway thinking that the tent would be gone. I slipped through the canvas doors wishing instead for a circus with clown acts and high-wire walking.

The whole crowd was on their feet, so it was easy to blend in. I started clapping my hands and singing along with the last verses of "He's Got the Whole World in His Hands." The crowd kept perfect time, nobody missed a beat, the poles vibrated, and I thought we might lift off into outer space. The top of the tent quaked as we kept clapping. Brother Saul shouted out the different things God held in His hands — little bitty babies, brothers and sisters — and we all sang "in His hands" afterward. The empty-cup-in-the-palm method of clapping was the least painful and probably made the biggest sound, like a paper bag full of air being stomped on each time my hands came together. When we finished and sat down, Brother Saul launched into his sermon.

He picked up on the lesson of the night before, about suffering for Jesus' sake and all the suffering Jesus had endured for the sake of washing away the sins of the world. The same world that put Him to death on the cross at the tender age of thirty-three, which seemed pretty old after all. Brother Saul must have figured that anyone left on Friday night who hadn't yet been saved needed to be scared out of his wits, because he started right in on the Book of Revelation and the great Tribulation that was just around the corner, maybe already here.

"You think there ain't rumblings of the coming storm? You think there ain't a storm upon us right as I speak these words to you tonight? Well, think again. Consider the uprisings across the campuses of colleges and universities today! Consider those forces that would turn our misguided sons and daughters of the affluent into Communists and you can judge what a storm it might be that's coming. And it's a-coming; it's a-coming in the blink of an eye."

People on either side of me erupted into applause, the prospect of flood and famine and war and destruction exciting them into glee. Brother Saul had struck a seam and he mined it, laying out the picture of the destruction that would befall the earth in the days of Tribulation. Then he paused to let it all sink in before he started up again.

"Assassinations are the least of the trials that are coming in the days and months ahead. Some of you might have traveled to Kentucky back in February and had the occasion to hear Bobby Kennedy speak of the poverty he saw there." Brother Saul was treading dangerous ground. Several men tapped their feet and cleared their throats. Poor people don't like the word *poverty* for one thing, and I thought for a minute that getting onto politics had lost Brother Saul his flock. At least he had sense enough not to mention the assassination of Martin Luther King directly. Poorwater people would just as soon stay off that subject, like they'd just as soon let the hippies and the yippies worry about Vietnam.

"There were people there and people here he wanted to help, but he never got the chance. It's no accident that a foreigner killed him!" Brother Saul, back on safe ground, once again had the crowd in the palms of his hands as he raised them in a sort of benediction over the throng. "Who ever heard of Sirhan Sirhan before two months ago, before a weapon in his hand made him a big man? But I'm telling you that as horrible as that instant was, as horrible as it was when a gun tore through JFK's head in Dallas, five short years ago, as bad as these events have been, when the Tribulation is upon us it'll be a million times worse. But I'm here tonight to offer you a way out! Praise Jesus, there is a way!"

Amens and clapping and low humming and raised hands rippled through the tent.

"The Bible says that the believers will be swept up; the Bible says the believers will be raised above the Tribulation. And you can be one of those believers who are sailing through the air into Heaven before the Tribulation takes hold of the land and for seven years lays down every kind of destruction from war to famine to tidal wave. Get smart! Get saved now!"

As soon as those words had left Brother Saul's lips a jerking sensation swept over him; his eyes rolled back into his head, then focused on infinity, and his hands stretched out. Willie appeared in the spotlight, out of the darkness, and set the cage on the table, once again unlocking and throwing back the lid. Brother Saul drove one hand in and raised up the cobra like it was a lightning bolt. He raised it over his head and I saw the snake race toward the empty air and wriggle backward, like it was traveling backward in time, like it was a loop of outrageous time in Brother Saul's stiffened hands. Around and around his neck the green head ran, swiftly entwining Brother Saul's body from neck to waist, while he stood firmly, legs spaced apart and arms suspended away from his body. The snake whipped its tail and kept circling until it had wound down Brother Saul's right leg and its tail had unwound from his ankle. The cobra shot straight across the floor and down the center aisle. Nobody screamed. Nobody breathed. Brother Saul snapped out of his trance and yelled, "Willie, catch that blasted snake!"

Willie was already in action; he gripped the cage in one hand and a long stick in the other. "Don't anybody move!" he shouted.

I stood stock still with the rest, having lost sight of the snake after it passed the first several rows and headed toward the heart of the tent. The spotlight followed Willie as he chased after the snake. The next sound I heard was the crack of a gunshot and a loud voice hollering "Freeze!" like they do on TV.

Willie stopped in his tracks, frozen in the spotlight. The sheriff and three of his men, guns pointed at Willie's head and heart, inched toward him. Willie raised the cage over his head; the stick clattered to the floor.

"There it goes!" someone yelled from the crowd. '
loose on the town!"

While Willie held on to the cage, and the sheriff and
encircled him, then took the cage from his raised arms
him, nose first, to the dirt floor, the crowd was pou⌐ ⌐ ⌐ ⌐
the tent, driven as if from flames. As I was swept out the door
with my row I craned my head and saw the flash of handcuffs
as they were whipped from a deputy's belt toward Willie, lying
flat on his stomach.

I waited outside in a group that had formed to see what happened
to Brother Saul and his right-hand man. Nobody seemed to
know Willie's name. A few minutes later the sheriff emerged
from the tent. Behind him, like faithful pups, followed his depu-
ties, and between them, handcuffed and quiet, came Willie and
Brother Saul.

"You can't arrest Brother Saul!" a brave man said.

"Hush, brother," Brother Saul spoke. "Trust the Lord to pro-
vide."

"Blessed are ye, when men shall hate you," Willie mumbled,
"and when they shall separate you from their company, and
shall reproach you, and cast out your name as evil, for the Son
of man's sake."

I caught Willie's eye as they lowered his head into the back
of the squad car and locked the door after him. Through the
window he flashed me a big smile. They tucked Brother Saul
into a twin car with a blinking cherry top, and off they screamed
into the night. The ride to the jail was only a couple of blocks,
so some of the crowd pressed after them on foot. I didn't see
what good that would do, so I watched them go and waited in
the field until only the cars of the most faithful were left.

When there was only the low rumble of a few remaining engines
starting up, I walked back inside the tent. The spotlight was
still trained on the spot where Willie had been caught. The
cage lay on its side against an overturned folding chair. I took

the cage by its handle and righted it. The whole time I kept looking over my shoulder, feeling like somebody or something was watching me, but nobody else seemed to be around. I sat down in one of the chairs and scanned the arc of the spotlight. On the farthest rim of light I finally found what I was looking for, an edge of green, coiled tight as a garden hose. The cobra's head jerked upright from its circled length when I fixed my eyes on it. It had been watching me from the dark for a while.

I went toward the snake, pushing the cage in front of me with both hands. The snake didn't move except to periscope its head about six more inches. I didn't know what I was going to do or why I was acting like a darn fool. I set down the cage and sat cross-legged about a yard from the sage snake, well within its striking range.

"Come here," I cooed. "You'll die out there if you don't."

The snake looked at me and exercised its tongue, flicking it in and out, in and out.

"Come on, now," I repeated, like I was calling home a reluctant dog.

The snake coiled, little by little, the length of its raised body back into a slacker circle. At last its head coiled into the circle, and rested on the loops of its body in a hangdog expression. I wished I had one of those fancy flutes to pipe the right music so the cobra would straighten and climb right up into the air and clean out of sight.

I lifted the weight of the snake in two hands and lowered it head first into the cage. I snapped the lid shut and wedged a stick into the U of the padlock. My hands went numb, tingling all over with the needling sensation of fear, like it felt to wake up after having slept wrong on your arm and cut off the blood. My arms were so weak I couldn't lift the cage. As the tingling left my hands, heat entered them. I stood in the spotlight staring into my palms, a pale blue light seeming to shine from them. The cobra looked half asleep and happy enough to be back in its cage. I don't know how long I stood there with my knees about to buckle, but when I left the tent, all the strange feelings had gone out of my hands and they were mine again.

Walking home, I felt like a spy on a mission to Russia. It reminded me of a story I saw on TV about a man who got his face transformed, even his eyes changed to a different color. I felt changed, like I'd had plastic surgery on the inside, though, not the outside. I looked at my hands over and over but they seemed the same. I decided to walk by the jail, across from the new post office, and see if anyone was hanging around.

Only a handful of hangers-on were stationed outside, on the sidewalk just beyond the jail. They were standing a ways off, I guess, because the sheriff had told them to move on. I started to walk right by them and on home, but one of them said something to me.

"Hey, aren't you Willie Parks's little sister?"

"Nope, never heard of him. Who's Willie Parks?"

"They've got him and Brother Saul locked up in there for handling deadly snakes inside the town limits," a man in a white suit said.

"Seems there's an ordinance," said an older man on crutches. "I could've sworn you were one of those Parkses."

"I don't know him," I repeated.

"There's a law against just about everything you can think of." The man in the suit sighed.

"I'm not so sure they ought to have been messing with snakes," the man on crutches said.

"It's right in the Bible," another man said.

"Sure is," said yet another.

They turned in my direction once again, and the suited man said, "Young lady, whoever you are, shouldn't you be home in bed?"

"Yes, sir," I said and dug my hands into my pockets and took giant steps to the corner. After I turned it, I ran most of the way home, thinking about Willie, and thinking about how it would feel to be in Russia, on a mission, and having to think in Russian or be caught, not being able to tell anyone the truth until maybe you'd forget who you really knew and who you didn't, maybe even forget who you were yourself. Now I was going to have to wake up Momma and Daddy; there was no way around it. And then I'd have to face the fit Momma would throw when she found out about Willie. I'd have to face Daddy's expression when I told him how I'd been sneaking out late at night, walking around town alone. It would be a lot easier if I just let them read about Willie in the newspaper. He might even be on the front page. But Willie was bound to tell them I'd been there, if he ever got to talk to anyone again. And there I'd be, caught. It was better to get it over with, I guessed.

The poor snake was left all alone in its cage in the middle of the tent without a soul to feed it. I hoped nobody went back and killed it just for sport. Some people would do anything to an animal that couldn't fight back.

6

Genie in a Bottle

I decided to wait until the morning to tell them about Willie. When I got back home all I could hear was Daddy snoring peacefully; Momma was asleep, too, or she would have been walking the floor, having tea, like she did whenever there was a rescue operation at the mines and Daddy was the head of a team. Willie wasn't going anywhere now, so I went to bed. I thought I'd catch them before Daddy left.

Momma always got up about four o'clock with Daddy and made his breakfast; then she usually went back to bed and got up again with me when school was in session. By four forty-five Daddy would catch his ride or be off in the truck if it was his turn to drive. I must have been tired, because when I got up it was nearing six. Momma sat at the counter, sipping coffee.

"Why you up so early?" she asked.

"I don't know. I'm just up, I guess." I rubbed the crusty sleep from the corners of my eyes.

"Run down and get the paper for me, will you? — Oh, forget it, it's Saturday."

I hadn't remembered that last night, but this morning as soon as she said it, it was clear as day. The local paper came out on Tuesday and Friday. Daddy went out and bought a Roanoke paper on Sunday, but Saturday there wasn't any news. I could wait until Tuesday if I wanted to.

"Dorie, what's a-matter with you? Your face is all screwed up. It'll stick that way if you don't watch out."

"I'm just thinking."

"What you got to think about on Saturday morning?"

"I'm thinking about Willie."

"He's probably three hundred miles down the road by now." Momma sighed and drained the last of her coffee.

"No, he isn't. He's in the jail." Now I was in trouble.

"Dorie, what's got into you? What do you mean, Willie's in the jail?"

"He is. He got arrested last night with Brother Saul for handling snakes inside the town limits."

"Willie handling snakes! That's the craziest thing I ever heard. Brother who?"

"It's true."

She made me sit down and tell her the whole story. I left out how I'd gone to the tent the first night, figuring she didn't need to know about that, but she wanted to know how I knew there was a tent meeting in the first place and how I knew where it was, so the unabridged story came out. It all started with Tiger howling Thursday night, I told her. She never liked cats anyway, least of all Tiger, because he belonged to the Graysons, so I thought she might go easier on me if I let her know it had been his fault from the beginning. I don't think she even heard the part about Tiger waking me up. She kept wanting to know who Brother Saul was and where he was from. I couldn't tell her much except what he looked like and where his home church was, in Chattanooga, Tennessee.

"What should we do?" Momma asked me when I was through talking.

"We could wait until Daddy gets home and see what he says."

"We better do something . . . I wonder if Willie's got anything to eat. At least I can keep my own son from starving."

I wanted to tell her that food wasn't going to do him a darn bit of good, but maybe it'd do her some good. She started another breakfast, like the one she'd made for Daddy a few hours before, while I put on my clothes and ran up and whistled for Tiger. It was the last day I'd have to feed him and earlier than usual, but he came running out from under the hedge and straight to his meat without saying much of anything to me. That's gratitude for you. Betty was supposed to be back by supper time. I sure had a lot to tell her.

Momma packed the picnic basket and we hopped into the truck with the basket balanced between us on the seat. It smelled pretty good.

"Can I have a biscuit?"

"Willie's in jail and you're all set to eat his breakfast," Momma said.

"But I'm hungry."

"Take *one* off the top and wrap them back up tight."

I popped half the biscuit into my mouth, letting a trail of butter slide down my chin before licking it. The last trace of butter was wiped off my face when we pulled up in front of the jail.

Momma parked, grabbed the basket, and marched right toward the jail. I felt like waiting in the truck, but she turned and stared at me hard as she went through the glass door. I climbed out of the truck and followed her.

There were only two cells. Willie saw us and came toward the front of his cell. With each hand holding a bar and his face outlined between them he called out, "Good morning, Momma." The sheriff got off his chair, taking the cigar out of his mouth to ask us who we were and why we were there. Momma told him. I thought the hour had finally come when Willie might have worn out his welcome with Momma, but that was the last thing on her mind. Sheriff Darnell opened the top of the basket, peered beneath the towel, and rustled through enough plates for three square meals. Finally he lifted the basket from his desk, unlocked Willie's cell, and handed in the food.

Willie reached into the basket, pulled out a steaming plate, and motioned for Darnell, who unlocked Willie's cell again and took the plate of food next door to Brother Saul's cell.

"I thank you, ma'am," Brother Saul said, taking the plate. Darnell turned both the keys and removed them. He walked back to his desk and sat down stiffly.

"What else can I do for you, Mrs. Parks?"

"You can tell me when you're planning to release my son."

"He can go at the end of his twenty-four hours if he promises to get out of town for good."

"But he was born in this town, at the Sally Thomas." Momma sounded like she was about ready to break down.

"Well, he can stay right here if he likes." Darnell stuck the cigar back into his mouth.

"Momma, go on back home," Willie said. "I'll come by and say goodbye before we leave."

"But Willie, why?" Momma looked like she needed a chair.

"I'm sorry, Momma. I didn't know it was against the law."

"That's not what I mean."

"Sometimes a man's got to follow his heart," Willie said.

"Let's go home," Momma said, turning to me.

I felt sort of sorry for Willie when we walked out and Momma didn't say another word to him.

"Bye, Willie," I called over my shoulder.

"See you later, alligator," Willie said.

"After while, crocodile," I whispered under my breath. It was Daddy, not Willie, who always said that.

We drove home with Momma looking all the way like she might cry, but she didn't until we got back inside the trailer. She sat down and put her head in her hands, but not much sound came out.

"You going to be all right?" I asked. "Is it okay if I make me some breakfast?"

"Go ahead, if you can eat. You can start some fresh coffee, too."

I looked at her because I didn't know how to do it.

"Oh, never mind," she said, and got up to fix it herself.

I poured corn flakes, sliced up a banana on top, and drenched it with milk. Momma sat back down, waiting for her coffee to perk. A crack of close thunder made us jump. Then the rain started.

"Why didn't you tell us about Willie right off?"

"I don't know. I was scared you'd get mad because I was out by myself."

"That ain't here nor there, now. Your daddy's not going to like it, though."

I gulped down some cereal. Daddy had never so much as spanked me, but it only made me dread his disapproval that much more. Whatever Willie had done, what I had done seemed worse. Momma wouldn't let me go out and play. It was raining cats and dogs anyway. I just had to stay and wait with her for Daddy, and it wasn't even lunch time yet. The rain kept up, slacking, then pounding again.

Lunch passed, and somehow it got to be near three o'clock, the time Daddy got off. He should be home around fifteen of four. The TV had been turned off since *Sky King,* because of lightning. I thought I'd never been so bored in my life, bored and frightened and antsy all at once. Something about the way Momma seemed to be taking it all so calmly made it worse than if she'd turned the blame on me. She just wasn't herself; she was acting like she did when someone died. When Daddy's daddy died, Momma took charge while he cried.

"Momma, can't I go out in the yard? It just stopped raining."

"It's dark enough out there to be night, Dorie. You don't need to go out in that."

I used the full authority of looking out the window. "But it's stopped."

"All right, go on, but don't you leave this yard, and I mean it. Your daddy'll be home soon."

I hopped out the door. There were mud puddles where the grass wouldn't grow, and my pansies looked about drowned. A couple of robins plopped down on the ground and started bobbing for worms. The storm must have been over. Tiger crawled out from under the trailer toward me, looking ruffed up but dry. He knew what he was doing. I found a ball and started throwing it for him to go fetch. He wasn't interested.

Cats are strange; they never want to do anything different.

"Hey, Tina," I called. I must have been desperate, to talk to Tina. She was always trying to get my attention.

"You want to play school?" she asked, tilting her head like one of the robins.

Brother. That was all Tina ever thought about. "Not right now. Why don't you go get your Hula Hoop and we can take turns."

Tina hurried inside to get the hoop. I guessed Momma wouldn't mind if I just went to Tina's. It was still our yard, sort of.

"I'll go first." Tina batted the hoop to the left and started jerking her middle around, but the hoop had already hit the ground.

"My turn," I said.

"I get another," Tina squeaked.

"No you don't. Fair's fair." I took the hoop out of her hands and stepped into it. I sent it swirling around my waist and began rocking back and forth to keep it going. When it raveled toward the tops of my legs, I bent and rocked it back up over my waist. Tina was getting mad. I was going to keep it going as long as I could. I thought maybe I could do it all day if I really decided to. Tina stuck out her fingers and scraped the hoop when it went past. It wobbled like an egg for a second and then tumbled down around my ankles like socks with old worn-out elastic.

"It's still my turn. You cheated," I said.

"It's mine." Tina gritted what was left of her baby teeth.

"No it's not." I grabbed the hoop back out of her hands.

"It's my Hula Hoop." She resorted to a brat's truth. I shoved the damn thing at her; she looked like she might start bawling. It was nearly as tall as she was; no wonder she was no good at it. Besides that, she didn't have any hips.

I slunk back over to my side of the yard and picked up Tiger from one of the folding chairs. He didn't want to be picked up, and squirmed. The chair was wet, too, so I don't know why he chose it in the first place. Daddy should have been home by then. If he didn't come soon I thought I'd die. There was nothing to do, so I went back inside. Momma was already lighting the stove. Maybe she thought she'd stuff Daddy full of his favorite dishes and then break the news.

Momma cooked and I helped now and then when there was something I could do.

"Go out and see if your daddy's coming," Momma said when things were about finished. "I wonder what's holding him up?"

I walked down the street and looked, but nothing was coming in either direction. I went back inside and reported.

"But he should have been here by now." Momma took some beans off the stove and started scooping them into a serving bowl just as if I'd said Daddy was coming down the street.

"The food'll get cold," I said.

Momma dumped the beans back into the pot, added water, and set them back on the eye. I could tell she was worried, but I didn't feel like anything could've happened to Daddy.

"He'll be here. We would've heard something by now," I said.

Momma busied herself filling a plate with steaming spoonfuls of beans, greens, and squash. "I'm sure he's all right. You stay here and wait for him. I'll run this down to Willie."

"Aren't you going to take some for Brother Saul?"

"He can take care of himself." She covered the plate and went out to the truck and drove off.

About five minutes after she left, Daddy came dragging in, carrying his gear, looking awful. I was scared to talk to him, but he said "Hi." So I said "Hi" back.

"Where's your momma?"

"She . . . she went to the store."

"There's been an accident." He rubbed his forehead. Then I saw a big tear slide down his face, making a muddy river in a sooty wrinkle on his cheek. Oh, Daddy, I thought, don't cry. I didn't think I could stand to see him broken up.

"It's Tina's daddy, and I've got to go over there in a minute and tell them what's happened."

"Is he going to be all right?"

"No." Daddy stripped off his shirt. "Help me get washed up."

I was afraid to ask any more questions while I hosed his head and neck and back. I didn't know whether Tina's daddy was crippled for life or dead, and Daddy didn't say any more about it.

He went back into the bedroom, changed into his spare jeans and a clean work shirt, and wet-combed his hair. By the time he'd finished dressing, Momma was back.

"Thank goodness you're home," Momma greeted him. She stopped at the look on his face.

"There was an accident," I said.

Momma collapsed into the nearest chair, like she'd been waiting to do that all day. "I knew it. I just knew it."

"Bud McGee's dead," Daddy said simply.

"Oh no!" Momma's hand flew to her mouth. "Anyone else?"

Daddy shook his head.

"What happened?" I asked.

"They're not sure yet. The inspector's already there. Some of the men think it's a gas leak." Daddy sounded like he was reading aloud. "Bud was the first man into the room. He turned on the cutter and it blew. Just like that." Daddy snapped his fingers. "Bill Whitten got blown back into the cross entry, but he's okay."

"What's the cross entry?" I asked.

"Hush, Dorie," Momma said.

"The cross entry's outside the room entry. It connects to the main entry, so it knocked Bill back about twelve feet. He was fine, though. We had to dig Bud out. It crushed him pretty bad. He'd stopped breathing. Didn't even blow up the tunnel, just brought down the roof. Freak thing . . ."

"Does Marjorie know?" Momma asked.

"I told the superintendent I'd tell her . . . I've got to go over there."

"I'll go with you," I said.

"No you won't," Momma said.

"I'll be back in a few minutes," Daddy said, and opened the door.

Momma and I sat down across the table from each other in our usual chairs. She looked at me and I looked at her.

"You going to tell him about Willie?"

"I guess we'll have to, since Willie's coming by here tonight." Momma was wringing her hands together.

"We could let Willie tell him when he gets here," I suggested.

"That wouldn't be fair. We'll have to tell him, but let's wait until after supper. He's got a lot on him now. Poor little Tina. Poor Marjorie." Momma's eyes looked far away. I knew she was thinking it could just as easily have been her.

"Do they get a pension?" I asked.

"Should. Bud was a union man. You be nice to Tina, you hear?"

"I'm always nice to Tina. Why'd they let Mr. McGee into that room if it was dangerous?"

"They didn't know it was."

"But why didn't they know?"

"I don't know, Dorie. Don't ask so many questions. How should I know? It was an accident, an accident."

"I bet Daddy knows."

"No he don't. And don't go asking him a thousand questions, either."

"I'd just like to know what happened."

"Didn't you hear what your daddy said? Nobody knows anything else. Now hush, here he comes." She got up and met him at the door.

"Let's eat supper" was all Daddy said. He took his usual place and waited for his plate to be filled.

Momma served supper and we ate without saying anything except that the food was good. Momma said thank you and Daddy asked if there was dessert. We each had a cupcake; I kept looking at Momma and she kept looking away, so I knew it wasn't time to tell him yet. After we finished our cupcakes and Daddy had asked for another, Momma said something that made me nearly lose it all.

"David, Dorie's got something to tell you."

Daddy looked at me and I stared, dumfounded, at Momma.

"Well, what is it?" Daddy asked. He sounded exhausted.

I could have choked. Now I had to tell him everything I knew about Willie and Brother Saul. Daddy didn't say much. He didn't interrupt with questions, but Momma kept egging me on whenever I'd wind down. "Tell about the cage with the snake," she prompted. "Tell about how you went past the jail," she said. Once again, I left out the part about my putting the cobra back in its cage. That part seemed pretty hard to believe, even for me. I wasn't sure anymore that it had really happened. I looked down at my hands when I'd finished the story.

"I just can't believe Willie's in with the Holy Rollers," Daddy said.

"There's worse things he could be doing," Momma said.

"I suppose so," Daddy said, halfheartedly.

"What's Holy Rollers?" I asked.

"Dorie!"

"Holy Rollers roll in the floor over Jesus," Daddy said. "You saw them, didn't you? Ask your momma; her family knows all about it."

"David, what they do is their business."

"But look what's happened to Willie." Daddy sighed. "I guess it couldn't be helped."

"Are you blaming me?" Momma asked.

"Certainly not."

Momma was already weeping.

"Oh, Mary, don't. Here we sit bickering; our son's in jail, and Marjorie's over there crying her eyes out."

Momma straightened up. "I ought to go over there right now." She wiped her face and stood. "Dorie, wash up the dishes."

"Momma — "

"Do what she says," Daddy said. "While you're washing those dishes you can figure out what a proper punishment should be for all your gallivanting."

"If I hadn't, you wouldn't even know about Willie."

"That's enough," Daddy said.

Momma let the screen door flop back with a snapping sound. She had her white Bible in her hand like she was on her way to church. She hadn't been in a couple of years; neither had Daddy. They said the Poorwater church didn't feel right to them and it was too far to drive back home every Sunday. I went by myself to both Sunday school and church. I usually sat with the Graysons during the service.

Momma and Daddy and I sat out in the folding chairs facing the truck until it was nearly pitch black, and still no Willie.

"He's probably ashamed to see us, after what's happened," Momma said.

"I doubt it."

"Dorie, can't you say anything without using that tone of yours?" Momma asked.

"I'm just telling my honest opinion."

"Well, nobody asked for it."

"You go on in to bed. It's almost ten. If Willie comes, we'll call you," Daddy said.

I said okay. I had my book to read, and every night it seemed like something got in the way. At this rate I wouldn't come close to finishing it, and Mrs. Moody had ordered me to read something educational over the summer. The library hardly had any real books worth reading, mostly picture books for little kids and some old classic novels for adults that looked lousy. At least *The Arabian Nights* was fat and had pictures, even if they were only black and white. I picked it up once I'd gotten settled in bed and went back to the introduction, something I'd skipped over before because introductions were always so boring. It was just the sort of thing Mrs. Moody would ask me about, and since I was waiting for Willie I didn't want to get too interested anyway.

But the introduction was the strangest introduction I'd ever seen. It was all about how a man killed his wife for sleeping with her slave and then went off to see his only brother after not having seen him for years and years. Then the brother up and killed his wife, too, for having a big party with her slaves while he was away on business. If Mrs. Moody asked about this one, she'd be sorry. Then the two brothers set out because they've decided that it isn't worth all the grief it takes to be a king if women are so ornery. A bunch of stories get told and finally a vizier takes his daughter, Shahrazad, who's smart because she's read a thousand books, to one of the mean brothers who's back home on his throne again. The king usually kills all the women brought to him, but this one tells good stories, so he lets her live until morning. Her story has lots of stories in it, like the introduction. Shahrazad's trying to save her own neck, so she keeps telling stories. Knowing that sort of changed some of the stories I'd read. I couldn't stop reading, her stories were so weird.

For instance, there was a fisherman who pulled up three things out of the sea that weren't fish. On his fourth try he pulled up a big pot he could sell for cash, so he was happy even though he still hadn't caught any fish. But he loosened the lead stopper with his knife and a big cloud of smoke billowed out. It was a genie as tall as the clouds, but he was a stupid genie because he went back into the pot just to prove to the fisherman that he had really come out of it in the first place. Anybody could have seen what was coming: the fisherman plugs up the stopper so the stupid genie can't kill him, like he's said he's going to. The genie keeps begging to be let out of the pot, and the fisherman threatens to throw it back into the sea, so the genie says how he won't kill the fisherman after all and promises instead to make him a rich man. The fisherman takes the pot to the edge of the water and calls the genie a liar. Then for some reason he starts telling the genie a story about King Yunan and the Sage

Duban. Folks in Arabia sure have funny names, but what about the genie? And was Shahrazad still alive?

I must have fallen asleep. When I woke up in the morning, my light had been turned off and the book marked in the middle of the fisherman's story. Willie had never shown up, and all anybody knew was that he and Brother Saul had left town in a hurry. I wasn't surprised, but I bit my tongue. Momma just sat in the kitchen, drinking cup after cup of coffee, while Daddy read the paper. I went on to Sunday school, mostly to see if Betty was there.

7

Wild Stories

I was over at Betty's, watching TV, trying to think up something good for us to do because school was going to start in three days. It was hard to believe how life barreled on despite accidents and arrests and disappearances. Labor Day would always be the end of summer. The midday news came on and we were just about to turn it off when a special report about a motorcycle accident caught our attention.

Ever since the Graysons had gotten back from the beach, Barbara had been going around with some guy named Sid, from Johnson City, who she had met at the Gay Dolphin doing whirl art. Betty had given me a couple of pictures she'd made and explained how a white card spun real fast while the painter squirted paint from little squeeze bottles. It smeared all around, sort of like sun rays, and if you got a good color combination it looked pretty. I stuck the two Betty gave me up on my wall with Scotch tape. One was real ugly — lots of green and purple and red and yellow and brown in the middle. The other one was nice, just purple and red, not too much paint. Sid was visiting his cousins in Poorwater. Betty said it was just so he could see Barbara and that it caused a big debate between her parents about whether or not Barbara was allowed to ride around with Sid on his motorcycle, but since she was sixteen they decided she could. Mrs. Grayson was kind of glad Barbara was finally getting out of her room.

The reporter said that a motorcycle had crashed on the way to the Breaks. Two people had been taken to the Bristol hospital, but he didn't give their names because their families hadn't been notified. Betty and I looked at each other.

"It can't be Barbara."

"Why not?" I asked.

"The Breaks is way past Grundy, and Barbara's only allowed to go to the country club and back."

I rolled my eyes. "Well, they didn't say who it was, so don't worry about it."

"I'd better say something to Mommy."

"She'll just get worked up, and you don't know if — "

"I'd better tell her."

Betty left the room and I followed her upstairs after about five minutes to see what was taking so long. Mrs. Grayson was on the phone, trying to reach Dr. Grayson at the hospital. He couldn't take the call, so she called the Bristol hospital. Her hands were shaking and I looked at Betty to let her know I thought she'd done it now. Mrs. Grayson asked about the motorcycle accident victims, but they wouldn't tell her anything much until she said she thought it might be her daughter. Then they asked her what Barbara looked like and how old she was and who she was with. They wouldn't confirm it — the girl was still unconscious — but when Mrs. Grayson got off the phone she said she had to go to Bristol because she felt like it was Barbara and Sid. Betty had to come home with me until her mother got back. She said it would take about three hours.

Tina was out in her yard, swinging the Hula Hoop around her skinny waist. "She has hair like a white poodle," Betty whispered. Any other time we would have stopped and laughed at her, but she'd gotten pretty weird since her daddy had died, so we just walked on by. I'd tried to be nice to her for a solid week after it happened, but she wouldn't say anything no matter what I suggested. I thought she'd probably snap out of it when school started. Momma told me to give her some time, but she wasn't worth it anyway. I was just trying to be nice. Tina's momma was worse off than Tina, and that was going some. She just cried all day long. Momma fixed up plates at supper time and took them over there, but Tina's momma wouldn't eat. She had dark circles under both eyes, Momma said, and wouldn't take a bath or go to the store. Momma was afraid

Tina might starve or something. She kept asking Mrs. McGee if she didn't have some family that could come and stay with her for a while, but she never got an answer. Daddy had looked into the pension for them and written all the right letters, but he hadn't heard anything yet. Mr. McGee had some insurance, so everything was all right for now. I didn't go to the funeral because for some reason Daddy wouldn't let me. Momma said I had to go to one sooner or later, but Daddy said it would be better if I didn't go to this one. I didn't care. It sounded sort of like church from Momma's description, except that a lot of miners came. Daddy gave a speech about Mr. McGee and how he was a good person. Momma said it was a great speech. Daddy told me it wasn't anything at all. He let Mrs. McGee have it, so I didn't get to read it.

"What do you want to do?" I asked Betty. Since we were at my house, the burden of entertainment fell on my shoulders.

"We could write poems for the contest."

"What contest?"

"It was in the newspaper. They're due the first day of school."

"What's it got to be about?"

"Anything you want."

I would rather have gone up to the tanks and dug some more on our holes, but since Betty was my company and her mommy was gone on a serious mission, I went inside and got us some notebook paper and pencils.

"How do you start a poem?" I asked.

"How should I know? You just start. Mine's going to be about Tiger."

"I think I'll write one about Tiger, too."

"He's my cat, and I picked him first, copy cat."

"Oh, all right. I'll write about something else. It's a secret."

We put our heads down and concentrated.

"How far have you gotten?" I asked.

"Be quiet, I'm trying to write." She sounded just like Barbara when she told us to leave her alone.

"But how far are you?"

"I'm halfway through. You know a word that rhymes with 'Tiger'?"

I decided I'd better get something started, but it was hard. As soon as I started to write something, something better popped into my head or the wind would blow the corners of the paper up or my pencil seemed too dull on the side I was writing on and I'd have to turn it around and then I'd forget what it was I wanted to write. Betty was scribbling away. When she got to the bottom of the page, her fingers wrapped tightly around the pencil, she started copying it all over onto a clean sheet in her neatest writing. I was just beginning mine.

"Let me see what you got," I said.

"If you show me yours."

"I don't have much yet," I confessed.

"Then you can't see mine."

Betty folded up her poem and put it into her pocket.

"Well, I already know what yours is about," I said.

"Let's pretend old Miss Reider's a witch!" Betty burst out.

"That's stupid."

"It is not."

"Yes it is, because she *is* a witch, and everybody knows it." Betty might be company, but she still needed setting straight.

"She's not a real witch."

"That's what you think. She killed a kid once because he stepped on her tomatoes. You should see what happens to rabbits who eat her lettuce."

"She never killed anybody. You're a liar, Dorie Parks!"

"That's what you think."

Betty took a deep breath to issue her dare. "Then prove it."

"It'll be dangerous. Are you sure you want to?"

"I don't believe you, and you're not scaring me one bit."

"We'll have to go to her house," I said. "Then you'll see."

"Your mommy won't let us."

I called inside, "Hey, Momma, Betty and I are walking over to Sixth Street, okay?"

"Don't stay long" was Momma's reply.

"See?" I said. "Let's go. If you want to, that is."

Sixth Street drew a squared-off semicircle around the hospital and was one of only two flat streets in town. The rest were great for sleigh riding, but for bikes or walking around, the hills could get old real fast. One time I was riding straight down Betty's street on Harry's bike and hit a rock and flew over the handlebars and landed on my right arm. I still have a scar running from my elbow to my wrist. I didn't get any stitches, but I probably should have. Harry said I couldn't borrow his bike anymore. All summer long I picked off the scab on the edges and let it grow back. It was so deep the middle didn't come off until that September.

Sleigh riding could be dangerous, too, if you missed the street and ran into a parked car or a tree. That happened to one of Betty's friends up the hill. She was trying to ride down the sidewalk because the snow had been salted off the road, but she hit a slick spot and ended up underneath the Graysons' Pontiac. Betty was riding behind her and got out of it all right. Mrs. Grayson had to pull Marie out and call the hospital because she thought her leg might be broken. It turned out to be bruised up bad. Sixth Street was safe, except when the dirty boys were out. They had dirty necks and carried long sticks to hit girls with. Waiting for the dirty boys to grow out of it was worse than waiting for snow days in October or summer in May. Momma said they'd grow out of it and we'd even like them again someday, but Betty and I kept hoping they'd get sent to reform school.

Miss Reider lived alone. She came out of her house a lot to pull the weeds from her beds that looked like the pictures I'd seen of bombed-out cities in World War II — no flowers in them, just large areas of empty dirt. In the fall she'd be out raking leaves, usually with her hair tied up in chiffon scarves from the dime store. Her yard was full of crab grass and chicory and thistles, but the flower beds were spotless, and she never let the leaves pile up. I don't think she could get anybody to mow her lawn. I wouldn't have. Around her yard ran a broken fence that hadn't been whitewashed in a thousand years. Momma said she thought someone said Miss Reider used to keep boarders. That house was certainly big enough. I kept wondering what she did in there all day and if she ever went on vacation or watched TV. Somehow I couldn't picture her sitting in front of *Star Trek* or *Gunsmoke*. A porch traced the front and side of her house, and a screened-in porch stacked up with tools sagged off the back. That's where she usually came out. The flower beds and the vegetable patch were out there. In the far back of the yard, just in front of the fence, stood a shed with broken windows up so high you couldn't look in unless someone boosted you. I'd stood on an oil drum and looked in once, but with the window shards caked with dirt and the open spaces so dark, there wasn't anything to see. It was probably full of bodies, though. Like the kid who walked on her tomatoes and was never seen again. She probably burned him at the stake.

Betty and I walked across Lee Street, the other flat street, and onto Sixth. Nobody was out: it seemed like a Sunday during church or the Fourth of July when everybody was with their families on picnics or home in their back yards doing the same.

"Don't talk," I said.

"I wasn't."

"She might hear us."

We were almost to her house. In a few more steps we could see if she was out or not. Good. She wasn't.

We walked around her fence and into the alley; you could walk around three sides of her place without going through anyone's yard and getting yelled or barked at. When we'd walked from the alley past the front of her house and back again to the alley, Betty suggested we try to see into the shed.

"There's nothing to see, unless you like dead bodies," I said.

"There aren't any bodies in there. Are there?" Betty was beginning to enjoy the idea.

"I saw them once. They were stacked up so deep — almost to the ceiling."

"That's another lie," she said. "Pinocchio nose."

"I'll show you."

I got down on my hands and knees so Betty could stand on my back. "Be careful. Don't step in the middle, just — there," I instructed.

"Be still. Put your head down. I can't see anything. It's too dark." Betty climbed down. "I couldn't see."

"You ought to be glad you couldn't. It's terrible in there. It gave me nightmares," I said.

"What's it look like?"

"Each body is wrapped up in a sheet, all dirty and slimy. There's big ones on the bottom and little ones on the top. Little children, first-graders and smaller."

"It must smell real bad," Betty said.

I hadn't thought of that. "Real bad." I held my nose.

"I wonder why the police don't smell it and arrest her?"

"I don't know," I said.

"Well, they arrested your brother."

"I know it." I paused, then went on, "Do you want to go see if we can look through her front windows?"

"I've tried that before, and you can't see anything from the sidewalk." Betty sounded like she was getting tired of the game.

"We might be able to see in if we went into the yard!"

"I'm not going through the gate. You can go if you want to."

"I need a guard if I do it. You'll have to keep a lookout."

We walked all the way past the front of the house on the sidewalk. Sure enough, you couldn't see anything beyond the venetian blinds. It must have been dark as night in there all day long. A couple of upstairs windows were cracked open, letting a breeze through, but of course we couldn't see into those.

"Okay, here's the plan," I said. "You stand at the corner and whistle if you see anyone coming. That includes cars. Whistle once for a car and twice for a person on the sidewalk. Got it?"

"One if by land and two if by sea," Betty said sarcastically and took her post at the corner by the stop sign.

She watched me jiggle the lock, lift the latch, and inch open the gate; it squeaked like a trapped rat. For each inch I opened it, a high-pitched whine sounded. I didn't think I could go through with it. With all those bodies in the shed, it wouldn't make any difference to her if she killed one more kid. I pushed the gate far enough to squeeze through, but I looked back at Betty first. She nodded her head to indicate all clear. If I could get up to one of the windows, I thought I could see between two of the slats of the blinds. If everything went as planned, I'd know what was behind each of the big windows on either side of the front porch. The biggest problem was the window on the right, because the only way to get to it was if I went up on the porch itself. I crawled toward the left window on hands and knees, looking right and left the whole time.

I was just about ready to stand up when I heard Betty whistle once. I scrambled back to the gate and waited until I heard the car pass. In a few seconds I crawled the ten feet back to the window and grabbed the sill. I pulled up slowly, then cupped my hands against the glass to see what I could see. A living room. A couple of couches and chairs, a coffee table; that was all. After checking the front porch and listening for Betty, growing braver as the minutes passed and still nothing had happened to me inside the witch's fence, I crawled toward the porch steps and tiptoed over to the right window.

I thought I heard footsteps from inside the house. I didn't wait to see for sure, deciding instantly to make a run for it. I covered the distance in giant steps, slammed the creaking gate, and raced by Betty, shouting "Run!"

She was right behind me. When we made Lee Street we stopped to catch our breath on the curb.

"That was a close call!" I gasped.

"What happened?"

"I heard her coming to the door. She must have heard me on the porch."

"What'd you see?"

"I didn't get to see in the other window."

"But did you see anything?"

"A living room!" It was hard to make it sound exciting.

"Is that all?" Betty sounded disgusted with the whole deal.

"A lot of stacked-up newspapers on the coffee table. Probably years' worth. And a black cat sitting on the couch."

"A real black cat?" Betty reveled in the thought.

"With yellow eyes. She won't let it outside. It looked pretty old, too. Just sitting there like an owl or something."

"Like a sphinx." Betty's eyes glowed. She was full of big words. She used them whenever she got the chance. It was sickening, but I had to ask her to explain *sphinx*.

"A stone monster with the head of a woman and the body of a lion. And wings. They're in Egypt. Real spooky. You ask them questions nobody else can answer."

"That doesn't sound spooky to me."

"Well, it is. They had dead kings inside sometimes and treasures and if you go in them you're cursed forever."

"Who'd go in them then, just people with hard questions?"

"Archaeologists."

"Oh." I knew that word had something to do with our digging at the holes.

"So, what else did you see in there?"

"The cat hissed at me."

"It'll tell her who you are."

"Cats can't talk."

"They use telepathy."

Everybody knows a cat can't use a telephone. Betty wasn't scaring me, and she knew it. I was about to just tell her there wasn't really a cat.

"Oh no," Betty said. "Look who's coming."

"Let's go!"

The dirty boys hadn't seen us yet, but they were at the other end of Lee Street on their bikes, riding our way.

"Where?" Betty ran after me.

"To the church. They'll never find us there."

To get to the church we had to either run past the dirty boys or Miss Reider's again. We ran back toward Sixth Street without even thinking about it. A car stopped just behind us when we'd run past the witch's house and through a vacant lot between Sixth and the church.

"Betty!" We heard a man's voice.

"It's Pop. I got to go." Betty turned and headed to the car. She slammed the door and they drove off, stranding me there. Betty was waving, and the only thing I could do then was double back and hope the dirty boys would be gone. If they caught me out alone, I'd be a goner for sure.

I made it home by keeping a sharp eye out and running most of the way in case they saw me. Momma met me at the door and asked why I looked like I'd seen a ghost.

"It's the dirty boys." I was panting.

"Where's Betty?"

"Her daddy picked her up in the car."

"It looks like they could've brought you home. You'd better get washed for supper. Lord, what happened to your shirt? It looks like somebody walked over it."

After supper I worked on my poem. I let Daddy read it, and he said he thought it ought to win but it needed a title. When fall and winter had taught me all I needed to learn about real fear, I thought back a lot to this late summer afternoon, in the wake of Mr. McGee's death, spent in imaginary terror while we waited to hear about Barbara and Sid.

First Quarter

On the Banks of the Wye, 1955

I said before that Daddy never took me fishing, but I guess there are just some things you do with a son that don't get done with a daughter no matter how much you love her. Maybe it has to do with my being the second child, and Momma and Daddy being older and working so hard all the time. But, face it or not, time goes on before and after you're born; that's hard to take sometimes, and I can't help speculating about all the things that happened before I was born, before these people who were already related became related to me. So maybe this is what it was like one time when Willie and Daddy used to go fishing.

He wonders how it might feel to look up at the perfect quarter moon, a half to his eye, all alone, with no one depending on him, with no one waiting for him, without his son, Willie, holding on to his hand, about to ask some question about the fish. As any father can, David can hear the spark of a question forming in Willie's mind, feel the lump rising in his own throat before the words of the impossible question tumble out of his son's mouth. David looks into space where the moon has been, stares hard: How might it feel to be twenty-six, with a job in the city, looking toward this same moon vanished behind a cloud after an office-job day and a beer or two under his belt? He stares at the spot and senses he'd probably not even be able to see this moon, any moon, in a city, with so much street light bouncing up. He feels Willie's grip tighten on his hand, as if he understands his existence is being tried on and off like a suit. Willie squeezes his daddy's hand to remind him of the truth. Better that things are the way they are: at twenty-six, he has a seven-year-old son who would rather go fishing than dream.

"Hey, Daddy," Willie says as they approach the narrow path to the river, "a penny for your thoughts."

"You don't have a penny," David says, startled. Where did Willie hear that old saying?

"I know it," Willie says, bounding ahead.

Willie stakes out their spot and waits for his daddy to unravel the poles and tie on the hooks. David takes out his pliers when he has the hooks set and squeezes a row of small sinkers onto each line. Willie already has his hand on the worm he wants.

"If you plan on being a fisherman," his granddaddy has said, "you got to bait the hook yourself. Got to take the hook out of the fish, too. Learn to clean it, cook it, too."

The worm squirms across Willie's open palm, leaving a trail of dark dirt. He lifts the worm by one end, pushes the single barb of the hook through the rubbery muscle and back again, and still the worm wiggles as its blood seeps from the wounds. It is silly to feel too sorry for an earthworm, Willie knows, and he feels sorrier, somehow, for the fish he plans to fool. The first time he went fishing he felt big salty tears boil up in his eyes as his granddaddy held his first catch by the gills to remove the deep hook. When he saw the blood on his granddaddy's fingers, the tears rolled down his face.

"You feel like going home, son?" Granddaddy asked.

"Nope," Willie said.

"You feel like fishing some more, then?"

"Yep," Willie said, sniffling. "I want to fish."

"Okay then, let 'er rip. But you might not catch another one like this."

But he had caught another, and another and another. His granddaddy taught him how to take them off the hook himself, after the second one.

"I'm not going to spend the day taking fish off your hook!" Granddaddy complained. But Willie heard the pride in his voice, and that kept him fishing. When blood covered his own hands, he thought of that voice again.

His granddaddy's line whipped through the air to disturb the surface of the water, then flew backward briefly before it was flung onto the water again, lightly. They fished half the day and Granddaddy didn't catch a single fish. Willie wondered how he could stand it, and if he'd ever want to come fishing again, since he hadn't caught anything.

"If I could wade out there like I used to do, I'd get a bite. When you have to wait on the fish to come to you, you've got a long wait coming."

"Why don't you use a pole like mine, Granddaddy?"

"I like to give 'em a fair shake." Granddaddy winked.

"Daddy," Willie asks. "Why didn't Granddaddy come with us?"

"Oh, this spring air hurts his lungs, you know that. He'll take you fishing when it's warmer, in the summer."

"Is he getting worse?"

"Some worse, I guess, but he's all right. He just has to be careful, you know."

"I wish he was here."

"Well, he's a far better fisherman than I am, I know that much."

"You're okay."

"Ha!" David says. "I know what that means. 'You're *okay*,' " he mimics, smiling. "We'll just have a little competition this morning so you won't get so bored. We'll just see which one of us catches the first fish."

Willie casts his line out into the stream. "Go!" he says. And David follows with his own cast, laughing as the line curves into the air, then settles into the river.

"Don't laugh so loud, the fish'll hear you," Willie says, seriously.

"I'm sorry," David whispers.

He can taste the breakfast he knows will be waiting whenever they give it up and walk home: hotcakes with butter and maple syrup. Steaming cups of coffee, poured by Mary. The thought of Mary's face in the morning, still puffy from dreams, can stir him to happiness so quickly he cannot think better of the feeling.

He holds her face in front of the tumble of the river over rocks as he winds in the line and tosses it out again to feel a nibble that may or may not be real. Then he sees Willie's line pull taut.

"You got a bite?" David asks.

"Yep."

"Need a hand?"

"Nope."

David watches the line waver through the water, Willie winding his catch into shore slow and sure. He readies the net as Willie works, his eyes seeming to pierce the surface of the water to catch a glimpse of the fish he means to land. David sees Willie's arms jerk back as if they've felt the backfire of a rifle; he sees the surface wrung into motion and the mouth of the bass touch the upper air for an instant. The net twists in his hand — the bass flutters just out of reach.

Mary's face reappears, then vanishes, and in its place David follows the hairpins and spirals of the Wye as though he traces on a map with one finger. The river lazes along, rounding bends to pause here, before barreling down small rapids farther along. Or is it flowing from this direction, south to north? Of course he knows which way the river flows.

"Daddy!" comes Willie's plea. "Get the net under him this time, quick!"

David sees his hands extend, the net dip, like an answer, beneath the swirling circle of the fish.

8

School

It had been a strange summer, but I couldn't say I was glad school had started. The only good part about it was picking out supplies. Paul McCartney would be staring back at me whenever I felt like looking at the covers of my new notebooks. Betty and I were in Mrs. Harper's class. After one day of fifth grade I figured out it wasn't going to be so hot after all. Seemed like every year I looked at the kids a grade ahead of me and thought they were getting to do better stuff, and then it turned out they didn't; it just looked that way. I had to ride the bus to the new school. I could walk to the old one. Momma kept saying how much I was going to enjoy the brand-new school building, but after a few days, when I knew where everything was, I stopped being aware of its being new; it was only a school. Betty's momma took her and some other country clubbers in the station wagon, so I didn't see her until we got into class. "Thank goodness we're in the same class," Betty said. "If you were in Miss Horton's I'd die."

The first thing that happened was that I had to sit beside one of the holler kids, who looked like he hadn't had a bath all summer. His name was Dudley and his shoes were brand-new — I knew somebody must have given them to him — but tight, so he walked funny when he got up to sharpen his pencil. I don't know why, but all those holler kids always licked their pencil points before they'd write anything, and their papers looked terrible because of it, smeared and nasty. All year I'd have to look at one of those papers because another holler kid, named Martha, sat behind me, and whenever she passed her paper to the front I'd be the first to see it.

Betty sat in the same row as me but three desks ahead. At

least we could pass notes, if the kids between us weren't a bunch of tattletales. You couldn't tell by looking; you had to find out the hard way.

The first thing Mrs. Harper did was write her name on the blackboard and tell us how to write our names on our papers; then she reached into her dress and pulled up her bra strap. If we didn't print our name in the top right-hand corner and print her name just below, with everything spelled correctly, she said she wouldn't even read it, and she'd put a zero in her grade book. The whole time she told us this, she was smiling. She explained how a zero was worse than an F and worked a sample math problem to prove it. When she reached for her strap again, Harry caught on and giggled. If she was going to tug her straps up every time she wrote on the board, she was sure going to have a rough row to hoe. I wrote her name and my name in the top right-hand corner of my notebook as a reminder. I couldn't wait until high school, when you got to change classes. But probably every teacher had a different way for you to write your name and you'd flunk out because you couldn't keep it straight. Ever since Barbara and Sid had had their wreck, I'd been thinking a lot about high school and how I didn't care whether or not I was popular. It's a good thing, because I wasn't popular yet, so I probably wouldn't be. But Betty says that Barbara was an ugly fat baby who didn't get any hair until she was three, so weirder things have happened. I never understood how Barbara could be Betty's sister and have such blond, silky hair when Betty's was so dark and coarse. They both had hazel eyes, though.

Barbara was going to look fine — all her stitches were out. In five years of cocoa butter nobody would ever know anything happened to her. Sid was another story — he'd be lucky if he ever used his right arm again, and he was still in traction. I guess he could learn to flash the peace sign with his other hand. He had fifty stitches in his face, and half his mouth gone. It looked like Sid was going to miss a whole year of school. Barbara claimed she'd never date anyone else; she was in love with Sid.

"What does going to the junior-senior prom matter?" she was already exclaiming, and the prom wasn't until the spring. Barbara drove to the Bristol hospital every chance she got, even though it took over an hour to get there. She took Sid *Lord of the Flies* and *Demian,* which she'd just finished, but he said he'd rather have some comics. Betty picked out some comics she liked, *Superman* and *Archie,* because Barbara acted like she'd never seen a comic book before. I wonder how Sid turned the pages. His motorcycle was a mess, too. Totaled. The account in the paper said the front wheel had not been found. That was hard to believe. Wheels don't just roll off the world and disappear.

The next thing Mrs. Harper did was announce that she was ready to take up the poems for the contest if anyone had written one. Betty and I and Betty's friend Marie were the only kids who passed in poems. Mrs. Harper studied each one carefully and then handed mine back. "Dorie, you must think of a title," she said. I tried all through lunch to come up with one. Betty said that if I'd let her read it she'd think of one for me, but I didn't want her to read it right then with everyone else looking over her shoulder. I told Mrs. Harper I couldn't think of one and she said, "That's unfortunate, indeed. Because it must have a title for the contest. It's one of the rules." Betty said that Mrs. Harper was right. I still think it had something to do with my not starting off the first day of fifth grade in a new outfit like Betty, who wore a pair of new shoes and a corduroy jumper with matching socks. I'd probably have bad luck all year. Later on, I folded the poem and saved it inside the front cover of my zippered Bible I got when I joined the church.

After lunch we had to be weighed for the charts. I dreaded this because after we got weighed I knew we'd get measured, and for two years I'd been the tallest kid in the class. I looked around, and a couple of the girls, who should have been in seventh grade, looked like they'd finally passed me. Even Dudley looked pretty tall. We lined up a row at a time and waited as each kid stepped onto the scales and Mrs. Harper wrote down the result, without comment, to the right of their name on the big chart.

Seemed like we'd only been in line about two minutes when one of the girls between Betty and me dropped to the floor like a coat off a hall tree. I didn't even notice it until I heard a girl next to her calling her name, "Jenny! Jenny!" then yell for Mrs. Harper. The girl who fell down, Jenny, was real skinny. Her face looked like a skull stretched over lightly with too-white skin, when most everyone else was tanned from the summer. Jenny started shaking all over and jerked onto her side. "Quick as a snap now, Harry, run down and alert Mr. Clarke that we have a problem on our hands requiring *immediate medical attention!*" Then Mrs. Harper grabbed her ruler and forced it into Jenny's mouth, pressing down her tongue.

Betty and I and most all of the other kids circled Jenny and Mrs. Harper, even though Mrs. Harper had instructed us to return to our desks. For some reason I bent down beside them. My hands felt hot as blazes, all tingly and bigger than usual. I blew on my hands before placing them on Jenny's forehead. Mrs. Harper didn't say a word. It all happened so fast — I guess she was glad to have some kind of help. Right away Jenny stopped jerking. She lay there real still, as if she had died. I got water from the fountain, cupped some in my hands, and sprinkled it over Jenny's head. She sat up and a thick sweat broke out on her face and neck, but some color slowly crept back into her lips, like she was putting on lipstick from one side to the other. The red climbed up her face little by little. And my hands all at once went cool again.

Mrs. Harper looked more shook up than Jenny by the time the principal, Mr. Clarke, got there. He took one look at Jenny and asked, "Is everything under control here, Mrs. Harper?" His bright red face looked like it might explode from the effort of running the stairs; he patted his face and neck with his handkerchief several times while waiting for an explanation.

Mrs. Harper peered at Jenny and took one of her frail hands. "How are you feeling, dear?"

"Better," Jenny whispered.

Mr. Clarke and Mrs. Harper stepped out into the hall after helping Jenny to a chair. We were too scared to talk to her and scuffed back to our desks. Jenny folded her hands into her lap and looked down at them while we stared at her, wondering, I guess, if she was real after all that. The rescue squad huffed in with a stretcher, but Jenny said she'd just call her mother to come and get her. Mr. Clarke looked worried but agreed, and they walked down to his office. It wasn't the first fit Jenny had had, it seemed.

In a few minutes we were back in line like nothing had happened, finding out who was the heaviest and the lightest and the shortest. Usually the skinniest was a girl named Carla, who had gone home last year and the year before because she was upset. Carla didn't get skinniest this year, so she stayed. I never understood why the short kids didn't cry and go home. I guess they were used to being short or didn't think they'd stay that way. Come to think of it, there really weren't any fat kids, just gawky ones, who were lucky, because there wasn't a test for that.

When everyone had been measured I felt kind of let down — I wasn't the tallest anymore. It was Dudley, of all people. He smiled great big and showed his rotten teeth. I felt good for Dudley, though, because people made fun of his shiny shoes. At least he was the tallest. The heaviest was the ring leader of the dirty boys. Michael Dale walked to the front of the room and took his place beside the shortest, raised his right arm, then bent it at the elbow slowly, while he made a fist, until his muscle popped right out of his skin. Stinking dirty boys. They're a pain one at a time and worse in a pack. Michael looked straight at Betty when he flexed his dirt-streaked arm. She turned around to me and whispered, "Yuck." The lightest turned out to be Martha, the girl behind me. It would have been Jenny, I think, if she hadn't gone home. Martha's legs looked like she'd fall over if given half a chance. Her dress came to her knees and her arms stuck out of the sleeves like stems. It made her look even smaller to stand beside that big creep, Michael Dale. We gave them a round of applause, and it was time to go home. I thought I was lucky not to have to stand in that line-up on account of how different I felt on the inside. It was only the outside that mattered at school.

Betty said she was riding the bus home, and hopped into the seat beside me. "Scoot over."

"Won't your momma wonder where you are?" I asked. "It takes twice as long on the bus."

"I told Belinda. Her mom's driving."

"I wouldn't ride this old bus if I didn't have to."

"It's not so bad," Betty said as we bumped out of the school lot. "Barbara says it's the only way to get material."

"What?"

"She's decided to be a writer instead of an artist."

"I bet your mom's glad," I said. "No more turpentine!"

Betty and I switched places so she could have the window.

"I want to know what you did to Jenny," she said. "She stopped shaking the second you touched her."

I turned around and asked Harry if he had a stick of gum. I waited while he dug one out of his pocket. "You're a bum," he said and handed it to me.

"Want half?" I asked Betty.

"He's stingy." Betty unwrapped her half and started chewing it up. "I saw what happened, with Jenny," she prodded.

"I didn't do anything."

"Yes, you did," Betty insisted.

"I don't remember." I popped my gum.

"Well, I do — you put your hands on her head. Everyone saw you!"

"So what?"

"It happened just like I said." Betty pulled a string of gum out of her mouth, rolled it up, and flipped it back into her mouth.

"Did you see Mrs. Harper's bra strap?" I asked.

I remembered what had happened clear as day — I was afraid it might have something to do with Brother Saul's cobra, but I sure couldn't tell Betty that. I already felt like a freak; if I told her about the tent meeting she'd probably croak or just say I was a big liar. Thankfully, Betty dropped the subject and asked to read my poem. I felt guilty about keeping my secret, so I showed it to her. She said it was better than hers. She titled it.

The Life Cycle

A bird will slurp a worm
While it squirms

A cat will gnaw a bird
Head first

A car will hit a cat
Like it was a rat

A train will strike a car
And that will end it all

Before the bus stopped in town we had to wind the back roads and let off all the holler kids. Some of the roads were so steep the bus hung off the sides of mountains. We couldn't go but about twenty on most of those roads, the curves were too sharp. We stopped at dirt paths that wound up mountainsides to warped wood shacks that looked stuck together with thumbtacks and Scotch tape. None of them were painted. No wonder the holler kids came to school with mud on their shoes and clothes. They had to slosh through mud puddles just to get to the bus stop. Some of the places those kids ran off to I couldn't see from the window. A path would hairpin up through trees and vanish.

"I've got a secret, but you have to promise you won't tell anybody. If Mommy found out I'd told anyone she'd kill me," Betty said.

"You know I won't tell." I was still gazing past Betty's head out the window.

"You have to promise." The urgency in her voice startled me.

"I promise," I said.

"No matter what?" She looked at me like she might cry.

I drew a cross over my heart and sealed my lips with crossed fingers.

"Pop is gone. He said he couldn't stand it anymore. Last night he packed up the Pontiac and drove off. Mommy cried on her bed for hours. I asked her when he's coming back, but she won't answer. She got on the phone late last night to Aunt Phyllis, in Charleston, and told her everything, with the door shut. Barbara listened at the door with a glass!"

"That's awful," I said. It really did sound bad. And probably half the kids left on the bus had heard, the way Betty's voice carried.

"Barbara says they'll probably get a divorce."

"Do you think they'll go on *Divorce Court?*"

"That's not real, stupid!"

"It's not?"

"No. Everyone knows it's just actors playing parts."

"I wonder why your mom won't ever let us watch it, then?"

"She says it's unhealthy. Worse than *Dark Shadows.*"

"Oh." I looked out the window. "I always thought those people were real." You couldn't count on a damn thing anymore.

We rode in silence to Lee Street, where the bus stopped for me. Betty was looking out the window, too, sort of like you'd fix your eyes on a fire in the fireplace or maybe on the ocean or on anything where you didn't expect the unexpected to happen. I always wanted just once to work the door handle, but the old bus driver wouldn't let me. "Regulations," he'd say with a smirk. We clumped down the bus steps and started walking down my street. Betty swung her Barbie lunch box with each step until she turned up the alley, the back way home.

"I'm sorry about your dad," I said. "I bet he comes back."

"Just don't tell anybody."

"I said I wouldn't."

"Well, you better not." Betty was digging a trench in the gravel with the toe of her new saddle oxford.

"You want to come down later?" I asked.

"Maybe. I might go to Bristol with Barbara, if she goes."

"You know she won't take you."

"You don't know, she might." Betty scraped the side of her shoe, filling the hole she'd dug, tamping it in place.

"Why'd you want to go to the hospital, anyway?"

Betty straightened up her notebooks and looked me in the eyes. "Because" — she paused dramatically — "I'm going to be a doctor, that's why."

If I hadn't been afraid she'd start in on me again about Jenny, I would have laughed out loud. Instead I kicked some gravel, trying to bite my tongue. Betty, a doctor! That was about the craziest thing anybody'd ever told me. She couldn't even stand the sight of blood and nearly fainted that time we cut our fingers with Barbara's microscope set of scalpels and pressed them together to be blood sisters. After that, when we needed blood to sign our names we used pokeweed berries. One day I went home with pokeberry stains on my hands and Daddy told me his grandmother would fry pokeweed stalks and call it "dry land fish." He claimed it really tasted like fish, but I've never tried it. Betty turned and marched up the alley like she'd told me something noteworthy.

"Come on over if you can," I called.

A week into school and we were already having to outline chapters of our history book to prove that we'd read them. I wished Mrs. Harper'd just give us a reading quiz. It took longer to outline than it did to read, by a long shot. It was starting to get cooler at night. I went for a long walk by myself on Saturday just to see what was going on. Lots of kids out throwing football, but I didn't feel like joining any of the games, even if anyone asked. It was the kind of day I called a *blue* day. All day the sky held puffs of three-dimensional cloud that moved around, making shadows on the mountains. I lay on my back for a long time after I got back home, counting clouds, picking out my favorites. There was a game where you called clouds by other names, matching cloud shapes to animals. I never have been able to see anything but a cloud in a cloud. I can see the man in the moon when it's full. But clouds look like clouds. And I like it that way. I lay on my back with a stick for a pointer and squinted up to each cloud I especially liked. On *blue* days the sky vibrated with blue and the mountains shimmered with green of a darker shade, like the tube of Barbara's marked Forest Green. I took my stick and traced from one peak to the top of another, ran the pointer across the ridge, then dropped it suddenly into one of the shadows that looked like a river but wasn't. From my distance I could trace the V shapes between mountains. Each V outlined a gap in time, like the spaces between the black second lines of the clock. If I left the safe outlines and poked my stick into the open space where all the rules were different, I could feel Willie's war raging inside me, pulling this way and that. I guess he and Brother Saul would say it was a necessary tug of war between good and evil, but I wasn't so sure. In those dark spaces where I lost the outline, time leaped a space, leaving out the spaces of time where things had happened that didn't fit in with the rest — the time I had taken to put that snake back in its cage was like that, and the time I touched Jenny. *Blue* days were magic days, when the mountains were closer than dreams but didn't seem to smother you.

I was still on my back, figuring things out and pointing up at a bulby cloud with a dark bubble across its middle when a whoosh of wind flipped my bangs into my eyes. I was letting them grow out, and it was a pain — too short to clip back and too long for me to see with them brushed straight down. The wind whipped through the grass, laying it flat for a second. A singing, sighing started in the branches as leaves bumped and turned over one by one. You can always tell when a storm's coming, if the leaves turn upside down and shimmy. The bottoms of leaves don't shine like their tops. It's a dull, light, watery moss-green, with all the veins sticking up.

I heard the door slam over at Tina's. She smiled once in a while now. Momma said she'd get over her daddy dying, because she was so young, but it was sad in a way to think that people really could get over such awful things that happened to them. It's easier on little ones, Momma said. That didn't make sense to me. If you looked at Tina and her mother, though, it must have been true. Mrs. McGee came outside now and then, but only as far as her chaise. In the sun, she'd throw her neck over the back of the chair and close her eyes. I wondered if she enjoyed squinted colors, but I tried it her way and it didn't really work like it did in the truck with the sunlight changing all the time, so I don't know why she sat like that, like she was afraid to open her eyes. If her housedress flapped open, she wouldn't even pull it together again. Maybe she thought she was invisible, or wanted to be.

If I was going up the hill to the holes, I had to get a move on. The sky looked pretty clear, but those leaves had turned and that was a sign to trust. I figured I still had an hour; though the clouds were moving faster, the light still sparkled. I hiked up the alley past Betty's — she'd gone to the skating rink — and on beyond all the other back yards bordering the alley on both sides. At the top I popped out on another street. All I had to do was walk to the top of that hill and then up past Marie's house and past the water tanks to the beginning of the woods, to the holes. I was at the top of the hill when I remembered I hadn't brought anything to dig with; I'd even left my pointer in the yard. All the way to the tanks I kept my head down, looking for big flat rocks or an old spoon or a stiff stick. Two of the tanks were aqua and the third, a newer, bigger one, was painted silver. The aqua ones said "Class of '65" and "Class of '66," and the silver said "Class of '67," with the 7 crossed through and an orange 8 painted beside it. I guess the class of 'sixty-eight hadn't cared enough to write the whole thing out.

I walked over the dried-up tadpole ponds where we caught tons in the spring. A big debate raged between Betty and me, trying to figure out how the tadpoles got back into the ponds after they dried up over the summer. It would have made a lot more sense if the ponds stayed full of water all the time, but they dried up right on schedule. I thought maybe the tadpoles dropped into the ponds with the rain that filled them. Betty said the tadpoles had to come from frog eggs. It couldn't be frogs, though, because we hadn't seen any frogs near the ponds, only tadpoles. Momma wouldn't let me keep the buckets, so Betty kept them underneath her back porch while we waited for the tadpoles to turn. Right after they got legs, they died. Betty said they must not want to grow up and be frogs and have to hop away and have babies of their own. This reminds me of something I'll have to come back to, something creepy we found in the Graysons' basement when we were getting our costumes ready for Halloween later in the fall. Anyway, one of Betty's friends claimed she'd kept the buckets until fully formed frogs hopped away. Fat chance, I thought. But you couldn't contradict some of Betty's friends. Because their fathers were doctors they thought they knew everything. I don't see how she put up with them. Every other week, it seemed, one of them was having a birthday party and Betty would have to go to the drugstore and pick out a present she'd rather keep for herself.

Since it was nearly fall, some of the mud in the center of the ponds was a little mushy. I pushed at it with the end of a stick. When completely dried, the ponds cracked into a string of small islands, each bordered with what looked like a creek. Betty said it looked like the quilt one of her grandmothers had made. It looked more like a baseball cover, if it could be stretched out flat instead of wrapped around the core, the red stitches, like Frankenstein scars, cinching the ball. The mud patterns were pretty but boring. My shoes weren't even muddy from walking out to the center. I'd found a good digging stick, though, so I scrambled up the bank and around a ledge to the holes.

I don't know what started the holes. Miss Reider probably tried to bury a body and conked out before shoveling the whole six feet. Betty and I had looked around in the woods for the body, but it was decayed by now for sure, and bones are easy to scatter around. Looking for that body, I'd found a snakeskin. Snakes just slither out head first in a shed. I had the whole length of one, about a yard long, until Momma cleaned it out of my underwear drawer. Betty said it looked like rice paper, and since I hadn't ever seen any of that I had to take her word for it.

One hole sank down about four feet and the other was a lot shallower. They lay side by side, lengthwise, in a flat tier just above a sharp drop-off. Beyond the holes you couldn't go far before you were slipping from one shrub to the next just to get down the slope in one piece. We usually stayed on the safe side of the holes and threw the dirt over the hill. We hadn't dug very deep, but we were going to bring some real tools up and find some arrowheads and other valuable stuff pretty soon. All I had was the stick, so I climbed down into the deepest hole and started scratching out a pile of red clay.

Scooping my hands around the pile I'd carved out, I gathered every bit I could and slung the handful from the hole, over my head, down the steep bank. Dirt blew like raindrops back down into the hole. I scraped out what looked like another good double handful and then some, to be sure I'd done enough. Handful by handful I carved out a little space, rounding out a corner of the hole. Stick digging was like standing on my head; it made me feel funny when I raised up. I sat down on the dirt and it was easier, but harder to throw dirt out of the hole. Digging longer between heaving out the handfuls was the answer, so I settled down for a good long dig. The only problem that way was that I couldn't see anything but the sides of the hole or, if I looked up for a minute to shake the hair out of my eyes, the sky. It looked a little darker, but the clouds still bounced along like puffs of smoke.

On the sides of the hole the earth looked like streaks of crayon, burnt orange and orange red, henna yellow, saffron, and ocher. I wondered what the whole earth looked like sliced down to its core. Not like an apple, the same pulp to the seeds, but layered with different colors, down past the limestone to where the black coal glittered. What was below the coal? What was below what was below the coal? In the side of the hill about a mile from the holes were two caves. Betty and I ducked into them sometimes, but without a flashlight we couldn't see very far, and beyond the first several feet we had to crawl. I would have gone farther if anyone had come with me.

I stood to shovel out the handfuls of dirt; it made my head swim to suddenly stand up; I'd dug a lot this time. The corner I'd worked on slumped now. I wished I'd evened it out more. I felt like I should go around to the other three corners and catch them up, but then maybe it wouldn't look like I'd done as much if I left it too neat. I brushed off my shorts, looking over my shoulders, first one side and then the other, and the seat looked clean enough. But my socks looked like they'd slid into second. Maybe Momma wouldn't notice. I threw the stick over the bank just to see it whip end over end through the air. For a second, before I released it, the stick felt solid, worth keeping, and my hands didn't want to let go.

Behind me I heard a commotion of wings high in the sugar gum tree. Some leaves rustled down around me like stars. I crushed one to breathe in the scent. I knew my trees but not my birds. Birds were too hard to see; they wouldn't stand still so I could get a good enough look at them. If I didn't recognize a tree, I could always strip off a leaf and take it home to Daddy, and nine times out of ten he'd know it. He knew more trees than anybody I knew. He said my granddaddy taught him. I don't remember my granddaddy who was Daddy's daddy too well. Willie does. Granddaddy Parks died of black lung; it's something people get in the mines. He was sixty when he died, but Daddy said he'd been staying at home for a long time before that. The last three years he couldn't sit up in bed to read his mail, and he coughed all the time. That's why Daddy had to come home from college after the first year. He took his daddy's place in the mine when he got his leg crushed and made Grandma proud. Granddaddy wanted him to stay in school, but there wasn't money enough. Daddy said he'd work for a year, then go back to school, that the university would still be there waiting for him. That's how he started and it's how a lot of people end up doing things they maybe didn't want to do. One day something happens and they have to do right by someone who needs them. Then their whole life gets based on that bond.

I made it home before the rain; the storm blew over and even the rain didn't last long enough to muddy up the ponds.

9

New Secrets

"You're as stubborn as the old-timers who'd still rather have soap money than showers!" I heard Momma say, as I climbed the step to the trailer after walking to the Rexall for a cherry smash. It was almost supper time, but it didn't look like we'd be eating any time soon. And I had something to tell them, too.

"It's not that simple, Mary. You know that," Daddy said in a level voice, trying to calm her down. She must have been going on a while now for him to say anything at all.

She stood at the stove stirring, staring into the pot of beans, her face already red.

"Dorie, that you?" she asked at the sound of the door.

"Yeah."

"Well, set out in the yard until I call you for supper."

I backtracked; something in the atmosphere stopped me from talking back. I kept close enough to hear them, though. I hoped it would be over soon, because I was beginning to have to go to the bathroom pretty bad.

"Something's wrong with the whole thing, don't you see?" Daddy said quietly. "That's why the old-timers would rather keep their soap money."

"All I know is that you've been after those owners to build showers for I don't know how long, and now that they've finally offered, you say you don't want them anymore. It sure would make things easier around here."

"I know it would." Daddy paused until I thought he wouldn't say anything more. It's funny how the more you think you can't get to the bathroom the more you really have to get there or else. "There's something I haven't told you," Daddy said then. "I've been meaning to; I just haven't — I don't want to see you hurt. I can see now that I should have told you, but I thought for a while it'd be better if you didn't even know."

"What are you talking about?"

"I've been, well, I mean, I was offered a promotion and a raise."

"That's wonderful!" Momma blurted. I hadn't heard her that happy in a million years.

"I turned it down, yesterday. I had to."

"Are you crazy? What are you saying?"

"It's just the truth, Mary. They offered me a raise and a promotion to foreman, and I had to turn them down. I didn't want to, but I had to."

"How could you do this to me? How could you? All this time you spent slaving like your daddy, and you see where it got him!"

"I couldn't live with myself if I'd taken that promotion."

I could hear tears in Momma's voice. It was like she'd been betrayed for good and all. "Dorie's only ten. Now, how do you think we're going to send her to college like you been always saying? You've thrown all that down the pipe. And you ain't even given me one good reason for it."

"It's a feeling I have about it. That's all I can say."

Now Momma's sobs turned furious, pitched high in her voice; her tears vanished away, along with all the gentleness left in the world between married people. "You don't!" she screamed. "You don't care about anyone but yourself. Throw away the future on a feeling. Me, I know I don't count — "

"That's just not how it is," Daddy interrupted.

" — but I thought you had plans for Dorie. I thought you cared about her more than anything. I guess you never know how wrong you can be. I guess I'm just finding out how wrong one person can be about another."

"I love Dorie, you know that. And I love you," Daddy said, his voice stronger than usual.

"Then how in the world are you going to explain this to her?"

"It's like I said, an intuition. But I'm not the only one who feels it. I've been talking to some of the men, and they're uneasy too. If I took that promotion and then regretted it, there'd be no going back; I'd be stuck in the middle no matter what happened after that."

"In the middle of what?"

"I'm not sure yet."

"You're driving me plumb crazy, that's all I know. You're driving me crazy. Wait till Doreen hears about this. You take the cake, you really do."

"You can't tell Doreen or anybody else. At least for now."

"Now you're telling me I don't have the right to talk to my own sister if I want to?"

"I'm asking you not to. Not until I know more about it; not until I'm sure about some things."

"Sure about what things?"

"I just can't say anything else. You've got to trust me on this. You've got to believe I wouldn't do anything unless I thought it was the best thing for us, not just for me. It's more than just a hunch. Trust me."

"Well, what else can I do?" Momma said. "You'd better call Dorie to the table."

"Mary, you'll see. It won't be long and I'll tell you everything I know. I've got to go out later. Some of the men are meeting at Fred's. I'll have to go right after supper."

I skipped a few steps into the yard so Daddy wouldn't know I'd been listening. When he stuck his head out and said, "Supper's on the table," I made a beeline for the bathroom.

At supper, Momma seemed calm, considering she'd been shouting her head off just a few minutes before. Daddy was his old quiet self, but they both kept asking me questions, like they needed somebody else to fill in the silence. I wanted to tell them what had happened to me on the way back from the Rexall. But the feeling that it wasn't the right time crept over me. It seemed like they had enough to worry about without knowing that a man in a suit had been following me. I had crossed behind the stores, then behind the houses, jumping fences, patting all the dogs along the way home, and lost him anyway.

It started while I was twisting my stool at the counter of the Rexall, listening to high school creeps shooting off their mouths about their cars. I noticed this guy, a little younger than Daddy, by himself, sipping through a straw in the booth next to the wall. A newspaper half hid his face. Judging from the heft of that paper, it wasn't local. I stared at him, but he kept reading and sipping. When I finished my smash I pinched the straw at right angles from top to bottom, watching the red stripe bend along the hills and valleys I was shaping. I always did that; it was a necessary part of the fountain experience, like blowing off the white straw paper or blowing into the ice after you'd sucked the liquid dry.

The guy with the paper had bad skin. I should have gotten more suspicious right away: an old guy like that having himself a float. I jumped down off the stool and headed out, after shaking the ice in my glass one last time. I wove through the hoods congregated on the sidewalk to whistle at girls. One of them wore cowboy boots pulled over his pants legs to show them off. Leaning against the telephone pole next to the sidewalk, he propped his heels on the edge of the curb to keep his balance while he smoked and tamped down his hair with a greasy comb. His pal stood beside him, smoking; his claim to fame was a stupid-looking straw cowboy hat with a peacock feather stuck in the band. I'd passed Betsy Farmer on my way out the door; she was about the prettiest girl in the high school and she knew it. She didn't take one look at those cowboys. I heard the one with the boots sigh "whew" under his breath, then whistle through his teeth like he was letting off steam. I made a face, and his sidekick with the hat turned around. "Mind yer own business." All his front teeth looked broken or black or both. It made my mouth hurt just to look at him. "Scram, brat!" his friend added.

It wasn't until I'd walked partway up the street past the jail that I realized the guy in the suit was behind me. I thought I'd

find out where he was going, just for fun, so I crossed over
and went inside the post office to watch what direction he took.
I stood far enough back from the tinted glass so that nobody
could have seen me. It was weird; that guy leaned up against a
brick wall and took out his paper like he was waiting for someone.

Since nobody was in line, the postman asked what I wanted,
so I had to leave. There's this lady who dresses in wild print
clothes and carries a suitcase back and forth in front of the post
office, looking both ways as she passes, and even she wasn't
around. I could never figure why she needed the suitcase when
it looked like she was wearing all her clothes at once.

I crossed the street and walked straight on to the corner.
The only time I checked behind me I bent down and pretended
to tie my shoe, sneaking a peek between my legs. There he
was, about twenty feet back. That's when I decided to cut behind
the Presbyterian church and tear through the yards.

I didn't look back, but the Lanes' dog started barking like
crazy just after I jumped their fence. The guy was back there
on my trail, all right.

I thought I'd sit down after supper and work a few word problems,
but I couldn't concentrate on them. Who really cared how much
Bob's wife Donna spent on her dress anyway? Daddy had gone
out and I asked Momma if I could go play until dark. With
summer a thing of the past, she was pretty sympathetic. Maybe
I could get up a game of hide-and-seek.

I looked into each yard as I meandered by, but we ate so
early that most everyone else was still stuck at the table. I knew
it was too early for Betty. I couldn't be sure she'd come out
anyway — lately she'd been studying all the time, trying to prove
she meant business about being a doctor. Maybe it had something
to do with her daddy being gone. I'd never known anyone whose
daddy left them on purpose. It was a mystery to me. I kept
thinking that he must have had to go do something, something
secret, the way my daddy had a secret he couldn't tell us yet.

As I walked I started having the strangest feeling; I thought

I heard little crunching sounds coming right after me; after each of my steps on the gravel, I'd hear a repeat, an echo. It was still daylight, so I just turned around, expecting one of the dirty boys with a rock in his hand. Nobody. I kept walking and hearing the echoes. I'd take a step forward, then hear another crunch. I checked the soles of both my shoes to see if anything was stuck on them. Nothing. I wondered who Fred was and where he lived. If Daddy would call people by their whole names I might be able to figure out who they were once in a while. When I got to the top of the alley with all the yards empty, I just turned around and started back, with my head down, looking for money. Two winters before, I had found a ten-dollar bill beside the Graysons' car, but it turned out to be Dr. Grayson's. I got all the way back to Betty's with my eyes combing the gravel. The echoes stopped as though I'd never heard them in the first place, and maybe I hadn't.

"What're you doing?" Betty's voice made me jump; she was lolling on her gate. "I've been waiting for you." She picked up a rock and tossed it toward me. "Catch!"

I caught the rock in front of my face. It weighed more than I'd expected and a sharp edge scraped my palm.

"Why didn't you throw a bigger rock?" I asked, ready to stuff it in her face.

"I guess I couldn't find a bigger one, is all. What's with you?"

"My hand's bleeding, if you haven't noticed." I waved it under her nose.

"I'm sorry. You got a Band-Aid?"

I looked at her. What kind of a person goes around carrying Band-Aids?·

"Wait right here. I'll get you one. You ought to wash it out first, though, or it'll get infected and swell up and they might have to saw off your hand," Betty said in a rush.

"Dadgum it, Betty, it's only a scratch."

"Then why do you need a Band-Aid?" Betty popped her eyes and placed one hand on her hip.

10

Riddles and Holes

In *The Arabian Nights* there're these mountains called the Kaf that are bigger than the mountains around here. Arabians think their Kaf mountains circle around the whole earth, but that's a crock. Though sometimes I think my mountains are like a fence that runs between this part of the world and the rest of creation. Nobody can see out and nobody can see in. You can tell it might be true if you listen to the TV news at night like I had to with Daddy. Nobody on TV ever sounds like they came from anywhere in particular. Hunt and Brink, as Daddy called them, talked like they were born in outer space. Just like the Jetsons. It's funny if you think about it, that all we know about other places gets told to us in a voice that doesn't sound real. How can you believe it? It's the news, but whose?

Everyone knows the moon isn't made of green cheese, and pretty soon, Mrs. Harper said, there'll be men walking around on the moon, stepping into the face of the man in the moon, I guess. But I used to think that the world seemed like a big piece of Swiss cheese, the kind Momma never bought, because she said with all those holes in it you couldn't get your money's worth. If Rainbo bread looked like that, she said, they'd never be able to sell it no matter how many chichi lies they told. Whoever heard of a sandwich chock full of holes, and so on.

John Glenn orbited around the earth, outside of everything that went on here. I don't see why he had to come back. I wouldn't have, if I'd had the chance to spin off like that. If you tried to walk an honest-to-God real line around the earth, something like the equator, you couldn't do it. Mountains and trees and jungles and deserts and rivers and oceans would get in your way, not to mention natives with spears. You'd be off the straight line before you even knew what happened. Look what happened to Columbus when he started west: a whole hunk of land he'd never even heard of welled up between him and the place he wanted to go. But Glenn circled us for real, not an imaginary line either. A real trip. He could look down and see the earth curving along beneath him. He didn't have to worry about finding a ship to get across the ocean and then a camel to cross the desert and then a big saber to hack his way across a jungle. The sailing was smooth up there, a clean chute.

All the questions I have about things are like the holes in the Swiss cheese, and all the answers that don't match make more and more holes. What holds us down when we walk? What holds down what holds us down? All right, if gravity is the answer to the first question, what answers the second? And what is gravity? How long does it last? What is the shape of eternity? What is God? Did God make snakes? There're so many questions that I can't begin to list them all right now. For a long time I wrote down questions in a notebook, the kind of questions you can't get an answer to right away. The list of questions kept getting longer and longer. Sometimes I'd come up with three new questions every five minutes. I got tired of writing them in the book after a while. I kept my question book under my bed with a lot of other stuff. Maybe it's still there. Sometimes I feel like taking it out, but it's depressing to think of all those questions, all those holes, just adding up. I thought I'd find out the answers, so I planned to leave a place in the back with one line for each answer, numbered to correspond to each question. It seemed like every time I did get an answer I'd think of another question because of it, so I stopped trying to write down anything but questions, and then I had to stop that too. There're just too many.

For instance, lots of questions just happen to you and you don't think of writing them down, like whenever Momma asked me what I thought I was doing. Or when she asked what I thought we should do about Willie in the jail. I don't know why she asked that. Was she just thinking out loud? Is that what questions are, after all? Just loud thoughts looking for an echo?

Solid parts of the cheese are easy to count on. They're like when you fall down and rip open your knee. Gravity, I guess, you can count on, whatever it is. I got the worst cut I ever got by just stumbling onto the edge of the sidewalk on my right knee. It got cut clean to the bone; I could see the bone in there. I didn't cry. It didn't really hurt or bleed that bad at first. That's when I learned that we really do have bones inside us, or at least I know I do. I was thinking about the bones, about how I had proof of the whole skeleton, and I got a little queasy. I sat down and put my head between my knees and the blood started running down my leg. I went numb all over. I was afraid to move a muscle because of the implications of it all. I didn't get any stitches. I've got a scar on my knee that probably will never go away, but I don't care because it means something.

When a rock hits your head, that's the solid part of the big cheese again. I ought to know about that. Betty threw a rock up once that came down on the top of my head with a vengeance. She didn't mean to do it. I did get stitches that time, and part of my hair shaved off. I can still remember having to walk home with blood in my eyes. I really thought I was going to die without being able to get Betty back or anything. When I rubbed my head and brought my hand down covered with blood, Betty ran into her house. The doctor told me I was lucky that I had such a hard head. Maybe my head hovers somewhere between the holey and the solid parts of the cheese.

Parents belong to the solid parts of the cheese. At least I'd always thought so. Lately I wasn't as sure. What if they really belonged to the holey part, like Tina's daddy, or Betty's? That was another question for the notebook. Tina's momma looked like she'd fallen through a hole, too. Brothers and sisters sometimes belonged on the solid side, sometimes on the holey. Take Willie — he'd been in and out of my life since I could remember. But then he would always be my brother no matter what happened, even if I never saw him again. See? Part holey, part solid cheese. We might never see him again until he did something so awful his picture wound up on the post office bulletin board saying WANTED. That didn't seem likely, though. I couldn't imagine Willie in a crowd of those hollow-eyed criminals who looked like they'd sooner take a bite out of your arm than say doodle-de-squat. One thing was sure — Willie wasn't mean-spirited. He was sort of like the landscape, and you couldn't really accuse it of anything.

If I felt good I'd touch a tree trunk and think its name and think how much a part of everything it was. Then I'd climb the tree to the top and jump down branch by branch before hanging from the lowest branch and skinning the cat to the ground. I could pick up a big bunch of dirt and watch it trickle through my fingers, through the long bones and back to the ground. Gravity. I'd pick up the dirt and watch it sift again, watch until it seemed more like water than dirt, a steady stream of water cascading onto the earth from my hand. If you knew the names of things, they became more solid. Daddy taught me the names of trees and the names of animals and I wanted to know more plants and birds. All I knew on sight were robins, blue jays, hawks, eagles (like the American eagle), cardinals (the state bird), doves, mockingbirds, whippoorwills when they called before night or daylight. If you only know the names of people, that's all that's real to you.

There's a point in time where the holes start seeming realer than the rest. And there's a point when the holes fill in. That's the past, when you're old enough to have one. If you know something has already happened, that it will never happen again, like a year gone by or a real good holiday, then which part of the cheese does it stay in? If you remember it, it seems solid. Then it's just as likely to drift from your mind while you live day after day, thinking you're solidly alive, that the past should sift through the holes. But instead it's like a memory has fallen into a hole inside my mind. Then one day I'll remember it because of something that happens or because of something somebody says or because I am sad and need a happy memory, or happy and need a sad memory to anchor the joy. Up from the hole it will come, proving it has never really fallen through, just sunk to the bottom of the pit, waiting to be dredged up when I called it. If you've ever spun around so many times that when you stopped the earth turned over and over like a piece of wrapping paper, then you know what I mean.

There's this game that Betty and I played all the time called "steps." We'd cut two squares of cardboard from a box, not too big, but big enough to hold one foot with a fringe of space left over — about ten inches square, I guess. Cutting the squares was the hardest part of the game, because Mrs. Grayson wouldn't let us use a razor blade, just scissors. It took forever, and cutting straight sides was impossible even if we traced first. What we'd finally come out with looked more like badly peeled eggs, but we called them squares. Usually, we'd set up in Betty's front yard, because it was flat. She'd start from one side of the yard and I'd start from the other. The trick was to see who could get to the opposite side first, by stepping only on squares. I'd place one square down for each step, then move from square to square without touching the ground. It required careful measurement. You had to know exactly how far you could stretch without falling between squares. If you settled on timid little steps, you'd cramp up and make a mistake. If you set a square too far out, you'd miss it or slip. Once you placed a square, you couldn't move it. If you missed a step, you had to start over from the beginning. I don't know why, but I never cheated. I'm sure Betty didn't either. Each of us was so involved in her own twist across the grass, it would have been easy to cheat, but the game wouldn't have lasted very long if we had. Sooner or later one of us fell between her squares, picked up the pieces, and ran back to start over. Hardly ever did we get across in one clean try. But what if you just kept on falling? What if you never hit the squares but fell down and down, through empty space? Where would it end? Were the squares the holes? Was the ground between them holey? Solid ground or solid squares? Is *nothing* full or empty? It's hard to tell.

Take a mountain: solid or holey? I always thought, for a long time anyway, that mountains were as solid as they come, but then what about the mines drilled into them? And tunnels blasted under them and roads going through them and caverns hollowing them out? Especially mines make you think twice. They can cut out the coal and never have to put anything back. How long do you think a mountain can take pit after pit, like some kind of cancer, and go on like always? Does a mountain have a skeleton holding it up from the inside? They have to bolt up rocks after cutting out coal or the roof of the shaft will cave in on the miners. Sometimes it does anyway. So a mountain must not be as solid as it seems from the outside. How does a tunnel dug through a mountain stay without having the mountain cave in? Somehow it's like the mountain doesn't even know the tunnel is there. The mountain goes on around a new road like nothing is the matter. Cars zoom through the mountain, into the dark of the mountain, burning headlights into the black-as-night inside of the mountain. The coal comes out and nothing goes back in. It's like taking the piece of cheese and gutting more and more holes until there's not any cheese to go around the holes. All hole, then, or nothing at all?

There're a lot of mountains in the world, but not all of them give coal. My mountains are so old they've got lots of it. Coal is the bodies of plants from prehistoric times pressed so tightly together that they melded into rock, black shiny rock. Carbon distinguishes life. I learned that in science. I'm not really sure yet exactly what carbon is, though. The weight of ninety million years pressed down the ferns; it happened so long ago that forests were where the mountains are, just like there's desert where there used to be ocean. Coal just sits there quietly all that time. Like a riddle. Old as the hills, a buried treasure. Somebody found it out. It must be worth a lot for all the trouble they go through getting it out. If you think about how long it took to make that coal, which didn't belong to anyone in particular, it seems like they dig it out too fast. Sometimes I think it would be better if it had stayed trees.

If you can take something like a mountain and turn it inside out, what can you say that's solid, and what can you say that's holey? I mean say for sure, and for sure is forever, not just a year or two. I worked out that definition in my notebook a long time ago. It might be the past; that's the only thing that stays on my list for very long. And I am making more of that every day; there's no way around it: the past follows me everywhere, like a caboose. Momma always says that if I feel like doing something I shouldn't, I should remember that whatever I do will always have been done once I do it. What is done can't be undone, she says. I can't say that's kept me from doing what I've felt like doing, but her words sure weigh on my mind.

I keep the past at the top of my list of solids, when it seems like most everything else just flutters back and forth between what is solid and what isn't. Even the mountains, like I said. Real and not real. Maybe it's things at a distance that always seem solid, and things in the palm of your hand that holes shine right through.

11

The Identity Number

When something happened, it happened, didn't it? What I mean is this: If something happened and nobody was sure exactly what happened, was it solid or holey? Had it happened even when you couldn't know what had really happened, when all you could know for sure was that it had changed things, that a man was dead and all the speculation in the world couldn't bring him back from the dead? Lately, even the past, the last thing on my mental list of solids, seemed to be losing its credibility. When the past wasn't sewed up either, when it acted more like a long dream, there was worse trouble than usual; when the most anyone has to deal with is knowing that each hour is slipping back into the past, it's comforting to think there's something solid forming back there, a sort of string trail pulled taut: things that happened and that is all, nothing more. You can't *do* anything about those things back there, so you're free to get on with what you can do. But when you're still in the dark, wondering what happened, you can't get on with it. You're looking backward, moving your feet forward. You're bound to step right square into a hole.

I was lying awake the night Daddy had gone out to Fred's, waiting for him to come home and thinking about things. Since he was more likely to talk if he thought I was asleep, I'd turned off my light and called good night, through the wall, to Momma. The only problem was that I was afraid that if he didn't come soon I really would fall asleep.

My eyes were growing heavy, like the hypnotists say. I'd pull open my eyes to feel the stinging underneath the lids, which always started when I was trying to stay awake but losing the battle little by little. I raised one hand and then the other into the air above my head, trying to concentrate on preventing the hand from falling. When it fell, I'd wake up if I had drifted off with a hand in the air. This worked for a while. Then I started reciting the multiplication tables we were learning. We hadn't gotten very far, but already I was confused over something no one else seemed the least bit worried about. It had to do with one times any number and zero times any number. Mrs. Harper wrote it on the board for us.

"One times any number equals that number.

"Zero times any number equals zero."

She worked out several problems, which I copied dutifully into my notebook. It seemed an easy concept. She didn't plan to spend much time on it.

$$1 \times 1 = 1 \qquad 0 \times 1 = 0$$
$$1 \times 2 = 2 \qquad 0 \times 2 = 0$$
$$1 \times 3 = 3 \qquad 0 \times 3 = 0$$

I raised my hand and asked, "Is the answer always zero, no matter how big the number gets?"

Mrs. Harper answered, "Always. Zero times a million would still be zero."

"What about a zillion times zero? Isn't that a zillion zeroes and don't they make something all together?" I asked.

She said that a zillion zeroes or more were still zero, just the same as one zero. I couldn't get that. A zillion of something had to be more than just zero. A zillion or a billion zeroes had to add up to something, even if they were only zeroes. They were still more than nothing, weren't they? I asked some more questions and Michael Dale said I was stupid so I shut up. He's the stupid butt, and everyone knows it. I should have kept asking questions until I got the answer, but I was ready to revive my questions-without-answers notebook anyway, and this would be a good one to start up with. Mrs. Harper tried to explain that numbers stand for things. Like apples. A 5 stands for five apples, or oranges if you don't like apples. So a 0 stands for something that doesn't exist, or a world without apples. No apples equals 0 apples. But what about the word *zero?* Wasn't it something?

I understood about *1* being the "identity number" right away. It looked a lot like *I*, so the concept made sense. I would think it was *I* times something, not *1,* or I'd think that *1* and *I* were the same thing. What's I × 1 = ?

Someone was chasing me, and the faster I ran the more I stumbled, the more my feet felt like bricks mortared into a walk-way. I raised one foot and felt a pull of bubble gum beneath it. And now I could see that it was a man coming after me, gaining steadily, each of his steps covering the distance of five of my anguished plods. My hands tugged at my ankles to dislodge my feet from the muck. The man's face pressed close to mine; his half mask turned him into a scavenger bird. My bed started gently shaking back and forth over the floor, the way it did when Momma or Daddy walked through the trailer. They made it rock just by walking normally, even if they were trying to be quiet. Was I awake or dreaming? When my bed shook like that it felt like I was in a boat. I was on a creaky old ship, big sails flapping, waves gently slapping its sides. The sheets were whitecaps. I could arrange them in wrinkles and sail my hand through the pits and peaks. *Was I awake?* Whose steps were nearing my door? I started seeing the birdman's beak in front of my face, hoping that it was only Daddy shaking the trailer on his way to the bedroom, that he had finally come home, and that I was still awake.

My door opened. I held my breath, opened one eye, and the door shut again, pulled silently until the crack of light vanished. I raised up in the bed and pressed my ear to the wall.

"David, is that you?" Momma asked.

"Yes. Go back to sleep."

I let out my breath all at once, feeling each pound of my heart. I multiplied myself to sleep.

*　　*　　*

I woke up having almost forgotten it was Sunday, and the day I was supposed to join the Methodist church. Each Sunday for several weeks, instead of Sunday school I'd been in the minister's class, studying all about the church with five other kids. I didn't understand half of what we read, but neither did the others, not even Betty. We were too blank to ask questions. The minister said we were the best class he'd ever had; we were all so smart, he said. And what could we have asked anyway? All the right questions were printed out in our little study books with the right answers beside them. All we had to do was memorize them. None of those printed questions were the things you really would like to know, though, like was Jesus black or white, and if He was Jewish, then why did the picture in our classroom show a blond Jesus with blue eyes? Something I'd always wondered was if the baby Jesus knew He was God's Son when He was a baby; you know, did He feel like a regular baby or did He think like a little God in a baby suit, like Mighty Mouse?

When I told Momma and Daddy about my joining the church and they said they thought they'd come and see it when it happened, my mouth must have fallen open, because Daddy said if I wasn't careful I'd wind up catching flies. Momma and Daddy were already eating breakfast when I got to the table. I'd stayed awake half the night and nearly missed it after all. I sat down, Momma poured me some milk, and they just kept right on with it, like I wasn't there.

"What it comes down to is this," Daddy said. "The company's accusing Bud of having caused the accident. Nobody else was down there with him, you know; they were right behind him, maybe only five seconds back. But the company's leaking that Bud struck a match to light a cigarette."

"It's against the code to light up down there," Momma said.

"Of course it is. Bud knew the code. The company won't have to pay any compensation if they can make it stick. Everyone knows Bud chewed, kept a plug in his hip pocket all the time. Why, there're probably some of his coffee can spittoons left over in the yard."

"Momma, I'm hungry."

"Hold your horses for a minute," Momma said. "I never saw Bud light a cigarette."

"He was always spitting. Fred said he thought it was a short in the miner that caused the blast. He said they had that continuous miner hot-wired so they wouldn't have to lose time having it repaired. Now that coal's moving again, seems nobody wants to stop long enough to make it safe." Daddy sipped his coffee.

"Should she be hearing all this?" Momma asked.

"I think she can keep it between these walls," Daddy said, looking at me. "She's old enough. These are family matters."

"I can keep a secret," I said.

"Well, this isn't exactly a secret, but all the same it'd be better if you kept it to yourself. Don't want Tina to hear about this."

"I just want my breakfast," I said.

Momma started heating a pan, and I was afraid they weren't going to go on with it, but they did.

"Why didn't Fred say something before now?" Momma asked from the stove, back turned.

"He said he did say something. But they told him to turn off the miner whenever the inspector came so he wouldn't see the sparks flying out of it. Just about everything down there, from the miner to the cars, was hotter than a firecracker, just ready to blow. Fred thinks Bud was electrocuted before any rock ever landed on him."

"Can the company prove anything?" Momma cracked the eggs into the pan and scrambled them with a spatula.

"Seems like they don't have to," Daddy said above the racket of the sizzling eggs. "They just say it to the right people. And unless we can prove what really happened, it'll be our word against theirs. We've got to have evidence, not just accusations, before we say anything at all. There had to be gas down there for it to blow in the first place, but nobody's talking about that." Daddy got up with his empty mug.

"What did the men say about all this? Dorie, here's your eggs. David, sit down. I'll get it." She filled his mug.

"We've got to get to church," I said, and blew on a forkful of egg.

"We'll be there in plenty of time. Eat your breakfast." Daddy sipped his coffee. "Well, some of the others want to let it go — they say we should have taken the showers and let it go at that. Let the union worry about the regulations. They say we got to get all the work we can get. A couple others said we ought to press for better safety, or something else is bound to go wrong down there. And it might be more than one man next time."

"Dorie," Momma said, "go get your dress on."

"I'm not finished."

The conversation stopped while I swallowed what was left without chewing. I went back to my room, ears cocked.

"David, do you think they could be right? Is it dangerous?" Momma tried to whisper.

"I just don't know. It's always dangerous. That inspector, Mr. Handcock from Grundy, sure seems to be a big buddy to Mr. Willis. They spend most of the time cracking jokes when Mr. Handcock's supposed to be going through the mine. Willis has us shut off that miner every time before the inspector gets there. But Handcock seems like a decent fellow. He writes notes. Willis just doesn't do anything. I'd sure like to get a look at one of those reports. I guess I should tell you that Fred and Bill and Mike want to strike. They say it's the only way to get the mine cleaned up. That if we keep going down there with things like they are, we deserve to get killed."

"A strike? But you don't think — "

"I can't promise it won't happen. I don't think it'll happen right away, though. We agreed to see what else we could learn, and we can't learn anything if we're pickets instead of miners. We've got to have good reasons, and we've got to have some proof the UMW can understand if we want their help, and unless we've got them behind us . . . Well, you can't eat air and promises."

"Do you really think it's so serious? We just can't get by, David."

"I don't think it'll happen, but if it does, we'll make do."

"Oh, I know, I know. I ain't saying you'd have a choice. Just be sure you can win before you go out. You'd better make sure you don't leap into something — "

"Everybody remembers what happened over in District Nineteen four years ago. Bill was *there;* he was part of it. That's why he moved on over here after the strike failed. His family nearly starved to death on that twenty-five-dollar-a-week food voucher. He's got five children. You know he wouldn't fly off at the handle over just anything. He's worried, or he wouldn't be breathing the word *strike.* And you know Tony Boyle's just as likely to turn the other way as help us if we get out on a limb. Who ever heard of a strike in a Poorwater mine, anyway? We're chicken feed."

"I hope you remember when you're talking Mr. Boyle down that he's the president, after all. And if Bill thinks he might not approve of the strike, I say that's good enough reason to forget it."

"Mary, I only said it was an option. You wanted the whole story and I'm trying to tell you everything I know. If the company thinks we're sniffing around, they'll fire some men. They're already suspicious as hell about us turning down the showers."

"You never should have. What about your promotion? Ain't they suspicious about that?"

"No. I don't think so, at least. It's a big step up to management. I just said that I appreciated it but I didn't think I could handle it right now. Willis'll just offer it to someone else, if he hasn't already. I told Willis I had my heart set on going after the fire boss certificate."

"What if the next man turns him down?"

"I don't know."

*   *   *

I thought maybe I'd tell them about the stranger on the way to church, but then I didn't. I wanted to tell them I could save my lunch money in case there was a strike, but I was afraid Momma'd get mad at me for listening. It was weird, walking between Momma and Daddy — like being a real little kid again. I almost felt like grabbing a hand from each of them, but I stopped myself and took a few steps ahead so they'd hurry up and walk faster. "You act like you're going to a fire!" Momma said.

Betty and her momma and Barbara were already seated when we walked in. As members of the special class we were supposed to sit together in the front row, so I got Betty and we went on up there, scooted onto the first bench, and started looking up the processional hymn on the program. Before too long the choir marched in from the foyer, singing "Holy, Holy, Holy," not one of my favorites. I liked "Onward Christian Soldiers" the best. The minister had the idea that there were lots of good songs in the hymnal that nobody knew because we never sang them, so he started the new hymn of the week. The choir practiced it all week and it was a good thing, because they were the only ones who ever sang the hymn of the week worth a damn. A couple of the old ladies, who had once been told they had great singing voices, tried to stay right with the choir. If they had been that great they would have been in the choir, but I guess they never thought of it that way. There was an old bald guy who lived up the street from us and had given the church a lot of money — he really could sing pretty good for his age, and he was in the choir. The first time through the hymn of the week that Sunday, he sang by himself. I got kind of worried about him, his face got so red when he hit a high note. I looked at Betty beside me, afraid she was going to crack up right before joining the church. I was sorry I'd looked at her, that was for sure. She got me tickled at that red-faced man, and I'd been trying lately to love everybody equally.

It's a lot harder than you might think, the business of loving everyone. Treating others as you would have them treat you is about the hardest thing in the world to actually do. And unless you try it you'll never go to Heaven; that's what the minister said. I tried it, but before a day was through I'd said something wrong to someone. It seemed like I could keep from doing things if I stopped to think first, but when it came to keeping my mouth shut I didn't stand a chance. I guess I wasn't blessed with a poker face. I don't know how many times Momma said to me, "You'd better watch out; your face'll stick that way." She's right. Everything I ever thought would wind up on my face. Before I could even think about it. That's the worst part. Nine times out of ten the wrong words would come rushing off my tongue and I'd be back at the beginning all over again, trying to be good. The second I'd forget, I'd say something worth regretting. It was always worse than not saying anything at all. If I didn't improve I'd probably be struck mute, my own little version of the tribulations of Job. I'd been working a lot on thinking before I spoke, though, and maybe I could improve. Momma hadn't yelled at me in a while, but maybe she'd given up on me.

She and Daddy looked as good as anyone when they dressed up and came to church. I'd forgotten how nice they looked together. Momma in her hat and Daddy in his blue suit and a striped tie that was too thin but still looked all right. At least he didn't wear white socks with everything like some people. It would put out your eyes — white socks between dark pants and black shiny shoes. Black socks didn't cost any more than white ones, Momma said. Everyone should have both kinds.

It was time for the confirmation class about halfway through the service. We lined up before the altar and all knelt together. Then our parents came up and stood behind us. I was glad Momma and Daddy had come when we got to that part. We promised to support the church with actions and prayers and with money. I wondered where I was going to get the money. The minister'd never mentioned that part in class. I'd have to get a job or something so I could give money to the church. Things are always more complicated than they start out seeming.

Our heads got sprinkled and we sat back down like ducks in a row. It felt pretty good, to tell the truth.

After the sermon we stood at the altar again and the whole congregation filed past to shake our hands and say how glad they were to have such fine new members. The old red-faced bald guy who sang shook my hand and called me his neighbor. I didn't know he knew where we lived. He had the pinkest hand you ever saw. I guess he didn't go outside much, with all the singing he did. I told him I liked his voice, and he smiled. "Someday *you* must join the choir!" he said. Having conversations with grownups is a turning point in your life. I kept thinking that Momma would interrupt and say something for me, but she wasn't paying any attention; she and Daddy walked outside to wait for me. I stood there at the front of the church and, for the first time, looked out into the rows of pews instead of up into the minister's face or toward the cross. Even during our ceremony we had stood facing the cross while the minister read to the church and we answered "I will" to each of his questions. The view was different from the altar.

I walked up the center steps to the flat stage where the minister stood most of the time preaching. He didn't like to stand behind the podiums with the banners and the big Bibles. He'd walk out into the middle. When he first started he didn't wear a robe, but since the choir wore robes somebody talked him into it. Every other preacher we'd had wore a robe, they told him, and it didn't mean anything. He said he felt like a big bird flapping around, getting above the human level. If he didn't wave his arms so much he wouldn't have to look like that, I said. Daddy laughed, but Momma told me to hush. From where I stood the sanctuary stretched back and back; it had a side area, too, where the Graysons and I usually sat. Red carpet parted the pews from the altar to the foyer, beyond the closed double doors that opened when the choir marched in each Sunday singing the opening hymn. Lots of people walked down the red carpet to get married. A worn streak ran along the center of the carpet. I wondered why people couldn't walk on the edges more. I decided that whenever I walked down the center aisle I'd step on the edges, close to the pews; maybe I could balance out the wear. Where the red was worn it turned pinkish. Only when light was on it a certain way, though.

A row of real stained glass windows ran the length of one wall of the church. They weren't just painted purple with scenes or something, like the big Christian church in Doran I sort of remembered going to once with Momma and Daddy; these windows were real mosaics. I think that red-faced man bought them. Lead bordered each little piece of glass until the whole picture was formed. We made drawings of them in Vacation Bible School one summer. I drew the nativity window. First I puzzled over the outlines, then spent the whole rest of the week coloring in each shape with crayon to match the real window. I didn't even know where that window I drew was now. I'd spent all that time on it and now I didn't even have it.

I could see the wooden beams of the ceiling suspended throughout the sanctuary. Once there'd been a rain leak up there and a bucket had been placed in the third row from the back during a service. That Sunday you could hear pings of water punctuating the sermon. Dark blotches still marked the spot where water had seeped through, if you looked really hard. I used to spend most of church looking up at the ceiling, following the center beam as it split the church in two equal halves; then I'd trace each intersecting beam, following them like spokes of a wheel. I'd counted the spokes a hundred times or more, but now I couldn't remember the total, as I stood at the top of the stage, gazing across the ceiling, over the heads of the lingering crowd as they filed slowly out the foyer doors. I felt like singing or screaming or something and then again I felt very quiet inside, like I was suddenly old, now that I was a real member of the church.

In the old days I liked to imagine myself hanging from one of those beams, swinging by my arms beam to beam, like a trapeze artist, out the front doors without anyone being the wiser. I liked to think that the dark water stain was really a bat asleep up there during the service, never knowing what was going on below it, never opening its eyes until the night came and no one was there to see it swoop out the doors into the night sky. I'd make myself small as an elf and pretend to balance along the beams, inching from beam to beam, then skipping and jumping, never falling, looking down on the people as they bowed their heads to pray. I might sprinkle star dust down on their heads, not anything mean, like what some kids did at the movies, not like that; I'd dust down some glitter. Fairy dust. When they stopped praying it would seem to them like they'd been praying for a century or more. They'd walk out the front doors and discover themselves in the future. Nothing in the world would look as it had when they'd entered the church that Sunday morning. I wondered as I stood there, remembering all the things I used to think about, if I would still have as much to imagine during the sermons, now that I was a real member. I guessed it was about time I started listening to the messages and trying to figure out what they were really all about. Already I'd let one go by. I couldn't remember a single thing that the minister had said after we got sprinkled and sat back down. Maybe I had brain damage or something. I couldn't even remember the last hymn — and it was usually a familiar one that everyone could sing. If my bat ever woke up during a sermon it'd be terrible.

Full Moon

Blue Moon at the Edge
of Summer, 1958

Two moons in one month
A month of bad weather.

Two moons in the month of May
Rain for a year and a day.

It seems strange to write about my own birth, but who else
would ever bother with it? The biggest puzzle goes on inside
my head when I try to think back to things and then realize
that the reason I can't is that I wasn't there. I write these pieces,
these little scraps of time, and they help me fill in the blanks.
You can live with your family all your life and still not really
know what goes on inside their heads. When I fill in the blanks,
I think maybe I really can know my brother after all, that I
can think my way inside his head, and I can think myself inside
Daddy's, even if he were silent forever.

"How long's Momma going to stay at the hospital?" Willie
watches trees and fences as they seem to move past the moving
truck while he and his daddy drive home from the Poorwater
hospital on the curving road.

"Oh, not long. Just one more night. They want to make sure
everything's all right."

"Is anything wrong?"

"No, son. They're healthy as horses. And they'll be home
tomorrow afternoon. Your momma's going to need our help
for a while. Good thing your school's let out, isn't it?"

"I guess so, but why's Momma going to be so tired?"

"From having the baby. It's hard work, having a child. Lots of things to tend to. You'll see."

"Nobody ever told me that."

"It's just part of living. I guess nobody ever thought to tell you. It's no secret. It's right there in the Bible."

"It's in the Bible about having babies?"

"The reason it's so hard to have them, I mean. It goes back to Adam and Eve."

"I remember."

Willie has a little sister now, and she's wrinkly and red, but sort of pretty at the same time. His momma has somebody new to think about, and he has more responsibility too. It is going to be hard, being a big brother. He feels the weight of it just as he felt it when his daddy first told him the news.

"Sure you do — you already know more about that book than I do."

When his daddy broke the news he felt a momentary disappointment that he would not have a little brother to teach things to. Somehow the idea of a brother had sustained him through the long months, the fall, winter, and spring of the pregnancy. The news came that it wasn't a boy, but a girl. And his daddy seemed just as happy, but it took some getting used to.

Maybe it would be better to have someone so different, he thought. She would never take his place, never be what he was to his parents and his grandparents. She would always be a girl. The more he thought about it, the more he liked the idea — it was simple relief, not happiness, though, until he saw her lying next to his mother. His age of ten felt heavy against his bones, a sort of fierce gravity that said he was much too old to do the thing he felt, to touch his sister with one fingertip and trace the warmth that linked his momma's arm to his sister's small body with a single curve. So he stared at them all, stared until his parents interrupted by looking at each other through the silence, wondering what in the world was wrong with him and then imagining that they knew, which was worse.

"You want to hold her?" his momma asked.

"No," he said, but he could not add that he was too afraid to hold her, too afraid he would injure her if he touched her.

"That's no way to act, now," his daddy said.

They did not know how he felt, but to show that they were wrong, that it was not jealousy holding him back, now he would have to lift her up into his trembling arms. Willie's arms felt rubbery as he took his sister. In his tight grip she immediately began to cry.

"Jiggle her up and down a bit" came his daddy's command, and Willie tried to obey as the crying increased, and he was more sure than before that he would drop her onto the hard hospital floor.

David looked into Mary's face as she watched her son with the baby. All of David's own fear seemed to subside in his pride. This is my family, he caught himself thinking; this is my family, mine. It was not for this moment that he had given up his education and returned home — he was here because of a former obligation, to his own daddy — but for a minute or more, as Willie gently shook the baby in his arms and her crying died down to quick gasps of sound, it made some sense. Without testing his feelings, with merely a recognition of them that would help him remember these minutes, his life and more seemed sealed in a web of sense. Not that he understood what any of it meant, or what it might add up to; he understood only that it did, it did mean something in the end, and he was part of it all, whatever it was.

The last hazy quarter of a moon hangs in the sky, more a memory of itself than an omen or simple light. The night is plenty dark. They slam the truck doors shut; nothing else stirs as they walk to the house.

"You back already?" Granddaddy asks from his rocker on the porch.

"It was past visiting hours. They kicked us out," David answers his father.

"How'd they look?"

"Fine," Willie says.

"I guess I'll just wait and see them when they get back home. When's that, David?"

"Tomorrow."

"Oh, well, then I don't have much longer to wait. Is she pretty?"

"I guess so," Willie says.

"I reckon so." His granddaddy chuckles. "How's the sky look to you?"

"It's so dark I can't see anything," Willie says. "Why?"

"Any stars a-tall?" Granddaddy rocks.

"Not that I see."

"Bad weather coming. I can feel it here." Granddaddy taps himself on the chest, breathes in deeply once, then lets out the breath gradually, invisibly. "It's going to rain this whole June, you mark my instruction. Cold one, too. Can you guess why?"

"Why, Granddaddy?"

"Blue moon. Full moon on the first, another one on the thirtieth. Don't happen too often, but I remember the last time it did. Sent me to the hospital, most. Wicked month, but that was a May, even worse they say."

"Don't fill his head up with superstitions," Grandma says, coming outside. "Y'all going to sit out here all evening?"

David kisses his mother, a peck on the cheek. "She's like a real live little doll," he says. "Just wait till you see her."

"I can't wait." She slips out of her apron, pats her silver hair, and turns back into the house to hang it on its nail behind the kitchen door. "I'll be right back. I want to hear all about her," she says.

12

"Open Simsim"

Betty came down to the court after school. I'd passed her a note in "Gold-Bug" code during reading lab when I was going to check my answers, and she passed one back that said she'd be there. Every time you passed a card by reading and answering the comprehension questions within the specified time, you moved up through the box to a new color. The print got smaller on the cards and the questions less direct, until it seemed like you'd do better if you read through the questions before reading the story, so that's what I did, even though it took up extra time. The early stories had been more like real stories and not so boring, but the latter cards were full of facts, what they called "fun facts," about the jungle or the Orient or agriculture (a real favorite of mine . . .) or animals. Mostly, the harder cards told about countries and their imports and exports. I felt like I was reading over my head, but the reading lab system was guaranteed to move you along at the proper rate. I think the fuchsia card, where I was, was already eleventh-grade level, whatever that meant. But I liked reading lab better than most everything else in school; after I'd sit there concentrating on a card, I could get up and walk around the room to get the next one. We were left alone while we read and were free to get up whenever we finished a color. You had to check the box for the answers; then you either took another card of the same color or moved up a color. For the first two weeks I moved up about five colors a day; now it was getting harder, and only a few new colors were left in the box.

Betty ran into the yard. "Well, here I am. What's up?"

"We've got to have a meeting." I gave her my mysterious raised-eyebrow look.

"Wow! A meeting. You do mean a *club* meeting?"

"Yeah. At headquarters. Right away. It's a state of emergency."

"I didn't wear the right shoes," Betty whined.

I looked down and sure enough she still had her oxfords on. And her school dress.

"I came as fast as I could," she explained.

"I'll meet you in ten minutes," I said.

Betty ran home to change. I threw my old Superball a few more times. I could shoot it into the air like a rocket and be there when it came back down. I could throw it so high it stung my hands on the catch. I sent it flying into space as nearly vertical as I could so I wouldn't have far to go in catching it. The game reminded me of summer. Now, it was getting cooler and cooler every night, the kind of time when you woke up thinking it was fall and came home from school with your jacket tied around your waist wishing for Saturday instead of homework. When I played after supper I had to wear a sweater and long pants. I could see the stars better night by night. I was beginning to understand what people meant about time flying. When I looked up into the sky I tried to imagine what it might be like to look down at the land, at the lights on the earth. I wondered if our lights had looked like stars to John Glenn. The ball snapped into my hands one last time and I headed up to Betty's just in time to see her running toward the back gate.

"What took you so long?" I asked.

"Diversionary tactics with the lady of the house," Betty said, breathlessly. "She wanted me to do my homework first, so I had to sneak out. Let's go!"

We started up the alley, trying to run without making a racket on the gravel, an impossible mission, so we slowed to a walk after Betty looked back to see if her mother was behind us. Almost to the top Betty said, "Hush," putting a finger to her lips.

"What is it?" I gasped.

"I heard something," she said, and turned back to check down the alley. "Oh no! Don't look now, Dorie, just run! Faster!"

My legs pounded the big hunks of gravel and clinkers, grinding against them; my ankles felt the sting of pelted rocks; my arms pumped and my heart jumped up and down at each step. Her mother was going to be mad as a hornet when Betty went home.

"Stop!" Betty said. "We made it."

I looked back, bending my head between my legs. I thought I saw Michael Dale and someone else vanishing into the bushes, but I wasn't sure. "Why didn't you say it was the dirty boys?"

"They were gaining on us. Boy, that was close. We've got to protect headquarters!"

"I hate those dirty boys. If I ever see their ugly faces around headquarters. . . ."

"Mommy says to ignore them, but how can we ignore them if they're coming after us with sticks?"

"Momma's the same way. We could have been beaten to death a million times by now if we listened to our mothers. Let's hurry. I don't want them getting any big ideas about following us."

We hadn't been to headquarters since the spring. The first time we'd discovered our hideout was like a dream. We'd been walking in the woods behind the tanks, farther up than we'd been before, when we saw a low entranceway, framed by little white bell flowers called Solomon's seal. When we climbed inside between the bells, beneath a thatch, feeling like rabbits, we came into a magical place, dappled over with sunlight and carpeted with thick furry moss, like no other moss you've ever seen before. Ferns grew up through the moss carpet, ferns as big as a toddler, some bigger, as tall as my head. We sat on the moss beneath a weeping tree that grew arched branches completely to the ground, so that nobody could see in from the outside. That was headquarters. Betty came up with the name for the whole place. I wanted to call it Dreamland, but Betty said Fairyland was better. Fairies and leprechauns probably lived there; she was right. Betty had me half convinced we shouldn't even go there at all, because it was magic territory. That was the only explanation for the low entranceway, the bell flowers, and the carpetlike moss.

We hiked past the holes; shadows rested in their depths, waiting for all the leaves to try to fill them up.

"If we brought rakes up here we could put all the leaves into one hole and take turns jumping into them. In a couple of weeks it'll be perfect," I said.

"The leaves would be wet," Betty said, sinking my plan. "Today's Sid's birthday, and the second day of fall. Barbara says it's symbolic. She's gone to take him a bunch of dumb presents."

"Like what?" I asked.

"A stuffed monkey, for one thing. It's some kind of joke between them. It cost twenty dollars. Can you believe it?"

"What else?"

"That's all I saw. She wrapped them in her room. A whole shopping bag of boxes. Mommy told her she was extravagant. You know Sid can't even open those presents by himself. I guess Barbara will unwrap them one at a time and make a big deal about it all."

"I think it's kind of nice," I said.

"How would you know? She's not your sister."

"Well, she doesn't get in our way."

"That's because she couldn't care less what we do as long as we stay out of her room."

"Do you think this is the right way?" I asked.

"Sure. There's the fence and here's the stump with the hole in the middle. Hey, look! It's full of water. It rained last night."

"It might have come from the inside," I said. "You don't know."

"It couldn't come from inside the stump!"

"Did you see it happen or what?"

"No, of course I didn't." Betty put her hand on her hip. "But neither did you."

"Well, I think it came up from the inside, like a fountain." I reached into my pocket and pulled out a penny. "I'm going to make a wish." I closed my eyes and tossed in the penny.

"What did you wish?" Betty asked.

"I can't tell you that. Make your own wish."

Betty dug into a pocket and came up with a dime. She closed her eyes and tossed it into the stump.

"It has to be a penny," I said.

"My wish has ten times more chance of coming true than yours."

"I've got to be home soon for supper. We better get going," I said. Maybe I should have saved that penny.

"Why do you eat so early?"

"Why do you eat so late?"

"Because that's when Pop gets home," Betty said.

I started to say that he wasn't even coming home anymore, but I stopped myself. She hadn't said anything about him lately and I hadn't asked, because it was supposed to be a secret. I think I know what Betty wasted her dime wishing for. But she'd never guess my wish.

We walked along the fence until it stopped; there we crossed onto an overgrown path that led up past an abandoned shack. Most of the wood had rotted and lay in stacks. Someone must have wanted the lumber at one time and then forgotten about it. Behind the main house stood a smaller shack that looked sturdier. The door was still on its hinges. This time we didn't stop to look through the three-sided doorframe to see what was left of the floor inside the main shack, or poke our heads through the window holes to scare each other.

The path turned rocky and vanished, but I knew the rest of the way like the back of my hand. Past a few more big rocks, around a crevice, and then through a stand of thick trees.

"Is that the opening?" Betty pointed to a dark hole, low to the ground, but the little bells weren't blooming, just bushes, with brownish leaves running up their stems. Rows of black berries hung beneath the leaves.

"Open Simsim!" I said.

"That's 'Sesame,' " Betty said. "I saw it on *Popeye*."

"It's not *Popeye,*" I told her. "It's 'Ali Baba and the Forty Thieves' in *The Arabian Nights,* and Ali Baba says, 'Open Simsim,' just like I said."

"Okay, already," Betty said. "You don't have to gloat."

Ducking beneath the thicket, we popped our heads and then our bodies into Fairyland but jumped back at a light rustling noise. A yellow snake scurried for cover.

"A baby rattler." I said. "You see his stripes?"

"Let's get out of here," Betty said, and started backing out of the entrance.

"Come on." I grabbed her hand. "We're having a meeting, remember? You're not afraid of a baby snake. It's scared of you."

We stood up inside Fairyland. A few leaves had dropped onto the moss, but otherwise it seemed the same. I missed the wildflowers, though. Back in the spring I had seen nodding trillium, with its purple-red center hanging toward the ground, and jack-in-the-pulpit about ready to bloom. Daddy told me you could boil that and eat it. May apples were flowering then, too. Their closed white flowers stayed hidden below green umbrellas, but whenever I saw a double umbrella I turned the leaves up, and there would be the cocoon of the flower. Bloodroot was poisonous, but it had a pretty white flower with a yellow center; its leaves curled up around the stem, showing blood-colored undersides, not green. Last spring when we went for a drive in the truck, Daddy pointed out the redbud on the hillsides and called it Judas tree. It looked so pretty, like somebody had planted it there. I wondered how something so nice got a name like that. The only thing blooming in September was yellow jewelweed. I thought maybe I'd take some home if I could find it and break it off clean.

The leaves of our weeping tree still looked green, but a darker green than before, like it was almost ready to change. We lifted up some branches and went inside to the trunk, headquarters.

"You think that snake could be in here with us?" Betty asked.

"No way," I said, and scanned the encircling branches. I knew that where there was one baby there were sure to be others.

The moss felt damp through my jeans, so I sat on my hands, then rocked up onto my feet, and stayed squatted that way. Betty just plopped down on the moss and started feathering her fingers over its soft surface like she was petting a puppy. She'd have a stain on the seat of her pants when she stood up.

"When I grow up I'm going to carpet a room with this," she said.

"You can't do that, can you?"

"You can do anything if you have enough money. I'm going to plant a tree in my living room."

"Inside the house?"

"Right in the middle of the moss."

"If anyone ever invented a carpet this soft it would cost a fortune. You can always come back here," I said.

"Not when we're old," Betty said. "Should we call the meeting to order?"

"Yeah. This meeting is now in session," I said.

"Well?" she asked.

"This is top secret. It's so secret that nobody but the club can know about it. Cross your heart and hope to die."

"Do I have to say that?"

"Yes. Or the meeting is canceled," I said.

"But it gives me the creeps." Betty raked her hands faster over the moss.

"Don't dig a hole!" I said. "I'd say it for you."

"Cross-my-heart-and-hope-to-die," Betty stuttered.

"Okay. We've got to spy. There's this man in a suit, and he tried to chase me home."

"Hold it. Why would anyone do that? We'll need a description of the suspect."

"His face looks like Bobby's arm did when it got spiked."

"Acne." Betty nodded her head like she was taking notes. "How old is he?"

"I don't know. Old."

"Then why's he got acne?"

"I didn't say that; you did. I said his face was full of moon craters. You never listen to me."

"Scars, then. How am I going to spy on him if I don't know what he looks like?"

"I'm trying to tell you, if you'd listen."

"I am listening."

"No you're not."

"I was just offering a diagnosis. You get mad over nothing."

"No I don't."

"Yes you do. And you're not the president of the club, either, so you can't boss me around. We're co-presidents, remember?"

"I called this meeting. If you don't want to help me, just say so."

"I didn't say that. Of course I want to. This guy might be dangerous, a Russian agent or worse."

I rolled my eyes.

"Well, you never know," Betty said. "What else do you know about him?"

I told her about how he followed me up the street and pretended to read a newspaper.

"It was probably a Russian paper," she said.

"It was in English," I said.

"A Russian paper could be in English."

"He's not a Russian."

"Well, we can find out. When do we start?"

"I've got to go home now," I said. "But right after supper we'll try and set a trap. I'm drawing a map. I'll start into town and you can trail me to all the marked places."

"But how will we trap him?"

"If he follows me, then you'll be following him. Get it? All you have to do is follow the map, about five minutes behind me, and watch for that guy."

We shook on it and crawled out of Fairyland on our hands and knees. "Shut Simsim," I said, and Betty gave me a dirty look. It seemed like every time we went in it was harder and harder to crawl out again, like we'd grown bigger while we were at headquarters. I wondered what Betty had meant about us not coming back to Fairyland when we were old. Wouldn't it still be there? Or had she meant that we wouldn't want to visit it anymore?

On the way home we talked about the election the seventh-graders were having in a couple of weeks, to see who the fifth-through the seventh-graders would elect for President. The seventh-graders had planned a public debate to illustrate the three sides. They had a hard time getting anyone to play George Wallace.

"Who're you for?" Betty asked.

"I'm waiting for the debate. I haven't made up my mind yet."

"I'm for Nixon."

"He wouldn't debate Humphrey, you know."

"He probably had better things to do, getting ready to be President and all that."

"But he might not win," I said.

"You're for Humphrey." Betty stared at me. "I can tell you're for Humphrey. Go ahead and say it."

"Daddy says Humphrey's for the unions."

"Your daddy's for Humphrey too, isn't he?"

"I don't know."

"Well, he's not going to win."

"How do you know? You know-it-all. You make me sick."

"I'm just telling you the truth. You'll see. Humphrey's a pharmacist, Nixon's a lawyer, and the lawyer always wins."

"I might not even vote." What in tarnation was a pharmacist?

"You have to vote!" Betty pulled me back by my arm, stopping us cold on the pathway. "What are you, a hippie or something?"

"Will you just drop it? Meet me after supper. I'll have the map."

"You better vote."

"In the alley," I said.

"Whistle when you get there. I might be at the table."

*   *   *

Before I started the map I sat down and read a little of *The Arabian Nights,* all about these two bad angel twins. Head first, hanging into a dark pit by their feet, Harut and Marut, the fallen angels, taught black magic to the Arabians. The pit was at Babel; I wonder if it's the same place that had the tower? I guess there's no connection between the tower and the pit of Babel, but there might be. Those angel twins started something terrible; they seemed to be behind a lot of what happens in *The Arabian Nights.* Unless it was magic, all that weird stuff couldn't really happen, could it? Imagine, two fallen angels — that's what Satan was too — tied at the ankles and dangling into a shaft. Whoever did that should have gagged them first. But you can't always predict what someone's going to do or say, especially ugly angels with names like Marut and Harut. For a long time I thought that Satan was the first and last fallen angel, but apparently, if you can believe Arabians, there were at least two more. Someday they ought to get all these books' stories straight and make one complete story out of them so people could know what really happened.

The first map I drew jumped off the page when I turned a corner because I hadn't left enough space. I got a good one the second time, though, labeled all the places, and drew a red dotted line for the whole route, from the X that marked the start and finish, so Betty could trail me. I traced a map for Betty and folded them both to fit into the back pockets of our jeans. All I had to do was wait for Betty to finish her supper and go whistle her outside. I still had some time, so I started filling in the slam book Betty had passed on to me.

On the first page, in various colors of ink, everyone who had answered the questions so far had written in a number to stand for their name. That way the answers were anonymous. The first thing I did was flip through the book to see if there was a page about me. There wasn't, but Betty had a page and so far the comments went like this: "cutest girl in school — 4"; "not a snob — 7"; "a very nice girl — 10." I turned back through, checking out number 4's comments to see if I could figure out who it was. The handwriting looked awkward, like a boy's. I never could figure out why boys couldn't write worth a damn. When we had the President's Physical Fitness Test a girl won everything except the pull-ups and the soft-ball throw. And that wasn't fair, because they didn't let girls do pull-ups. We did something called the flexed-arm hang. It was the only thing I was really good at; I could hang there as long as I wanted, way past the thirty-second "excellent" rating. I think I stayed up there two minutes. The teacher finally told me to come on down because there wasn't going to be time for everyone else to try. Betty was good at sit-ups and the standing broad jump. The broad jump was hard, but the shuttle run was worse. It loused me up every time, so I couldn't get a certificate.

The first question in the slam book was "Who's your favorite girl/boy?" I wrote, "I don't know — 007." The second page asked, "Who would you like to kiss?" I answered, "Nobody — 007." There had to be some good questions in there somewhere. I kept turning pages and squeezing out a dumb answer to a dumb mushy question. Sometimes I just put "No comment — 007," like on that question about who would you like to have with you on a desert island. All I had left were the people pages. I couldn't believe it, Michael Dale had a page all to himself, and somebody, number 10, had written "Dreamboat." About a dirty boy!

I scrawled "Sucks eggs for a living — 007" across my line. I don't know why I had to write that. I tried to scratch out my number and the word *sucks* as best I could. I drew over *eggs* about a thousand times until I finally succeeded in digging a hole through the paper. I thought about tearing his page out, but I left well enough alone. When Betty saw it she said, "Michael Dale will bludgeon you to death with an ax if he finds out who did that." I slapped the slam book closed, grabbed the maps, leaving Momma and Daddy in front of the TV set like two bad children forced to serve corner time. I arrived in the alley, whistled for Betty, and when she came toward the gate I waved the maps like signal flags.

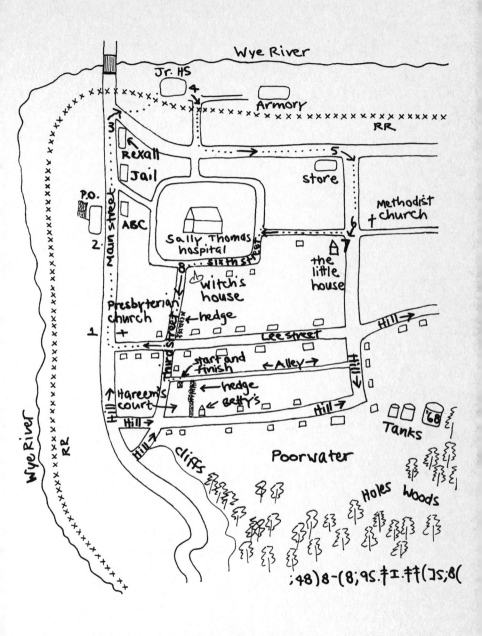

Wye River

Jr. HS

4

Armory

RR

3

Rexall

Jail

store

5

Methodist
church

P.O.

ABC

2

Main street

Sally Thomas
hospital

the
little
house

6

7

8

Sixth street

Witch's
house

Presbyterian
church

1

hedge

Third street

Lee street

start and
finish

Alley

Hill

Hareem's
court

hedge

Betty's

Hill

Hill

Hill

Tanks

'68

Hill

cliffs

Poorwater

Holes woods

Wye River

RR

;48)8-(8;95.‡I.‡‡(]s;8(

13

Spies

I explained the loop I'd follow, and Betty said it looked like a cinch.

"Ambush!" Her eyes brightened.

"No. Just watch him," I instructed.

Betty quickly translated the Gold-Bug in the lower right-hand corner of her map without a key and penciled it in: *The Secret Map of Poorwater*. It pleased her no end.

"I'll be right behind you. If you need anything, just whistle," she said.

Neither of us had a watch, so I had to go inside and ask Momma to tell Betty when five minutes had gone by; then I started off. It was getting late, but some kids were still out throwing football. At the Presbyterian church I checked the map and turned right, down Main Street to the post office. I looked over my shoulder, but I didn't see Betty or anyone else. Maybe he'd left town. Betty would never believe me. At times like these I wished I had Maxwell Smart's shoe phone.

Walking around by myself seemed to bring out a habit of mine. Daddy said he liked to hear me humming, but I always stopped if anyone noticed it. While I walked along that night I was humming "Gospel Ship," trying to remember the words, but all I could remember was "going to take a trip . . . going to take a trip." I kept getting the tune confused with my real favorite Carter Family song, "Keep on the Sunny Side." Daddy said it was a sign of happiness that I could hum involuntarily, like breathing, but it seemed more like an attack of nerves that night when I was walking from place to place, following my map, like I was on a high wire without a net. When I got to the third stop, the Rexall, I decided to take a break. I sat twisting the stool until Mac asked what I'd have. My throat felt dry as a desert, but I didn't have a wooden nickel.

"Nothing, Mac." I twisted the stool.

He filled a glass with vanilla ice cream, poured Dr. Pepper over it, and set it down in front of me with a straw, a silver iced tea spoon, and a napkin.

"On the house, from me to you. Just keep it under your hat," Mac said.

He looked me dead in the eye, like he would have me swear a blood oath of silence before I could taste the float. He straightened his paper hat, pulled the towel from his shoulder to wipe the counter. It already sparkled like a freshly washed window. A couple of swipes of Mac's towel erased the trail of water beads my glass had left.

"You're giving me this for free?"

"Just remember what I said. Between you and me and the fly on the wall, you hear?"

"Yes, sir!"

"I thought so. I looked at you and I thought I could trust you. Ice cream's melting; now dig in."

I've had a lot of floats in my life, but honestly, Mac's float that night was the best he'd ever made. I could have sat savoring the last of it on the end of the straw, but the clock over the counter was pushing eight.

"Where's Doc?" I asked.

"Home eating supper. He'll be back in a few minutes. You through with that glass? Let me have it."

Doc came through the door in his light green coat, nodded at Mac, who winked at me. I slipped down from the stool as Doc called from the drug department that it was time to close the fountain.

"Thanks, Mac," I said.

"Just remember what I said," Mac whispered.

I headed back out to the sidewalk. Out of the corner of my eye I saw Betty coming toward me, walking faster and faster before breaking into a run. "Wait up!" she shouted when I turned and started walking to the fourth target. "Wait up!" she called again. Darn it, she was supposed to shadow me silently. It wasn't going to work if she couldn't stay back. I felt like running off, but her face was all red and she sounded desperate. When she caught up, she had to put her head down and pant before she could speak.

"You've spoiled everything," I said. "I thought I could count on you, and we're not even to number four yet." I traced the projected path with one finger, unfurling the map beneath her nose. The more I thought about it, the madder I got. It had been a pretty good plan and she'd loused it up royally.

"But I saw him!" Betty finally blurted in a hoarse voice. "He's real!"

"Where was he?"

"At the corner, watching you. I had to stop and wait for him to move before I could trail him."

"Are you sure it was him?"

"Positive. He had a newspaper. He was wearing a suit. I saw his face — scars, I think. Gosh, Dorie, I believed you and all, but that guy is really after you."

"I told you."

"Let's go home. It's getting late and that guy gives me the creeps," Betty said.

"You shouldn't have come running after me like that. He'll know we're together."

"He left while you were in the Rexall. What took you so long anyway?"

"What if he's waiting for me? Which way did he go?"

"I'm not sure." Betty's eyes dropped to the sidewalk. "I mean, one minute he was leaning over there and the next he wasn't. He must have —"

"He could be watching us right this minute, you know."

"Let's go home, Dorie. Come on. He's not going to bother us once we're home. Not with our parents right there and everything."

"Let's take the short cut. Keep your map. We might need them later."

"I —" Betty dug around in her pockets, then pulled out an empty hand. "You're going to kill me, but I think I lost it."

"I can't believe you. We've got to hurry. Come on! He's got our map."

We cut around the hospital, afraid to run, because that would mean someone was after us, and we didn't want to look back. We walked past Miss Reider's just about to breathe a sigh of relief when he popped out from behind her shed like a cat set to pounce.

We nearly ran right into him before we realized who it was. Betty grabbed my hand and took off as fast as she could go. He just stood there in the middle of the sidewalk and pushed back his hat as we brushed by. As we raced down the middle of the street, two scared rabbits zigzagging across the road, I heard him say, "Hello, girls," in a voice like honey-flavored acid. He laughed three low hurried *ha-ha-ha*'s, which he seemed to force up from his gut like carbonation burps that were burning their way through his gullet. Betty never let go of my hand; she tugged me along, although usually I could outrun her. I couldn't stop myself from looking back at the pitted face of the stranger as he stared after us and laughed.

A car beeped and swerved to one side, missing us by a hair.

"Betty, you're going to get us killed. Let go of my hand!" I shook free.

"Stop turning around. Are you crazy or what?"

"He's just standing there, watching us," I said.

"I don't care what he's doing. I'm going straight home and tell Mommy."

"You can't do that. It's club business."

"That guy, Dorie. That guy — you don't know what he'll do. He probably is a Russian spy."

"You promised, remember? If you tell this, it's the end of the club — FOREVER." I issued my ultimatum.

"Oh, all right," Betty said. "You want to come over to my room and do homework?"

"Cross your heart?"

"I said I wouldn't tell. But you ought to tell your parents."

I stopped off to pick up my books. Momma didn't seem very keen on my going, but when I told her it was to do homework she said I could stay an hour.

Up in Betty's pink room, we spread our books over the floor and started with history. We decided to read one page aloud and then the next, taking turns until it was finished.

Barbara was home early from taking Sid his birthday loot, judging from the rock-and-roll wafting through the wall. It seemed like I hadn't seen Barbara in about two years. She was always gone or locked in her room when I came over. Betty said that all Barbara did anymore was talk about Sid and how she was going to write a novel about their great love affair and the wreck and Sid's recovery. She had two notebooks full of notes. If she wasn't playing music or scribbling in her notebooks, she was reading novels by people you never heard of. Last week, Betty said, she'd been reading *As I Lay Dying* by William Faulkner. Barbara said it was a masterpiece, and when she'd gotten to the end she'd started the whole thing over again. Who ever heard of reading a book twice in a row, like riding a roller coaster? You already knew what happened. It was about the most boring thing I could imagine. Barbara said it was even better the second time around and decided to take it to Sid so they could discuss it. If I ever got through *The Arabian Nights* one time, it'd be a miracle. Just like it'd be a miracle if Sid ever cracked open Barbara's novel. The title didn't seem all that appropriate, somehow, anyway.

Betty said the music coming through the wall was a Beatles' album called "Sgt. Pepper's Lonely Hearts Club Band." It, too, according to Barbara, was a masterpiece.

"I've got the whole thing about memorized," Betty said. "She plays it a hundred times in a row. It's got some good songs, but I'm sick of it."

"I like their new song, 'Hey Jude,' " I said.

"Sergeant Pepper is a whole concept. There's this song about fixing a hole. It's a pretty good song. It comes after this one."

"What's this one?"

" 'Getting Better.' I don't like it. Wait till you hear the one about the hole. And there's one that sounds like a circus." Betty closed her history book and then the door to her room before she continued. "Pop wrote us a letter. He's coming back pretty soon."

"What'd he say?"

"He said he was tired of playing golf by himself. He's in North Carolina at the Pines."

"That's good. But why'd he leave?"

"I guess he thought he wanted to play golf."

"Oh," I said.

"And then he decided he'd rather not play so much. Here's the hole song; listen."

"I can't understand the words."

"I'm singing them."

Betty sang along with the record, slapping one hand against the floor in time. It was a pretty good song about keeping out the rain, and keeping people out who don't understand things. Barbara probably liked the part about painting in your room. I could hear Barbara's voice echoing through the wall. She and Betty made a good duet, but they didn't know it.

"Barbara's not allowed to play Janis Joplin when Mommy's home. She screams a lot. Mommy's philosophical about the Beatles, but there's a new song by Janis Joplin, 'Piece of My Heart,' that Mommy would like to scratch."

"I better go home," I said.

"But we're not through."

I gathered my books and notebooks, stuffed them under my arm, slid the pencils into my back pocket.

"I'll see you tomorrow. We've got to make a plan," I said.

"Are we still on duty?" Betty asked.

"From now on — if you're not too scared," I said.

"I'm not scared, even if he is a Russian agent."

It was the worst dream I'd had since the night after I watched *King Kong* on TV and dreamed he stuck his fingers into my room and filled my window with his nose. I'd reasoned my way out of my terror by reminding myself that the window was so low to the ground that King Kong could never scrunch down that short, not even to kill me. I can still see his nose in the window, though, dripping with sweat and inhaling enough oxygen to leave me breathless and faint. His hairy fingers groped in the air, the window too narrow to let his head through. Why he didn't just bust the trailer down, I'll never understand. Dreams, I guess, have safety nets.

This one began with a pounding noise, maybe native drumming, up and down my spine until I half believed I was dreaming and half believed I was awake, unable to escape the assault of the persistent rhythm. It could have been a scene straight out of Tarzan. Drums kept beating while I tried to thrash my way to sleep. The jungle was growing, taking over the dream. A tiger swayed, circling the fire, around and around. Like the tiger in "Little Black Sambo," it steadily turned into a streak of butter — or a streak of light. The light got brighter and brighter, forming a ball. My ears, still pelted with drumbeats, were suddenly cuffed by that ball of light. At first it was fun and I laughed, but the pounding of the drums and the ball against my ears began to scare me. I couldn't stop it. I reached up and touched my ears — hot as coals. They burned my hands and I cried out. I tried to run away from the ball. It chased me as I tripped through the jungle, followed by the sound of those damn drums, which seemed to get louder instead of dimmer, the farther I ran.

My legs pumped faster than I'd ever run and my heart felt heavy. A burning started in my chest, but I was afraid to stop running because of that burning ball, like a disembodied hand, still closing in on me the faster I ran. I knew I was losing the

race, that the ball was toying with me. It could overtake me
any time it wished. I slowed, feeling sure it would bounce against
my spine and burn me. It hung back until I got my breath,
then kept following me, inches away. I couldn't run anymore,
but just at the edge of what looked like a clearing I put on a
final burst of speed. My legs pumped into empty space before
I started falling, sinking like a stone, into a ravine. The ball
danced above my head as I sank, my stomach rising into my
throat like a water balloon as my speed increased.

When I hit, I thought, I will die. Not in the dream; in real
life. Someone must have told me that once, I guess, for it to
have occurred to me in the middle of my dream of falling. As I
fell into the dark hole, thinking that at any minute I would
smack the bottom and it would be all over, I tried to rouse
myself from the dream, aware then that it was a dream and not
a ravine I was lost inside, falling. If I can scream, I thought. If
I can just open my mouth and scream. It seemed like a year
before I woke myself with my own moaning. Daddy rushed in,
shook me awake, and pulled me forward into his arms.

"It's only a dream. Only a dream," he said.

He rocked me against his chest; then I lay back against the
pillows, breathing heavily. A line of sweat broke across my upper
lip.

"There, now. You must have been dreaming about cows!
Sounded just like a cow in here." He rubbed my hands. "Your
hands are hot as blazes."

"Something was chasing me." My hands seemed to glow in
the dark. I wanted to hide them under the covers, but Daddy
still held them.

"A cow, I expect. Was it a big one?"

"It wasn't a cow, Daddy." I should have told him it was a
man. He'd never understand about the ball of light, how it could
scare me so.

"Well, whatever it was, it can't get you now. Go back to
sleep. The sun's still dreaming, but it's near time for me to rise
and shine." He let my hands go. They felt far away, almost

detached, like they had lives of their own I could only sit back and watch.

"I'm sorry, Daddy."

"I've got to get up anyway."

"Daddy?" I wanted to tell him about the man with the pitted face.

I must have been asleep before he shut my door; he never answered. It took me all day to remember the dream. When I finally remembered, I couldn't believe I'd forgotten it. With Betty on the lookout for the agent, I felt a lot better. At least if anything happened to me — if I was kidnaped or something — at least she'd know who was responsible. I didn't really think he'd kidnap me, but what did he want? The more I remembered his voice, the voice he'd spoken to us with, the spookier it sounded. A real low, soft voice, like you'd use if you didn't want anyone to know you had said anything. That way, if they didn't answer, you wouldn't be embarrassed. I kept hearing it over and over: "Hello, girls." The more I thought about it, the worse it sounded, like something was so secret you'd never want to know what it was. The secret was so awful that it wasn't any fun to keep but could never be revealed.

The second day of fall had been more like the longest day of the year. I felt so glad when I finally woke up and it was morning and the third day of fall, and there wouldn't be another day like yesterday, at least for a year. I ate two bowls of corn flakes; I felt so hungry, like I hadn't eaten in a long, long time. If I breathed in deeply, my chest burned, like it did whenever I'd stayed in swimming too long.

14

Up in the Air

October started with orange and yellow leaves, deepened into flashes of crimson, and ended with brown and empty limbs swept by cold air. It was the longest month I can remember. That October, my shadow kept growing larger and larger, straight toward Halloween and beyond. It got to where whenever I stepped outside I could feel another foot pressing down on top of my own, like a dancing doll I used to have that you could strap her feet on top of your own. I couldn't forget about the shadow without getting skittish and then suddenly remembering that wherever I went I was never alone. Just me and my shadow, and I still didn't know his intent. He didn't bother hiding anymore. He knew that I knew he was watching me; sometimes he even smiled at me, and then when I looked away as fast as I could, I'd feel a chill pass down my collar, down my back, and out, until it ran over the ground at my feet where I could run and run and never run fast enough to lose my shadow among the eventide shadows of houses and fences and the changing trees.

On Friday, the eleventh of October, three things happened. The first was that Apollo 7 blasted off with three men inside suffering from bad colds. The second was that the letter came back about Mr. McGee's compensation, saying that the union couldn't pay a cent because Mr. McGee had died due to a safety violation, and besides that, he had once worked in a nonunion mine, so his dependents were ineligible under the current plan. Daddy called it a bunch of hogwash and worse and sat right down to write another letter. He stopped in the middle of a sentence, tore up the letter, and said, "I'm just going over there and tell her what they said; no use putting it off. See if she knows anything about Bud ever working in a nonunion mine. About like he lit a cigarette that day, I expect." Daddy slammed the door on his way to the McGees'.

The third thing that happened, happened in the middle of the night, so it rightly occurred on the twelfth, but it was so awful that half of the town woke up and went to see about it in their nightclothes. If someone had shaken me awake, I would have been more thankful than I'd ever been after waking from a nightmare. First thing I knew about the fire was sirens running like lightning through the town. It sounded like a descent from the sky, a landing from the air. It nearly split my eardrums, like so many tolling bells and wind-up toys let loose at once. Half awake for half a minute, tossing my head side to side, I shook my first instinct to cover my ears with my pillow as best I could and get back to sleep. The more penetrating the sirens became, the more I wanted to sleep and to know what was happening at the same time. I couldn't see a thing from my window, so I went out into the kitchen. A light was burning.

"What's going on?" I asked.

Momma said she didn't know. About that time Daddy rolled out of the bedroom, rubbing his face from top to bottom, a one-handed mashing motion, like he could rip the sleep from his face if he tried hard enough.

"Do you smell smoke?" Momma asked.

"Let's go take a look-see, since we're all up. It must be close," Daddy said.

As soon as we hit Lee Street we could see the flames shooting toward the sky in furies of beautiful color and sparkles of ash. We couldn't tell yet which building it was, but it had to be something big, Daddy said, because of the height of the blaze. A sick feeling started in my stomach as we wove around the hospital into sight of our church, like a burning wreck on the ocean. Water plumed into it, crisscrossing the flames, but the water seemed to be feeding the fire, along with the breeze and those hundred-year-old wooden beams.

Firemen had roped off the street around the church. More and more people gathered, some with hands across their mouths or eyes as they watched. It was a gesture of shock, more than a protection from the fumes or the amazing heat. I squeezed a hand from Momma and one from Daddy. I thought I'd never let them go. Tears stinging down my cheeks, I looked up at Momma to catch her crying, too.

Daddy shook free and walked through the crowd to chat with some of the men he knew well. I could see the little dots of red from their cigarettes punctuating the darkness. Pretty soon it seemed like everyone in town was standing there — not just Methodists, but Presbyterians and Baptists and Christians and probably some Holy Rollers, too. There were people there who'd never been so close to a church before, and some called back before their usual Christmas visits.

Over next to a tree, a solitary cigarette flickered intermittently. When the man stepped closer to the blaze, out of the shadows so I could see his face, a shiver vibrated the muscles in my shoulders, like the door of a shack had suddenly blown open and slammed shut on its hinges. The pitted face of the shadow shone in the strange orange fire glow, along with all the faces of the people I knew. He gazed toward me and my brief advantage vanished. I couldn't be sure he had located me in the crowd, but I backed to let Momma block his face, the light, and the heat of the fire. I wished Daddy would stop talking and find us again. Maybe the man had only come out of curiosity, like everyone else, but I felt like he had come to see me or to laugh at the fire. We stood there, all together, the town along with that demon, in the fire and brimstone of our burning church, eyes watering and skin roasting, unable to turn away, unable to see anything beyond the sure fact of the end of a landmark. It was the worst fire in Poorwater since anybody could remember. The atmosphere seemed so fitting for the shadow that I believed he might go the way of the fire and burn his way out. I thought he might have started the fire just to bring us all out. Later they said it had had something to do with the ancient electric wiring — I still don't understand it. I peeked out from behind Momma, and he had vanished before the smoke, like the specter he'd become.

We left the church, knowing the fire would continue into morning, knowing that before long there would be little left to burn.

Saturday, Betty and I walked down to the corner where our church had been to see what we could see. Yellow ropes quarantined the block and held us well back into the street. No cars passed that way, but drivers pulled up to the ropes and stopped to gawk. In spots, the rubble still sent up staggered plumes of smoke. The front concrete steps led to nothing more than a shell. The sanctuary had been cored out, as if a meteor had plunked down exactly on the center of the roof and singed through whatever lay in its path to the earth. The brick walls still partially stood, along with three of the stained glass windows that the heat hadn't managed to blast from their casings. Some said it was a miracle that the big sanctuary cross had been spared. Some people can always find a miracle, even in the worst of circumstances.

Betty and I must have walked around those ropes twenty times or more, trying to see into the gutted remains, trying to imagine how one night something as solid as a hundred-year-old church could be standing there big as life and the next day be gone.

The wall that faced the railroad tracks and the river had housed a million snails. We'd stuck our hands back there, through the hemlock, to blindly scrape snails off by their shells. Once I had been stung or bitten by a spider or something and my hand had swollen up fatter than a rubber glove full of water. It bulged around the knuckles like it wanted to bust open like a kernel of popcorn. When we brought the snails out into the light we'd sometimes scratch our faces on the hedge, sometimes nearly poke out our eyes, trying to get to what lived on the wall where nobody could see it. The snail shells weren't much to look at —

mostly gray or brown — not anywhere near as pretty as Betty's seashells, but when I looked at them I turned them into pinkish seashells with mother of pearl inside in place of slimy snails. Now the hemlock was charred and would probably die during the winter. The exposed brick wall looked blank as a cloudless sky. I couldn't get those snails out of my mind. How translucent and frail their feelers had been.

"What do you think we'll do tomorrow?" Betty asked.

"What do you mean?"

"It's Sunday. I guess we can't have church anymore," she said.

For a minute I was sad, but when I remembered all those people who'd never missed a Sunday in their lives, and all their attendance bars, such long strings of them that they hung like rope ladders past their waists, the whole predicament started getting a little funny. They only got to wear their pins one Sunday out of the whole year, but they knew we knew who they were, all the same. They came with colds, flu, fevers, and headaches, and ten minutes before they were supposed to deliver twins, bringing their children with measles and mumps and chicken pox disguised with calamine lotion, and claimed that the infectious stage had passed. The more I considered their persistence, the more I realized that we'd have to have a sermon, building or no. The minister couldn't let a Sunday go by, especially with such a bloody shirt to wave; we'd need a lot of collection money and special gifts if we were going to rebuild a church.

When Daddy came in from work he said he'd heard it on the radio that our services were going to be held in the high school auditorium, where we'd gone to take vaccinated sugar cubes. The congregation was urged to attend. Car pools were being organized. When we saw the choir file in that first Sunday after the fire, in their regular clothes, singing "Holy, Holy, Holy" like nothing had happened, half of us cried. Of course even the choir robes, stored in the practice room, had been destroyed.

*   *   *

I went up to Betty's to watch the astronauts on her new RCA color TV, and Dr. Grayson was there. He just said hello, like always. Most of the time he was at the hospital anyway, so it had seemed pretty much the same to me when he'd been gone. I know Betty was glad to see him, though. He led us into the den and switched on the new set just as they were showing what the inside of the space capsule looked like.

"That's not really the astronauts; it's actors," Betty pronounced.

"It certainly is our astronauts," Dr. Grayson corrected. "They're up there in space right this minute, give or take a few seconds of transmission delay."

"It's not like *Divorce Court*," I said, and wished I hadn't. Dr. Grayson seemed to jump. "There's not any gravity up there," I said quickly. "Remember what Mrs. Harper said?"

"Oh, I remember," Betty said. "It's just so, so different seeing it. We've got to watch this for school," Betty said to her daddy. She gazed intently at the screen, as if into the future through a crystal ball.

I sat back in the Graysons' Barcalounger, crossed my legs, and looked at what was left over after Betty had soaked most of the pictures in through her eyes. It was her color TV set.

One of the astronauts added water to a plastic bag of food that looked like glue. He squeezed the contents of the bag into his mouth like toothpaste from a tube.

"That's so it can't float away, in weightlessness," I said. "If they put beans on a plate they'd bounce right off it."

"Yuck, look at that stuff!" Betty said.

It looked pretty neat. I wondered if Betty and I could mix up some stuff in plastic bags and save it to eat the next time we went up to the holes on an expedition. I was going to ask Mrs. Harper what kind of food she thought would work. The astronauts' food started out dry; then they added water. It would be pretty hard to take jugs of water with us to the holes, but a canteen might be enough.

"What's that?" Betty asked.

"It's us," Dr. Grayson said. "The earth."

A fuzzy ball through a cloudy window — it couldn't be the earth. Who was taking the picture? The astronauts, of course. There we were, floating on a ball, looking at ourselves, looking at the astronauts floating up in space and looking back at us while we looked not up, but into a screen, at them, at ourselves. It was like a set of crazy mirrors held up to each other, but the simple truth was the fuzzy little ball of earth, filling a window clouded over by ice crystals, partially obscuring our view.

That night I looked up into the sky toward the moon, and saw nothing but the faintest sliver of light, not a ball at all, hardly anything but the tiniest slit of light. Venus was far brighter. Everything moved around the still point of Polaris, in its place in the handle of the Little Dipper. I decided that I wanted to be an astronaut, but I wasn't going to tell anyone. Betty hadn't said anything directly about being a doctor since that day she first announced it, but she continued to take a keen interest in all things vaguely scientific or related to accidents or diseases. I wished she'd find out how to get rid of warts. I had a cluster of them, shaped like an airplane, next to a knuckle on my right hand. Every time I scraped them off they bled and stung, then grew back in the same place. I put acid on them every day for two weeks and they dried up and fell off before they grew back, pretty as you please. It didn't take as long for them to grow back as it had taken for the acid to take them off. Daddy said his daddy had known how to charm warts, but he died before telling my daddy the secret. All Daddy remembered was that it had something to do with a full moon. Momma told me my warts would up and leave someday if I just stopped pestering them. I wanted so badly to find out how a full moon could take off a wart that I sat down one day and wrote Granddaddy a letter. I'm not crazy or anything; I knew he was dead. But I thought there might be a way to get an answer. I folded the letter into my question book. Someday I'd find out the answer. Sometimes I'd go out when the moon was full and then remember about my warts. Whatever it is, I'd think, let it happen. So far it hadn't. But I knew that was only because I wasn't doing it right.

It was getting close to Halloween, but all the seventh-graders could think about was their stupid presidential debate. They got the whole school out of class for two hours, though, while they held it in the gym. Mr. Clarke introduced them as each candidate stood behind his podium, which bore a giant nameplate. Each debater was allowed a staff of five, seated at a table behind him to write out questions and keep notes. Nixon sounded the best in the debate, because Harry's big brother Larry played Nixon, and everyone was in love with Larry. Wallace was played by a short pudgy kid who had plastered his hair down so flat he looked bald; he didn't know what to say either. Humphrey was so short the microphone wouldn't reach down low enough, so he had to stand on his tiptoes and shout. What he said was pretty sensible, but he started out talking about joy without smiling.

I don't think many of the fifth-graders were listening worth a damn. Betty asked me what I was wearing to her Halloween party right in the middle of the closing remarks, and she was supposedly the one so civic-minded about voting and all. Right after the debate we lined up to cast our votes. In a couple of days they announced the winner, and it wasn't who I'd voted for, but it wasn't the real election, so it didn't really matter. The whole thing just gave the seventh-graders an opportunity to become more stuck-up than ever. Now, a fifth-grader couldn't even get a drink of water if seventh-graders happened to be passing through the hall, because they'd rush over to the fountain, butt in, and hog the water until the bell rang. You could die of thirst waiting for those bullies to quit gulping and slurping. A crowd of them would gather and snigger when the bell rang. "Boy, that water sure is good," one of them would say. "I'll bet you're mighty thirsty, standing there with your tongue hang-

ing out," one of his buddies would add. Then they'd all laugh
like hyenas, until I was ready to spit.

The Saturday before Halloween, Betty invited me up to rummage
through the trunks in her basement where her parents kept
their old clothes. On Halloween we could wear costumes to
school, and there'd be a contest at lunch; that night Betty was
having a party, so we figured we'd need two costumes each.
This was when we found the weird things I can't forget.

The trunks sat in the corner of a big room where we played
when it was rainy out. Once we'd set up a maze of linked cardboard
boxes. We got the biggest boxes we could find and taped them
end to end, after opening the bottoms so they'd fit together. It
had looked like a kind of crazy plumbing, stretched out across
the floor. Inside it was too dark to see until we punched holes
along the tops of the boxes like we were lightning bugs caught
in jars. The Graysons' new refrigerator had come in the center
box, our main room. We laid a rug in there and hung a flashlight
from the ceiling. We had stayed there all one afternoon reading
magazines, eating sandwiches, and drinking a thermos of hot
chocolate. Today the floor looked barren — only a corner stacked
with trunks and scattered racks of old dresses and suits covered
in plastic.

"Let's start with the black one," Betty said, pointing to the
nearest trunk. We each took hold of a handle, scooted the trunk
apart from the others, and set it beneath the bare bulb in the
center of the room, right on top of the drain.

We set aside the tray of costume jewelry fitted over the clothes
inside the trunk. Once we'd planned our costumes, we'd go
through the jewelry for the right accessories. Dipping through
layers of clothes, we recalled other years as we lifted each piece
into the light. The velvet skirt, cape, and sequined blouse Betty
had worn as Cinderella two years before were there. So were
the Gypsy pants and tuxedo cummerbund I had worn last year
and won second prize. It helped if you sort of had in mind

what you wanted to be before you looked through the clothes, because there were so many possibilities. Betty said something about being tired of all the usual things, like ghosts, or characters from fairy tales. She wanted something that no one would be able to guess was her. We could wear masks at night but not to school, though we could paint our faces, so this presented a consideration. Also, the daytime costume had to be something that wouldn't give the nighttime costume away.

Some of Betty's friends would show up, as usual, with store-bought costumes. They'd be Superman, or Captain Kirk, Mr. Spock, whose ears were popular, Batman, Robin, Frankenstein, Cousin It, Porky the Pig, and all that. We didn't go for those kinds of things. All you had to do was look through the shelves at the dime store and you'd know what they'd be on Halloween. That's why they never won the prize for the best costume. Mrs. Grayson was old-fashioned about some things. She'd saved all the clothes so Barbara and Betty could play dress-up. Now and then she'd slip downstairs while we were going through the clothes. She'd sit on the steps and just watch us so quietly you couldn't tell she was there.

I thought maybe I'd go for the traditional — but with a costume so great it would stun the judges into awarding me the prize. First prize was usually something seasonal, like candy, but it was the glory of winning that mattered. You could always give the candy away, if it was some kind you didn't like, and be doubly well thought of. I was thinking maybe something black, a vampire, or better yet, a bat, a vampire bat.

I flipped my bangs out of my eyes, but they kept falling across them as I sifted through the trunk. I snatched every scrap of black material, though I was a little worried about how I would ever construct the wings.

"You can't have *all* the black!" Betty said. "I might need some of that."

"I'm not taking it all. I'm just saving it out."

"What are you going to be?"

"A vampire, I think."

"Haven't you been that before?"

"This time I'm going to be a vampire *bat.*"

"That's different. Help me think of something," Betty said.

"You could be a pumpkin," I said.

"But I want to be an animal."

"But you could stuff your orange poncho with pillows and make a stem out of cardboard and paint it green. Don't you have some orange tights?"

"I don't want to be a pumpkin!"

"Can I borrow your poncho, then?" I asked.

"If you don't punch any holes in it. Even for the stem. Phooey, you've got two ideas, and I don't even have one yet."

Betty pulled the last item from the black trunk, a long satin dress with some brown circle stains down the front. I grabbed some black lace for my pile. "I like this dress," Betty said. "Do you?"

"Yeah. I don't remember it. Stand up so I can see it better."

She stood and held the dress, letting it unwind like a scroll in front of her body.

"I've got it!" I said. "One of Dracula's brides!"

"Hey, that's good. But what about my face?"

"All you have to do is powder it and get a veil."

Betty flung our discard pile back into the trunk. We pushed it aside and pulled the smaller, brown trunk under the light.

"Help me look for a veil," Betty said.

"I've got an idea for your other costume," I said. "You could be a cat. I'm going to be a vampire bat and you could be a black cat. There's enough black here for two."

"What about a tail?" Betty asked.

"What about my wings? A tail is easy pie. You just take a coat hanger and straighten it out and wrap material around it."

"Like when we were mice?"

"Yeah! I wish we still had those tails from the play."

"They weren't black, and they probably wouldn't be long enough anyway. That play was a long time ago; first grade."

It was right after this that we found a veil from an old hat and abandoned the trunks to scavenge in the other storage room, where Mrs. Grayson had told us not to go. We were hoping to turn up some shoes, and since we hadn't really understood her command, we didn't see any harm in just taking a look. As I think back, I suppose it was bound to happen that we'd eventually hit on the very pattern of that first fall long ago: find ourselves doing the only forbidden thing and find out something that we'd rather not have known.

An old wardrobe leaned against the far wall, and once we'd switched on the light we seemed to be drawn toward it like flies to syrup. It looked like the very place to find shoes, if there were any to be found. Betty tried the right-hand door and it creaked open. A row of ancient suits hung across the rod. And beneath the suits was a neat row of shiny brown and black shoes. When I started to pick up a pair, Betty told me not to touch them. She carefully opened the three drawers to the right of the suits. The first contained handkerchiefs, some of them still plastic-wrapped. The second drawer was stuffed with black and brown socks, and the third contained boxer shorts and old-style ribbed undershirts, yellowed with age. Then Betty said, "These are my grandfather's." She pulled out one of the handkerchiefs and showed me the monogram.

"Why'd he want to leave all his stuff here?" I asked.

"He's dead, stupid. But these are his clothes."

It got a little creepy after that, thinking how I'd touched a dead man's handkerchief and even rubbed my fingertips over his initials. The whole thing made me feel sad and scared at the same time. It was like someone expected him to walk right in there and need his wardrobe.

Betty opened the other door. That side was full of bigger drawers containing shirts with the paper laundry bands still around them and a few sweaters. Inside a kind of cabinet door there must have been three hundred ties, so many that when I tried to grab a handful so I could look at them in the light, half of the others tumbled off their hooks. I thought we'd never get all those slippery silk ties balanced and the door shut on them again.

With Betty in some kind of sulk so she wasn't saying anything, we wandered around the room and glanced beneath plastic. All we unearthed was a few of Betty's old games and a rusty pair of ice skates Betty said belonged to her pop and we'd better not move them. Right before we gave it up, I opened a closet door.

The light was pretty dim, but I know I'm not mistaken about what we saw on those closet shelves. At first we couldn't make sense of them at all, just jar after jar. Jars like you can tomatoes in, only bigger — gallon size, I guess — but with something floating inside. When our eyes adjusted to the sparse light of the closet, we began to see something recognizable inside a few of the jars. As the shapes came into focus, I tried to make the information fade as quickly as it formed.

"We'd better not," Betty said, and pushed the door closed.

I followed her into the safe room.

"Wait here," she said.

I sat down on a trunk while she ran upstairs. My heart was beating fast, but all the same I was disappointed we'd given up. In a couple of minutes she came down the steps, carrying a flashlight. I followed her back into the forbidden room and straight to the closet.

She shone a beam into each jar, and we were amazed. What did it mean? Babies in jars. Some of them seemed perfectly formed; we counted their delicate, nearly translucent fingers and toes, looked through their eyelids to see the curves of their eyes. We took long looks at their private parts, to see whether they were boys or girls. I was scared to touch the jars, but Betty chinked her fingernail against the glass to point at specific parts; she even tried to lift one jar off the shelf, but it weighed too much or else she decided not to take the risk just as she nearly moved it. It reminded me of the story of "Ali Baba and the Forty Thieves," the part where the thieves are hiding in the big oil jars, waiting to attack, and Ali Baba's faithful servant girl discovers them and manages to kill each one by pouring boiling oil down on their heads. I think she had a crush on Ali Baba, but anyway the thieves never saw it coming, and they died curled up in the jars before they could surprise Ali Baba and murder him.

But some of the jars we found held monsters, things that seemed more reptile than human. Betty quickly passed over them with her light, but those quick flashes remain most vivid in my memory — the jars that contained babies that were never born whole, but born all the same and kept for study. I still wonder who their parents were and if they knew what had happened to their children.

When a nightmare brings back the discovery, the monsters break out of their jars, slink and ooze across the floor. They even speak to me, and I've tried more than once in a dream to make them whole, to heal them. When I try to touch them I always hold back, unable to lay my hands on them, unable to touch their deformity. Whenever they speak, they seem to hold me responsible. I awake from the dream feeling like a monster myself. Because I know that it is true. If I use my gift I am a freak, and if I refuse, if I could refuse, I'd be bound for destruction from the inside out.

Betty said that the specimens must belong to her pop, that he must have gotten them in medical school. That was a relief, because I thought at first that somebody had murdered them for no reason. I never felt the same about Dr. Grayson after that, even though he was just as nice to me, and I knew that even Leonardo da Vinci was supposed to have carved up corpses to find out how the body works. It just didn't seem the same, taking little tiny babies and making them float in jars for the rest of their lives. It didn't seem like they could tell you anything you didn't already know.

We spent the rest of that afternoon trying to forget what we'd seen and piecing together our finds from the trunk. I had a vest and a cummerbund and a cape to make into wings. Betty was going to let me borrow some of her black tights and her orange ones. I drew a stem for the pumpkin on green construction paper, cut it out, and pasted it over a piece of strong cardboard. Then I taped it on top of the hood and pulled the poncho over my head for a trial run. It worked. So I helped Betty with her cat. She planned to wear black tights, a leotard with a turtleneck dickie underneath it, and a black half mask and black mittens. The tails were harder than I remembered. We must have had help with those mice tails before. Mrs. Grayson straightened out the coat hangers for us and broke a nail without complaining very much. First we taped paper towel strips around the wires, then wrapped them with black cloth. Betty's had to be longer than mine. Sometimes she could be so stubborn; she had her mind set on doing costumes and nothing else could distract her. I kept thinking about those jars. I wanted to ask a million questions about them, but I didn't start because I knew we'd be in big trouble if we let Mrs. Grayson know.

When we'd accomplished everything but my wings, I persuaded Betty we should go for a walk. There was no mistaking the scent of burning leaves. The air was full of little trails of smoke. All up and down the alley people stirred their leaves in big barrels, standing watch as smoke spiraled into the sky. We hadn't gotten in a good afternoon of jumping into them, and here everyone was already burning them up. At least one pile was left in the Graysons' back yard, so we cut short our tour and each settled into a swing. We alternated swinging up and back so we wouldn't pull the concrete loose any more than it already was. We were growing too heavy for the swings. My stomach heaved and lowered as I lifted forward and fell backward, higher and higher in the air each time. I stretched my legs into the emptiness and tilted up in the swing, saving my descent until the last possible instant.

In a swing it was easy to imagine the world upside down. Half of the time I leaned backward in defiance of my own upward push toward the sky. When I swung back behind the center bar, I'd lean forward ready to tap the ground hard, to push with all my might when I went by.

"I'm higher," I said.

"No — your legs are just longer."

Betty gave the ground a tremendous push, like she was trying to knock it away from her, and propelled into the open space. The intensity on her face complained that the chains were too short, that gravity was a punishment, and she'd much rather leave the ground altogether than continue the push-me, pull-you of swinging back and forth between the earth and the clouds. She sprang from her seat, like a spark set off in the dark, and rustled into the big pile of leaves Mrs. Grayson had been raking up for a solid week.

"I'm going to jump!" I warned.

Betty scrambled out of the pile, turned back and scooped up armloads of leaves, heaved them onto the top of the pile for my landing.

"Okay," she said. "Jump!"

I released my grip on the chains and pushed off from the seat. I kept my eyes on the leaf pile. My legs arched toward it, but it seemed I hit seat first, not feet first. It was hard to keep balanced while falling through the air. And it happened so quickly — the way my stomach sent a brief wave of nausea to my hands just as they jerked free of the chains, and I managed to jolt from my seat. Leaves splashed out in all directions from my landing. Betty was already back in her swing, gaining altitude, so I rose quickly and heaped the leaves into a pyramid for her second jump.

Betty dove toward the pile, legs and arms sprawling, swimming through the air, and came up covered with frail fragments of dry leaves that looked like a million butterfly wings stuck to her hair and sweater. She was all smiles.

"Did you see me?"

"Yeah!" I brushed some of the leaves from her back.

"You try it! It's just like flying!"

I didn't know why, but I was too afraid, afraid to do what

she'd just shown me could be done without breaking an arm.
Something told me to hang back instead of trying it for myself.

"I don't think so," I said.

Betty looked at me, hardly believing that I would pass up a
chance like that, to join in one of her best discoveries. She treated
it like an insult. I felt like someone who might prefer two paper
cups and a string to a walkie-talkie with batteries. I didn't know
why I wasn't ashamed of myself. I just knew I didn't have to
do it, no matter what Betty said. But thankfully she didn't rub
it in.

"You want to go look at the grave?" I asked.

"I guess."

The grave was a sacred subject that made us afraid of ourselves.
We went back to it over and over but would have rather forgotten
about it if we could. I didn't really want to see it again, but I
guess I suggested it because it was secrets like that that glued
together a friendship. We scuffed the worn toes of our summer
sneakers through the gravel on our way up to the tanks. The
grave was near the holes, marked with a flat rock and a stick
cross. It had been there two years.

One night in the middle of a hide-and-seek tournament a sickly
gray-and-white-striped cat had staggered into our play, into the
center of the shrub-lined back yard where an old barbecue marked
home-free. One by one, as we were either tagged out or beaten
back to base, we noticed the cat. In a few minutes the striped
cat had become the center of attention and the game vanished.
Bile caked its neck, and foam lathered its mouth and nose. It
collapsed in our circle and panted heavily, more like a horse
than a cat. The breathing seemed to echo through each of us
as we held our breath and watched the cat's dying. Finally one
of the boys suggested we kill it, put it out of its misery. It was
going to die anyway.

I stepped out of the circle and pulled Betty up to her feet.
We ran back into her yard across the alley and watched as the
boys pounded the cat's head with their sticks, then pelted it

with rocks. In a few minutes they called that it was dead, and lost interest. I guess that was the beginning of the dirty boys.

We couldn't leave the poor thing there, so I got a shovel and Betty got a dress box out of her basement. We carted the cat up to the tanks in a wheelbarrow. It was harder to dig a hole big and deep enough for that box than I'd thought. We took turns and finally were able to wriggle the box into place. I thought we ought to say something over the cat, but we couldn't think of anything — neither of us had been to a funeral — so we just scraped the dirt back into the hole. I found the big marker rock and Betty made the cross.

My nightmares about the cat being buried alive had faded, but if anything could bring them back it was a trip to the grave. The rock had sunk down and only the vertical part of the cross remained.

"I ought to bring some string up here and fix that cross," Betty said.

"Let's go," I said.

Just standing there staring at the marker was making me feel like a criminal returned to the scene of his crime. The moon was rising just at the horizon. It hung between two mountains, an overinflated ball, blood orange, the hunter's moon. It had been a bad idea to come up to the grave with Halloween only a few days away. As we ran back home, twisting our ankles on the path, I couldn't get it out of my mind that I heard breathing.

The afternoon before Halloween Betty came down to help me with my wings. She brought her old bat kite and some black electrical tape. We stripped the plastic from her kite and tore out the supports — a plastic T hooked the crossbars together. But when we pulled out the bars they broke into four separate pieces. Betty suggested we tape them together and use each set to support one of my wings.

It sounded like a good idea, except that it took a lot longer than expected. Once we'd get one wing up, the other one would collapse. We succeeded in the end by belting the bottom of the cape around me instead of letting it hang free. It didn't look as good, but the wings really stood out. I thought we should celebrate at the Rexall with cherry smashes, so we did.

On the way home, something funny happened. We were just past the Presbyterian church when we heard a big boom, like thunder but higher pitched, close but faraway-sounding at the same time. It seemed to shake the birds off the ground into flight. A whole bush of birds took off when it boomed. I'd never heard them flap and chirp so much at once. A little bird got left on the ground, trying to flap its wings. I thought maybe it had a broken wing, so I bent over it to look. Betty told me not to touch it. "Its mother will abandon it if she smells you." I thought it would probably die anyway, so I picked it up. A baby blue jay. A second later it peeled into flight after the others. My hands felt scorched. I watched as it perched on the guttering of the church.

"Hey, what'd you do to that bird?" Betty asked.

"Nothing," I said. "Do you think that was a car backfiring?"

"No, I don't."

I felt like running toward the fallout shelter sign above the basement steps of the church and banging on the door. We had had one of those yellow-and-black signs at our church, too, before it burned down. Maybe there were rows of canned goods stacked up to the ceiling: carrots, tomatoes, Vienna sausages, and all different flavors of Campbell's soup, so a person could live in there and never have to come out. I should have stayed away from that jay. Why'd I have to pick it up, anyway? I couldn't help myself. I guess it was as natural to me as breathing, as necessary as telling my story.

The booming sound seemed to have come from inside the ground. My teeth hurt when I got home, and I didn't know whether it was because of the ice I'd eaten or the sound we'd heard or because I had gritted my teeth so hard after Betty asked me that about the bird.

I could still feel the rapid beating of that little blue jay's heart, like it was there and not there at the same time. So light, like air. It was easy to see how it could fly to the top of the roof. My hands felt like they did when I ran them quickly through bath water, to cup a waterfish, then let it go.

15

Halloween

Halloween morning was dark as evening; heavy clouds hung in streaks across the sky. Momma said for me to dress warm, because it had turned suddenly cold. I wore a sweater beneath the pillows and the orange poncho that would make a pumpkin out of me. At least I'd be dressed for rain.

On the bus I squeezed in beside a devil carrying a pitchfork. The real thing. I was afraid one of my eyes was going to be put out at any minute. The devil really made a ruckus; he kept whipping around to point his pitchfork at the pair of mummies in the seat behind us. I could barely sit down, with all those pillows belted around me. The devil acted like he didn't know what I was. He thought he was going to win the prize with that bit. The first thing Mr. Halley, the bus monitor, did when we filed off was confiscate that pitchfork. He took it straight to Mr. Clarke's office and told the devil he couldn't carry it home unless his parents came and got him. The devil pitched a fit about them ruining his costume, but they wouldn't let him have it back.

Tina came to school as a princess. It suited her perfectly. She'd made a little cardboard crown and covered it with Reynolds Wrap and a stick wand with a glitter star on the end. She pointed the wand at me and said, "I'm going to turn you into a magic coach." It took me a minute to remember what she was talking about. Tina could be pretty sharp on her fairy tales for a little kid, except that she mixed them up. It turned out she wasn't a princess, but the good witch, Glinda, from *The Wizard of Oz*. Momma must have been right when she said Tina would get over her dad; she seemed back to normal, for Tina, I mean.

The worst part of school was waiting for the contest. And we had a test to take right before lunch. It covered twenty-five states and their capital cities. If the words weren't spelled correctly, they wouldn't count either. When Mrs. Harper pointed to a state on the map, we had to write its name and capital and one thing we knew about the state while she searched for her bra strap. A whole class full of goblins, hoboes, and superheroes sitting there trying to remember how to spell Tennessee, heads bent over their papers, pencils scribbling, was enough to make anybody fall out of a chair laughing. Mrs. Harper didn't believe in wasting a single minute of school. "I can't abide foolishness," she'd lament whenever something like dress-up day was declared. Whoever won the candy, if they were in her class, wouldn't be allowed to open it until after school, no matter how much they promised to *share,* a magic word with most teachers.

Lunch was a far worse trial. Pinto beans just made me sick to look at them in the middle of the day. I wanted to take all the rest of my lunch tickets and cut them to shreds, even if they were cheap, nutritionally balanced meals. I stared a hole in Betty's peanut butter sandwich, so she set it back into her lunch box between bites. I ate the corn bread and bargained my way into another piece by pretending I didn't want to give up the beans. Worked every time on most people — seemed like all they needed to know was that you liked something and that made them want it all the more. So I ate two pieces of corn bread and milk and Jell-O without fruit. J-e-l-l-O without fruit cocktail isn't worth beans, but at least I could squish it through my teeth.

Michael Dale tried to start a bean-shooting contest and got sent home. That would put him in a great mood for trick-or-treating. Pinto beans happened to fit perfectly into hollows of spoons, to fire one at a time by flipping the handles. If Michael Dale hadn't done it first, it might have been fun. All those beans did was cause trouble; bean fights weren't the half of it by later into the afternoon.

After lunch the judges established themselves behind a long

table at the front of the lunch room. Each teacher kept a pad and pencil for note taking. By classes, starting with the lowest grade, we were to file by the judges' table — for a few seconds each of us commanding the undivided attention of the judges before the next kid started out from the black tape mark.

I hadn't seen another pumpkin in the whole patch when it came my turn to step beyond the black line and strut before the judges. I puffed my stomach, hitched up the pillows in the back, and walked out. Snickers started from the audience, but not from the judges. I walked deliberately; I wanted the judges to appreciate my originality. Those kids probably never saw a pumpkin before.

When the head judge said thank you, my turn was over. As I made my way back to one of the long tables, Batman, probably one of the dirty boys, nudged me in the arm. "What are you, anyway? A life preserver?" I should have belted him in the mouth then and there.

At long last, after the umpteenth ghost had been scribbled about, the ice cream descended from on high. Every year a few of the mothers donated ice cream for the whole elementary school. This year it was going right for a change; I got my first choice, strawberry, and a wooden stick that didn't splinter the first time I dipped it. Betty said those sticks looked like tongue depressors. The ice cream was the beginning of a long afternoon of sweets. Betty wasn't that interested in treats, maybe because Mrs. Grayson didn't approve of sugar, but she always tried to collect the most anyway. Once we'd counted all our candy to see who'd done the best, she'd throw her whole bag into the bottom of her closet and forget about it. You could smell it up in her room. Sometimes I felt like rushing to the closet and pushing back the clothes and grabbing a handful of candy bars. There were a couple of treats that if we got them Mrs. Grayson wouldn't let us keep. Apples were one. With Mrs. Grayson being such a health fanatic you'd think she'd let us eat apples above all else. Her apple phobia stemmed from an incident where an unsuspecting kid had cut his lip on a razor blade stuck in a caramel apple. So anything wrapped up by hand was off limits. We could include them in our count, but then we had to hand them straight over. Betty would trade anything, even a Zero, for a Snickers or a Baby Ruth. We usually collected a lot of suckers and little Tootsie Rolls.

I scraped the bottom of my ice cream cup and tried to lick the wooden paddle without actually touching my tongue to the wood. If I licked the wood it made my teeth ache down to the soles of my feet. In marched the judges from their deliberations. For once I licked the paddle clean without losing the taste of strawberry. I caught a drip of melted ice cream running down Betty's poncho. Wearing plastic was hot, but it had advantages.

I couldn't believe it — one of the boring ghosts won third place. A first-grader! They must have done it just to spread the prizes out. The ghost plowed through the crowd, jumping up and down and clapping its hands. "What do I win?" it asked. The judges handed the ghost a wrapped package; everyone applauded. Second place was worse than first — it went to a store-bought cowboy suit worn by a third-grade girl who looked more like Trigger than Dale or Roy. She'd added her own real leather boots and checked shirt, jeans, and hat to the ready-made chaps, vest, and gun set. She wound her six-shooter around one finger and pointed it at her audience: "Pow! You're all dead!" Her mother was one of the ice cream ladies.

When first prize was announced I almost shouted out loud. I jumped to my feet as happy as if I'd won it myself. It was Betty as Dracula's bride! Her dress billowed out as she stepped to the front to accept her package. I kept repeating "Oh, boy!" to myself.

"Now we must all return to our classes," the center judge said. "But first let's give the winners and the mothers who provided us the ice cream a big round of applause!" We whistled, stomped our feet, clapped hands until they stung. As soon as I could, I rushed up to Betty to see what she'd won.

"I haven't opened it yet. I'm going to wait until I get home so I can show Mommy the wrapping paper," Betty said.

"Oh, come on, open it," I said.

That only cemented her resolve to save it. We walked back to class. I did get her to rattle the box a few times. At least I'd see what she'd won later on, at her party.

"I think you should have won," Betty said. "Nobody's ever been a pumpkin before."

"Maybe that's why I lost. I'm glad you won."

"It was your idea."

Only a really best friend would've said that.

"A dead weight hung upon us. It hung upon our limbs — upon the household furniture — upon the goblets from which we drank; and all things were depressed, and borne down thereby — all things save only the flames of the seven iron lamps which illumined our revel." Mrs. Grayson was reading the first of two Poe stories she'd promised us before we set out to trick-or-treat. I was stuffed so full of hamburger and carrot cake that I didn't think I could walk. She read the stories while we tried to digest. In spite of the lump in my stomach and the wiggling of some of Betty's dumb guests, I was caught up in the story, about a shadow. It got better as it went along, but then it stopped all of a sudden, right after the shadow spoke its name and told where it was from: *". . . the tones in the voice of the shadow were not the tones of any one being, but of a multitude of beings, and, varying in their cadences from syllable to syllable, fell duskily upon our ears in the well remembered and familiar accents of many thousand departed friends."*

Mrs. Grayson paused, then said, "Well, that's the end of the first story. The next one's a bit longer; are you sure you want to hear it?"

"Yes, please," we all answered and leaned forward, propping our elbows on the table, forgetting our manners.

Before we had listened half a minute, Henriette broke in and demanded, "What is the Black Hole of Calcutta?"

"I don't know," Mrs. Grayson said. "But we could look it up in the *Britannica*. Get the index, Betty."

"What's Calcutta?" Marie asked.

"Calcutta's a city in India," Mrs. Grayson said.

"I knew that," Betty said.

"Get volume four," Mrs. Grayson instructed. When she'd found the page she wanted, she began to read silently.

"Just read the story, please," I said. "It's nearly dark and we haven't —"

Marie kicked me under the table and left a footprint on Betty's black tights I'd have to rinse out.

Mrs. Grayson finally raised her head. "It was named the 'Black Hole' by J. Z. Holwell, a survivor of the incident. In 1756, in Calcutta, Fort William was captured by the nawab of Bengal, Siraj-ud-Daula. He held close to a hundred and fifty prisoners in a tiny room with only two tiny windows on a very hot night. The next morning only about twenty-some were alive."

"Oh," Marie said.

She wouldn't know a nawab if he bit her behind.

"Now everyone be quiet, and I'll finish the story. Okay, girls?"

I bit my tongue and Mrs. Grayson continued the story. The worst part was that it kept saying it was true but that nobody would believe it. I believed from the beginning. Some nights I felt just like the man in the story, waking up in my room and thinking I was underground instead. He woke up on a narrow bunk in the hold of a ship, having forgotten where he was. He reached up and felt the wooden ceiling six inches above him, smelled the moldy air, and assumed he'd been buried alive. He'd read so much about premature burial that his mind was crawling with it. It was the heat of summer that did it to me, that made me feel like I was suffocating. The little window in my room didn't let the air flow through. I'd wake up with my pillow stuffed over my head, holding it down with my own hands, unable to take a deep breath. It was like somebody else was holding the pillow down. I must have only been trying, in my sleep, to keep the moonlight out of my eyes.

The best way to avoid being buried alive is to be cremated;

that way, if you aren't dead you will be soon enough. Betty told me that it couldn't happen now anyway, because people have to be embalmed before they're buried; it's a law. It isn't exactly comforting to think about having all your blood sucked out by a Dracula machine, but at least you'll be dead afterward.

The night air blew so cold it felt like it might snow, but the sky between the mountains was clear as glass, and the pumpkin moon like a giant waning headlight, when we started out to trick-or-treat. Betty carried the plastic trick-or-treat bag she'd won slung over one arm. A jack-o'-lantern grinned on one side and a black cat arched its back on the other. Since Betty wore her cat costume, she carried the bag cat side out. She left the candy bars she'd won in the bottom, for ballast. Her theory was that if it looked like she already had a lot she'd get even more. Seems like a weird idea, but if you take a look at the haves and the have-nots, she understood the basics. I thought she'd offer me a Zero, but she saved it.

The seven of us walked up the Graysons' hill, weaving from one side of the street to the other without missing a house. We never knocked on the neighbors' doors at any other time. We looked inside as far as we could see. Some of the houses were nicer than others. The bald man's foyer had a real slate floor and silk wallpaper. You could tell how much money each family had by what kind of candy they gave you and how much they gave and whether they let you pick out what you wanted or just handed you one of something. Whatever they did, we said thank you and walked on to the next house, shaking our candy up in our bags. If a house ran out of candy the light would go off, and the next day there might be eggs smashed on that porch or smeared across the windshield of the car. We never did anything like that, but the older kids did. And the dirty boys. They didn't even care about the candy.

Mrs. Grayson had given Betty a flashlight and instructed us to walk only on the sidewalks and to look carefully if we must cross the street. We had permission to roam the entire downtown.

And that was enough, because by the time we finished we'd be so tired it wouldn't matter how much more candy might be waiting just out of reach.

On Halloween night all the kids from the hollers came down into Poorwater in pickup trucks and spread out over the town like ants looking for sweets. If they wore a costume, it would just be some smears of paint across their faces and some big old clothes not much different from what they had to wear everyday. They put their candy in paper sacks so creased and recreased, they might split open at any minute. One year the holler crowd arrived just when everyone was about to call it a night and go to bed. Lights were flicking off one by one up and down the streets, but the holler kids knocked on the doors anyway, saying their halfhearted "trick or treat" and stuffing anything they could get into their bags. A holler kid would walk around with his mouth chock full of candy. They couldn't wait to eat it until they got home — it was like they thought someone was going to steal their Butterfingers if they didn't gobble them as fast as possible.

When we came to the door of anyone's house who was in our group we'd get twice as much candy. Marie's mother pretended not to know who we were. We looked so good, she said she was scared to death just seeing us at her door. Sounded just like something a mother of Marie might exclaim. "Oh, Mom," Marie said. We held out our bags and Twinkies tumbled into them. "Wow!" Betty said. "What a great idea!" Marie said she'd picked out the Twinkies, that they had some other stuff not as good her mother was saving for later on. Sarah's mother gave us cookies in the foyer and M&Ms in our bags. Momma had bought Boston Baked Beans. I'd been nibbling on them for a week, stealing them, I guess. Daddy loved to see all us kids dressed up. Usually he'd sit outside the trailer beside a little table that held our jack-o'-lantern and hand out the candy. That's where he was when we cruised through on our way to Belinda's.

"Halt, who goes there?" It was Daddy's voice, of course.

"A vampire bat," I said.

"Haven't we met?" Daddy asked.

"And a black cat," Betty said.

"I'm a mummy," Sarah said.

"But you look too young," Daddy said. "And who are *you?*"

"Belinda."

"He means your costume," I said.

"Why don't you see if you can guess, Mr. Parks," Belinda said.

"Well, the black mask . . . Let me see."

"Do you give up?"

"Of course. You're the Lone Ranger!"

"How'd you know?" Belinda whined.

"A lucky guess. And you're," he said, turning to Marie, "a skeleton."

She waved her pirate flag. The pinned-on bones shivered on her chest.

"I bet you can't guess me," Pinkie said.

"You're a monkey."

"But *what kind* of monkey?" Pinkie turned so he could see her red wings.

"The strangest monkey I've ever seen. I give up completely."

"I'm a mean *Wizard of Oz* monkey." Pinkie growled through her missing teeth.

Pinkie gave me the creeps; I wished Betty hadn't had to invite her to the party. She only got invited because her mother was in the bridge club. Like I only got invited because I was Betty's unofficial best friend. Pinkie's real name was Prescott, honest to God.

"Guess me!" a little voice piped up.

"You're a princess," Daddy said.

Oh no, I thought. It's Tina.

Daddy dropped Boston Baked Beans into each of our bags, including Tina's, and she'd just come over because she heard us talking.

"Well," I said, glancing up at the moon, "we'd better go."

"Can I go with you?" Tina asked.

I knew it was coming.

"No," I said.

"Well," Daddy said, "I don't see why you can't take Tina."

I was caught. If I didn't let her tag along, Daddy would think I was being mean to an orphan.

"Well, come on," I said.

"If anything happens to her, I'm not responsible," Betty said. I think her mind worked more naturally like a lawyer than a doctor.

"Stay out of the street," Daddy said. "And if you meet any suspicious characters, don't tangle with them, you hear?"

"See you later, Daddy."

I heard him say, "After while, crocodile," even though I hadn't said "alligator" in front of the others.

So "Glinda" joined our troupe. She and Pinkie walked together, since they both came from the same movie. On Lee Street, tons of kids clambered up and down both sidewalks and waited in line at each house. The dirty boys pedaled down to the end of the street fast enough to break their necks, like the Wicked Witch in Dorothy's dream. They turned the corner and disappeared. I didn't know what they were up to, and I didn't care, as long as they left us alone. But Betty gulped when she saw them, and I probably did too. They sped out of the picture, and we decided to split up into teams of four. Pinkie and Tina stayed with Betty and me: a vampire bat, a black cat, a winged monkey, and Glinda, the good witch. We were ready for anything. Pinkie grabbed Tina's hand and they bounced into a chorus of the Monkees' theme song. Betty and I didn't sing along, but we were too close behind to pretend we weren't with them.

Pinkie was a real brat, a genuine pain in the butt. "People say we monkee around," Pinkie screamed. She could make Tina seem like an angel. Of course Pinkie had to go to the bathroom almost immediately.

"I know this next lady. She'll let me in," Pinkie said.

We stepped up on the porch and knocked on the storm door. An old lady shuffled toward us in her house shoes. As soon as she opened the door a crack we shouted, "Trick or treat!" She smiled a quivering smile and dipped a liver-spotted hand into a basket, stooped to count candy into each of our bags. As the candy plunked we said, "Thank you." "You're welcome," she said each time.

Pinkie piped up, "I'm Prescott Wilson. Do you mind if I use your bathroom?"

"Who?"

"Prescott Wilson. You know my mother."

"I don't think I do."

"She helped you plant your flowers. It'll only take me a minute."

I wished Pinkie would give it up, but it wasn't in her to admit defeat.

Then the old lady said, "Oh, now I remember. Yes, we planted perennials and two rose bushes. One was Mr. Lincoln and the other — I can't remember. But dear, I'm afraid I don't have a telephone."

"I need to use your *bathroom,*" Pinkie said.

The kids were packed in behind us, pushing and shouting, "Stop holding up the line!"

"Come right in, Miss Prescott," the old lady finally said.

"Wait for me," Pinkie warned.

We made it off the porch by swinging beneath the iron railing into some boxwoods. Tina had trouble with her dress and crown, but she made it.

"Let's hide and make Pinkie think we've left," Betty said.

We edged around the house to where we still had a good view of the sidewalk. When Pinkie came back down the steps we would watch her search up and down the street before we sprang out at her, screaming bloody murder.

"I don't think this is very nice," Tina said.

"Then go home," I said.

Betty got the giggles almost immediately. Then I got tickled, too. We were laughing so hard I thought I might pee in my pants, and I didn't have to go. My stomach hurt more and more, but once you get started it's hard to stop laughing. I held my breath but it came busting out a second later, with a funny sound that started Betty laughing harder than before. Tina wouldn't laugh.

"She'll hear us," I managed to say.

Betty tried to hold it in; she pressed her face against her hands against the brick of the house, and after a few bursts of hysteria she got it under control.

"Do you think we could have missed her?" Betty asked.

"I've been watching," Tina said. "She hasn't come out."

"You know something?" Betty said.

"What?"

"I think I have to go to the bathroom."

We both started giggling again.

"Really," Betty said. "What am I going to do?"

"I'll look out. Nobody'll see you. It's too dark."

Betty headed around back with the flashlight. I held her bag of candy in one hand and mine in the other and stared toward the sidewalk with Tina in case Pinkie appeared. My hands were starting to freeze, so I dropped the bags on the ground beside me and rubbed my palms together. I should have worn gloves. I blew into my hands, but the warmth didn't last long. I wished Betty would hurry; I felt like going home. What had happened to Pinkie? It was just like her to get lost. Here I was stuck with Tina, on Halloween, too.

"Oh, look!" Tina said.

Thinking how I'd rather be at home crunching on the rest of the Boston Baked Beans, I glanced into the street, and there were the dirty boys on their bikes, coming right toward the old lady's house. They were carrying something. Each of them steered with one hand. They wore ski masks, but I recognized Michael Dale by his big head. "Heigh-ho, Silver!" he cried and skidded to a stop. His bully boys tried to imitate him but piled up like dominoes just behind him. I took a step backward and pulled Tina into the shadows. A second later we heard the first rapid firing of Chinese firecrackers and the hissing of squibs.

Another second passed before the screaming of the trick-or-treaters added into that confusion.

"Betty!" I called, a little too loudly.

I'd caught the attention of one of Michael's henchmen. Me and my big mouth again. I grabbed at our candy bags, but before I could get a good grip on either one, a boy ran toward us and shouted, "Hostages!"

The first thing he did, of course, was fasten his fingers on our candy bags. I pulled backward and he pulled forward, nearly toppling me onto my face. His mask rode up and I found myself staring right into Harry's face. Harry, a dirty boy? "You traitor!" I shouted. I felt Betty's arms lock around my middle, and the tug of war continued. Harry's monster teeth rattled in his mouth as we tugged. Tina took the opportunity to run away.

The whole gang of dirty boys, fresh from having scared all the other kids off the sidewalk, swaggered, impressed with themselves. They must have collected fifteen bags of candy. Most of their victims just dropped their candy and ran when they realized who was setting off the firecrackers. Being a boy and not being a dirty boy could be worse for your health than being a girl and excluded by birth. Better to have been born a sissy than to have opted for it. As the rank and file of the vile dirty boys closed in on us, Betty let go and urged me to do the same. Who cared about the damn candy? It just rotted your teeth.

"Run, Dorie! Run!"

Pulled forward toward the clutches of doom, I let go of the bags, sent Harry stumbling backward, and skidded after Betty into the back yard. I hoped Harry fell flat on his ass. I knew there was an old oil drum in the back yard where we could hide. But I wanted deep down to make those dirty boys pay, once and for all. They'd stolen candy from the whole neighborhood.

"They'll sell back the candy, like always," Betty said.

"But it's not fair."

"Where's Pinkie?" Betty asked.

"Over here" came a hoarse whisper.

"Pinkie?"

"I think I sat on Mr. Lincoln."

One of her red wings had fallen off. And the torn wing that was left looked like a gash down her back in the shadowy light. We pulled her free.

"How'd you *end up* out here, anyway?" I asked.

"Very funny," Pinkie said. "The old ninny made me give out her candy while she made me some nice hot chocolate. I told her I didn't want any. I had to stand there at the door. Then — Bang! Bang! You should have seen them dancing over the sidewalk! It was so cool."

"Whose side are you on?" Betty asked.

"Drat! I left my candy in there."

"The dirty boys got ours, and we're going to get it back," I said.

"How?"

"I've got to go get my candy," Pinkie said.

"The old lady's not going to eat it," Betty said. "You can get yours tomorrow. We don't even have any, and they got my prize, too."

"If it was *your* candy in there, we'd go get it." Pinkie sulked.

"We're going after them. Now," I said.

"Are you coming or not? We've got to find Sarah and Belinda and Marie and Henriette," Betty said. "Where do you think they are?"

"Probably at Belinda's. Do you think they lost their candy?"

"My butt hurts." Pinkie moaned.

Without warning, the dirty boys came shrieking and popping wheelies into the back yard. Each of their handlebars was strung with several bags of candy. They circled in on us and slammed their breaks.

"Why aren't you home in bed?" Michael started in.

"Yeah," Harry echoed. "Why aren't you little girls home in bed?"

There we stood like the three little pigs surrounded by wolves, and my blood began to breeze through my body faster than the puffs of steam that shot out of my nose and mouth as if I was a train trying to climb a steep grade. But I'd had it. Enough! was the message pulsing to my brain. If I felt like a scared rabbit, damn if I was going to let Harry know it. I opened my mouth and let fly.

"You creeps! Who do you think you are? Just who do you think you are? You're not going to get away with this!"

"Dorie, shut up," Betty said.

Pinkie stomped on my foot. I stepped toward Michael and his big fat face. He was built a lot like Popeye. His big fat arms crossed over his big fat chest beneath his big fat short neck; he was solid as a mountain towering over his big fat feet.

"And who do you think's stopping us?" Michael said.

"I'm going to stop you."

I took one more step toward him before he reached out and twisted me to the ground by one arm. One of my knees burned across the grass, right through Betty's tights. One more scab wasn't going to make much difference.

"My tights!" Betty sounded mad, but not at me.

"Your daddy's a doctor," Michael said. "He can buy you some more."

He released his grip on me.

It was more his tone than his words — maybe he pointed up a difference between Betty and me that I could never erase, no matter what good friends we tried to be — but I was hotter than I'd ever been in my life, and strangely calm. I picked up a rock and brought it down squarely on the top of Michael's head, near the back of his neck. The rock broke up on impact like a clod of dirt. Michael's head must have been hard as a diamond. He staggered to his knees. Too shocked to say one word, his buddies gathered around him. Then they turned toward me all at once.

"Grab the candy!" I shouted.

Betty and Pinkie ran to the bikes and pulled the candy bags from the handlebars. Not just ours but all of them. We couldn't even think about making a run for it with all those bags. This is crazy, I thought. They're going to kill us, and I'll be first. But they just stood there, waiting for their fallen leader's next order.

Michael rose up and looked me eyeball to eyeball. I thought I could see myself, upside down in his eyes. I guess he could see himself, too. We didn't blink. I felt a strain of energy running through me from top to bottom, like an incredibly intense light that wouldn't burn but all the same was too strong for words. I knew then that the healing power that ran into my hands had its source in this light, and that it could do evil as easily as good if I wasn't careful. It could pull me into a pit so deep I'd never be able to climb out again. It could strand me so deep I'd go falling forever, alone, untouchable. I knew that it had me and would never let me go. Michael was afraid of what he saw. He blinked.

"Don't mess with her," he said, then collapsed to the ground. He rubbed his bloody neck with one hand. Blood had pooled at the collar of his shirt; it beaded in his palm when he touched himself. He looked down at his bloody hand and gagged, almost threw up.

"Don't look back. Just keep walking," I said.

Betty and Pinkie and I trudged along, dragging as many bags as we could.

"We're lunch meat," Pinkie whispered, "and it's your fault, Dorie."

"No. They're not even coming," I said.

Pinkie looked back to the group of boys huddled around Michael. "They're not coming, they're not!"

"Not for now," Betty said. "At least we can count candy tonight."

"We've got to give it all back."

"Come on, Dorie. It's ours," Pinkie said.

"How will we ever sort it out?" Betty asked.

"We'll have to announce it at school."

"Did you see the look on Michael Dale's face when he saw the blood?" Pinkie asked.

"Yeah," Betty said. "He'll probably sue."

My knee felt like a splitting headache. Betty told me not to worry about her tights, but it still made me mad. I left the others at Belinda's house and started limping home, trying to avoid the dirty boys, even though I felt certain they wouldn't bother me anymore. It's best not to rub in a victory. I could still hear the pounding of my heart in my ears as I hobbled along, swinging my bag of candy in a show of confidence I didn't feel. The night had started off so quietly, and then the dirty boys had to spoil everything. It wasn't as bad as the year a carload of holler kids crashed into a rock cliff going back home from Poorwater and two of them got killed, or the time some teenagers decided to egg some of the holler kids and sent a second-grader to the emergency room to get ten stitches in his lip. After those firecrackers, the sheriff would probably try to find a way to cancel Halloween or roll back the ten o'clock curfew.

Cold air cut through my sweater as I swung my arms to keep my momentum. Everything was rhythm: my arms back and forth, the shuffling of the candy against the inside of the bag, my eyes tearing in the wind, and my heart beating with my breathing, with the clicking of my heels on the concrete walk. I looked up and made the eerie moon bounce in time with my step. Concentration on movement kept my mind occupied but empty and hard to rouse until an alien shifting of weight, one foot to the other, finally broke into my rhythm and into my range of hearing, more like a gong than footsteps. I knew exactly what it was, though, from the instant it registered and moved up my spine in a physical sensation of the presence, once again, of something that had taken up residence just at the edge of my consciousness, never far from mind. It speeded up behind me. I tried to quicken my pace, skipping a few steps to test the strength of my hurt knee. A hot pain shot through it when my weight fell from the height of a jump. I knew I couldn't run. It was better to walk, to walk as fast as I could. Two minutes before, I hadn't given a thought to walking home alone. It wasn't far, not very far. I'd walked farther alone in the dark and made it home each time. Why not this time?

As I walked I remembered one morning when I had climbed out of bed and poured myself a bowl of cereal. I'd dressed and set out for the bus stop without having seen Momma. A terrible fear washed through me, so that it controlled me and I had no choice: *I must run back home as fast as the wind to make sure my mother isn't dead.* My stomach hurts as I run. I think I may be sick. I climb up on her side of my parents' double bed and listen, holding my breath until it burns inside my chest, for her steady breathing. I can see her chest rising and falling, but it may be my breathing that I see. I take a mirror and hold it beneath her nose. I draw a circle in the fog: *She is alive.*

Now, as I walk, each cloud of breath from my own nose and mouth confirms the distance I have crossed and the distance left before I will be home, safe. It is like a game of freeze tag: if I am touched I will remain frozen, I will die, no one will find my body — he will hide it in the darkness; I will become a shadow. My legs are almost paralyzed with these thoughts as they strain, with impossible dream steps, against the force of gravity, of nightmare. If only I can open my mouth and scream, I think. I try to convince myself that the dirty boys have returned, or that Miss Reider is out riding her broomstick on this perfect witch's night of the wicked year. I translate the ordered footfall, footfall, into a rustling of leaves, wind through brittle leaves as they catch in the air, footfall, footfall, just before touching down. Animals scurry as I move forward; their feet scamper over fallen leaves, not the shadow's. My arms pump like wings through the chill air. I hold tight to my bag of candy. Footfall, footfall. I don't care if my bat wings tear loose or if the hole in Betty's tights gets wide as a softball; I simply steam ahead, my ears hot with listening for the shadow between the popcorn beating of my heart.

I jag left, into the court. Just a few more steps; count them to the trailer door. One, two, three . . . arms wrap around me, and I scream the scream I've been holding back. It snaps from my throat like a viper as I hear the word "Boo!"

The arms shake me. "Dorie!" I hear. And I scream louder. I try to break free. Someone is shaking me, but this isn't a dream.

"Dorie! It's Daddy. It's Daddy, I say. Now calm down; I never meant to scare you so badly."

My gasping turns into sobs that come from deep inside my stomach. I've never felt these twisting knots as I cry. Something seems to break loose inside and stream out through my hot tears.

"Get a-hold on yourself. Nobody's going to hurt you," Daddy says.

"Daddy," I say and fling my arms around his neck and cling with all my might.

"You're going to squeeze the life out of me!" Daddy jokes.

He gently released my grip, took my hand, and led me inside. When there were lights shining between us and cups of steaming hot chocolate, he asked me what happened.

"The shadow," I said. "It was after me again."

"What shadow? Some kid in a costume?"

"No — a man. A man's been following me. Not just tonight. He's out there right now."

"No one's out there, sweetheart. Believe me. You just imagined it. It's Halloween night."

"The shadow is always there."

I told him the history of my shadow, everything I knew. Daddy's face grew stern, then angry.

"It's my fault," he said. "That man's just trying to scare you."

"But why, Daddy?"

"It has to do with coal. It has nothing to do with you."

"I'm not afraid of that guy."

"From now on I don't want you to leave this yard without me or your mother."

"But, Daddy, I'm not scared of him, not anymore."

"Please, Dorie. It's just for a little while. Until I can get this straightened out. And believe me that man won't bother you again."

16

Facing the Shadow

That morning it was all over the radio: three men on the cat-eye shift had been trapped inside the mine. Some blamed it on the frequent blasting that had been going on to open up a new seam. It must have been dynamite that Betty and I heard boom that day at the church when the blue jay flew away. Some said it was the cold snap caused the explosion, that the sudden change of the barometer opened the way for methane gas from deep inside the earth. Others claimed that theory was pure superstition, that weather had less to do with it than the company's policies. Momma was of her usual mind-set: mining was a dangerous profession and anyone who climbed into the elevator to be lowered down into the pit had to know he might not come out one day. It was just the chance men took to earn their pay.

Daddy volunteered for the rescue. We sat in our nervous rows in school, waiting for the bell and the weekend. A few of the desks were empty. And I knew it meant that those kids waited at home with their mothers for the news. This explosion wasn't so bad, as they went. Miners were trained how to act when it happened. They were probably barricaded against the smoke and fire, near an air shaft. Not a sign had been heard from the pit, but as soon as the fire burned out, I felt sure Daddy would pull those men out.

When I got home from school Momma wasn't there and the truck was missing. I made myself a peanut butter sandwich and washed it down with RC. I wasn't usually so hungry after school, but we'd had meat loaf and I could live without it. I ate a couple of Oreos, too, from the inside out. My books were stacked on the table, like always, to wait for Sunday night. But for some reason I flipped open my math book as I idly licked a cream center. And there, written in Gold-Bug, was a message: 988;985;;48418).

My translation didn't take more than forty seconds: *Meet me at the hoes.*

I set off up the alley, in spite of my promise to Daddy. It was important business if Betty had used Gold-Bug; funny how she'd forgotten the *l* in *holes.* I could be back home before Momma if I lucked out.

Old jack-o'-lanterns topped garbage cans in the alley. So far the dirty boys hadn't come along and smashed them. But a couple of the pumpkins looked the worse for wear; they'd met direct hits. One had been gashed through its face. An open scar zig-zagged from the corner of an eye to its teeth. It had had excellent teeth, too, the hardest part to carve, in my opinion. Somehow, no matter how careful I was, I'd manage to cut through at least one of the fierce-looking teeth I'd drawn and turn out a jack-o'-lantern smiling a lopsided, snaggle-toothed, stupid grin, when it should have been scary.

At the top of the alley I turned and looked back, out to the mountains, which seemed closer than usual, like they leaned in on the town. The clear air singled out each tree; each rock was turned into a white flashing mound. It's hard to describe what colors look like through pure fall air — not bleached out by sunshine or pumped up with rainy shadows. The reds of the leaves jumped out, the golden browns laced the hillsides with depth, the already empty limbs etched into the background against shades of burnt orange and yellow. I stood there held by that vision, thinking how I'd like to be able to fold back the mountains, peel them easily as bananas, even if they were so golden, fold them back and fly out so I could see the stars, all of them for once, from horizon to horizon.

I drew away and up the hill past the tanks on my way to the holes, where Betty would be waiting. We hadn't held a meeting since I'd first told her about the spy.

I edged around the ledge just before the holes, sure that I'd see Betty sitting on the edge of the first hole, dangling her feet into it impatiently. But when I stepped out where I could see, both holes lay bare in front of me.

I called, "Where are you?"

At that same moment someone wrenched my arm behind my back and pulled my hand up between my shoulder blades so sharply that I cried out, "Stop!" Another hand clamped over my mouth and nose, mashed my lips hard against my teeth. All I could do was kick as I was raised a foot into the air by my arm and head, tasting my own blood. A sharp pain snapped through my wrist, through my elbow and back. My shoulders felt ripped in two, flung back toward my hand.

I wanted it to be Michael Dale, as I struggled in the air. A rushing, like water, pulsed inside my temples. If the hand didn't let go of my mouth, I would suffocate. I knew that the black circles would bounce toward me and then I would fall into the darkness, only this time no one would be there to make sure I woke up. I stopped kicking. My nose poked out between a finger and thumb. I took a breath that couldn't fill my lungs but kept me from passing out.

I kicked again, more desperately, and the hand clamped down like a trap on my nose and mouth. Sweat broke over my forehead; I could feel it drip down my side from beneath my wedged arm. I was drowning, and I meant to take him with me. I kicked and clawed with my free hand, but I couldn't see his face. I whirled him around but couldn't free myself. We were twined double stars, tied to each other by mysterious gravity. My life depended on pulling free.

"Now, I'm going to let go of your mouth and you're going to be very quiet and still."

Slowly he unfurled his fingers. The pressure seemed to ease up on my arm, and he jerked me around. I could count the pits in his face. I shut my eyes and he shook me by my shoulders, then clenched them, holding my face close to his. I was the varmint for his soup. He would not let me go.

"There, now. Let's have our little talk."

I said nothing.

"All you have to do is tell your daddy about our chat this afternoon. You can do that. You're a smart girl."

He laughed his kind of *ha-ha*, which sounded just like the words were written out on a page of comics. Then he stopped cold.

"You just tell your daddy to keep his nose out of the book."

"I'm not going to tell him anything for you," I said.

"We'll see about that."

His eyes flashed, then practically disappeared into their sockets; he let one of my shoulders go and I twisted to free myself, but in a second my arm was twisted backward like before, only this time it snapped like an overwound main spring. The zip of the cracking bone echoed in my ears as I was thrown head first into the deepest hole. Now it seemed like I'd dug my own grave. Through the dark whizzing circles that were finally closing, I thought I saw the shadow straighten up his tie as he towered over me.

The world made whorls of pain around me, circling outward from my arm. I flailed around at the bottom of the hole; I had to see my wound. With a quick movement I doubled over as nausea hit me fast and my arm tumbled like a clipped wing. When I saw the white bone through the torn skin, I passed out; a memory was replaying: a tiny bird, still down-covered, flies into the plate glass of the Rexall while I'm having a milkshake. Such a loud thud against the glass, more like a bumper crumpling than a bird. The glass shudders. I run to the window, look down. Fluffy red down, feathered by the breeze — the young bird draws small circles in the air with its feet; its head lies limp, skewed to one side. My hands, stiff, stay frozen at my sides.

I wake after what could have been years. All I can smell is earth and decaying leaves. I've swallowed blood. The walls of this hole rise around me, a layering of dirt, down to red clay, down to rock, down to fossil, where I am kept, swollen and numb. I can count the layers of my hole and everything is clear:

I can see my daddy, a union man by birth, with all the other black-faced miners — their bones support the rest of the soil. The only bones beneath these are their wives'. I can see the union and the company on top of them, in the same layer, holding hands. Then the factory workers and the sellers and the mailmen and the small farmers and businessmen. On top of all these layers, pressed between the top and the lower ones, are the mayor and the sheriff. Above them, pressing with all of their weight, are the operators, the owners of the pits, and the bankers and lawyers and doctors who help them stay on top. I am buried beneath them all. I have found the black hole. The darkness circles me again, like a vulture.

In my darkness I hear a noise like the buzzing of an angry hive of bees. In the leaves beside me something black lies frightened and menacing. I have awakened it, tossing around in its bed. It coils tightly, hisses, and rattles its tail, the black spring of its body welling up. *If a snake should bite you, you must kill the snake yourself, carve out its heart and swallow it whole.*

Leaves shower us. Away from the cold wind, the earth feels warm, a constant fifty-five degrees. I know that my mind is divided and weak. Part of me belongs to the shadow.

17

The Breaks

It's funny how before my arm got broken, I used to wish I'd break something so I could have a cast and collect autographs. Now I wished I could be just normal again, and that everyone would ignore me like they used to. But one good thing was that maybe the funny power had left my hands because of the break. Maybe when the cast finally got cut off I'd really be back to my old self. It made me feel lost, in a way, though, so I tried to put it out of my mind. One of my first thoughts when I woke up in the hospital was that I probably should stop wishing for glasses, because I might get them, and then, chances were, I wouldn't want them anymore. I couldn't even move my left arm, and my collarbone was broken, too, on the same side. It hurt pretty bad, but not as much as the doctors seemed to think. They had my arm stuck up in the air like I was terminal. When you're in the hospital you're usually so bored that you're happy to see anyone who comes into your room, even if they're bringing you a vial of poison painkillers that'll knock your socks off right before you turn into a zombie. While I was taking their pills I couldn't tell the past from the future. Up from down was immaterial.

Dr. Grayson was real nice to me. He explained everything to Momma and Daddy and told me not to worry, because my arm would be good as new after a while. "Young bones knit in a snap," Dr. Grayson said and cleared his throat.

When I first saw Daddy he was staring down into my face, so sad-looking that I thought maybe I had died, so I smiled at him and watched his eyes get wet.

Betty came to visit me at the hospital and brought a Zero bar I didn't feel up to eating. Every time I'd wake up I'd have to see that Zero lying there and wonder when some candy striper was going to stick it in her pocket. The day I finally could eat it, it tasted better than I'd remembered. After about two weeks I went back to school, but I didn't have to ride the bus anymore. Momma drove me in the truck. My right arm was fine — I could write and all. "What a lucky break!" Mrs. Harper said without the slightest notion of irony. I never realized how much the left arm helps the right when it's trying to write until I had to do it with only one hand. The paper would slip and slide all over my desk. I couldn't write a straight sentence to save myself. Betty worked out a system of weighing down the corner of my paper with a dictionary. I tried not to let my left hand know what my right hand was doing.

When Mrs. Harper finally announced the winners of the poetry contest, it wasn't anyone in our class. I still think mine would have won, especially after Betty added the title. Something else I missed while I was in the hospital was that the men who had been trapped in the mine didn't make it out alive.

"Dorie, are you awake, sweetheart?"

It was Daddy. I opened my eyes.

"You have to tell me now what happened. You've been hurt bad, but you're going to be all right."

"I fell into the hole. I already told you."

"I don't care if you went out of the yard when you shouldn't. I just need to know what really happened up there. Nobody nearly wrings an arm off falling into a hole full of leaves. I don't care what you said before. Right now I'm asking you for the truth."

I looked up into his weary face. He seemed so tired, but his voice sounded patient.

"I wasn't lying — exactly."

"I don't care if you were. Please, I've got to know what happened. A lot of things are going on that you're too young to understand."

"You mean about the men getting killed in the mine?"

"Yes. That's part of it."

"Mr. McGee?"

Daddy took my good hand and looked at my cast. "You're collecting a load of autographs on that."

"You want to sign?"

"But I'm not a celebrity like these folks here."

"Daddy, I did fall into the hole. But not exactly like I said."

"Well?"

"The shadow was there. He pushed me. But I told him I wasn't going to tell you. I wasn't scared of him, Daddy."

"What did he tell you to tell me?"

"He said you'd better stay out of . . . of the book, or something like that. Then he pushed me."

"Are you sure he said 'the book'?"

"I think so. What does it mean?"

"Just a record book that the fire boss keeps. He checks between shifts to make sure the mine's safe."

"I'm sorry I lied."

"You're very brave, you know that?"

Daddy turned to leave. I could see the muscles and the ribs beneath his blue work shirt. He seemed thinner; the back of his shirt sent waves of wrinkles up between his shoulder blades that I'd never noticed before.

"Daddy?"

He looked back at me.

"Be careful," I said.

"Don't you worry, crocodile."

"If we can just get through to headquarters," Daddy was telling Momma, "then we might get some backing. They just can't keep on saying the mine's as safe as possible, after this."

I sat on the couch, trying to tie my shoes with one hand. I was holding down one shoestring with my free foot and grasping the other string in my good hand, pulling the laces taut by adjusting the foot between them. It would work if the string stopped slipping out from under my heel.

"So there's going to be a strike?" Momma set her coffee firmly on the table.

"Not until we get some assurance. The men are scared. Scabs'll come rolling in. Without UMW backing, there's not much point."

"Maybe the company's right." Momma shook her head as she said it, though. The remnant of her home perm left her hair lying against the edge of her housecoat like limp dishrags.

Now, I thought, if I can just tie a knot and pull this string tight. Why couldn't they make shoes that snapped?

"They're sitting pretty. Hell, they've got enough equipment running in there that's been 'nonpermissible' for fifteen years to choke a horse, but it's still *legal*. So there you go. It's been rebuilt until it's so hot, you wouldn't believe it if you saw it. I saw an electric cord snap up and down like a python one day, hissing."

"Doesn't anyone care anymore about the men?" Momma asked.

"It's not even classified as a 'major' until five men get blown to bits at the same time. Three men — that's small potatoes."

There, I had the knot. Now for the bow.

"Somebody's got to care." Momma bent over her coffee.

"Oh, they care whether or not the mine stays productive. We've been working like hounds to make up for the three-day shutdown after the explosion. Roof's caved in. They just move us to another section and leave it. They post little 'danger' signs over that entrance. Willis'll open it all as soon as he can. Every few hours they take a reading and claim the gas is diminished to safe levels, but I haven't seen Willis go down. It's the dusting that caused the blow. I bet we haven't dusted with limestone in a year — takes too long, costs too much. The union still gets its forty cents a ton."

"But that's for the Welfare and Retirement Fund."

"So they say. All I know is we've got to make a judgment before long."

"What about us? How're we going to survive a long strike? Dorie's done got her arm broke. What makes you think they're going to stop there? Anyone who'd break a child's arm. I never thought I'd see the day come, but I wish you'd just walk out of there and find some other work."

"I know it's my fault. But I can't quit."

"I ain't blaming you, Lord knows. I just can't go on wondering what's next, who's going to get hurt."

"I'm not going to get hurt."

Daddy reached over the table and squeezed Momma's hand around the handle of her cup. Then he placed a hand briefly on her shoulder when he stood up. She stared into her coffee. His touching her made the situation seem even graver.

"You ready for school, Dorie?" Daddy asked.

"Yeah, if I can get my damn shoes tied."

Daddy's eyes popped and then he smiled. Momma still didn't say anything. She hadn't called me a smart aleck once since my arm. Every so often she'd ask me, "How's your arm, Dorie Ann?" One night at the hospital I woke up and thought I saw her standing over me like an angel. I guess I'll never understand my momma.

"Here, let me help you out." He bent to the task.

"Why aren't you at work?" I asked.

"I took a day off."

"Why?"

"Don't you think I deserve a day off once in a blue moon?"

"Sure," I said. "You don't have to take my head off."

"Watch your mouth!" Momma said. She must have thought I was nearly recovered.

The day Tina and her mother moved out it rained and rained. I talked to Tina about how she'd like it down at Raven. They were going to live with Tina's grandparents, because their trailer got repossessed; somebody was coming the next day to tow it down to Grundy. Mrs. McGee just stood there, trembling in the rain. "Shit," she kept mumbling under her breath. "Shit, damn," she kept repeating, and tears rolled down her face. Momma gave her some coffee and Kleenex while Daddy finished the packing. "I don't think it's safe for her to drive that child,"

Momma said. "But what can we do?" Daddy asked. Tina left me her Hula Hoop, because it wouldn't fit in. I wonder how she thought I was going to use it, with my arm hard as a brick.

I'd never seen such an ugly spot as what was left once the McGees' trailer was gone. The spot looked like a crater, so dark, like a person could fall into it. Black ground, like the center of the church where it burned down.

I was starting to itch under the cast, which Betty said was a good sign. But how would she know? She'd never broken her arm. It felt pretty rotten. Half of my autographs were already rubbing off, and the white plaster had turned sort of gray. Momma said my cast was the nastiest thing she'd ever seen and that she might just cut it off herself. My arm was slung at an odd angle, out to the side. It was hard to get through doors.

At first Betty didn't believe me when I told her what had really happened that day at the holes. Then she said it was her fault for having lost her map.

While I was still in the hospital Nixon won and Humphrey lost, just like Betty had predicted. At least it was close. Betty told me the results and waited for a reaction. She still wanted me to tell her who I'd voted for in our mock election so she could officially lord it over me for picking a loser. But what difference did it make after all? If a person couldn't tell the owners from the union leaders, then what difference did it make anymore who got elected? I didn't say that to Betty, though, because she wouldn't have understood it. My injury was playing right into her future plans. Betty appointed herself my doctor. She'd pumped her daddy about broken bones and was full of all the information anyone would ever want to know about how bones broke and how bones healed and how long it took and every single thing that could go wrong in the process. My x-rays were classics, she assured me.

"If they hadn't found you when they did," Betty told me one day in the lunch room, "you'd have died of shock. If you hadn't bled to death first."

That's the kind of remark I had to put up with because she was nice enough to stand in line with me and carry my tray.

Betty opened my milk carton and slid the straw in.

"Thanks," I said.

"Did I tell you Barbara's got a new boyfriend?"

"What happened to Sid?"

"He got well."

"Oh." I sampled my hamburger. I could lift it with one hand. For once I was glad our school served the smallest hamburgers on the planet.

"It turned out he was a fast healer." Betty scratched quickly at her leg beneath the table and pulled up her knee sock.

"What's his name?"

"Who? Oh, Pudge or Pooge or something. I don't like him, but he's got a convertible."

"What kind?"

"An orange one."

Some kid walked between our table and the next and managed to shove my cast. I made a face and said, "Ouch!"

"Sorry," he said. "Why don't you keep your arms to yourself next time?"

"Her arm's *broken,* stupid," Betty said.

"Sor-ry," he said.

"Brother," Betty said. "Some people. Did I tell you Barbara's decided not to write her novel?"

"How come?"

"She says that writing's too isolating. Pooge is a drummer in a band. Barbara wants to be a singer. But she's terrible."

Betty found an apple in her lunch box. She polished it on her skirt before she took a bite. "You want these?" She lifted up a bag of ginger snaps her mother had made.

I shook the bag and a cookie fell out. I don't think that cookie had a teaspoon of sugar in it.

"Pop's moving out," Betty said.

"Oh, I'm sorry," I said. I swallowed the ginger snap and washed it down with milk.

"Those are the breaks. He's buying a house at Cedar Run."

"He's staying here?"

"If he's buying a house, I guess so. I'm going to have a room there. He said I could pick out any kind of wallpaper I want."

"That's neat!" I said, a bit too enthusiastically. "But what do you need with another room?"

"So I can visit him."

"But if he's staying in town, why can't he live with you?"

"He's not going to anymore."

"Why?"

"I don't know! I shouldn't have told you anyway."

"Are they getting a divorce?"

"Not yet. Maybe they'll get back together, if I don't mess it up."

"What does Barbara think?"

"She says they're being childish, and she wants to go to boarding school."

"What's that?"

"Don't you know *anything?*"

"I just asked a question."

"Just don't tell anyone about this."

"I won't. But what's boarding school?"

"I don't know what it is. So just shut up, okay?"

18

Doors

Just past November, over in West Virginia, a mine disaster shook through that made Poorwater's explosion look like nothing. An elevator shot up into the sky like a fountain, followed by a plume of flame two hundred feet high. Seventy-eight miners got incinerated in that mine. They couldn't even get down there to pull out the remains. I'd never seen Daddy so fired up. He kept saying, "Why won't somebody *do* something?" and calling Mr. Boyle a son of a bitch for not speaking out about safety hazards.

"He agrees with the operators — they say it's inevitable, that men have to die. Like hell, they do," he said, pacing the trailer.

"You want some coffee?" Momma asked him. "Finish that pie in your room," she told me.

"I'll just get it on the bedspread."

"Let her be, Mary. My own daddy died from black lung and never got a cent compensation."

"He got money for his leg," Momma said.

"That's not what killed him!"

I looked at Daddy as he pivoted in his tracks, like a rat in a cage, with no room to the right or left on his path between the bedroom and the kitchen stove. He worked up a sweat as he talked it out, and Momma tried to calm him.

"Nobody in this state's ever collected a red cent for black lung. I've been doing some reading on the subject. Sure, it's on the list, but not a single claim's been paid, and it's not because no one's filed. You saw what happened to Bud's family."

"They're going to do all right."

"We just stood there and watched them go!"

"Will you get off your high horse? Weren't nothing you could do. You helped them pack. Do you want this coffee now?"

"Coffee?"

"Then sit down."

"I can't sit down." He continued to pace. "I've been on my ass too long as it is."

When Daddy finally took a seat he was panting. He ran his fingers through his short dark hair several times until his big forehead stuck out. He was losing his hair at the temples. I'd never really noticed it before. I thought he was calming himself down, but then he looked me in the eye and asked a funny question. "Do you know what the *natural* death rate is for miners?"

"What's 'natural death'?" I asked.

"*Natural* death is when you just die, from old age or sickness, not from an accident. Well, it's eight times what it is for other people. Do you know what that means?"

"She doesn't know what it means, David."

"Black lung," Daddy said.

Momma poured his coffee and picked up the knife, slid it beneath a slice of apple pie. Just as she lowered it onto his plate, Daddy said, "I can't eat. I'm going over to Fred's." She dumped the pie back into the pan and licked her fingers.

Daddy went out the door without a word.

I took my plate to Momma, already busy at the sink. I stood there holding a towel, waiting for my usual part. She let the scalding tap water pound the detergent into a mound of steaming bubbles before slipping the dishes into the soap.

"What's eating him?" I asked.

"He's got a right to be upset. Your daddy's a smart man, and don't you forget it. Put down that towel! How in tarnation do you think you can dry dishes with one arm?"

I couldn't win with her no matter how hard I tried. Whenever I tried to be on her side it turned out she was really on Daddy's all along. I sulked on the couch with *The Arabian Nights* until she'd stacked the dishes in the drainer; then I remembered something I had to do and jumped toward the door.

"Just where do you think you're going?"

"I promised Betty."

"It's too late."

"Come on, Momma. Barbara's going to the dance with Pooge, and I promised Betty I'd come up and help her watch."

"Half an hour — that's the limit."

Barbara answered the door. "Mom!" she shrieked when she saw me, and ran back up the stairs to her room. Betty heard her scream and came running, bounding past Barbara down the stairs. "Good," she greeted me. "You're just in time."

"What's the plan?"

"The den," Betty said. "We'll set up by the french door."

Mrs. Grayson followed. "I hope you girls aren't planning anything you'll regret."

"Mommy, we just want to watch," Betty said. "We won't even come out, I promise."

"How would you feel if it were your date?"

"Sick to my stomach," I said.

Mrs. Grayson shot me her look.

"But Mommy," Betty said, "we're not going to *do* a thing."

"You and Dorie stay right in here. Don't move a muscle and don't make a sound. Barbara's nervous about her dress."

"Barbara's a bitch," Betty whispered the second Mrs. Grayson turned her back.

Wheels screeched to a halt; we flew to the french door and pulled back the curtains. Pooge slammed his car door and started toward the steps while we watched.

"What's that he's got on?"

"A tux. It's formal."

"He looks like his shoes hurt him," I said. He was hobbling toward the front door. When the bell rang, we switched our attention inside. Barbara came down the stairs, hair flying, in her new minidress and high heels. She invited him in.

"Wow!" Pooge said. "You're looking cool tonight. Give me a kiss?"

"Pooge," Barbara cooed.

"Hello." Mrs. Grayson interrupted the smooch. "You both look so nice I thought I'd take a few pictures."

"Mom," Barbara said wearily and looked to Pooge for sympathy. Her long blond hair divided her face in half, almost covering one eye. The other side she flipped behind her ear.

"It won't take but a minute. I think the living room would make a nice background."

Since the living room was between the foyer and the den, we were in luck. Barbara plopped into the wing chair, flipping her hair. Pooge stood behind her, grinning like an ax murderer. His hair grew down over his collar. Little Beatle bangs sprouted along the line of his eyelashes so that he had to blink a lot to see. I could tell he thought he looked like a million bucks in that suit and bow tie.

"I'm sorry Dr. Grayson couldn't be here. He works all the time, you know."

"That's cool," Pooge said.

"He really wouldn't have missed this." Mrs. Grayson snapped the shutter as Pooge attempted to pin a corsage of black roses on Barbara's chest. She snapped another as Barbara pinned the black carnation on Pooge's lapel.

"Enjoyed meeting you, Mrs. G.," Pooge said.

"What time will you be home?"

"Ciao!" Barbara said. And they slipped out.

We posted ourselves again at the french door and watched them to the car. Pooge didn't open the door for Barbara but unlocked it from the inside. I was wondering how Willie would look in a tux and if he even knew how to dance and if he'd ever kissed a girl on the mouth before, and I was wondering where he was, as Barbara and Pooge spun out like somebody was after them.

"A real Nowhere Man," Betty said.

19

The Story of the Humpback

"I'm a blue meanie, and I'm coming to get you," Betty said, knocking on the trailer below my window one Saturday morning.

I crawled out of bed. Betty had Tiger on a leash and was dragging him around. Poor ole Tiger scrunched so low to the ground, his nose rubbed the dirt; he'd gained weight and now he looked like a winter slug.

"What's wrong with Tiger?"

"I don't know — maybe it's the leash."

"I've never seen a cat on a leash."

"It's an experiment."

"I don't think it's working, do you?"

Betty unhooked him and he waddled beneath the trailer.

"You want to go to the movies with us? It's *Yellow Submarine*," Betty said.

"Oh, I don't know."

"I've seen it twice already. It's good!"

Going to the movies was hard work in Poorwater. You had to wear the worst shoes you could find and worry the whole time whether or not some jerk would throw a Coke on your head from the balcony, or maybe something worse. If you sat in the front row you could avoid all that, but the crick might never leave your neck. My favorite movie that I'd seen was *Robinson Crusoe on Mars*. I'd sat in the front row and screamed each time the evil ship passed over Mars and made all the slaves' arms clang together so hard they couldn't pull them apart. The evil tyrants in the ship had put these metal bracelets on all the natives' wrists, and whenever they wanted to they flew over

and lasered the people with red light and made their wrists
clang together and an electrical current run through their bodies
like lightning. Finally, there was a war. I liked the chimp, too.
The movie wasn't anything like the book *Robinson Crusoe*, except
on Mars Robinson still named his helper Friday.

Whenever that evil ship returned and shot those red lasers
down, I curled my legs into the seat and screamed along with
the natives. I didn't leave my seat for popcorn, either. I didn't
like to leave my seat for anything, because there was this humpback who hung around the theater. He'd follow little girls to
the concession area and grunt behind them. One time he touched
a girl's hair. She had long curly hair hanging way down her
back. He just reached out and stroked it like you'd pet a kitten.
But she squealed and told her mother, and her mother said she
was going to call the police if the manager didn't get rid of the
humpback. But, still, the humpback was usually there at the
matinees. I felt kind of sorry for him when he touched that
girl's hair, but he scared me, too, and I wore a pony tail when
I went to the movies.

"Well, are you coming or not?"

"Thanks. But I don't think so."

"Oh, well, see you later, I guess. Tiger! Tiger! Come on,
boy. Here, kitty, kitty. Come on, will you?"

Tiger peeked out from his hiding place and observed Betty
as she continued to call his name over and over. Each time she
grabbed for his collar, he scuttled out of range. When she gave
up and went home he came right out and curled up beside my
feet.

My arm was cold in the air even though the sun was shining.
Ever since the cast had come off it'd felt like someone else's
arm, shriveled, naked, and pale-looking. About the only thing
I could do with it was stroke Tiger. Dr. Grayson told me I
had to be extra careful so I wouldn't break it again while it
was still "vulnerable." He told me to learn how to juggle. "Great
exercise for building coordination — amaze your friends, too."

I probably should have gone to the movies. The wind wafted, ruffled Tiger's fur, sent a cold wave onto my face. I shivered, starting with my arm. I went inside and finished the story of the humpback in *The Arabian Nights*. It was one of the longest I'd read, but it had a happy ending. I had to go back and reread the beginning, so many stories had come between the start of the humpback's tale and its ending. It all began with a tailor and his wife who invited this humpback in for dinner so they could laugh at him. They succeeded in having him choke on a fish bone. Thinking they'd killed him, they bundled his body in a blanket, pretended he was a sick child, and took him to a Jewish doctor.

The doctor by mistake pushed the humpback down a flight of stairs and believed he had killed him, so he carried the humpback outside his house to another house. The owner of this house thought the humpback was a robber and beat him. When he thought he'd killed his intruder, he moved the humpback to another location, outside a store, where a drunk Christian came along and also beat the humpback, before he was stopped by a Muslim, who arrested the Christian for killing the humpback.

Before the Christian could be executed, the other three men wised up and came forth — the homeowner, the doctor, and the tailor — all claiming to have killed the humpback. So before any of the men could be punished they had to tell stories. They promised that the stories they would tell would outshine the case of the humpback.

Of course their stories go on and on, like all stories do in Arabia, until someone else comes along and discovers that the old humpback isn't really dead after all, removes the fish bone from his throat, and revives him so he's healthy as a horse. All those stories on account of the death of the humpback — they were just about to bury him and build a monument in honor of all the good fiction his death had brought about for the entertainment of the king — and it turns out this humpback isn't even dead! When I found the tale of the humpback, I was about halfway through the book. Whether I would ever finish it was anyone's guess.

If only Daddy could have thought up a story that night, he might not have gotten bruised ribs and a black eye. I guess he couldn't think of anything to tell but the truth.

I'm still not sure what happened, but it had something to do with that record book the fire boss kept, and Mr. McGee and the other men who died. Daddy's friend Fred got beaten up too. Sheriff Darnell found them on the side of the road next to our truck. They were taken to the hospital, bandaged, and released. For all anyone knew it was just another wreck on a winding road. "Another foot and you'd a-been down the mountainside, quicker'n a jackrabbit," Sheriff Darnell said. "Somebody can count their lucky stars tonight."

Daddy told Momma he didn't know who'd run them off the road. He couldn't point a finger at the company, since he hadn't gotten a good look at any of the men. "Could have been some lunatic, for all I know," Daddy said. But he didn't believe it. He and Fred had decided to keep their mouths shut and let it be an accident. "It's not over yet" was all Daddy would say.

Just before Christmas, the Secretary of the Interior called a National Coal Safety Conference. Daddy said it was a good sign, and about time — maybe not everyone believed that explosions happened in *safe* mines. Maybe Boyle would quit taking the side of the companies. "Maybe there'll be a cold day in hell," Momma said.

"That new bureau director, O'Leary, he's got them scared," Daddy said at supper one night. "Inspectors have new orders: they've got to close the mines when they're ready to blow, not just issue a warning. And they can inspect any time they feel like it. They don't have to call ahead."

"Sounds like times are changing," Momma said.

"When they really change we'll know it without having to ask. What do you want for Christmas, Dorie?"

"Oh, I don't know."

"You'd better be letting Santa Claus know, or you'll wind up with switches and coal in your sock."

"You know what I want, Daddy." I stuffed my mouth with potato.

"What's that?" Daddy asked.

I pointed to my mouth and tried to swallow.

"Well? You'd better refresh my memory."

I hesitated.

"You don't still want a bicycle, do you?" Daddy looked at Momma and cut a slice of meat loaf. "Pass your plate."

"No, thank you," I said, trying to sound nonchalant. "You can get me some juggling balls."

"Can't you juggle eggs?"

"Not yet."

"Why not try apples?" Daddy speared his meat loaf, reached for his coffee, chewed the bite, and slurped the coffee. His hand was already on the last biscuit when he asked, "Anybody care for this?"

When Daddy started working double shifts two weeks before Christmas, I figured the bicycle was on its way.

Christmas Eve we drove down into the valley to take a wreath to Granddaddy Parks's grave. We'd been doing that since we moved to Poorwater. The only thing different this year was the big dent on the driver's side of the truck. Momma crafted the wreath from hemlock and holly. Her hands always looked like she'd run them through a briar patch when she finished. Whether it snowed or not we'd be driving to the cemetery with the hand-made wreath in the back of the truck underneath a wool blanket so the wind wouldn't blow it apart.

Snow was spitting by the time we had traveled ten miles.

"Do you think it's sticking?" Momma asked.

"It's not doing much right now, but you never can tell." Daddy looked at me, knowing my wish for snow. "Have you seen any rings around the moon?" he asked thoughtfully.

"Last night," I said.

"Good possibility, then. Good sign of a deep snow."

It seemed like the minute he said it the snow sped up, bounced against the windshield, some melting on impact, but most of the flakes piling up in the spaces where the wipers couldn't reach.

"How'd Granddaddy's leg get hurt?" I asked. It was a story I didn't tire of hearing, because Daddy would supply a new detail with each telling.

"Haven't I told you that story?"

"You just said some rock fell on him, that's all."

"That's about it. He was what was called a shot-firer."

"A what?"

"That was his job — shot-firer. After the drilling, one man would go in and blast down the coal. He got paid good, but it was real dangerous work. That's why they only sent in one man to do it — in case anything went wrong. Your granddaddy was doing his job one day and the roof caved in on him when he let off a blast. It could have happened any time, any day at all."

"But you said black lung killed him."

"That's right."

Snow splattered the windshield. Daddy turned the wipers up a notch and gripped the steering wheel. We seemed to be driving deeper and deeper into memory, with the snow swirling around our truck like it could carry us off, up into the air and away. "Don't worry," Daddy said, looking past me to Momma. "I put the chains in the back, just in case."

"I'm sure glad you thought of that."

I turned the radio on.

Momma snapped it off before I could find a station. "We don't need that right now. He's got to concentrate on his driving."

"We might hear some Christmas carols," Daddy said.

"Oh, all right." Momma's shoulders relaxed.

On WMTN a choir was singing "We Three Kings" and "It Came Upon a Midnight Clear" after that. Then a banjo picked out "Here Comes Santa Claus." I liked that better than the angel choir's sticky singing.

The old cemetery sat on top of a hill. No matter that we always seemed to visit in winter, it was colder there than any other place on earth. The minute we parked the truck and walked toward the stone, the weather got worse. Snow whipped down our collars and up our sleeves. Of course I'd forgotten my gloves. The pockets of my coat seemed smaller than usual as I burrowed my hands and balled them into fists. The sleeves of my coat had grown shorter over the summer, so the wind rubbed my wrists red. Our shoes mashed the spongy new snow, leaving three sets of side-by-side footprints. Daddy carried the wreath with both hands, slipping now and then. For some reason he would wear his Sunday shoes up to the cemetery no matter what the weather. We just stood there, Momma and I, as Daddy placed the wreath against the headstone that said WILLIAM GEORGE PARKS. It was always a little creepy, seeing Willie's name there, chiseled into marble.

Daddy balanced on one knee, unmindful of the snow soaking through his pants, to adjust the wreath; he propped it back at just the right angle so it wouldn't fall over in the wind. "Happy Christmas, Daddy," he said. It didn't ever seem real to hear my daddy calling someone Daddy.

All the way back to the truck, stamping my feet before I climbed inside, riding home through the swirling snow, I kept hearing Daddy's soft voice, like a snowflake dissolving on my tongue, like a prayer, wishing my dead granddaddy a happy Christmas. And it didn't seem weird at all.

"They've been around the moon five times," Daddy called toward the kitchen. He was watching the news while we got the supper ready. Christmas Eve, Momma went all out, even if it was just the three of us. Every year Momma's family invited us down to eat with them and every year we said maybe we'd come and then just promised to see them after the new year. Momma had baked a turkey with stuffing and green beans seasoned with fatback. Dessert was supposed to be a surprise, but I'd seen it already — boiled custard, Daddy's favorite.

"I just can't believe it," Daddy said, sitting down to the table. I thought he meant the food. Momma beamed. "They're up there," he continued, "circling the moon. Think of that. The moon, and we're flying right around it."

"We're not flying anywhere," Momma said. "We're setting down to supper if I got anything to say about it."

"But oh yes we are! We're tagging along. It might as well be Dorie up there as anyone! It won't be long before there's an American flag planted right smack dab in the snoot of the old man in the moon. You think about it."

"They'll never walk on the moon," Momma said, watching Daddy carve her bird.

"You just wait and see, just wait . . . and see. Somebody's been *cooking*, I'll tell you that. This turkey's so done it carves itself."

Like the scent of turkey in the air had been a cue, a knock that could only have been Willie's shook the door before we could sample a bite of that famous bird.

"It's Willie!" Momma rose to open the door, and a gust of frigid wind and a fizzling of snow flew in with him. "We're just setting down," she said. "Here, let me have your coat. You must be frozen stiff. Get him a plate, Dorie. Set him a place. Oh, Willie" — she hugged him — "you're the answer to my prayer."

"Good to see you, son," Daddy said, getting up to shake hands. "Have a seat. Can't let this feast get cold."

"No, sir!" Willie said.

I watched Willie unload an armful of wrapped packages and place them carefully beneath the little round table our cedar tree stood on. No room for a tall tree, but at least this one wasn't silver or pink. It smelled like the outside and made the inside part of the outside, like Willie's coat, covered with snow. I still had some cuts on my hands and a tiny splinter in my thumb from helping to set the tree in the stand and hanging the ornaments. Momma had strung the lights, all different colors, shaped like unopened tulips, and I'd hooked each gold ball. I had wanted to spray some canned snow on the tips of the branches but now I was glad Daddy had talked me out of it.

"Do you like the tree?" I asked Willie.

"A masterpiece, I reckon," Willie said. "Did you decorate it yourself?"

"Momma helped."

"You two did a fine job."

"Let's eat," Daddy said and dipped green beans onto his own plate.

I don't know if Daddy was that starved or if he'd just rather eat than talk. We hardly said anything again until we were finished. Momma sat there watchdogging our plates, helping everyone but herself, especially Willie, like he might up and fly away if she didn't see to stuffing him good.

I thought we were going to communion at the high school after supper, but Momma said that with the snow she'd as soon not go out again. It also had something to do with Willie's being home to unwrap the present marked with his name that Momma never failed to place beneath the tree, like a hopeful beacon to the one she wished would make it home. I hadn't given his return much thought this Christmas, because I knew Willie wasn't supposed to come back to town. I guess even Sheriff Darnell was home eating his turkey by that time Christmas Eve; he probably wasn't interested one bit in whether or not Willie Parks was back.

Every family has its own Christmas rituals, and we'd just finished part one, supper. Now we were beginning part two, the long wait to midnight when we could open our presents, leaving only the stockings for when we woke up Christmas Day. This year, for the first time, I had presents to give that I'd picked out myself. For once Momma didn't know what Daddy and Willie were getting from me, and she hadn't had to wrap her own so she wouldn't have to pretend to be surprised by her gift. It was fun back when I believed in Santa Claus wholeheartedly, but buying presents for other people wasn't bad either.

I was dying to know where Willie had been all this time and what he'd been up to, but no one asked him, so I focused my curiosity on the boxes he'd placed beneath the tree. We passed the hours to midnight reminiscing about our Christmases past, and how Momma and Daddy used to spend Christmas when they were little, up in the hollers, without much hope of getting anything. Daddy told how, when he was thirteen and the war was on, the first Christmas Train had come through the mountains, dropping free toys and dolls and candy canes behind it on the tracks.

"I felt lucky to get an orange, and that's the truth," Momma said.

"Is that *all?*" I asked.

"A stocking full of candy and nuts, and a Florida orange at the bottom. We didn't get oranges in the stores all year round back then, so it was a treat. We'd cut a hole in the top and suck out all the juice first."

The hours passed and finally it was time for the gifts. Any other midnight I would have been asleep, or sleepy, but never on Christmas Eve.

Daddy glanced at his watch, the official timepiece of Christmas. "Merry Christmas, everyone!"

"Merry Christmas," we echoed.

"I feel like it's really Christmas now." Momma looked at Willie.

Daddy ducked into the kitchen to mix up his special eggnog while we stacked the packages before each other's chairs.

"Put a lot of nutmeg on mine," I called.

Daddy emptied the last from a jar of something that my other granddaddy had sent into Momma's and Willie's and his glasses. I had my eggnog straight, Daddy said, and he didn't spare the nutmeg.

I watched Daddy and Willie open their ties from me, and they really seemed to like them. Momma said she liked her perfume, too. It was White Shoulders, from the Rexall. Willie gave Momma a robe and Daddy a wool shirt and me a snow coat. When I opened the coat, Momma said, "Willie! You spent too much!" Willie didn't say much of anything. It sure was a neat coat, and it fit. I got some red socks and new blue jeans and a sweater and shoes. Willie and I both got underwear.

I modeled all my new clothes and tried to forget about the bicycle with butterfly handlebars and a banana seat. I wasn't going to say anything about it, ever again. I still had my stocking to open in the morning. And Momma was happy — Willie was home.

The Fall of Law and Order, 1968

I'll never know exactly what happened the night of the wreck. But I have seen it in my mind a thousand and one times. It marked the beginning of the worst for my daddy.

He drives to Fred's house, his foot heavy on the gas. He thinks he'll only talk with Fred; then he might feel better. Fred can always make sense. More than 120,000 men dead, he thinks, an average of a hundred a month for a century. A lot of accidents, so many that it seems futile to be as upset as he is by a few more. Just a few more accidents, a few more men. But somewhere else, he thinks, not here. He can line up all of these dead men in the back of his mind and feel as if he recognizes their faces, so much the same, black crow's feet around their eyes. In the front of the line-up stands his own daddy, a number not even included among the 120,000, because he died from black lung, not in an accident underground. The line lengthens — string on all the victims of black and brown lung, like unpolished pearls, he thinks.

Fred's porch light burns. David knocks several times, banging the screen door into its frame, before Fred appears, sees him, ducks his tall head through the doorway, and asks him to have a seat on the porch. It is chilly, but the look in David's eyes has made Fred hesitate.

"Thank you," David says, "but I won't stay long. I'm going up to check on the cat eye, and I thought maybe you'd want to come along."

"I'll get my jacket." Fred pops inside and reappears, wearing his old brown corduroy jacket. He snaps off the porch light, as if it has been on only waiting for David to arrive.

They do not need to talk it over; they are going to the mine to learn whatever they can learn. For weeks they've talked it out, and now, without warning, they are headed up there. Fred knows the fire boss on the cat-eye shift and figures he'll look the other way. And if he will not, it is past time anyway.

There is a plan. Fred will ask Hardy outside for a smoke, get him to telling his jokes. David will slip into the office, take a good look at that record book. Then they will know. It is as if David has already seen the erasure marks along the ruled line on the day McGee died. He thinks he knows what he will find: a scratched-out number or a torn-out page, an erasure smudge beneath a new number. The form it takes is the last thing that matters. The meaning will be the same in every case: that the owners knew the air was bad, that the "braddishes," as the old men say, could not carry enough oxygen to mix out the fatal gas rising invisibly from the rock, and that the owners knew the shaft was not safe.

But the fire bosses take their readings like clockwork before and after each shift and copy down the numbers. Part of the story will be written in that book.

When David and Fred arrive at the mine, a car pulls up beside them. Without thinking, they jump out of the truck, slam the doors, and start toward the opening of the mine.

"What you boys looking for?" a voice calls from behind them.

They turn to see only a dark shape and the flare of a cigarette. They do not recognize the shadow.

"We're just stopping by to see a friend of mine," Fred answers. "Who in the heck are you? Like to made me jump a mile, sneaking up like that."

"I'm very sorry," the voice says. "And I think you had better get back in your truck and go on home."

"Come on," David says, reading something in the honeyed voice he does not trust. "Fred, let's go."

"Who is this guy, anyway?" Fred says.

"None of your business," the voice returns.

As they turn slowly back to the truck, the figure recedes like water. They hear his car door slam before they shut their own. Their lights illuminate a bare rock wall just beyond the truck's nose. David backs around and grinds into first. The road from the mine twists and hairpins, one of the steepest in the county of hundreds of back roads that wind, with ravines on one side and blasted rock on the other. Halfway down the mountainside a pair of brights blares in their rearview mirror.

"Some son of a bitch is tailgating us," David says.

Fred turns to try to get a look at the driver. "Too dark to make out," he says. "Those damn lights."

"I'm not going any faster. He'll just have to hold his horses or pass."

"Make him pass — it's probably some fool teenager drunk as a skunk. If he barrels into us, it'll be his funeral."

"He's signaling to pass," David says.

In a few seconds the headlights vanish from the mirror, lost in the brief blind spot between the truck's bumper and side. Then they feel the bash that rams Fred into the passenger door, whips his head back. David struggles to keep the front wheels on the road. Another sharp jar sends them off the road, onto loose gravel. They spin as if on ice.

When the truck stops, it is clinging like a fly to the soft shoulder. Gravel still sputters into the ravine just beyond.

All they can hear is a whoosh of air; all they have seen is a sudden blinding light. The shadow disappears, and the night rushes in.

20

The Red Bird

I kept remembering what the astronauts had said about the earth, how it was an oasis in space, blue water, white clouds, brown land whirling, but mostly blue, an incredible blue, marbled gazing ball. They could see the earth all at once, at least one side of it, the way we always saw the moon until they went around the dark side. For half an hour the astronauts were all alone, circling the dark side of the moon, drinking Tang, with Houston listening in to nothing, or only to static left behind the Big Bang, waiting for the voices of the astronauts to return, to bounce down again. It seemed like all those astronauts found was a gray moon, gray matter, dust, rocks. If the moon were an ordinary piece of land down here, no one would want it.

It's strange how full of light the moon seems from the earth, but up close it's empty and lonely, a big zero drifting along with us through space. It was enough to make you homesick for a place you'd never left, just looking up at the moon and knowing it wasn't all it seemed.

I still wanted to be an astronaut, but I set my sights higher than the moon — someplace beautiful and green. Or red. Maybe by the time I got out and walked around on it, the moon would look different. Or maybe I'd go to Mars instead. See what kind of no-good those tyrants were up to.

On Christmas Day, in the late afternoon, after opening my stocking and after we'd had our dinner, I walked up to see how Santa had done by Betty. She met me at the door and said that Barbara had the Hong Kong flu, and I could come in at my own risk.

I stepped into the foyer in my new coat. Even Betty admired

it when she hung it up. I could hear music blaring from Barbara's room.

"She's been in there since ten A.M., playing the white album over and over," Betty said. "If I hear 'Blackbird' one more time, I'll puke."

I pulled off my rubber boots and followed Betty to the den, where her presents were stashed.

Betty liked games and she'd gotten a pile of them, card games I'd never heard of and some board games. She got a game called Operation, where you took a pair of tweezers and tried to extract bones and organs without making a buzzer go off. Betty thought if she really stuck with Operation it would improve her coordination for real live brain surgery. She also got the last of her Little Women set, Meg, and a bunch of new clothes.

"I haven't gotten Pop's yet. We're supposed to go over there tonight and open what he's got us, if Barbara feels like it. I might have to go alone. Mommy said she'd wait in the car for me, but it'd be a lot better if Barbara could drive us."

"Willie's home," I said. As soon as I said it I thought better and added, "Don't tell anyone. He could get in big trouble. He's not supposed to be here."

Betty just looked at me like I was a fool to think I had to ask for her silence.

"Have you been down the hill yet?" I changed the subject.

Snow covered the trees and the sidewalk and the road. It was cloudy, so it wasn't melting either. I didn't have a sled, so I hadn't been down the hill. We could both fit on Betty's without any trouble, but she had to go to her daddy's house, so she wasn't interested in getting out her sled just for an hour or so. I thought she might let me borrow it, but I guess she didn't think about it, and I didn't ask.

When I got tired of Operation, with that horrible buzzer, I left Betty's and walked up the sidewalk to the top of the hill just to see if anyone was out. The cold stung my nose and made my lungs ache if I breathed in very deep. I got to the top of the Graysons' street, crunching a path through the crusty snow, and looked down the other side of the hill. Only three sleds, all the way at the bottom. It must have been pretty slick, because they'd made it way to the corner where the church used to be. The sledders made tiny blurs of color struggling to climb back up.

Tonight there'd probably be a fire at the top of the hill, and the teenagers would escape from their families to gather here. No cars would be out to mess up the party; it'd be way too slick when the sun went down. The wind was picking up already — that would make the bonfire seem better than ever. Betty and I usually kicked through the remnants of the fire the next morning. The parties happened too late for us. I guess when we got to be in high school we would build the fire ourselves and it wouldn't be so mysterious anymore.

I started down the hill, trying not to fall and break my neck. The few tracks the sleds had left had only packed down the snow. I slid down one of their runs until I met two sledders trudging back up — a couple of high school jerks with a kid I recognized as Belinda. She was sitting on the sled, being pulled back to the top of the hill like a queen. She didn't speak. One of the boys, probably her brother, told me I'd better not walk down the middle of the hill because they were coming through again just as soon as they made it to the top. I trekked over to where the sidewalk usually was and took giant steps up to midcalf until their sled whooshed by. My hands were red, my arm ached, and I'd gotten some snow inside my boots.

I stood across the street from the corner where the church had been, and I just looked into the mess of charred bricks. Snow covered the stacks of rubble, changing them into weird sculptures. What was left of our church could have been a bombed-out city after World War II — blown-out windows, just the sills in place. The wind had pitched the snow over to one side and made the pitted sanctuary appear lopsided, like it might sink.

In the limbs of the big oak, still standing in the back yard of

the church, I could make out a pair of cardinals, a bright male
and an orangey female. There's nothing more startling than cardinals against a background of snow, red on white. The birds
stand out like drops of blood. I stood still, my hands warm in
my new fur-lined pockets, and studied them as they perched,
feathers puffed against the cold afternoon air. I remembered that
cardinals mate for life. Those birds are married like Momma
and Daddy, I thought. A song came back to me. I'll never understand how suddenly the past can overcome the present, as easily
as an envelope conceals a letter, and an old song can overtake
you, a song from memory. I watched the red birds on the snow-
lined limbs and listened to the pure voice of my grandma singing
"Red River Valley" as she leaned over my crib: "Come and sit
by my side if you love me. Do not hasten to bid me adieu. But
remember the Red River Valley, and the one that has loved
you so true."

The grocery store, a block down on the opposite corner, always
tossed out its stale bread for the birds. Watching those cardinals
reminded me, so after a while I walked on down the street past
the church to the parking lot to see if any birds were out.

I pounded my way through the snow, warming up a little
the faster I walked. The more I swung my arms, shaking the
blood to my fingertips, the more I could feel them. My new
coat was water-repellent, a shiny red, lined with red fur. I drew
up the hood and tied it around my face. Without turning my
head and pushing back the sides of the hood, I couldn't see
clearly in any direction except straight ahead.

Sure enough, the birds were there, a bunch of old black birds,
scattered out across the parking lot, pecking crumbs off the snow.
I could have walked right into the middle of them. They paid
about as much attention to me as if I'd been a scarecrow. I
wished I had something to feed the birds to make them notice
me. Daddy said I'd never make a good bird watcher because I
got too excited when I saw one. I'd throw my hands into the

air and point at them as they flew away. But these birds couldn't care less. I could have shot and dropped one without upsetting the bird beside it.

Inside a holiday, everyone finds their own time. For Momma I think it was the minute after the knock came on the door and she knew Willie had made it home. Her face tensed and relaxed at the same time, and opened, almost like a child's. For Daddy it was the trip to the cemetery, when he bent and straightened the wreath on his daddy's grave, with Momma and me standing quietly by. Willie's Christmas seemed harder to pinpoint — maybe it was the taste of the turkey one minute, or a sip of Daddy's eggnog, or seeing the look of happy shock on Momma's face when he came in the door.

My Christmas was made up of the snowfall that the ring around the moon had promised and my solitary walk. As I stood watching those cardinals in the tree, I could feel Christmas open up inside me, bringing me in, all at once, from the cold of the afternoon.

21

The Revelations

Christmas night Barbara stayed in bed with the flu, the arm of her new record player worn hot from constantly replaying "Blackbird." Betty said her mother had agreed to drive her over to Cedar Run to see Dr. Grayson; then she sat out in the freezing car. After half an hour Betty heard the car horn blow. Mrs. Grayson was stuck in a ditch and ended up having to come inside after all to wait for the wrecker. While the wrecker saw to other disasters, Dr. Grayson drank four dry martinis and kept offering Mrs. Grayson one, but she wouldn't "give him the satisfaction." Betty said it was the worst Christmas in her life, even though she got more presents than ever before. She said that now she knew her pop might even move away and leave them altogether if he got a girlfriend.

At our house, Momma understood that home was just a way station for Willie, but she rolled out the red carpet all the same. Willie had to sleep on the sofa this time, and we had to climb over his stuff all day long. Momma had wanted to give him my room; thank God he'd had sense enough not to take it. Meanwhile it was like having an invalid in the house — because Willie never went out. He was afraid he'd be arrested, although we never discussed it. And we didn't let anyone know he was there. Willie didn't seem to care that all he could do was lie around in the trailer watching TV and eating Momma's cooking. He spent every day lost in his Bible and scribbling into a notebook like there was no tomorrow. When he wasn't stretched out asleep, he sat on the couch beneath the only decent reading light, with a pencil pushed behind one ear and the Bible spread across his knees the way Momma spread out her knitting. Hunched over the pages, very still, he'd remove the pencil from behind his ear and write several careful sentences before turning another thin page and reading on. Plates of cake and brownies and glass after glass of Coke disappeared as he studied. I thought Christmas vacation would never be over. In the morning it would be coffee in a mug, and in the afternoon tea, but in between it was Coke after Coke, a constant ring of moisture on the old coffee table.

If I said anything above a whisper, "Hush," Momma would say, "Willie's studying."

If I asked Willie what he was reading he would answer, "The Book of Revelation."

If I asked why, he would reply, "I'm a-figuring out how close to the end times we really are."

One afternoon he continued, "I've got this theory, and if I'm right I'll be the first to ever pinpoint the exact date of the end of the world as we know it."

"Why would you want to know that?" I asked. "I mean, what good will it do just to know something like that? Could you do something about it?"

"That's the beauty of it, Dorie. That's just the reason I want to know — nobody can't *do* nothing about it."

"That's what I said."

"You see, nobody can do one thing to stop it from happening. Everything they try will only fulfill what is written here." He patted the open page. "And the more they deny it, the more they fulfill it. Like all those who told Noah he was crazy for building the ark."

"But what good will it do?"

"As soon as I'm sure I'm right about the end of the world, I'm going to start telling people. I know won't half of them listen, but I'm going to shout it from the mountaintops. They'll call me every kind of lunatic they can think of, but it won't change a thing that's written." Willie's eyes got bigger and wilder as he went on. "A few people will hear me out, though, and little by little, maybe more and more people will believe me. You see, it's just like faith in Jesus Himself: nobody can prove it; you just have to believe it or you don't. Some people, when they hear the news, will have sense enough to wake up and smell the coffee. Now do you understand?"

"You mean they'll have to believe in Jesus because it's the end of the world?"

"It goes hand in hand. You can't believe part of the Word and not all of the Word. It says here about Jesus saving us from our sins, and it says about the end of the world just as plain, if you know how to read it." He held his place in a particular passage with the eraser of his pencil. "You can't take one thing and leave the other. You got to believe it all, whole hog. But once people know for *sure* that the end is coming, and *exactly* when it's going to transpire, then they won't be able to avoid the important things any longer. They'll start seeing the signs and coming to Jesus. It's the best opportunity for saving souls this world has ever seen. Imagine! A whole world of folks on their deathbeds, willing to listen, willing to believe the truth in exchange for eternal life!" Willie remained seated but hopped several times on the cushions.

"It sounds like a trick to me."

"But Dorie, that's the way He planned it. He wrote it down that way. Don't matter that our little minds ain't big enough to understand someone smarter than us. Most people don't understand how black their soul is." Willie's face clouded over.

I thought about that story where a man hides a letter right out in the open, where no one would think to look for it. Part of what Willie was saying made sense, but part of it didn't add up. The main problem I kept turning over in my mind was why God would make people so messed up in the first place. Why would He plant that tree in the garden, of all places? Why were people so bad to start out with that the first thing they would think of doing was the one thing they weren't supposed to do in all of creation? And what was so great about eternal life? I had a strange mixed-up picture of what Heaven was like. I knew that when you went to Heaven you didn't look like yourself anymore, that you were changed into an angel and got an angel body that wasn't like the real one you walked around on earth in. Or maybe it was the real body you got when you died; who could know for sure? But after you got there, however you did and being however you became, sort of still you and sort of changed, why was Heaven full of gold and riches like the Inca Indians had in Peru? Or was all that gold in the pictures just an illusion to give poor folks something to hope for, to make them think they wouldn't always be poor if they lived forever? However I thought about it, they would always *have been* poor, no matter what happened to them afterward. Even Jesus said the poor are always with us.

Willie was my brother and he almost had everything figured out. I felt proud of him even if I was suspicious at the same time.

"How long do you think it's going to take you to work it all out?"

"I can't say for sure — a week, maybe a month. I've got to check out all the possibilities before I announce it. Unless I'm convinced myself, how can I expect anyone else to believe it? It's not going to be a picnic, but I'm going to do it right. There've been too many Chicken Littles as it is, running around shouting the sky is falling, and then nothing happens. It gives us all a bad name. No, if I can't figure out the exact date, I'm not going to preach a word. But I can feel that it's time, and I know I've been appointed to look inside the book and pull out the answer." Willie turned grave. "I've been praying over this question for six months before I started to working. I wanted to be sure it wasn't just me who wanted it done, you know? Sometimes a man can fool hisself. But I'm sure now I was *called* to do this. The minute I opened the Book of Revelation, I knew I was called."

"How's Brother Saul?" It just popped out of my mouth. Now that Willie was talking, I must have thought, maybe he'll really spill the beans.

"He's gone his own way."

"You're not with him anymore?"

"We've parted ways, yes," Willie said quietly.

"How come?"

"It wasn't meant to be, that's all. There're things I have to do alone. I can't be a grown man following after someone else all my life. Do you think you could get me a Coke out of the refrigerator? I've got to get back to work on this chapter."

"Dorie, stop bothering your brother and get him a Coke," Momma chimed in. She seemed afraid that if everything wasn't just right Willie would up and leave.

But we all knew Willie would leave in his own good time, unless the sheriff got wind of him and cut his visit short. Willie came and went as it pleased him, bringing his concerns into our lives without bothering to discover any of ours. He didn't know anything about what Daddy had been going through, what I had gone through, and nothing about the deaths in the mines. He never asked. Willie turned off like a light if anyone mentioned the mines. For some reason, he'd been convinced from an early age that he was supposed to go to work in them, carry on the family tradition, or some bunk like that, even though Daddy had said he didn't want Willie digging coal, no matter what he did. I think that's why Daddy didn't ask much about what Willie was doing. As long as his son wasn't slaving in the mines, he felt that things must be rolling along smoothly.

And of course if Willie had up and become a saint, it wouldn't have surprised Momma. She'd always treated him like one. It was only a matter of time before he made his mark and the outside world understood him for the genius she'd always known he was. I think Momma was torn between wanting Willie to just stay in Poorwater and raise a nice family and wanting him to succeed at something great, far away from Poorwater. Maybe in Bristol or Bluefield or even Roanoke or Richmond. She wanted people to know that Willie was more than a high school dropout.

Willie was one of many dropouts. Some of them went to work in the mines; some left town for Detroit or Chicago factories that turned out to be worse drudgery than mining. Some of them just stayed up in the hills, doing what their daddies and granddaddies had done — scratch farming and a little moonshining. Maybe they'd raise some sheep or goats, go to work in a city factory for a season, then come back home the first chance they got to buy themselves a piece of land.

The one thing Momma was beginning to nag Willie about was getting married, something nearly everyone his age, in Momma's opinion, had already done, if they weren't maimed or ugly or off fighting in Vietnam. I didn't know enough at the time to wonder how on earth Willie had kept himself from being drafted away from God's army into Uncle Sam's.

"It's not natural," Momma said. "A man needs a wife like a dog needs a bone. You're thin as a rail. You need someone. I can't follow you around, looking after you. Ain't there someone you could ask?"

"I ain't ready, Momma."

"Sure you are. I'm not prying. I just don't want you to be alone."

"I'm never alone."

"So there is someone!" Momma brightened.

"I told you, Momma. I don't have a girlfriend. I just mean I've got work to do that maybe a man can't do if he's tied down."

"Leave him alone," Daddy said. "He's got time."

"You were married when you were his age. You had a little boy, if you ain't forgotten. It didn't hurt you none, did it?"

"Momma," Willie said, "things are different now. Not everyone gets married right away. I promise you that by the time I'm thirty-three I'll be married."

"Thirty-three!" Momma shook her head. "Did you hear that, David? He thinks he's going to find someone when he's thirty-three."

"That's not what I meant," Willie said wearily, closing his Bible.

"I heard what you said. I ain't deaf yet." Momma fell into her chair and took up her knitting.

"Mary," Daddy said, "how can he get married if he doesn't have a girlfriend?"

"That's what he *says*."

I think Momma was just curious about Willie's secret love life. She'd nag him but then seem relieved when he told her there wasn't anyone. I wasn't ever getting married, but I didn't tell her or Daddy. If I was going to be an astronaut I couldn't get into a fix where I'd have to cook and clean and have babies. Even if they let fathers go into outer space, I bet they wouldn't let a mother any closer to a spaceship than they'd let a lit blowtorch. The best thing was not to take any chances. I hoped the end of the world wasn't any time soon, either, even if postponement would mess up Willie's plans to become the Billy Graham of doom. I had a lot of things I wanted to do first. What if the end of the world came while Willie was still trying to figure out the date?

22

Question

One day in January, Willie up and left. Two days before, he took the truck for several hours in the afternoon and came home with a complete suit of new clothes for himself; not just a pair of jeans and a flannel shirt, but a real suit with matching coat and slacks. He bought a dress shirt and tie to go with it. Momma made him try on the whole outfit. Willie looked better than Pooge in his tux. Of course Momma made plans to take Willie to church on Sunday so she could show him off. Seeming to oblige her, he spent an hour polishing his old dress shoes. Then he decided he had to have a new pair and took Momma to the men's store with him that time. They brought home a pair of brown wingtips, but Willie immediately got to worrying about them.

"Does brown go with blue? I mean, is it all right if I wear brown shoes with a blue suit?"

I told him nobody was going to look at his feet while he preached.

"But I don't want to distract anyone from the Word with the wrong shoes," Willie said. I could tell it made perfect sense to him, too.

We woke up that morning and found Willie's note. He'd left after midnight, it said, on the last bus. He didn't know when he'd be back, but it wouldn't be too long this time, and he left some money on the kitchen table to help out. A crisp Mr. Hamilton was sitting on top, and just as I reached for it Momma palmed the whole stack and started thumbing through, counting.

"I was just going to count it," I said.

"I'd like to know where that boy gets his money." Momma fanned the bills like a hand of face cards.

"He probably just prays for it."

"Dorie, your mouth needs the soap worse than a dog's behind. You shouldn't make fun of Willie's calling; that's like making fun of the Lord."

"I wasn't."

"Don't tell me what you wasn't doing, because I heard you loud and clear." Momma pushed the folded bills into the pocket of her robe. "Don't tell your daddy about this."

"Why?"

Momma cocked her head to one side. "You know it'll just worry him. And he don't need any more worries. You want some hotcakes this morning?"

I wished she hadn't known me so well. I accepted the bribe and gobbled down every bite. The maple syrup pooled around the neat stacks I cut and soaked into the cakes from the bottom. Momma even melted butter to pour over the top.

"Willie used to like these," she said and sampled one.

That same afternoon, before Daddy got home, Sheriff Darnell knocked on the trailer door.

"Good afternoon, Mrs. Parks," he said when Momma answered his knock.

"Why, Sheriff Darnell, what can I do for you?" She didn't invite him in.

"I ain't going to beat around the bush, Mrs. Parks. Is that your truck sitting out there?"

"Of course it is. Paid for too." Momma backed inside and Darnell followed, pulling the door behind him.

"You want some coffee?" Momma asked.

"No, this won't take but a minute, but I'm afraid you're not going to like what I have to say."

"Why don't you just say it, then?" I asked.

"Dorie, go to your room."

"Hold on. Maybe she can help us out." Darnell got a twinkle in his runny eyes. "You love your brother, don't you?" he asked, turning his red nose in my direction.

"Of course she does. What's that got to do with our truck?"

Momma walked to the kitchen and started coffee anyway.

"Your truck matches the description of a truck that was used in a delivery of illegally produced goods. Now our witness didn't get the tag number, but the make and the color and the dent all match."

"There must be a hundred trucks like ours in this county," Momma said. "Eyewitness —"

"There's more to it. I know your boy was here over Christmas."

"Don't everybody have a right to spend Christmas with their family?"

"I'm not against that, Mrs. Parks. Matter of fact I knew he was here, and I didn't lift a finger during the holidays. My mistake. If I'd run him out then, we'd both be better off right now."

Momma pointed to our worn corduroy couch. "Willie sat right there studying his Bible every day. He didn't go out anywhere — except to buy him a suit of new clothes."

"Where'd he get the money?"

"I don't know. But he didn't steal it."

"I don't think he stole any money. I think he sold something and was paid for it. Until I find him I won't know for sure. I need you to tell me where he is, that's all. Where is he?"

Momma twisted in her chair. The percolator popped and gurgled. She pulled her sweater tighter and answered, "I don't know where he is."

"Maybe you can help me out," he asked me.

"He never tells us where he's going," I said. "Honest."

"You know the draft board would like to know where he is, too. I bet they could find him."

"We don't have no idea. I'm sorry," Momma said.

"Let me just ask you one more question." Darnell sat on the edge of his chair, dangling his hat between his legs.

"He left last night," Momma said.

"On the bus," I added. "That's what the note said."

Darnell perked up and asked to see Willie's note.

"I threw it out," Momma said. She looked at me and I got

the message better than if she'd used Western Union: Don't mention that money. I was already kicking myself for having brought up the note.

"Well, well, well." The sheriff mock-sighed, rose, and placed his hat back on his square head. "You've been very helpful. Now if you hear anything, anything at all from Willie, you'll be sure and let me know?"

"He don't write much," Momma said.

"And you be sure and call me if you find that note." He gave Momma a hard look and let himself out.

As soon as Darnell was gone I said, "What do you think he did? What's 'illegal goods'?"

"That Darnell's out to get your brother, and don't forget it."

"But what about the money?" I asked. "Where'd it come from then?"

"Just because we don't know, that's no reason to turn against your brother. Just as soon as we hear from him I'll ask him about that money, and I know there's going to be a good explanation. You just wait and see."

"Shouldn't we tell the sheriff about the money, just in case?"

"I don't want to hear nothing else about it. Forget that money, all right?"

But that's all I could think about, the money, and Willie, and if he really was on drugs like that kid Barry had said. I could still see the mean look on his face across the lunch table. "Your brother's on *drugs*." Like he could have been saying, "Your brother's a rapist and a murderous snake."

It seems impossible when there's something bad on your mind that the world keeps turning around, around and around like nothing ever happened, like each day was always the same. When you walk outside and the sun is shining and the inside of you feels caved in, it's worse than if the rain was falling on your head or the wind was racing away with your favorite hat. At least then you'd know that everything was of a piece, that everything in the world, even the wind and the weather, was against you and it wasn't your imagination, and there was nothing you could do about any of it. Just some evil fate. But the day Darnell came by the trailer was a sunny one — cold, windy, and sunny all at once. That night the stars glittered and shone, with hardly any atmosphere between us and them. If I'd had a telescope I could have seen the moons of Jupiter and counted Saturn's rings.

If I closed my eyes I could see the giant map of the United States that I'd memorized for Mrs. Harper's test. Tracing down from Virginia, through Tennessee and Kentucky, or down through North Carolina, or up by way of West Virginia, I kept wondering where on earth Willie might be. And how far he could have gotten. Could he be crossing the Atlantic by now? He probably didn't even know where he was going. I kept hoping he'd go far enough away that the sheriff and the draft board wouldn't be able to catch him, because if they did I was sure they'd put Willie in jail, and maybe Momma, too, because she'd kept that money.

Willie left without saying whether or not he'd discovered the date of the end of the world. If he'd found out, I think he would have tried it out on us first. I thought when he left it would be because he'd found conclusive evidence and was ready to set out on his preaching tour. When he bought that shiny suit I was sure he must be close to the answer.

I reached underneath my bed and pulled out my question book. I'd been thinking I was going to start it up again, but somehow I hadn't gotten around to it until now. I flipped to the last page I'd used and wrote:

203. QUESTION: The exact date of the end of the world.

A blank line beneath the question waited for the answer. Answers never seemed to take up much space when I finally found them.

The worst thing about knowing secrets is not being able to tell them. This time I knew I couldn't even tell Betty. Every time I looked at Daddy I felt guilty, so sick to my stomach no amount of sassafras tea could have eased it, and I knew I would keep feeling that way even if I told him, because I could never erase all the time that I'd known about that money and kept it a secret. I could blame Momma, but that would only make it worse. If anything happened to Daddy before I could tell him, I thought, I would never forgive myself. I kept wondering about the end of the world and how convinced Willie had been. Was that why he'd left in such a hurry? I couldn't seem to think about anything else. I even dreamed about the end of the world. It looked like a big sea of fire sloshing across the land, washing people away no matter who they were or what they said they believed. No matter how special they used to be.

One night I closed my eyes knowing that fiery sea was out there, or in there, waiting for me. I had hold of Daddy's hand. I depended on his strength, not my own. He felt so sturdy, like a tree. I was home free. Then I looked and it *was* a tree I held so tight, and Daddy was out swimming in the fire, bobbing up and down, while I knew I was empty as a hollow stump. My power dry as a bone. I pushed my fingernails into the thick bark of that tree as far as they would go without breaking. Afraid to leave my safety, I just watched him drown in the fire.

23

Every Man for Himself

The new Secretary of the Interior surprised everyone, especially everyone who had voted for the Democrats. He proposed to limit coal mining because of the safety risks. Daddy said he didn't know which side of anything he was on anymore. He'd voted Democratic all his life and now the elephants were speaking out more about mining safety than all the donkeys ever had before. Likewise, he'd always been a union man, but the union, and "that son of a bitch Boyle," seemed to want high production at any cost, just like the "damn operators" always had. "Unexamined allegiance" to any one side had turned into a bad habit. "But a man can go crazy having to keep changing day to day," Daddy said, "moving every which way the wind blows. I like to know where I stand. What it boils down to is every man for himself."

"Yeah, we're here to make someone else rich," Momma said. "Ain't that always the way? Some things don't change."

Daddy heard that a group of miners in West Virginia were organizing a Black Lung Association to push for compensation. Even though Virginia already officially listed black lung, it didn't mean anything, since no one had been able to collect. Daddy by now was urging a sympathy strike to support the West Virginia miners in February. Time for the strike neared, and the company warned that whoever walked would lose his job the same day. They said Virginia already had compensation for black lung, so there wasn't any sense to the strike. Daddy couldn't ask his friends to give up their jobs, but he said he had to do what he thought was right, no matter what the others decided.

"I'm doing it in memory of my daddy," he told Momma.

"No you're not. You're doing it to spite Mr. Willis."

Daddy looked at her like she'd cut him in two without the use of a magic trick.

"I'm not against you," Momma said. "But I think you're wrong this time. No good's going to come of it. You'll lose your job, we'll go hungry, and what will that prove? I don't know what you're thinking of anymore. Ever since Bud died you been acting like you're the only one who knows what's right. Been walking around here like you're all alone in the world. You near got yourself and Fred killed." Momma faced him, standing far enough away to look up into his tired eyes. There were dark circles under her own. "What'd that prove?"

Daddy looked back into her eyes for a second. "I thought you understood."

"How could I? You don't confide in me anymore."

"I can't go on like I always have. I've only got one choice. Can't you see?" Daddy stepped toward her, and she stepped back.

"I can see one thing," she said quietly; "your family's been the last thing on your mind."

"How can you say that? I'm thinking of you and Dorie. About Dorie's future, and the kind of life she'd have if things didn't change around here. Don't you see there's nothing here for her?"

"There's nothing here for me either," Momma mumbled.

"What?"

"You don't listen to me anymore."

"Yes I do. More than you know."

"It would have to be," Momma said. "Because it seems to me you got your mind made up — so why don't you just leave me out of it? You don't want my opinion."

Daddy left without another word. I heard the truck start, crunch over gravel, and go. If he came home that night, he was gone again before I woke up.

I knew better than to ask Momma what was going on. And I couldn't even talk it over with Betty this time. I couldn't tell her about the money or the sheriff and least of all about Daddy's trouble with the strike. I felt myself drawn back into the small circle of my family like an arrow not allowed to be released. Everyone else lived outside the circle of our problems. Betty seemed farther away day by day, especially when she told me her thoughts and worries and I couldn't reveal my own. Betty said she was glad her parents had moved into different houses, because she'd felt sick all the time, having to listen to them shout at each other. She'd close her door, crush her pillow around her ears, and still be able to hear them, one minute yelling at each other and the next minute hushing each other so the children wouldn't hear. I never knew that the Graysons had fought. Since they were getting a divorce, what Betty said had to be true, but it was still science fiction when she talked about how her mother had thrown one of her pumps at Dr. Grayson, and he'd cut his palm open on the spike heel when he tried to block her shot. When Momma and Daddy started their fighting, I was more worried about whether or not they'd get a divorce like the Graysons than I was about the subject matter.

I couldn't understand how Momma and Daddy could say those things to each other and then sleep in the same bed and get up morning after morning like nothing had happened. Momma would scramble his eggs, butter his toast. They'd sit at the breakfast table with it still pitch black outside, saying no more and no less than they usually said to each other in the morning. Neither apologized; things just rolled along. Marriage was a mystery. Sometimes I felt like I could go crazy just looking at them, not knowing from one day to the next what they were thinking about.

When something happened to Daddy, I was almost relieved; we'd been feeling the tremors long before it happened, and our worst fears were finally made real.

It was a day of spitting snow and quick bursts of furious wind that left you gasping. I walked home from the bus stop with that air burning like coals inside my lungs, trying not to breathe unless I absolutely had to. Momma had the heat turned up as far as it would go, but the cold found all the cracks and left us bundled in sweaters. "I wish we had a fireplace," Momma said. "The only way to keep warm on a day like this is just to set as close to the fire as you can get." Everything she conjured about the fireplace she'd grown up with left me feeling that much colder. I tried to read, but my hands froze holding up the book. I played at my homework until Momma said, "Why don't you make some brownies?" So I started mixing. I only needed to add water and pour the batter into an eight-inch pan. Daddy liked my brownies even if they weren't homemade from scratch. If you cooked it yourself, it was still sort of homemade, I thought.

After four o'clock Momma started looking for Daddy without saying that she was. It reminded me too much of the day Mr. McGee hadn't come home and Daddy had been so late because of it. I never thought, though, that Daddy would be the one who didn't come home.

At five-thirty we sat down to eat without him, an act of faith. Momma seemed torn between worry and anger. She pushed her food around the plate and was overly upset by my picking at my food. Before long a knock came at the door. The message was short, delivered by a man I didn't think I'd seen before, but Momma seemed to know his name. He didn't come all the way inside. Momma leaned out, holding the door open. He pressed his face close to hers, the blustery cold blew onto my face, cooled my plate of red beans and rice. He said that Daddy had been taken to the hospital, and he offered to drive us there in his car. It had been Daddy's turn to drive and his truck was still parked at the mine.

"What's wrong with him?" I asked.

"I'm not sure," Momma said.

"What happened?"

"Get your coat. Mr. Jones will take us to the hospital."

Momma had turned icy calm, soft-spoken, assured. She held herself straight; she wasn't about to cry, I could see that. It was as if the part she'd been rehearsing to play for a long time had arrived. It seemed to suit her, or to bring to the surface all of her strength. It scared me to see her in control when I felt like lightning was racing through my mind, bouncing from one dark corner to another, pointing up every terrible possibility imaginable. I was sure he would die. As impossible as it seemed, I couldn't keep it out of my mind. The short ride to the hospital could have been hours long. I felt dazed and weak. I could hardly keep my eyes open. It was as if he was already dead.

The nurses told us surgery was still in progress. We waited for the doctors. All we knew was that some rock had fallen, that he had internal injuries, that maybe his arm was hurt. I felt guilty for having thought he was dead, almost like I'd wished for it. But to learn he was still alive shocked me more than if they'd just shaken their heads when we arrived at the hospital door. I might see him again. He might live.

Waiting for his surgery to end, I could fit all the small pieces we knew about the accident into a million variations of what Daddy had suffered and what the doctors might be doing to him at that very second, at that second, and at the next. I could feel the time tick forward, from one black line to the next. When I breathed in, I imagined I was breathing for him too, making him breathe along with me. I hardly let any breath out. My chest ached. If I could hold the air inside my lungs long enough, he could use it too. Make it pass from my lungs into his blood, I prayed. The beat of my heart kept him alive, stroke after stroke. I couldn't talk or move, my mind too busy with counting breaths, with holding it inside.

How long can surgery last? I felt my heart, his heart, beat. One second the thought swept through me, along the back of my neck, that he was dead and there was nothing, nothing I could do to stop it. I waited for the doctors to emerge from the dim hallway, for them to approach with their solemn faces, and tell us, like we were in some movie, that they had done all they could but that it hadn't been enough. I waited a long minute, two minutes, five, and still no one came. I flushed the scene out of my mind for fear that I might make it come true. I might wish death on him. If not for my thoughts, he might still live. My faith must make him well.

I hadn't been to the hospital since my cast had been cut off. To be a patient in a hospital is nothing like waiting to hear about someone else. I sat there waiting as Daddy had waited for me. And Momma was here once again. The waiting room smelled like fear — stale cigarettes, cigarettes smoldering in sand, vinyl, sweat. The linoleum sparkled except for occasional dark shoe streaks, like burned rubber. Each sound echoed between the tiled walls — it was like being inside a giant bathroom. If I whispered to Momma, the words would travel clear across the room to the man who had driven us, who sat quietly by himself turning the pages of a *Life* magazine. As I looked at Mr. Jones's face, dirt-caked and streaked, the light lines around each of his eyes filled with dust, he still didn't look very old. The more I looked at him, the more he seemed to be about the same age as Willie. "Don't stare, Dorie," Momma interrupted, and I gazed down at my hands again. For a long time every grownup person had been the same age to me. Now that I was beginning to distinguish between them, I felt older, too. If Momma and Daddy had had me first, I'd be as old as Willie, I thought. Would that make him as young as me?

The minutes kept passing like days as we waited. Other people started piling in. A little boy with a cut finger. A man who'd wrecked his motorcycle walked in holding a bloody towel to the side of his head. We all waited there together, wrapped up in our own questions. A woman raced through the glass doors, looked around the room, and rushed to the man holding the towel. A nurse called the man's name and he left her to disappear down a corridor. Half an hour later he emerged with stitches around his ear. He embraced the woman and they walked out together.

"Mrs. Parks?" a voice called at last. A nurse clipped in. Momma raised her hand and answered, "Yes?"

He was in recovery with stable signs. He was sleeping and

we couldn't see him until the morning. "If he does well tonight, he'll be out of danger," she said. "Dr. Grayson will be out in a minute to talk with you."

If tonight, I thought, *if tonight, if tonight. I've got to see him. If I can just see him.* Dr. Grayson took Momma aside and told her something that made her close her mouth into a line.

Three days later I was finally allowed to visit him. The night before, I dreamed he was sitting up in bed, perfectly well, but I could tell he was worried about something. His hands rested in his lap as he leaned against the pillows. Though he was smiling, his position looked awkward. His shoulders hunched and one of his feet was stretched out toward the floor as if he'd been frozen in a game of statues. It startled me when his lips moved and words flowed out. "If we can just get through this," he said.

Momma tried to prepare me. "His face is blue and swollen. He might not recognize you, he's taking so much painkiller. You don't have to go, you know."

"I have to see him," I said, my heart fluttering, part of me hoping I might be able to do for him whatever I'd done for that blue jay, and the same part of me afraid that I might.

"Then I guess there's something else you should know." She gazed out the window. "He's lost his arm."

I could see myself walking down an endless hospital corridor, passing closed door after closed door until I found his room, the only room with an open door. I'd walk in alone, Momma waiting for me in the hall, and move near to his bed. He would open his eyes and know me no matter how bad he felt, and take my hand in his.

Or — I walk down the corridor, faces turn toward me. They know where I am going and why, and they know what I don't yet know: that he's died in the night and I'll never see him again. The panic makes me run, though I know now there is nothing I can do. I run into the open room, and his bed, empty as my hands, lies ready for another victim.

24

The Hook

Two tables held a spread of casseroles and cakes, pies, breads, baked beans, potato salad, and platters heaped high with fried chicken. The women made sure all the food was arranged from salad through dessert so the buffet would go smoothly. It was like a church potluck, except that it was happening at Hareem's Court, right in our yard. My job was to see that each of the ten eating tables had enough plastic forks and knives and napkins. Betty helped me count each item into neat stacks.

The day was shining, warm, the first spring picnic, and everyone had come just to welcome Daddy home. Momma had gone to get him. And when they drove up, the whole crowd gathered around, cheering, patting, and hugging them. I was afraid they'd hurt Daddy's arm, pushing in on him like that. I held back and watched. When he'd first jumped out of the truck he'd looked the same as always, and I'd wanted to run to him; then he turned toward me and he was different, like he'd always be from then on. I felt shy. I didn't know him anymore.

Within fifteen minutes the chairs groaned with big eaters. I filled a plate and wandered to the farthest table, set smack over the dark spot left by the McGees' trailer. The ground felt hard as rock when I brushed the soles of my school shoes over it, swinging my legs before settling. I knew people were staring at Daddy, but I felt like they stared at me more, like they could see how afraid I felt of my own daddy because he'd been hurt and changed.

I could see him through the crowd, eating chicken. He held a drumstick still and sank his teeth into the meat to saw it away from the bone. He lowered the chicken and picked up a napkin, wiped his mouth while he swallowed, then speared in a bite of beans and chewed. I caught his eye and looked away, down into the plate of food I'd hardly begun. I picked up a breast with two hands and sank my teeth into the thickest part of the white meat, then set it back on the edge of my plate. I watched my hand wrap around the fork, feeling each tendon and joint, each cramped finger bone. What hands do they seem to do alone, without connection to the rest of the body. All the things they know so well — the heft of a fork, the way to stab the beans until a line collects on each separate prong, the balancing act of knife in one hand and fork in the other, of knife cutting while fork holds the place. The more I studied my hands while they moved, the less real they became; and the more I tried to concentrate on exactly how each movement felt, the less real I became. I ought to have gone and wrapped my arms around his neck.

I looked across the table to Betty. I'd forgotten she was there. "Earth to Dorie: Come in."

I tried to smile at her joke. "I wish they'd just go home."

"Your daddy seems to like it."

It was true. I could hear his laughter rolling across the crowd like a fifty-yard pass. When he laughed, the laughter spread. "Yeah," I said, "he always liked picnics."

"Don't you?" Betty looked amazed.

"I'm just not very hungry, I guess."

"Try the chocolate cake Mommy sent. Boy, is it good." Betty stuffed a forkful into her mouth and rolled her eyes in delight. I wondered why her mother hadn't brought it herself. But she probably didn't know these people. Most of them worked with Daddy. And maybe she wasn't even invited. Before recent events, I had thought all grownups knew each other and got along equally well, but I'd learned a different story.

I headed toward the dessert table. Before I could turn back Momma had already spotted me as she leaned over the desserts and selected pie for herself and Daddy. "Where have you been hiding? You ain't said hello to him yet."

"I will." I located the big chocolate cake.

"He's been looking for you."

"All these people." I turned and made my way back to my table.

"Where's your cake?" Betty asked.

"It was all gone."

"Shoot. I wanted some more."

He wandered into my room in the dark just before I fell asleep, his body silhouetted by the hall light.

"Hey," he said, his voice very low and quiet, as if I might be asleep, "are you mad at me?"

No, I thought with all my heart, but the word stuck in my throat like an aspirin.

"It's all right if you are."

I pushed my head into the pillow. I was angry, but why? Because he'd come home? Because he'd been away? Because he'd lost his arm and couldn't get it back? Because he hadn't died? Because he had to live like this? And I was mad at myself because I felt so little, because I couldn't help. No one expected me to, but that didn't change the responsibility I secretly felt. I'd probably never really healed Jenny or the blue jay, I thought; it had all been Betty's imagination flaring up again. And the tingling in my hands, and the warmth, had been in my head. Now it was all like a memory of pain, impossible to recall. My arm seemed good as new. That no one noticed my dilemma only made it worse.

He turned to leave as I peeked out from the covers. Light outlined his body. Where the curve of his arm should have continued alongside his hip, the shape came to a stop, squared off. From behind it looked like he must be holding something in his arm, with his forearm bent in front of his stomach as he walked.

"Daddy," I asked, "will there always be miners?"

"What kind of a question is that?"

"I was just wondering if there would, still — all the time."

Daddy laughed. I was talking to him again. "As long as the Wye flows and the green grass grows," he said.

"Be serious," I said.

"I'm serious."

"You're laughing at me."

"Laugh at you? Never. Sleep tight. Good night."

"Daddy?"

"Yes, sweetheart."

"Good night."

He understood what I meant to say but couldn't. He came back and patted my hair twice before leaving me.

I slammed the trailer door and threw my schoolbooks down. Just one more week, then summer vacation. Three of those days were to make up snow days, which never seemed fair. Nature gave you snow and the school board made you pay for it. Daddy stood over the newspaper spread across the counter. His coffee cup worked as a paper weight.

"Fellow here named Yablonski," he said without looking up, "who's going to run against Boyle and be the next president of the UMWA."

"What if he loses?"

"He can't lose."

"Where's Momma?"

"She's working late today."

One more change in our lives was Momma getting a sales job. She had to miss her program, but she didn't seem to mind. *Edge of Night* just went right along without her. It felt strange to walk in the door and find Daddy standing in the kitchen finishing another cup of coffee. Lord knows how many he'd drunk. I'd been back riding the bus and the shadow seemed to have gotten what he wanted and sunk out of sight, but not without leaving our lives in a mess.

"Dorie, we've been waiting to tell you something. No use waiting any longer now." He looked up from his paper and straight at me. "How do you think you'd feel about your momma having another baby?"

My mouth was hanging open.

"Well, she's going to," he said simply.

"You can't have a baby! You're too old!"

"Well, maybe we're not as old as you think."

"How old?"

"I'm thirty-nine, and so is your momma. And the doctor says she's doing just fine. There's nothing to worry about."

Nothing to worry about, I thought. He really is crazy.

"When?" I managed to squeak.

"Oh, it's due around Christmas; there's plenty of time."

"This Christmas?"

"Of course, this Christmas."

"Great," I muttered.

"You just wait and see. Your momma's going to need your cooperation. A lot of things to do to get ready, you know. Plenty of time, though. Now, what do you want for your birthday?"

"I don't know." The bike with butterfly handlebars and banana seat had been shocked out of my system by Daddy's announcement. I felt like a paper doll fluttering in the wind. How could he stay so calm?

"If you don't know, I guess you can't help me. I guess I'll have to think of something myself."

Daddy walked with springy steps, a silver hook attached to his right arm. I couldn't keep my eyes off it. As he stepped inside, the hook caught the sun angled off the metal door and nearly blinded me.

"Well?" he asked. "What do you think? I can tie my shoes now."

"Does it hurt?"

"Not really. You want to see how it works?"

Before I could answer, he unbuttoned his shirt from the collar. "Help me with this."

I took his striped shirt and T-shirt and folded them over a

chair. Black leather straps circled the shoulder of his bad arm and his chest. He pulled on one strap and lifted the whole contraption over his head. Something like a flesh-colored sock protected his stump from the holster of the hook. I watched as he examined the metal of his new hand.

"There's a wire that runs up from here. Pressure makes it open and close. Like this."

I could see it work, open and close. He handed it to me. I held the icy hook up to one eye and looked through: Daddy smiled back.

25

Happy Birthday

Sometimes when I talk I have to stop because I can see the sentences I'm trying to say cascade through the air and vanish into the listener's ear — if I'm lucky. Or more often the stream shoots up from my lips and bounces off the listener's hearing like a shot in the dark. When I can *see* what is happening to my words, it's all I can do to keep talking along, pretending in a trapeze of talk that everything's normal. And if I can't go along they might ask, "Cat got your tongue?" I've learned not to tell anyone about the water words — it only causes trouble.

When Momma and Daddy argued I could see the water jumping back and forth. Daddy didn't want her to work, but she had to all the same. The streamers unfurled across the kitchen. "Don't go to work," he'd asked, though he knew we needed the income. "I have to," she'd said. And that was the end of it.

The day after my birthday was the first day of summer vacation. Even though it was a Saturday and we never had school on Saturday, it felt like more of a holiday just knowing that this time Monday would come and school wouldn't. I had the strangest birthday of my life in some ways. Not because I finally got the bike with butterfly handlebars and a banana seat and rode it around the neighborhood until I thought I might fall over dead tired. My birthday was strange because of what happened at school.

There was always a party on the last day of school — and my birthday didn't always fall on the same day we got out. Those ladies who supplied ice cream for Halloween, or others like them, supplied the ice cream for the last day of school. We didn't have to stay all day, so lunch and ice cream were always the last you'd remember of the year before when Labor Day rolled back around. Probably a plot to keep us coming back. Well, we're there in the lunch room, waiting for the ice cream, which we're used to getting but must treat as a surprise to be polite, when the door to the kitchen pops open and a few ladies step out behind a cart that holds a giant sheet cake glowing with candles. We leap up, applauding. It's not only ice cream, but cake! All the ladies smile as they wheel the cart to the front of the cafeteria.

Mr. Clarke waves his arm for us to hush, the candles keep burning, and I can feel eyes on me but I don't know why or if it's only my big ego. I shake off the feeling and sit back down. Then the singing begins, "Happy birthday to you, happy birthday to you . . ." The whole school sings together. I'm singing even though it's my birthday. It must be someone else's birthday too, I think, so I sing along, but I'm blushing because Betty might think that I think they're singing to me or something dumb like that. One time I heard my name called and turned around and an old woman looked up and caught the eye of the person who wanted her — it was her name, too. I felt like an idiot. It seems wrong that everyone in the world can't at least have their own name so mix-ups like that won't happen. Now I'm worried it's happening all over again in the lunch room in front of everyone, because when they get to the part where the name goes I hear the ladies singing "dear Dorie." It's so embarrassing, but then they're pointing at me and I turn around to look and there's no one else behind me named Dorie. "Go on!" Betty says. "You're supposed to go up and cut the cake!"

I weave my way through this dream to the front of the cafeteria. Kids fall in line smacking their lips, and I stick the knife into the cake, right through the icing message: HAPPY BIRTHDAY DORIE PARKS FROM YOUR FRIENDS AT TORNADO ELEMENTARY. Lucky it was a giant-size cake or they'd never have gotten all that written on it. As I slice a line through the cake from top to bottom and begin cutting at right angles from the line, a lady beside me says she'll finish for me, dips the first piece onto a paper plate, and hands it to me, along with a fork and a polka-dot napkin. Then she hands me an envelope with my name on it and tells me to open it at home.

The sound of all those voices still echoes around me. I remember them clearly as I return to my seat — all their mouths going at once, even Harry and the other dirty boys singing right along. Jenny's singing; I can see her thin face stretch around each word. Mrs. Harper's singing, even though it's foolishness. I'm singing it too: Happy birthday to you.

"What you got there?" Daddy asked.

"A card or something. You'll never believe what happened at school today." Daddy looked at me, his eyes asking, Well, what? "They had a big cake with my name on it and everybody ate a piece. I brought you one." I unwrapped the cake dripping with sugary icing. Part of TORNADO, an open-ended O, had melted.

I tore open the card while Daddy pinched off a bite of the cake. He licked his fingers as I read the card.

"What's this?" I asked, holding up a rectangle of paper.

"Let me see." Daddy took the paper, and I watched him read and reread it. He fell into a chair, still holding the paper. I was almost afraid to ask "What is it?" But I did.

"It's a check. It's made out to me. It's a check for five hundred dollars and it says it's from the Methodist church. Of course we can't keep it."

"But what's it for?"

"It's for us. To help us out. It probably came out of the rebuilding fund. But we can't keep this."

"Sure we can. They'd be sad if you gave it back."

"I guess we could save it — for your education. For college. What do you think?"

"What about the hospital bills?"

"I've got something up my sleeve. And your Momma can stretch a dollar as far as taffy. I don't intend to sit around here. I've got a plan."

"What're you going to do?"

"It's a secret, but I guess I can trust you. I'm going to be a mine inspector. How does that sound?"

His trusting his secret to me reminded me of the secret Momma and I had kept from him all this time. Willie's money. I felt like a dog because of that, and because I thought Daddy's plan sounded kind of crazy. But after all the things that had happened, it was as likely as anything else. I thought he would probably be the best inspector there was, if he felt like doing it. It was just like him to take the first chance he'd had to get away from the mines and turn it around some way to stay there. He had a job to do and he hadn't finished it; that's how he saw it. His only reason for living had to do with changing things in the mines. I didn't understand then how a life could end up being so predictable after all the chance it took to move it along.

There was Willie, and there was me, whoever I would turn out to be, and now there was going to be someone else, someone related to me that I didn't know yet, someone I had nothing to do with, but no matter what happened they would always be related to me and to Willie. And right now they didn't know anything about us either. My parents could have been anyone, but they turned out to be who they were, and I was who I was only because of them, or somehow in spite of them. But really, no matter what happened in the long run, it was *because,* not in spite of. My little brother or sister would have a one-armed daddy — he'd never be any other way to them.

And all of this will be as if it never happened, it will slide so far into the past. That baby will never be able to remember it. But if that baby was mine, I'd make it remember.

26

Willie and the Snake

I guess it was only a matter of time before Willie showed up in our lives again. No matter how deep a secret burrows, it's down there clawing toward the light, never moving in the opposite direction.

The afternoon before Willie turned up I had a tingling in my fingertips, not the itch in the palm that means company's coming, but a tickling feeling. Nothing like it used to feel, though. It seemed like the minute Willie's knock interrupted our supper, the strange feeling vanished. Willie nearly always arrived home in time for supper.

"Oh, Willie!" Momma greeted him. "I was beginning to think I'd never see you again."

Willie's mouth turned serious; instead of his usual homecoming grin he put on his Mona Lisa smile. "I've been having this feeling I ought to come home. I've been waking up in the middle of the night and seeing your faces."

"You been eating dill pickles late at night?" I asked.

"We're glad you're home," Daddy said, rising from the table.

I watched Willie's eyes rivet to the hook. He didn't say anything at first; he just sat down, holding the chair back. "Seems like I've been gone a long time this time."

"Just had a fall, that's all," Daddy said. "The big news is that your momma's going to have a baby in December."

"You're — not!" Willie said. "Well, why didn't you say so?"

"He just did," I said.

Willie grabbed Momma around the neck. "Oh, Momma! That's the most wondrous news."

"Yeah," I said, "and it's going to be a girl."

"That so? Then you know more than I do," Momma said. "But that ain't nothing new."

"I'm going to let her play with all my old toys."

"Ain't that nice," Willie said. "Real nice. I just can't get over it. A baby."

After supper Daddy tried to get Willie to take a walk with him, but Willie didn't want to go and kept making up excuses. First he said his leg hurt him: "Must have cramped up on the Hound. You know those seats just ain't made for a long-legged fellow like me." Then he said he had some work to do and pulled his raggedy old spiral notebook out of his pack. I thought Momma might just tell Daddy the truth and save Willie the trouble of pretending to write notes. She knew he was a wanted man and shouldn't be seen on the street, but she couldn't say it before she got him alone and found out about that money. Daddy kept on about the walk and waited out Willie's cramps; he wanted to talk to his son alone too. About sundown they headed out. I guess Willie figured luck was with him in the dusk.

I followed on my bike after a few minutes. Daddy had been building up his strength by walking around the town every evening. He'd gotten pretty swift. I looked all around but I couldn't see them right off. I decided to ride down Main Street.

As I rode toward the post office, it seemed like time had compressed and I was riding down the street all the times I had gone down it in my whole life, walking or riding, seeing all the same things as they had been and as how they were, an overlapping past and present. Not much had changed since first grade except for the new post office building and the trees the council'd planted in little pots along the sidewalk to beautify the street.

As I pedaled I began to make out a circle of people on the sidewalk. For a second I believed I was seeing the past, seeing the night when Willie and Brother Saul had been thrown in jail and folks had milled around on the sidewalk, wondering what to do next. I shook my head and blinked against that feeling and the wind rushed into my eyes, and the crowd didn't vanish. As I rode nearer I picked out Sheriff Darnell's hat in the circle. I stopped riding and walked my bike up next to the crowd. The door of the jail hung open. Flies buzzed against the windowpanes, trying to get inside in their confusion.

A siren blasted behind me, drowning out the voices. I couldn't see anything more until the rescue van pulled up to the curb and the circle of people drew back to make way. When the figures drew back I saw Daddy kneeling on the sidewalk. "Hurry!" he kept repeating while the stretcher rolled toward the body he shielded. Then I knew it was Willie lying there.

The rescue squad raised Willie onto the stretcher at the count of three. In their arms he swayed briefly before striking the white sheet. His chest looked red. Daddy looked up at me. "Go home," he said. "Get your momma. Meet us at the hospital." I wanted to ask what had happened but instead I threw a leg over my bike and rode home like the devil was chasing me, without touching down once on the banana seat. Coils of warm air rose toward me from the pavement. Night air fanned my face. And all I could think of was the snake. Willie's red, red blood. And the green coil of that snake rising up like a smoke signal.

We huddled in the waiting room, Momma and me. Daddy was still with Willie. Whenever I closed my eyes I could see the spreading circle of blood on Willie's chest and the pool of blood he'd left on the sidewalk. His blood exploded out of neat circles into unformed shapes each time I blinked against the glare of the fluorescent overhead light of the familiar waiting room.

"I never should've let him go," Momma said, looking down into her hands, talking to herself. "I should've told him not to go out."

"Sheriff Darnell was right there. He must have called for the ambulance right after he shot Willie," I said.

"It's all my fault," Momma continued as if I hadn't said a

word. "He didn't know they were after him. I should've told him. Oh, why did I let him go?" Momma cried into her hands.

"It's not your fault." No one's fault, I wanted to say. Because Willie's life was a natural force, like a flood, that would go where it went. But I said, "Darnell ambushed him. He was after Willie, like you said."

"I know Willie never knew what hit him."

I glanced up and saw Daddy walking toward us.

"It's all my fault," Momma was murmuring between muffled sobs.

"He's in surgery." Daddy sat down. "It's bad — one of his lungs collapsed." He rubbed at the corner of one eye. "I'll never forgive myself."

I looked at the stunned faces of my parents and turned away. I wanted to tell them that it wasn't their fault, that I was responsible, just like I was responsible for Daddy's losing his arm. And chills rippled through my body and lodged in my teeth. I couldn't keep them from chattering wildly. An old remedy popped into my head: *To relieve chills place a pair of shoes under your bed with the soles pressed together pointing toward the head.* A lot of good that would do me now. I'd kept Willie's money a secret from Daddy, while he trusted me. But how could I have told him? Momma had asked me not to. I couldn't betray her trust. I felt out of balance, as if loud music was pounding on one eardrum and not the other. I thought I might throw up on one of the black squares of the checked floor.

Had I tried to give back my gift like an Indian giver? The door swung open, allowing a gust of humid air into the waiting room, along with Sheriff Darnell and a deputy. Darnell pulled his hat off and held it in front of his belt in both hands before opening his mouth. He was waiting for Momma or Daddy to look up; I tried to stare a hole in his badge.

"Folks, I realize this ain't a good time, but I need to ask you some questions while things is still fresh in your mind."

Momma began to sob out loud at the sound of the sheriff's

voice. "You shot my boy," she said. "You shot my Willie."

"He didn't shoot anybody, Mary," Daddy said.

I felt my heart jump. Daddy wouldn't lie. Momma couldn't stop crying. Daddy wrapped his good arm around her. "She's too upset right now to know what she's saying. I'm sorry."

"I understand," Darnell said. "I guess I come at a bad time." Darnell replaced his hat but made no move toward the door. "But the sooner I can get a few details, the sooner I might turn something up. You see, I was back in the back when I heard the shot. By the time I got out there it was all over. And Pete here says he didn't see a thing. He was out on patrol."

With his mask still dangling around his neck, Dr. Grayson walked into the waiting room, straight toward us. I could see what he was going to say before he said it. "I'm sorry." He almost mouthed the words, and repeated them so their meaning could sink into us and fall like a shadow across the freshly waxed linoleum. Unless one of us spoke to Dr. Grayson the shadow would just keep spreading. *Bind the heart of the offending snake to the bite.*

"He's gone?" Daddy asked.

"I'm afraid there was nothing we could do. His blood pressure dropped suddenly."

I thought for a second that Momma hadn't heard, but then her chest heaved and Daddy wrapped his arm tighter around her. Daddy's touch reversed the freeze tag rules they'd always operated under in public and in front of me. And instead of freezing, Momma collapsed, woke up to the misery of losing Willie, something they'd probably been waiting for longer than I could remember. But she wasn't alone. That moment made me understand how many meanings a touch, like a word, can carry.

"It had to be a forty-five. Nothing else leaves a hole that big."

Momma gasped. Dr. Grayson added, "I'm sorry." Willie's bloodstain was already drying on his white coat. There was a pause in which Dr. Grayson turned and said, "If there's anything I can do, call me." Knowing that we wouldn't call him didn't take the comfort out of his routine words. Daddy rose and shook his hand.

"Mr. Parks, did you get a good look at the vehicle?" Darnell asked.

"A pickup, a dark red pickup." Daddy's voice came from under water.

"Did you get the license number?"

"No."

"Any part of it?"

"I didn't pay any attention to the truck until I heard the shot. Willie fell. I tried to cover him. I didn't see the gun; the truck pulled out from the curb in front of where we'd been walking. I heard the tires spin out." Daddy still cradled Momma. "They meant to hit me, you know. Why'd they have to miss?"

"You say they were trying to kill you, Mr. Parks?" Darnell scratched his temple. His hat bobbed up and down. When he finished scratching he pulled the hat off again. "Pete, you getting this down?"

"Yep." Pete kept scribbling on a pad.

"How do you know?" Darnell asked.

"Well . . ." Daddy paused. "Why would anyone shoot at Willie?"

"I ain't deaf and blind, much as some would like it to be true." Darnell lowered his voice. "I know you got yourself into a bind with Willis, but I thought that was settled now."

"I'll never forgive myself, that's all." Daddy's mouth snapped shut into a straight line. He didn't mean to say another word.

"It ain't your fault," Momma said. Her eyes were red, her face puffy, splotched purple in places.

"I got reason to believe," Darnell interrupted, "that shot was meant for your son."

Daddy looked at Momma and she nodded.

Darnell faced Daddy, Pete's scribbling stopped, and Momma started filling in the story.

"David, after Willie left the last time, after Christmas, Sheriff Darnell came by the house."

Daddy raised his eyebrows for a second, reminding me of the way he used to look whenever he found something interesting in the newspaper.

"That's right," Darnell said. "I been keeping an ear out for Willie ever since. I don't know how to tell you this, but I'm ninety-nine percent certain he was mixed up in running whiskey down into North Carolina. I think he might have double-crossed his partners, left them without dividing up the money. I'm not the only one who's been trying to find your son. I think I can find out who killed him, but there's something I ain't been able to locate. The money. Must've hid it. Maybe here in Poorwater. He came back for something."

I sat there wondering, in the small pause after Darnell's revelations, whether Momma would say what she knew or keep depending on me to be silent.

"I know where it is," Momma said. "But I'm afraid it's gone. I spent it. I had to."

Darnell rubbed his forehead. Daddy's mouth opened suddenly. "That was stolen property," Darnell said. "I'm going to have to —" He stopped. "Pete!"

Pete stopped staring at Momma and started writing again at top speed.

"Oh, forget it," Darnell said. "Stop that scribbling! You going to wear your pencil to a nub. Mrs. Parks, come down to the station in a few days and we'll sort this out. Looks like you folks have some things to see to."

Daddy had been dazed but managed to say thank you.

Darnell hitched up his trousers. He was always twitching at himself. "Don't mention it. I mean that," he whispered. "Don't mention this to anyone. Come on, Pete, we got to get while the trail's still smoking."

Pete tipped his hat and strutted out behind the sheriff.

"Why'd Willie come home if he was a sitting duck?" Daddy asked.

"To visit," I said.

"He's gone, David." Momma began to cry all over again. "Willie's gone. He's gone."

The next time we come to the hospital, I thought, it'll be to see Momma when the baby's born. I was sinking into a trance, when all at once it hit me that Willie didn't have to be dead. He's in there right now, I thought, laughing his fool head off at his own joke like the humpback who swallowed that fish bone. Willie just needs to be waked up good. I tried to break out of the waiting room, to find him, but Momma held one hand and Daddy clasped the other tight. "But he's alive," I said. "He's in there alive. And I can help him."

Willie's Blue Horse Notebook

Last Things

I was sent to planet earth
to publish facts of the truth
at any cost up to a dying life time
night and day, with or without support.

— The Reverend Howard Finster

1. We spin through the night, dive through the night like
ghosts shooting through solid oak doors. The road spins under
us instead of us driving dreams over it. We drive and drive,
tires churning, and I'm dreaming at the wheel. My little shipmate
sits beside me in a preacher's stupor. Out like a light after the
show is over. Traveling salesman. I want to keep straight and
narrow, charge straight into one side of a curve that elbows
down into Tennessee, and shove myself right into a rock face,
out of this preacher's dream and into another, but I am steady
at the wheel. "Going to take a trip on that old Gospel Ship," I
hum. Easy Jesus, quick as greased lightning. But uh-oh, oh
no. I feel that big old snake shifting gears in the trunk. Yes,
sir. He's going to bite my head off someday. Drive his fangs
into my neck and shake my head till it cracks and colors pop
out and streamers and the four winds and a creature with the
head of a dragon and a red Corvette sleek as a polyester pimp
and a black leather book with nothing but my name on every
page, no address, I ain't that dumb, and a girlie show like on
Bourbon Street — "Biggest titties in the city" — girls swinging
in and out of windows and Lord knows what-all in their
G-strings and a tiny little pillbox you think send your head to
sweet Jesus and back with one swallow and some angels singing
over my lost and found soul. Light up and fly through the corners.

Take it easy. My burden's light. Strike a match to my plant and inhale like sipping shine. Shine's dead. Clicking bottles in the trunk like it ain't, but it is. Snake ain't got no ears. I never touched it. I fly away by my own lights. I don't want to wake Brother up. When he's angry he's a mean mean man. Snake bite him — hell, no! Brother my ass. Bugger my ass before that. I can't stop laughing. I might take this next curve too fast —

2. 1948 plus one generation. Forty years more. No — I can't wait that long for it. The bitter End got to be coming sooner not later. This crazy sideshow can't last now, can it? Can't outlast me. Make love not war. Shit. Got to take me on up. I'm not waiting. I'm not hesitating. I ain't that dumb. I'm waiting on the love of the One not the many bouncing titties, not that crap, that disease in the heart. Hippie Free Love going to destroy us all in the end. If your heart ain't clean it'll move into your balls, drop like mumps. I've felt it and I know the unclean from the clean. Porky Pig and all. Pigs kiss mine and die young. Make your brother stumble and you fall. Make love too often and you turn into a big hot dog with a woman's place for a brain. Never get one near to the other after that, hard as you try, sucker. I cut it out of a man oncet. But he kept on coming back for more. He don't know yet how dead he is. But I do. I know.

3. I'm no jungle bunny. Catch me if you can. I'm a flying-away man — but not to enemy country. Kill all us traitors and more will come. Cut the snake into little pieces and you get more snakes. Wiggly worms multiply faster than hamsters. Don't need anybody else to do it, either. Let the Marines take out the swamp. Canada, shit. I got business elsewhere, down south. Got a letter from Uncle Sam in the toe of my shoe, divided it up like that — letter in one shoe and envelope in the other. Always drag it along step by step, just being polite, because he can't never catch up to me. I render unto Caesar just exactly the amount he can strip off of me, whatever flies off my backside as I go along. Catch what you can stomach, I say. For every man

who lives by the sword will die by the sword. Not I, Brother
Rat, not I —

4. "They shall take up serpents; and if they drink any deadly
thing, it shall not hurt them; they shall lay hands on the sick,
and they shall recover." Mark 16:18.

5. False prophets and miracles shall abound in the last days.
Many will claim to be sent by the living God and really come
out of the devil's mouth. Many miracles will be performed
in Jesus' name with Satan as their backer. If I should happen to walk across the river, I won't know anymore who kept me
afloat —

6. I had a woman and she was not my wife. I used her till
she took a knife and threatened to cut out my eyeballs. Then
she turned the point of the knife on herself, stuck it in her wrist
right through the ligaments. She never used that hand for nothing
else. Sat in the waiting room while they pumped blood back
into her, sat there being a hero. I'd saved her life. Hell if I had.
I drowned her in drink first, poured myself down her throat.
Did everything but shit on her. What did I think about while
I waited to hear if she'd live or die? How that night I picked
her up and did her over good in the back of the car while Brother
slept like a baby in the front and the damn snake rattled his
cage. Gagged her with the handkerchief Momma sent so she
couldn't wake Brother and pushed in on her till she stopped
trying to stop me. Then I let her fall in love with me. I never
touched another woman, and I never touched her again. Not
yet. Whenever I felt it coming on I'd smoke my plant and roll
too fast over the roads. Helen told Brother what I did to her
and I said she was a lying bitch. We dumped her on the roadside
outside of Nashville, but she thumbed a ride straight to the
next tent. Sat there like a temple whore, ran up claiming her
soul was touched. And she got to be Brother's woman after
that. I thought she might take me back, but she drew that knife.
Had to sleep in the same room with them whenever we stopped,
had to listen to them doing it, had to listen to Brother's yells

from the pulpit, had to watch him saving souls from the likes of himself —

7. Without there being a sacrifice of blood there is no redemption. Without bloodshed. Without blood there is no grace. Old-timey warriors used to drink cups of their victims' blood, take their souls into their own strength that way. Blood shed, body eaten like bread. Bread of life was shed for thee. I can't eat it. I can't drink it. I can't eat it. I'm a dead man. Save me —

8. He will make a miraculous recovery from a fatal wound. Not JFK, he's DOA. He will arise from his deathbed and all the people will deem him great, follow his direction. The Anti-Christ will cut a fine figure in a suit — 666 — probably wear one of those funny collars that stick up all around like a priest's. He'll be riding pale horses when he comes. Greased Jesus cleanse my heart like a dose of salts. I don't want to live to see it. If I can't believe by myself, will you take me up into the air? I can't do anything. I can't do it. I can't sleep or drink. I can't sip the holy grape juice or swallow the holy Ritz. I want to, but it ain't easy. Whole world turning black as oil slick. Black against White and White and Black against Slants, North hating South again, and fire falling and skulls busting open like I crunch over a polecat on the highway. Pigs bashing scholars. Jesus seal me. In a couple of nights it'll be too late.

9. Helen spit in my face and put out the fire. Launched a thousand ships, shit. Like to cut that night out of my head and bind it for good and all to the wound. Like to take back that Act, like to fix it out of my mind with a needle and thread into my arm. But I can't forget what I'm always ready to do again —

10. "When the unclean spirit is gone out of a man, he walketh through dry places, seeking rest, and findeth none . . . Then goeth he, and taketh with himself seven other spirits more wicked than himself, and they enter in and dwell there: and the last state of that man is worse than the first. Even so shall it be also unto this wicked generation." Matthew 12:43, 45.

11. I see a girl standing on the side of the road. Only a scant

prissy dress covering her nakedness. No shoes. I stop the car. Good Samaritan. Go ask how far she wants to go. I see her up close. Before you can say Rumpelstiltskin I'm tying my clean handkerchief around her painted mouth, drawing blood from her lips. Drag her to the car. Get in on top of her. Rub her titties. She wants me to kill her but I won't. Her arms lay at her sides. She knows how far she can go. Push it in until she wants it just like this, but she never will again. Should have put a gun to her head instead. Gotten free myself. Should kill myself instead. Nothing's free in this dead world. Had myself a time and now I'm paying —

12. "This know also, that in the last days perilous times shall come. For men shall be lovers of their own selves, covetous, boasters, proud, blasphemers, disobedient to parents, unthankful, unholy, without natural affection, trucebreakers, false accusers, incontinent, fierce, despisers of those that are good, traitors, heady, highminded, lovers of pleasures more than lovers of God; having a form of godliness, but denying the power thereof: from such turn away. For of this sort are they which creep into houses, and lead captive silly women laden with sins, led away with divers lusts, ever learning, and never able to come to the knowledge of the truth." II Tim. 3:1–7.

13. Mysteries. "And the third angel followed them, saying with a loud voice, If any man worship the beast and his image, and receive his mark . . ." Rev. 14:10. God will destroy them. I'm shouting for a sign and Jonah is all there is or ever shall be in the way of signs. For three days buried, then kick away the stone door, angels watching over me. I am too low to hope for wings. Unclean. Send me a sign of the last times and I will preach until my throat swells shut, rots black with pain. I will bring sinners to their knees, where I belong night and day, especially in the nighttime when I can't make up my mind.

14. My dreams wake me, send me the devils I deserve for my time with the Beast and his Jezebel. My Brother, the Beast. He wrapped his snake around my middle. Let it hiss at me, let it crawl over my naked skin while he watched. "Hit won't hurt

you, Willie, my son." "How do you know?" "Too smart to sink a bite into the likes of you." "Get him off me, Brother." "Be still and know that I am God." "But Brother, I'm sweating like a pig." "If he smells your fear he'll strike the life out of you. Now be still."

15. First and last of all got to shed this darkness. Black cave of stinking despair. My guilt runneth to meet me in the black cave of shadows. Nothing in the bottom of these hills but black guilt. I don't dig it. I don't dig to the soul of despair. Pry out my pride with a pickax. I don't want to die in the dark of a black cave slimy with coal dust. And I looked and I saw the Snake let loose on my town and my people. I saw the Snake Coal strangling my generations, my children choking on coal. But I still got to pay my own debt. Eat my dust, demons, eat my dust. Not my body. Not my flesh and bones turned to fossils in the dark, dead eye dark —

16. She comes slinking round the mountain on her beast. Twenty-eight million dollars day by day on studying War. Vietnam, you eat dogs and skin cats and teethe my meat when I ain't even coming to meet you if'n it's the last thing I do in this sorry world. Help yourself out, by God. Carry your children to meet the Lord of Lords Most High. Don't slug through the jungle biting mosquitoes for blood. Before it gets better it's going to get worse. Take your leeches and your jungle rot and your America and your Canada and your AWOL and shove it where the sun don't try to shine because it's too smart for your greedy words.

17. Doubting Thomas take my hand, push it into the wound of life everlasting, A-men. Take my eyes and make them see the Truth of Truths. Crown of Thorns. And I looked and I saw a spaceman coming to take me across the river to the other side of time, where time slips aside like a bad joke and space opens up my eyes on the insides.

18. "Behold, I will cast her into a bed, and them that commit adultery with her into great tribulation, except they repent of

their deeds. And I will kill her children with death . . ." Rev.
2:22–23.

19. I want to be sealed as a Lamb in the army of Sweet
Jesus. Every morning I stand on my head before anyone's up,
let blood cleanse my spirit while it rushes to my head. If my
eyes bug I don't give a shit. If they pop I might begin to see
the real honest light. I want a sign but I don't deserve it. My
faith's as sincere as a fox's smile. But I can make them listen to
the truth —

20. D-Day, Delivery Day. I shall be released. Let them take
my garbage and get high one last time before the Snake climbs
out of his pit and makes War on the planet. I'll take their silver
and run to Jesus. I paid my debt and then some —

21. That man's coming back to me now. I killed a man and
he's my everlasting yoke. Why the lamp of my soul turned black.
Turned my knife in his belly one dark night. Stand on my head
and all things rush. Sold pills by the barrel. Sold weed by the
bushel. Sold clear liquid poison that'd blind eyes and rot gut —
all like ice to an Eskimo, all like venom to a viper. Water to a
drowning man. I turned myself into Jesus and He told me it
was settled, debt paid COD. That His blood was the True and
certified Real Life. Now try to peddle the Good Book and can't
give it away, that's the truth. Before this generation is passed
away into dust there will come a great darkness screaming over
the earth, and firefall and earthquake and hunger and sickness
and a wasting plague that will separate goats from sheep and
separate the living spirits from the dead and separate son from
mother and daughter from father and brother from sister and
lover from lover, A-men.

22. And I looked and I saw the River of Blood flowing through
the streets of the earth, spreading panic and terror. I saw children
killing themselves before they were old enough to think and I
saw teenagers ramming their cars into solid brick walls so they
wouldn't have to think and I heard their music telling them to
slit their own gullets because they couldn't grow into manhood

whole and complete. And I dreamed I was falling, flung off a cliff and falling and screaming for mercy and clawing the bare air. Then I was stopped in the midst of His thin air and felt myself rising, rising, and I never touched the ground and I went flying through the air toward Heaven and Jesus met me at the gates of His plan for my heart, and I said, Yes, I will do it. Yes, I will. And He wrapped His white robe around my bleeding limbs and made them well —

23. Blessed are the poor in spirit and the poor, period: all those who never kick up a fuss no matter how many times they get kicked. Blessed are those who hold their peace and talk inwardly with the Spirit of God Himself, indivisible, one nation under God, A-men. Blessed are those who despise the meek, for they shall never see God, but are part of His plan same as Judas who hanged himself when he saw the fruits his very hands had wrought. Blessed is pain and suffering, for those who endure learn to trust in the Lord. Blessed is disease, for it sows patience in the hearts of its sufferers and brings them near to God Almighty, in Whom is all rest and all proper health, A-men.

24. If I have not loved I am no better than a flea on a dog's behind. Have I forgotten my people? No, I have not forgotten them, and I shall return home to lead them out of the valley of their misery into the Spiritual Tomorrow. While they sweat in their bodies they shall rejoice in their hearts because they know Him and they are His Own Flock. They are become Free Men. "He alone comforts them in the caves of despair. He comforts them in the blackness. He converts their labor into holiness. He anoints them with oil and seals them with His blood, for they drink of His suffering day by day. A-men.

25. Blessed are the addicts, for they wrestle with demons and therefore must avail themselves of Jesus and His opposite works. Blessed are the blue chicory flowers and the green mountains and the white snow mountains and the twisting goat paths and the sheep and every rock that breaks a plow and every voice that utters music and everything and everyone that lives

and breathes in the mountains because they are closer to Him
Who is Most High. A-men.

26. When I was a child I fished the Wye for sport and caught
His fish like they were peanuts instead of living creatures. I
fished the waters and I stalked His creatures in the woods and
I raked my saw-toothed knife over the skins of His creatures
and I severed the heads of His creatures and I ate of the flesh
of His creatures, after draining them of His blood. And it was
clean flesh but my emptiness was black as death, black and
bloated as death. Until I knew Him everything I did in innocence
was unclean because I was not baptized by the Spirit of the
Living God —

27. And I looked and I saw a New Heaven and a New Earth
where Death had disappeared and there was no more crying,
where all blood had been shed and we were rinsed of despair.
I took myself back to the mountains and there I met my God.
He was setting out to look for me, thinking I was lost in the
land of the dead —

28. All the seals of prophecy are broken open and the scroll
rolls out into my hands as it was in the ancient of days. "And I
heard a voice from heaven saying unto me, Write, Blessed are
the dead which die in the Lord from henceforth: Yea, saith the
Spirit, that they may rest from their labours; and their works
do follow them." Rev. 14:13.

29. He floated down on His magic carpet of cloud wearing a
golden crown. And the next day I looked into the sky and began
to apprehend the wisdom and the loveliness of clouds and to
see His image etched in their shapes. And I looked into the
garden of earthly delights and I saw the face of the dead one,
pus oozing from his sores. And I saw that he could never be
satisfied but ever vainly striving after success because he did
not choose to know God.

30. "A double minded man is unstable in all his ways." James
1:8. Every time I looked into the face of a woman and saw the
face of my own lust I am chastened. Every time I returned to

my home and was filled with wanderlust and pride I am beside myself with my shame. Every time I spoke His Holy Word and did not believe I am not worthy to breathe His precious air, for I am to be passed away like a season of flowers and no man knows when his time is nigh.

31. "Blessed is he that readeth, and they that hear the words of this prophecy, and keep those things which are written therein, for the time is at hand." Rev. 1:3.

32. I've come home for the End — July 20, 1969, a month away. In my dreams I have seen the faces of my father and mother and sister, and they were crying. So I have come home and the signs of the End are scattered around me like the grass and the trees. I want to wander Bald Mountain before the end. Take Momma and Dorie for a picnic. Pack cold chicken and potato salad, pickles, biscuits, jug tea. Oil the ball gloves for a catch game. I can see the wildflowers blooming and dancing on Bald Mountain and the new yellow-green grasses bowing their heads and the cleansed shining air and the old picnic blanket spread out beneath a shade tree, a beech tree fanning us with its multitude of small hands. Dorie, quiet as a cucumber, what goes on in your head? Do you hate your brother like a stranger? Golden dappled light runs fingers over your face. And I looked and I saw that this was the only miracle: a summer's day on Bald Mountain. The signs are clear as my eyes. His covenant permeates everything, even the crab apple, even the invisible air, even the least of these —

33. ———

27

A Puzzle

203. QUESTION: The exact date of the end of the world.
ANSWER: June 20, 1969.

The twentieth of June was the day Willie died. I remembered what Daddy had said about Mr. McGee's funeral and how I would have time enough to go to funerals when I was older. This time no one raised an objection, and I kept wishing they would. That was the difference between ten and eleven. I was clearly over the hill. More and more of the old solid parts of the world turned steadily into holes as I watched. After a while, I guessed I'd just get used to the holes, and the spaces between the holes would start to seem more and more like the imaginary parts of the picture. Only the holes would be real.

Can you find a frog in this picture? (There are five frogs.) Can you find a car? (There is one car.) Can you find a rabbit? (There are many rabbits, none of them white.) Now, can you find a girl?

The long black car speeds a girl and her parents to a graveyard far, far away. Their car winds through mountains while sunshine beats down on its shiny hood like a giant bird's wings. Between her parents, the girl sits still as a mouse. Her mother cries a little into a handkerchief. Her father tilts his head back to catch a glimpse of sun through the rear window. Behind their shiny car another follows, another black car with no one inside it but a driver and a box affixed with silver handles so its weight can be held aloft by hands. Can you find the hole in the puzzle where this box must fit?

Now the girl naps, her head on her father's lap. Her mother looks out the tinted window of the car, presses an open palm to the glass in farewell, as the road hairpins, quickly losing the place they have only just left.

28

Fireflies

A month after Willie left us I sat with Momma and Daddy and half of the inhabitants of planet Earth, watching two astronauts bounce around on the surface of the moon. As Daddy had predicted, men were walking on the moon and they even stuck an American flag up there. Momma gave in: it was happening; it was on TV.

The surface of the moon takes footprints easy as damp sand, but no ocean rushes in to erase them and there's no wind. Sharp shadows, stark black against gray dust — the white of space suits is the whitest white ever seen on the face of the moon, an electric contrast. I could feel my weight reduce, my buoyancy begin. Each giant step they took pulled me along, piggyback with the rest of creation. I understand why some people still insist that the moonwalk, like the Holocaust, could not have really happened. At least those people still balk in the face of the miraculous, even if they don't have the faith of a mustard seed.

"You're going to stare a hole in them," Momma said. "She's going to ruin her eyes. Sit back."

"But Momma, they're on the moon."

The astronauts laid a plaque in the Sea of Tranquillity:

HERE MEN FROM THE PLANET EARTH
FIRST SET FOOT UPON THE MOON
JULY 1969 A.D.
WE CAME IN PEACE FOR ALL MANKIND

Our first instinct, of course, was to start a museum.

I guessed I would get over it, like everything else in life. The daily would carry me along until I simply grew out of my amazement. But I didn't want to forget those footsteps on the moon, and if I didn't want to, would I have to? I would wind up in a zoo, where all the people who remembered were kept. I got out my question book and found the page where I had written a long lost question: Is there life on the Moon? I scrawled on the blank answer line: Yes.

But so many spaces were still left without answers in my original question book. I thought about copying all the questions that now had answers into another book, but it all seemed so artificial. It made more sense to me now to have some questions with answers but the vast lot left with nothing but the empty space.

Some things are meant to stay hidden, like some animals, like the future itself. You can't rip a turtle out of its shell and expect it to thank you.

I never finished *The Arabian Nights,* but I hear that Shahrazad found a way out of the bargain. Her husband the king didn't have the heart to kill her after having spent night after night hearing story after story. A wise king learns to live with his beauty.

So I did go to college, and Betty's working for a firm in Richmond between one L and two. Her last letter would have me believe that somehow torts are attempting to kill her. Barbara's a conceptual artist living in New York City. I'm home for the summer and I don't have a job, and writing this story hasn't rid me of my problem. What did I expect?

Every few seconds I can hear Williann's ball smack the oiled palm of her glove. She's the best pitcher the league's ever seen, and she knows it. When she's not pitching or signing autographs, she throws a ball into the sky, straight up, then poises in position for gravity to work its magic, bring it home, right on target. If Williann's not thinking softball, she's either curled up on the end of the sofa with her nose stuck in a Harlequin romance or she's telling me to "shut up." Half the time she wakes up saying she's Willie Stargell in disguise. It doesn't faze her a bit when Daddy reminds her that Stargell's not even a pitcher. The other half of the time she unbraids her hair, shakes it down her back, aching to change her name to Fawn or Lauren or Mandoline and insisting that in the meanwhile we at least allow her to add an *e* to the end of Williann. I've tried to prepare her for Mrs. Harper, explain the ins and outs of outlining and other Harper esoterica, but Williann won't listen. She's sure she's scheduled for the pretty new teacher, Mrs. Adarre. Even Momma gets into it: "Ain't never been a Parks that got past Mrs. Harper, mark my words." But Williann just shrugs; it's no skin off her nose. "Mrs. Adarre," she might say in a near whisper as if she likes the sound of it. Williann throws her ball into the air, waits between the up and down, and knows she'll catch the ball before it hits the ground.

It's dusk on a summer evening and I'm out for a walk. I can feel the heat of the day passing up through the soles of my shoes and the cool of the coming night as my arms swing free in the mountain air, propelling me along the circuit of the neighborhood. And the circle of the year is closing, summer to summer, as I walk west to reach east again, to reach home. Someone is waiting. All along this path, where I walk and have walked, I pass through myself, through points along an unending line. Fireflies spin a web of specks between the stars and the grass, a spectacle like the sparks that fly up from burning wood, burning carbon, life itself.

No matter how far or how fast I walk I can still see the intermittent patterns of firefly light just ahead, as if dozens of specters are taking drags on dozens of cigarettes at once in the dark of a stadium. I try to count their beacons. If I look into the night sky, beyond the streetlights and their glare, each star presents itself as if it were alone. But it is seldom true; their faint partners would become visible if I could look at the bright stars another way.

Flashes of heat lightning divide the sky, but only briefly. This danger isn't real or lasting, but the excitement of a possible storm begins to rise along my spine. Should I look into the flashes or look away? Should I walk faster just in case the rain beats me home?

Wind knocks against the trees, shakes the leaves, stirring them into sound. Broken twigs settle softly to the ground. I step over them, creep silent as a brave. I am stalking the little flashing lights I can hold in my hands. I used to take a jar and fan it through the air until I'd caught too many bugs to count, then punch lopsided holes in the metal lid and hope they'd live. Now there's a gift like a star that burns a hole in my pocket. And I have nothing but my hands to give. So I send one cupped hand through the air until I feel the tickle of a bug inside. I run the other hand through the air, catch another bug. Soon I have to cup both hands together to hold them all.

More and more lights flicker just a few steps ahead, weightless in the night. Without gravity, they wouldn't need to fly. I stop; the fireflies pinned inside my hands, like butterflies, must change.

When my hands open, one hand like a lid popping off, I expect to see the contents flower into the air, but nothing moves. The lights just hang there, blink off and on. Walking lights now trace the chains of my two lifelines as if they were tightropes to be danced. Left hand the right hand's twin, the given fulfilled in the will. The bugs keep blinking off and on, as I stare into my hands and wait for the transformation that will send us back where we belong.

Up there the moon stays hidden behind a cloud or a mountain. As soon as I shift my attention the fireflies light and rise, taking their formation back into the sky, where it drifts beyond my reach and I can see it more clearly. "Escape velocity" depends upon the mass of the body you're trying to leave. For fireflies to leave my hands is easy. Not much speed required for their getaway. They couldn't live anywhere else, I think, but in this place, this cool, blue sphere. But I might leave them, fly away. I take my hands out of my pockets, where I will never be able to hide them again. If I must leave, and I will, I'll take these mountains with me.